The Sorcerer's
ABYSS

BROCK E.
DESKINS

"**W**itch!" a man cried out, trying to pull the wild-eyed girl off Brad before she killed him. "Let him go!"

Ellyssa turned and faced the man grabbing at her and saw Sonjay's big black face twisted in anger, ready to lash her with his whip once again. A scream tore from Ellyssa's throat, drowning out the hoarse wailing of the tortured man now falling from his chair. Outside, passers-by stopped and stared at the front of the diner from where those horrible screams emanated.

The walls exploded outward, blasted the onlookers from their feet, and pelted them with splinters and planks of wood. The entire roof caved in and crashed down with a billowing cloud of dust. Even as the astonished spectators struggled to their feet, a second explosion turned a portion of the roof into splinters and shards of clay tiles and sent them arcing hundreds of feet over the tops of the neighboring buildings.

Like a demon emerging from the shadowy recesses of the abyss, Ellyssa burst from the cloud of dust, skidded across the loose pieces of wreckage, and sprinted down the street. She made a mindless dash through the city, fueling her body by drawing in the Source and feeding it directly to her muscles. It was something briefly talked about in class, but they were warned that it was a very dangerous practice to use. It was very easy to push oneself so hard that the heart gave out and literally burst in the chest.

Ellyssa did not care and would not even if she were of a mind to form such a rational thought. Her terrified mind put her in full flight with no energy spared for any other kind of thought or reason. She rounded a corner and found her way blocked by a large wagon laden with cargo. With a cry of fury, Ellyssa hurled the Source at the unfortunate conveyance and blasted it to pieces, sending bits of it and its cargo flying in all directions.

To my readers
Thank you for your outstanding support.

CHAPTER 1

Ellyssa gasped as the sting of Sonjay's cruel whip ripped open the back of her blouse and the tender flesh beneath. She instinctually grabbed at the Source, but the shackles on her wrists prevented her from reaching it. Tired of being the target of the quartermaster's abuse, she sprang to her feet and hurled her bucket of mop water at his head. The unexpected attack clipped his forehead and opened a gash above his left eye.

The dark-skinned slaver roared and pulled his arm back to give her the lashing of a lifetime. Ellyssa was not about to stand around and allow him to beat her. She would throw herself overboard and drown before suffering more abuse. She spun and ran toward the stern railing.

Several slavers tried to block her path, but they were not close enough to stop her. She pumped her legs furiously, but they felt leaden and sluggish. The air felt as thick as water, and the railing looked as though it were receding with every step she took. Stars filled her vision when a belaying pin collided with the back of her skull. Ellyssa stumbled and fell painfully onto the hard deck. She rolled onto her back and looked up at the glaring visage of Captain Jake.

"I've had enough of your trouble, girl," he said. "I told you what I'd do if you didn't behave, and I'm a man of my word."

The slaver captain pulled her up by the chain joining her wrists and dragged her to one of the cargo hold's hatches. He flipped it up with the toe of his boot and pushed Ellyssa to the edge of the opening. She stared down in horror at the mob of filthy, bedraggled men milling about in the darkness below, all shoving and pressing together to get a glimpse of precious sunlight.

What little remained of their clothing was nothing more than strips of cloth. Their flesh was as white as a fish's underbelly in the few places it shone through the black filth, clothing them far better than their rags. Desiccated hands reached up, clawing at her with eager anticipation.

"I have a present for you; just make sure you keep her alive, or I'll drown the lot of you." He smiled, flashing his gold tooth with its small diamond set in the center.

Ellyssa tried to look back at Captain Jake, to promise she would behave, but he shoved her through the open hatch into the grasping hands hungrily awaiting their gift. She screamed as fingers tore at her clothing. She thought she had faced the greatest terror of her life until Captain Jake kicked the hatch shut and darkness enveloped her.

Ellyssa awoke with a ragged gasp and fell to the floor as she tried to kick free of the blankets constricting her body and covering her head. She took several deep, shuddering breaths, mentally commanding herself not to cry. She was strong and refused to weep, especially from a mere nightmare. She had been having night terrors for the past year, ever since Azerick died, but they were coming more frequently.

This was the fourth time her dreams had woken her this night. She glanced at her window and saw the sun was beginning to peek over the trees to the east. Knowing she would get no more sleep, Ellyssa decided to grab some food from the kitchens before the others were up and about.

It was a little earlier than she normally got up, but not by much. Ellyssa always awoke early to get to the kitchens for her morning repast in hopes she could avoid most of the tower staff. Avoid them and their accusing eyes. Everyone blamed her for Azerick's death. They were right, of course, even though most of them denied it. Even a year later, those eyes still held contempt and condemnation. Especially the ones in the mirror. Those eyes held the most contempt of all. Ellyssa had long been avoiding the mirror so she would not be forced to look into those hazel-green orbs of scorn.

Even the kitchen staff was not around when Ellyssa picked through the cupboards for some bread and cheese. Normally, she would take her meager breakfast to the woods where she spent most of her time these days, practicing there instead of going to class as she was supposed to. She was too tired to practice this morning, and she needed to go to class often enough to keep Allister and the other instructors from making a fuss over her truancy.

She hid out in her room until it was time to make her way to class. Ellyssa plodded down the stairs, avoiding everyone she saw until she reached the magical theory class and dropped into her seat. Her head thudded dully against the wood desktop.

"Congratulations, you look worse than usual. A feat to be proud of, to be sure."

Ellyssa rotated her head without lifting it from the desktop and stuck her tongue out at Roger.

"More bad dreams?" he asked.

"No more or less than usual."

"You think you're going to be able to stay awake through the entire lecture?"

"I sure hope not," Ellyssa replied. "It's the one reason I came to this class."

"Well, you better pay attention. How are you going to learn anything when you never come to class?"

"I do come to class, sometimes, and there is a lot more to magic than reading books and listening to lectures. Sometimes, I feel like I am being held back when I sit in class."

"You are being held back for your own good," Roger said seriously. "You in particular need someone to keep you in check so you don't hurt yourself or others by exceeding your abilities."

Ellyssa worked up the strength to glare at her friend. "You have no idea what my abilities are."

"Do you?"

Before Ellyssa could issue a retort, Wizard Maira entered the room and commanded everyone's attention. As Ellyssa had hoped, it took only a few minutes of droning lecture before she felt her eyes close and her mind drift away.

"Ellyssa, wake up!"

Ellyssa's eyes flew open and she bolted upright. "Yes, Chain Mistress!"

Misha glared down at the stubborn girl. "What do I have to do to you to make you pay attention?"

Ellyssa's mouth worked up and down, trying to find the words to prevent the sadistic woman from unleashing agony through her chains.

"Maybe this will help you focus," her chain mistress snapped.

Ellyssa stood and backed away as Misha stepped angrily forward. She looked at her hands and saw that the chains were no longer there. The bracelets and collar they once joined were gone as well. Ellyssa did not hesitate. She grabbed at the Source and felt it flood into her a moment before unleashing it against her cruel mistress.

Misha brought up a ward to shield herself from the young girl's magical onslaught, feeding more power into it as Ellyssa's arcane strikes forced her back across the room. Ellyssa punctuated each attack with screams of unbridled rage driven by fear. Other screams soon mixed with hers. The shouting was so loud, she barely heard Misha crying out her name, begging her to stop.

"Ellyssa, wake up! Stop this!"

The different tone of her voice finally broke through Ellyssa's subconscious. She blinked several times and saw Wizard Maira pressed against the far wall, the remnants of her ward little more than a fragile eggshell. Her next strike would have surely shattered it and possibly killed the young instructor.

Ellyssa stared down at her hands and felt the tingling of the Source as it slowly drained away. She looked around the room at the terrified faces of the other students standing rooted in shock, certain their psychotic classmate was about to murder their teacher.

Her jaw trembled as she tried to form words to apologize but could not force them past the lump in her throat. Unable to speak, she turned and fled the classroom, racing across the grounds and through the southern gate. On she ran, pushing her muscles well past the point of exhaustion. Only when her legs finally collapsed and her breath became so ragged and painful it was barely able to bring air into her lungs did she stop.

Ellyssa heaved until she purged the last bit of bile from her stomach. She lay next to her pool of vomit and wept until even her tears ran dry.

"What is wrong with me?" she shouted into the woods, but the trees did not answer.

Ellyssa clamped her eyes shut but dared not fall asleep no matter how powerful the urge to do so. When she finally opened her eyes once more, the sun had set and darkness filled the woods around her. Her stomach ached from heaving and sobbing, and her legs were as stiff and unyielding as the trees. She looked in the direction of the school and dreaded returning, but she had nowhere else to go. She hated the thought of making the walk back, but the evenings were too cold to stay in the open.

It took almost half an hour just to get her legs to obey and carry her back home. She was miles from the school, and it seemed an eternity before she finally reached the flickering orange glow of the torches and lamps lit upon the walls. Ellyssa collapsed onto her bed, terrified of going back to sleep but powerless to prevent it.

If the nightmares returned that night, she did not remember them. Pale light seeped through her window, heralding a new day. A new day of the same old pain, the same accusing stares, and the same unrelenting ocean of guilt.

She ran a quick brush blindly through her long, tangled hair and grabbed whatever clothes lay close at hand. She stole down the stairs of the old tower and darted into the kitchen. Agnes was there, as usual, along with several other kitchen staff, busily preparing enough food to feed nearly a thousand hungry mouths. Agnes, rushing between the three full kitchens, one of which was in the new tower, paid Ellyssa no heed and would not have even if she were not so busy. The cook was fully aware of the girl's ritual and was one of those who preferred not to have anything to do with her.

Ellyssa dodged the bodies milling around, which was far easier than avoiding the accusing looks, and snatched up morsels of food before escaping into the dining room. She was barely halfway through her breakfast when the sound of voices preceded the appearance of nearly everyone she wanted to elude.

Allister, Rusty, Colleen, and worst of all, Lady Miranda strode into the dining hall earlier than was their normal routine. All conversation ceased as the arrivals stopped and looked at Ellyssa who stared back like a trapped animal, her half-chewed food filling her mouth with the taste of ashes. That moment of silence spoke volumes before Ellyssa bolted for the kitchen, the remains of her breakfast left half-eaten on her plate. Agnes and half a dozen scullery maids thwarted her escape by trying to enter the dining room with trays bearing the morning meals for the school's masters.

Her retreat blocked, Ellyssa spun, ran along the far side of the table, and fled through the door through which the others had emerged with her head down and her arms crossed defensively across her chest.

"Ellyssa," Allister began to say, but Ellyssa was already past and sprinting for the doors leading outside. The old mage sighed loudly. "More than a year and the girl still can't bear to be in the same room with us. I'm surprised she can tolerate sitting through her classes."

"Other than her frequent truancy, she has been doing exceptionally well, until yesterday." Rusty said.

"What happened?" Allister asked.

Rusty and the others took their seats around the table. "She attacked Maira. She fell asleep in class, and I think her night terrors have returned. When Maira tried to wake her, Ellyssa called her Misha and Chain Mistress. She said Ellyssa looked at her like a trapped animal and lashed out at her. If some of the other students had not helped reinforce her ward, Ellyssa may have killed her before coming to her senses."

"Dear gods," Allister muttered.

They all knew of Ellyssa's nightmares, but there had never been an episode this serious before. They had tried various potions and even had Brother Thomas use his divine powers to try to bring her a measure of peace. It seemed to have helped a little, but that no longer appeared to hold true.

Rusty continued. "Except for yesterday, she has shown more effort than I have seen from any other student, including Roger. It's just too bad a tragedy had to occur to make her take her studies seriously."

Allister harrumphed. "Too seriously if you ask me. The girl does nothing but study and practice. I fear for her sanity if she keeps herself locked in Azerick's lab all day and night. Perhaps my fears are borne out."

"Do you think it is wise to leave her alone with Azerick's book?" Rusty asked. "The tome contains a lot of information on advanced magic and has already gotten her into trouble once. With this new development, the last thing she needs is more power."

"I do, actually," Allister replied with a nod. "She is not the frivolous little girl she was before the…accident, and I think Azerick would want her to use it to reach her full potential since she has matured."

"How can you call what happened an accident?" Miranda practically snapped.

Allister laid a gentling hand upon Miranda's forearm. "I know how painful this has been for you. Azerick was the son I never had. But you need to let go and forgive Ellyssa. She was young and foolish, but she loved him as much as any of us, and her pain is just as great. Greater, probably, since she refuses to unload the additional burden of being responsible. We all need to try and bring her back to us instead of pushing her further away."

"I have told her I forgive her; when I can keep her in the same room long enough to say it."

"Yes, you have said the words, but such pain and guilt need far more than the words, my dear."

Miranda' took in and released a deep breath. "I try, Allister. The gods know how I try, but every time I see her, when I look at my son, all I see is the girl who led my husband to his death. I know in my mind it is not fair to think in that way, but I cannot convince my heart, and my heart speaks the truth when I try to say otherwise."

"You would not be human otherwise, my dear," Allister told the still grieving widow. "Perhaps we all just need more time. Speaking of young Daebian, Aggie and I believe we have done what we can to shed some light on his…condition. This is all more of her expertise, so let us wait for her to come down to explain what we have found."

As if she were a stage actor awaiting her cue, Aggie burst through the dining room door, putting the finishing touches on her tightly bound bun of hair. "I tell you, it would almost be worth being a man just so I could stick my feet in a pair of slippers, drop a robe over my head, and be ready to start my day. Miranda, I don't know how you manage to look as lovely as you do by the sixth hour."

"Easy," Miranda said with a smile, "I get up at the fifth."

"Ugh, no thank you. I will settle for second…" The elder lady mage looked at Colleen. "…well, a distant third best."

"You are beyond lovely, Aggie. You are majestic," Colleen told the venerable wizard.

"Majestic! Yes, that's the word," Allister barked. "Like a mountain: tall, old, and frigid!"

"Oh shut up, you old goat. You're lucky I'm too tired to beat you to within an inch of your miserable life."

"Aggie, Allister said you discovered something about Daebian," Miranda interjected.

"Yes. Demonology is not my specialty, but when you mess around with transdimensional magic, it's good to have some knowledge of otherworldly beings. Now, we all know about Azerick's affliction with the demon Klaraxis. When there is a possession the likes of which Azerick experienced, more happens than an entity residing in a human vessel. Their souls entwined, and Azerick's very essence became mixed to the point that one cannot be separated from the other. Most people think of the soul as a separate entity from the body, that the body is simply a container for the spirit, but others insist that the soul fills every nook and cranny of our bodies like water absorbed by a sponge. The soul does not simply reside inside the body; it melds with it and becomes every part of it."

Miranda raised her hand to her mouth. "Are you telling me my son is some kind of demon?"

"Of course not. Daebian is a sweet boy, but he has obviously inherited some of the changes made in his father. When demons are…hatched, for lack of a better word, they are forced into a very hostile world and largely left to fend for themselves. They must grow rapidly in order to defend themselves from the other predatory creatures of the abyss. Daebian has obviously taken on this trait, which is why you have a one-year-old toddler."

Daebian's birth had been an epic ordeal for Miranda, one many thought she would not survive. Miranda had grown so large during her pregnancy that they all thought she was having twins or even triplets. It was not until she went into labor that the former field surgeon, Evan, realized it was something else entirely. The man had to use a blade to open Miranda's womb and pull the twenty-pound baby boy out. If not for Brother Thomas's healing ability and weeks of imbibing healing draughts, Miranda surely would have perished. Even with magical aid, it was a full six months before she could leave the bed unassisted, and she still showed signs of the strain Daebian's birth had put on her.

At first, he seemed to be like any baby, only very large. The only thing that appeared out of sorts was the fact he never cried. He would fuss when hungry or needed changed, but he never wailed. At four months, he began walking; at five, he began talking and he grew at a rate that could almost be seen if you watched long enough; at a year old, he looked like a child of two and talked like a child of four. Even those who did not know his peculiar state noticed something very different about him.

It was in his eyes, those dark orbs seemingly able to look through the flesh and into the very soul of a person. Other than his unusual growth, it was the one thing marking him as something more than the union of Azerick and Miranda. Daebian's eyes were a brown so dark it was difficult to see where the iris ended and the pupil began. When he looked at you, it was as if every secret you ever held laid itself open like a book for him to read. It made people very uncomfortable.

Allister asked, "Have you seen anything unusual or worrisome in his behavior?"

"Not at all. He is a happy, loving little boy who likes to sing and make up poems," Miranda answered. "He is different, but otherwise a perfect child."

"Then unless we see something to the contrary, I think it reasonable to assume there is nothing more to it and treat him in accordance with his level of maturity."

"Speaking of worrisome events, have you heard about Ellyssa's episode yesterday?" Aggie asked.

Allister nodded. "We discussed it just before you came down. Rusty is concerned about allowing her access to Azerick's tome."

"He damn well should be, as should we all. I have studied magic in that book even I find daunting."

"What you all say is true, and if she is losing the grip on her sanity, we will have to make efforts to keep her from harming herself or others. I will check in on her more often to ensure she is not reaching beyond her abilities again, but I also do not want to take away the one thing that may be offering her a measure of comfort. I fear taking away her only substantial link to Azerick may push her over the edge. On to school business. Our rolls are growing once again and we need to construct another classroom and billets."

Ellyssa leapt the short flight of steps leading into the tower and stalked purposefully toward the gates. She had barely made it out of the tower when the sound of a wordlessly sung tune reached her ears. Her heart skipped a beat as she stopped and spotted Daebian hopping down the steps leading from the new tower. She looked around, frantically seeking another route of escape before he saw her, but it was too late.

"Ellyssa!" Daebian called out in his tiny, shrill voice, racing toward her. "I made up a new poem! You wanna hear it?"

Guilt-ridden anxiety clutched her heart in an iron grip, and she found it difficult to draw a breath. She did not usually react this badly, but the past day and a half had already inflicted more stress than she was willing to bear. Daebian looked so much like Azerick it made her ache with guilt. The fact he was so unique only served to remind her how much like her former mentor he was. Barely a year old, he was the size of a two-year-old with the speech and vocabulary of a child twice that.

Ellyssa swallowed the lump in her throat and slung her head from side to side. "No. I'm sorry, I have to go."

She hugged her arms around her body even tighter and broke into a run. She passed through the gate without hassle. No one bothered her anymore. The playful annoyances the melee students once gave her died with Azerick. All they had for her now were looks of reproach and condemnation.

Ellyssa decided there was no way she could go to her classes today, perhaps maybe ever again. Her mind was a jumble, and her emotions were frayed to the point of breaking, so she simply ran. She raced down the cobbled road leading to the city. Maybe a day of browsing the markets would ease her nerves. Even though the city had mourned Azerick's death, Ellyssa doubted anyone would recognize her and direct their scornful looks upon her.

A flash of movement out of the corner of her eye caught her attention. She peered into the deep shadows of the nearby forest but saw nothing. It was likely Wolf and Ghost, ever vigilant for intruders. Ever since their capture and near death in Sumara, the pair had redoubled their unofficial sentry duty. Gone was Wolf's constant grin and carefree attitude. Like her and Sandy, part of him had died during their captivity.

A massive shadow danced upon the uneven ground as Sandy flew overhead, getting a dragon's eye view of everything and everyone for miles around. The young dragon and Wolf's closeness had increased proportionally with the distance they put between Ellyssa and themselves. Sandy was growing at a phenomenal rate. Young dragons grew largely in accordance with the availability of their food source, and Sandy's food was practically unlimited. Although she now did a great deal of hunting on her own, the large stockpiles of food kept at the school ensured her belly was always full, and the energy it provided went mostly to growth.

Sandy spent almost her entire time in the woods with Wolf hunting, flying, and practicing her innate dragon magic. Allister had found several references to dragon magic in Azerick's big book. Those, along with her egg memories, gave her the knowledge she needed. Ellyssa knew Sandy's breaking had been much like her own, and the experience had created a similar change in the young dragon. She was wary and worked daily to improve her strength, flying, and magic so no one would ever be able to abuse her again.

Ellyssa did not know how much longer she could tolerate living in a place where every face reminded her of her responsibility for Azerick's death. She needed the school so she could practice and learn. She had already increased her skill considerably by devoting her full attention and nearly every waking minute of her life to practice. She knew Allister and the others were worried her newfound devotion was becoming an obsession, but they did not understand. None of them could ever understand.

It was a long walk to North Haven, but the desire to be anywhere else right now motivated her, and the inner turmoil fueled her muscles. In little more than an hour, Ellyssa was walking amongst the numerous trade tables and stalls, many of which were still being set up. She was early and the walk burned off her half-eaten breakfast, so Ellyssa bought a roll fresh from the oven and wandered aimlessly for another hour before the majority of the proprietors set their wares out to sell. She navigated the booths and tables at random, looking for nothing in particular. The one thing she wanted could not be found here, or anywhere.

Ellyssa watched some children moving amongst the tables. Some were older than she was and a few others were younger. She knew they were sneak thieves, ready to pilfer a trinket or bite of food if they got the chance. Azerick's school had removed many kids like these from the streets, but not all. This was a way of life for them, one many of them willingly chose. The school was where those kids who desired to escape this life lived. The streets were where those who did not want to go to the school found refuge and did what it took to survive.

It was still early, but Ellyssa was growing bored and much of the stress and anxiety had finally ebbed to the point where she could at least go back home. She still dreaded the thought of sitting in class, but she would not squander her time. She would go down to Azerick's laboratory where he kept the big book and practice her spells. She was just about to leave the square when a light hand hesitantly touched her elbow.

"Ellyssa."

Ellyssa turned and looked at the woman who had stopped her. She appeared almost middle-aged but was probably ten years younger than the deep lines created by a lifetime of hard, meager living indicated. She wore a thin homespun dress meticulously repaired and kept together by numerous stitches and patches.

"It's me, your mother," the woman said as she withdrew her trembling hand. "I saw you, and I wanted to know if you were all right."

"You want to know if I'm all right after I got the man you sold me to killed?" Ellyssa asked cruelly. "No, *Mother*, I am not all right, but you gave up the right to pretend you cared when you sold me."

"Ellyssa, please. We never stopped loving you. We think of you all the time. He came to us, you know. He came every few months to make sure we were doing okay and to tell us how wonderful you were doing at the...the school."

Ellyssa furrowed her brow, surprised by the revelation. "When he took me in, he said I was his and you would have no more contact."

Ellyssa's mother smiled. "He was a kind man, much kinder than he liked to show. He was a good man."

"He was a great man! And because you sold me to him, he is a dead man!"

The woman took a step back in the face of her daughter's fury. "We had no choice. We were all going to starve. We would have died otherwise."

"Then we should have died!" The nearby crowd of shoppers all stopped and stared as the scene unfolded. "He helped people! All I have done is cause everyone around me pain. You say you never stopped caring. Azerick died before letting me go! He cared, not you! Others loved him so much; strangers who barely knew him, but knew how great a person he was, died for him to come rescue me! Selling me was not your last act of desperation, it was your first. He was my true parent, and now I have none."

Ellyssa picked a direction at random and found herself running once again. She could run from her mother, run from the accusing eyes of everyone at the school, but no matter how furiously she ran, she could not escape the pain in her heart. How much worse could this day get? She had not felt this bad in almost a year. It felt like everything that could go wrong had gathered and waited for this day to leap from the shadows and bury her beneath a mountain of emotional torment.

People stared at her as she ran down street after street, looking behind her to see if the Watch was giving chase. Ellyssa eventually found herself in the lower common quarter. Eyes still followed her everywhere despite her having slowed to a purposeful walk. Let them look! Let them stare at her with their judgmental eyes!

Ellyssa spotted a stray dog sniffing around for a scrap of food and realized how hungry and thirsty her flight had made her. She searched the area and found a kitchen and bar three blocks over. It was not the nicest establishment in North Haven by any means, but she would probably have to cross the entire district to find a better one. The smell of food wafting through the open doors was sufficient to entice her inside.

The distraught girl stepped inside and found the place packed with diners. Every table in the place was filled to capacity and beyond. The din of dozens of voices was a physical assault on her ears. She was about to turn away and find somewhere less crowded and noisy when a voice accosted her.

"Come here, honey!" a grizzled older man with the look of a logger called out, beckoning her with a wave of his arm. "You look a bit rough. Let ol' Brad smooth ya out!"

At barely fourteen, Ellyssa was still within her girlhood, but her disheveled appearance, sunken eyes, and the rapid maturity brutal captivity brought on made her look several years older. Although it was not even yet noon, the man was obviously getting a jump on a day of drinking.

"Brad, you leave that girl alone! She looks like she has enough troubles without you making the usual ass of yourself."

A rotund serving woman with a matronly bearing and kind smile approached and took Ellyssa by the elbow. Ellyssa flinched but allowed the woman to guide her toward the bar.

"You don't pay the old goat no mind. He likes to bother anyone with a new face, especially a pretty one. You look hungry. Would you like something to eat?"

Ellyssa nodded.

"Can ya pay?" the woman asked, seemingly abashed at making such a request.

Ellyssa nodded again and fished a silver coin from her pocket.

"Well there's a nice change of pace. Most folks looking like you come in here without two coppers to rub together. I have a big skillet of logger's omelet cooked up and ready. I'll go fix you a plate."

The woman reappeared from the kitchen barely a minute later with a plate heaped full of scrambled eggs topped with chunks of pork sausage and melted cheese. She set a glass of water down next to the plate at the corner of the bar. Ellyssa took the plate in one hand and picked up the water with the other. She looked around the room and made for an empty chair set against the wall. There was no table, but she would make do.

Her attention focused on navigating through the crowd, Ellyssa did not notice she was passing right by the table where the obstinate logger was sitting. The cup of water Ellyssa was holding fell to the ground when Brad grabbed her by the wrist and pulled her toward him.

"I was just playin' with ya, girl. Here now, give Brad a little peck on the cheek to show there's no hard feelin's."

Ellyssa's throat closed and her lungs froze as she looked at the man's grinning face. A bright gold tooth set in the front of his mouth winked mockingly when the light of a nearby lamp struck it. It was unadorned and occupied the space next to his left incisor, but Ellyssa's tormented mind moved it back and elongated it into a canine tooth with a glittering diamond set in its middle. The deep creases of his sun-aged face smoothed out, and his somewhat humorous laughter turned mocking and cruel.

Ellyssa stared into Captain Jake's face and her blood boiled. She dropped her plate of food, grabbed the wrist of the offending hand, and tore madly at the Source. Ellyssa poured white-hot electrical fire into the man's arm. Other patrons cried out and leapt away in fear as Brad screamed in anguish, helpless to do anything as the smell of burnt flesh and hair filled the room.

"Witch!" a man cried out, trying to pull the wild-eyed girl off Brad before she killed him. "Let him go!"

Ellyssa turned and faced the man grabbing at her and saw Sonjay's big black face twisted in anger, ready to lash her with his whip once again. A scream tore from Ellyssa's throat, drowning out the hoarse wailing of the tortured man now falling from his chair. Outside, passers-by stopped and stared at the front of the diner from where those horrible screams emanated.

The walls exploded outward, blasted the onlookers from their feet, and pelted them with splinters and planks of wood. The entire roof caved in and crashed down with a billowing cloud of dust. Even as the astonished spectators struggled to their feet, a second explosion turned a portion of the roof into splinters and shards of clay tiles and sent them arcing hundreds of feet over the tops of the neighboring buildings.

Like a demon emerging from the shadowy recesses of the abyss, Ellyssa burst from the cloud of dust, skidded across the loose pieces of wreckage, and sprinted down the street. She made a mindless dash through the city, fueling her body by drawing in the Source and feeding it directly to her muscles. It was something briefly talked about in class, but they were warned that it was a very dangerous practice to use. It was very easy to push oneself so hard that the heart gave out and literally burst in the chest.

Ellyssa did not care and would not even if she were of a mind to form such a rational thought. Her terrified mind put her in full flight with no energy spared for any other kind of thought or reason. She rounded a corner and found her way blocked by a large wagon laden with cargo. With a cry of fury, Ellyssa hurled the Source at the unfortunate conveyance and blasted it to pieces, sending bits of it and its cargo flying in all directions.

On she ran through the city, out of the gates, and up the road to her home. Ellyssa made the ninety-minute walk into a twenty-minute sprint. By the time she reached the safety of the tower, she was certain her heart was going to explode, and almost welcomed the freedom it would bring; freedom from the fear, uncertainty, and shame that defined the majority of her life.

Ellyssa staggered drunkenly up the stairs, snatched the blanket from the top of her bed, and wedged herself in the small space between her wardrobe and the wall next to it. She collapsed into the corner nook and huddled under her blanket, trembling. This was the worst day of her life since she had been captured. All those horrible memories had come flooding back. The feeling of weakness and helplessness drove her to the brink of insanity. Just before exhaustion pulled her into the numbing folds of unconsciousness, Ellyssa wondered how much more it would take to push her forever over that edge.

A soft rapping on her door startled her awake. Ellyssa peered over the top of the blanket and saw only blackness through the small window of her room. The rapping sounded again, this time followed by Allister's soft, rumbling voice.

"Ellyssa, it's me, Allister. May I come in?"

When Ellyssa did not answer, the old mage slowly pushed open the door and stuck his head inside. He spotted the huddled lump of blanket in the corner. Allister entered the room fully and touched the dimly glowing glass globe on the wall, filling the room with soft white light.

"Ah, there you are. Are you all right?"

Ellyssa's only response was to bury herself deeper into the blanket and try to melt into the wall by sheer force of will.

"A lot of people were hurt today."

"Did anyone die?" The muffled question came from under the blanket.

"No, thankfully, although that in itself is a miracle," Allister answered. "The man will lose the arm."

"No remorse," Ellyssa whispered, almost hypnotically.

"What was that?"

Ellyssa pulled the blanket down and looked at the kindly old wizard. "He should not have grabbed me."

Allister shook his head. "No. No, he should not have, but you must learn to control yourself. I know you hurt, and I know you were scared, but you must conquer the fear and the pain. You have an amazing amount of power within you, and you have yet to tap your full potential. Your studies have been going extremely well, but I fear you are becoming too isolated. It is not good for people to be alone with their own thoughts for too long. The mind has a remarkable ability to confuse and trap us within its ramblings. It is then we do something foolish."

"No one else wants me around. They all blame me and hate me."

"That's not true, Ellyssa."

"Yes it is!" Ellyssa shouted. "I see it every time they look at me. Especially Miranda. She tries to hide it. She's too nice not to try, but it's still there. Especially when Daebian is around. I look at him and I imagine him riding on Azerick's shoulders around the school, but I know it will never happen because of me, and it hurts so much! It's all I can do to lose myself in my studies. It's the only way I can stop thinking about it, to ignore the pain."

Allister let out a sigh. "Oh, child, you must not ignore it. Pain cannot be ignored. It will only come back, often at the most inopportune time. Like yesterday and today. You must face it, accept it, and move past it. If you do not, then you become a slave to it. Remember what I told you. Be strong for Azerick. It is what he would want, and hiding from the unpleasant is not what a strong person does."

Ellyssa bobbed her head. Allister patted her on the knee and left her alone. Ellyssa's stomach growled angrily, reminding her she had eaten next to nothing all day. She eventually mustered the strength to shed the blanket providing a rather flimsy shield from the world outside her bedroom and quietly snuck downstairs.

The lower level was empty with the exception of the hideously ugly dog, Lord Crowley, who lay as always in front of the fireplace despite no fire burning on this moderate night. Ellyssa made it to the kitchens uninterrupted and scavenged through the cupboards and pantry for something to eat. Mission accomplished, she began to make her way back upstairs where her bed demanded her undivided attention.

As Ellyssa passed the open stairwell leading down to Azerick's laboratory, she paused and looked down the stairs. "Hello? Is someone in the lab?"

When no answer was forthcoming, Ellyssa cautiously crept down the stairs, trailing a nervous hand along the wall as she descended. When she reached the bottom, she found the heavy steel door firmly shut. Having permission to use the laboratory, it opened with the touch of her hand. Inside, it was dark and felt empty. Touching the magical globe on the wall confirmed it when the orb, along with several others attached all along the walls, flared into a bright light and illuminated the entire chamber.

Ellyssa took one more look around, letting her eyes pause at the thick tome resting on a tall podium like an orchestra conductor's sheet music—if his stack of music was six inches thick. With a shrug of her shoulders, Ellyssa doused the lights and retired to her room.

CHAPTER 2

The seven heads of the Magus Academy convened in the massive, dark, and austere Hall of Judgment. It was a vast chamber with seven cathedral-style pointed arches supporting the granite roof thirty feet overhead. The seven Magus Academy councilors occupied throne-like seats of the same rigid and unyielding stone atop a long dais ten feet above the hall floor.

Beyond that, the room was practically bare, bereft of art or furnishings except for a few rows of backless benches. The hall was the central point of all major decision-making for the Academy. Everything from Academy rules to legal inquisitions was debated and decided here. All seven council seats were occupied, each by an archmage of the Academy wearing formal robes. Several members of the Academy stood in front of or sat upon the stone benches as the council members took their seats.

"Magus Robert Harvey," Headmaster Florent called down to the man standing below, "you have requested this emergency convening of the council. What is it you feel necessitates our immediate attention?"

A man in his mid-forties, of average build, and with the thin line of a black beard took a step forward from the few others in attendance. "Headmaster, esteemed council members; an associate of mine has sent me word of an event which has occurred in North Haven, and I believe it requires the Academy's swift response."

"What is this event, Magus?"

"Several days ago, a young woman believed to be a member of the orphans' academy, as the locals call it, used magic in a populated eating establishment resulting in numerous severe injuries, the destruction of the building, and damage to several nearby structures. I feel this so-called school has operated for far too long without being under the auspices of the Academy. I have voiced my opinion before regarding this renegade school of magic and the dangers its teaching of unregulated magic poses."

Headmaster Florent's lips compressed into a thin line of disapproval. "Yes, you have made your concerns clear. Do we know for certain the wizard belongs to this school?"

"I do not have that level of detailed information at this time, Headmaster, but if you give me leave to conduct an investigation so we can bring this renegade wizard to heel, I will certainly get it. Then, with that information in hand, I will recommend the unlawful school either falls under the control of the Academy or is permanently shut down."

"Magus Harvey, may I remind you this school is now being run by two of the Academy's most esteemed archmages and a wizard-level Academy graduate?"

"I understand that, and only that fact keeps me from filing a formal petition to have the school shut down immediately. The argument remains that a renegade whose teaching doctrine does not follow Academy guidelines, moral standards, or rigid attendance requirements founded it. This may be the biggest disaster created by one of their poorly trained students of magic thus far, but it is far from an isolated event. If the school does not fall under full Academy oversight, I feel this is just the beginning. We may soon be facing numerous renegades of substantial power with little to no discipline. We must act before another tragedy occurs."

"Do we know the identity of the mage in question?" Headmaster Florent asked.

"No, but she is described as a young woman between sixteen and twenty years of age. If the council will grant me a writ of inquisition, I am certain I can find out very quickly."

A fit man in his late forties or early fifties stood up and addressed the council. "Before you go and do something irrevocably stupid, I can tell you who it was."

"Ambassador Sabaht, you know the identity of the woman?" the headmaster asked.

"I do." Devlin, Azerick's former master, turned his eyes toward Magus Harvey. "I too have *associates* who pass important information to me, and it would seem they do a significantly better job. The mage is Ellyssa Jensen, and she is hardly a woman, but a girl who only recently turned fourteen. She was Sorcerer Azerick's ward and apprentice."

Magus Harvey sneered. "Well, that certainly explains a great deal. It hardly comes as a surprise that a renegade would beget a renegade. This only proves my point that the practices being taught in North Haven are a very real danger to the kingdom and should be stopped immediately. Need I remind the council this was the same man who murdered the former headmaster?"

"Headmaster Dondrian was involved in a scheme to overthrow King Jarvin, which goes against the strict laws of Academy neutrality," Devlin pointed out.

"A fact that only came to light after he killed Dondrian. He also took Academy wizards to End's Run in the support of King Jarvin, thus breaking the law of neutrality himself!" Magus Harvey countered.

"A law Azerick is not beholden to since he never made it to the level required to take the oaths of an official member of the Academy. It could be argued that he acted as his oaths to the King required in his station as the future duke of North Haven. Magus Allister and Magus Cossington's involvement can be attributed to dealing with the near-disastrous necromantic summoning in the region."

"You again make my point, Ambassador! Azerick is a runaway from the Academy, after murdering a fellow student, who then continued to practice magic without Academy training or oversight. He then founded a school teaching the lowest members of society in the same manner; a manner resulting in severe injury and loss of property."

"Enough," Headmaster Florent called down as Devlin was about to make another retort. "Ambassador, you seem to know more about the particulars of what happened. What can you tell us of this event?"

Devlin shot a final glare at the wizard next to him before he responded. "Ellyssa was taken by slavers nearly a year and a half ago. She was then sold to the vila of Bakhtaran, a rogue province in Sumara. Vila Mushadan had been recruiting and enslaving spellcasters for years. Those he obtained unwillingly were mercilessly tortured as part of their training and breaking. A man in the destroyed establishment grabbed Ms. Jensen, and I believe she suffered an episode of some sort. In a state of panic, she used her magic against what she perceived as a threat. This is not a case of a renegade wizard, but the reaction of a terrified child."

"Headmaster, this is all irrelevant! If the girl is emotionally unbalanced, then all the more reason to bring her in before she commits even worse crimes."

"I have heard enough," the headmaster declared. "Council, what say you in this matter?"

Magus Dorothy Sorenson, an elder wizard spoke up. "I believe Magus Harvey's points are valid. Regardless of the circumstances, this school is producing mages of respectable power without proper safeguards and oversight. I think we have humored its existence for far too long. It is time to rein it in."

"I think we should take something of a diplomatic approach," Magus Morgarum, the cherubic alchemy instructor replied. "Let us not forget Sorcerer Azerick was not only married to the duchess of North Haven's daughter, but was a friend of the king as well. This school of theirs has had a very important impact upon the city, and we do not wish to alienate some very notable people by acting abruptly."

The other four councilors were evenly split between taking immediate action to either shut the school down or bring it under the direct auspices of the Academy, and simply opening a line of dialog. It came to the headmaster to break the stalemate.

"Magus Harvey, I will grant you leave to perform a cursory investigation and to speak with the heads of this orphans' academy so we may gauge the curriculum and safeguards they have in place. This is not an inquisition. This is a fact-finding and discourse mission only. Do I make myself clear?"

"Of course, Headmaster. I have no doubt that when I return I will have no problem convincing the entire council that allowing this sort of unauthorized teaching of magic is a serious danger."

"I hope you will try to keep an open mind, Magus," Headmaster Florent suggested. "You will take Magus Brown and Magus Parkes with you."

"Yes, Headmaster."

The seated assembly stood as the council members shuffled out of the room. Once the senior mages cleared the chamber, Devlin turned to Magus Harvey.

"Have you ever been tortured, Magus Harvey?" Devlin asked. "Have you ever been made to feel helpless as someone stripped away all your power and dignity?"

The wizard set his jaw. "I hardly see the relevance."

"I spent very little time with the girl, but I like to think I do know her master. If you screw this up, you might just find out."

"M-master Allister," Simon stammered, "there are some, ah, um, people here to, ah, see you."

Allister was sitting in the large living area of the old tower, taking advantage of the solitude to read. Rusty and Colleen were out with the twins on a picnic, which left only Simon, Theresa, Jansen, and Ellyssa. Jansen was out on the drill grounds, Ellyssa was rarely seen and was certainly off practicing somewhere, and Simon and Theresa were practically invisible unless something was needed—like now.

Allister set his book on the table next to him and stood up. "Show them in, if you would, Simon."

The little accountant and de facto school steward disappeared back through the doors and then reappeared a moment later with two men and a woman in tow. Allister's stomach clenched. He recognized the trio as being from the Academy. He had been dreading their arrival since Ellyssa's violent and public episode. His expectation did little to make him feel any better about their appearance.

"Magus Allister, I am Robert Harvey, and this is Oliver Parkes and Melanie Brown of the Academy," Magus Harvey said before Simon could make any introductions.

Allister leaned down and whispered something in Simon's ear and the little man darted upstairs. He then gave each of the Academy wizards a nod. "To what do I owe the pleasure of this visit?"

Magus Harvey smiled, aware that the old archmage knew exactly why he was here. "We are investigating an attack within the city by a young girl by the name of Ellyssa Jensen."

"It was hardly an attack. A man accosted her and she panicked in defense of herself."

"Ah, so you are aware of what happened. Good, I was concerned this *school* and its students were completely without oversight. So, do you simply choose to ignore the criminal behavior of all your students, or just this one?"

Allister was taken aback by the man's unexpected hostility. "Criminal behavior? What are you going on about? This incident has been investigated and all damage recompensed."

"By whom, the duchess and your cadre? Hardly an objective body to conduct a proper investigation. It is why such matters fall fully under the jurisprudence of the Academy. We shall decide guilt and punishment. Where is the girl?"

"She is not here. I imagine she is off studying somewhere," Allister answered tersely. "If that is all, I bid you good day."

Magus Harvey knew the old archmage was giving him the brush-off. "Please send someone to fetch her. We will be taking her back to the Academy for questioning."

"Like hell you will," Allister bristled. "I assume you have a writ of apprehension?"

"I can get one if you insist upon being uncooperative."

"I doubt that. If the council felt it necessary for you to arrest the child, they would have sent one with you. Now, what is it you are really doing here, Harvey?"

"I, along with many at the Academy, see your *school* as a threat. You not only operate outside the purview of the Academy, you teach magic to commoners. We have no idea what your agenda is or what it is you are teaching this riffraff!"

"Simon," Allister called upstairs.

Simon appeared instantly, descended the stairs, and handed the Academy wizard a book.

"You will find our training curriculum in there, and you will see the tenets nearly mirror those of the Academy. As to whom we are teaching, there has never been a mandate restricting Academy attendance. The current state of elitism is an artificial construct created by pretentious snobs like you. Now, if there is nothing else, you may show yourselves out."

Magus Harvey sneered at the book in his hand. "It really does not matter what is in this book. The fact remains this school is no more legitimate than the Black Tower. Continue to train and harbor criminals like the girl, and we shall shut you down, by force if necessary."

Magus Allister's face clouded in fury. "This school hosts two of the premier archmages in the kingdom, five full wizards, and nearly five hundred journeymen and apprentice level mages. Threaten this school and you will find your threat very difficult to carry out!"

"Put away your bluster, Allister. We both know your bluff for what it is. The former master of this school may have been willing to throw away his life and the lives of these children, but not you."

"Get out of my school! It is no longer a request," Allister snarled through clenched teeth.

Magus Harvey sneered contemptuously before he and his two companions departed the tower. Allister tried to calm his nerves by taking several deep breaths. Magus Harvey had been right. Azerick would not have hesitated to fight the Academy if they had threatened him. Had he been here, Azerick would likely already be halfway to Southport to challenge the entire council. But he would not. He would not jeopardize the lives of the people at the school in open conflict with the Academy. Allister was certain given the king and Duchess Mellina's backing, the Academy would not press too hard unless something catastrophic occurred.

Ellyssa listened to the terse conversation from the safety of the laboratory stairwell. Her stomach churned as the Academy mage threatened to take her in and close down the school. She hastened back down the stairs the moment the other wizards left and paced about the laboratory.

"If Azerick were here, they would not dare make such threats! But he's not here. Because of me. Because of Captain Jake. I swear I will kill Captain Jake and every slaver in the city. They took me, they took Azerick, and they need to die. I need to be stronger though. I can't let them or the Academy take me." Ellyssa spun around. "Who's there?"

She looked around the room, but it was barren except for her and the big tome resting upon its podium. Ellyssa studied the book more closely. Was it glowing, or was it just a trick of the light? She stepped toward the book Azerick had liberated from the psyling city and fought a dragon to reclaim.

"Is it you? How is this possible? You can help me? How?" Ellyssa took a deep breath. "Show me."

The book practically jumped on the podium when its cover flipped open and the pages fluttered as it fanned open. Line after line of text swam about on the pages as if alive and rearranged themselves to give her what she needed. Ellyssa looked down upon the spells laid out for her to see, the light of the glowing text illuminating her face, and she smiled.

CHAPTER 3

Azerick was engrossed in yet another obscure tome, plucked from the black stone shelves of what passed for a library within the shadowy, foreboding halls of Klaraxis's massive citadel. It was impossible to tell how long he had dwelled within the onyx halls. Only the number of books he pored over in his quest to discover a way out of this abyssal prison gave him any indication of the passage of time.

He soon discovered he no longer needed sleep or food—at least not in the way a human viewed such things. Demons fed on the energy contained within a shade, which was essentially the soul of the damned. Not all shades were damned, however. Lesser shades were little more than a shadow of the soul belonging to anyone who died. Those souls who were not damned to the abyss went to the kingdom of the god who chose them, but a portion, a shadow copy of the soul, went to the abyss as food for the demons who dwelled there. Sharrellan was the goddess of death, and Death always got her due. It was only the truly wicked people whose true souls went to the abyss to writhe in torment until the demons devoured them. Such an end to misery could take centuries.

I do not understand why you continue to toil away down here, Klaraxis complained. This same argument invaded Azerick's mind for probably the hundredth time.

"Because I refuse to accept that there is no way out." Azerick responded as he always did, when he bothered to reply to the largely rhetorical statement at all.

I have been the master of this dismal realm for almost two thousand years. If there were a way out, I would have found it long ago.

"The wizard, Shakrill, she brought you out of the abyss, so there must be a way."

Shakrill transferred the bulk of my soul into a human vessel. I was little more than the shades you see here, only I had the strength to possess another. That was the plan anyway. Besides, I truly doubt anyone you know would be willing to make the blood sacrifices required simply to contact you much less attempt to transfer your essence into another body.

"Regardless, I have never given up on anything before, and I am not about to start now. It is not as though I have anything better to do with my time."

On the contrary, you have very pressing matters to which you must attend. You have an entire realm requiring your guidance and judgment. The denizens of this place require constant attention to keep them from battling one another. You are the balance upon which the scales rest. Ruling this place requires a swift iron fist to crush any concerted uprising.

"I prefer to rule by detached ambivalence. Let these disgusting creatures destroy one another. What is it to me if they kill each other?"

Fool! Your lack of interest is perceived as an inability to rule. Anything appearing as weakness is a call to replace you by anyone capable of doing so. Even now, we could easily crush any of these lesser creatures, but there are other lords in the other circles who ache to claim my position nearest the dark goddess's side.

"Again, why should I care? I want nothing to do with Sharrellan, this place, or the foul creatures within it. Let them and everything around them rot."

For a creature who has shown such remarkable cleverness, you are amazingly stupid and shortsighted at times. You think you and your humanity are so much better than we are, but who are the real monsters? Who is truly depraved? Yes, any demon worthy of being called such will lie and tear you apart the instant it becomes beneficial to do so. But anyone who is not a fool knows that when they make any pact with our ilk. It is you humans who are true creatures of chaos. You smile to each other's faces and destroy everything around you, sometimes simply on a whim. You can never be certain who your friends and allies are, or who will plunge a dagger into your heart. We demons are vile, cruel, and malicious, but it is humans who are truly disgusting.

The little demog, Skulk, fluttered into the chamber, noisily flapping his undersized wings. "Supreme Master, several unworthy succubi and balrogs request your attention. I told them you were busy, but they were insistent and threatened to tear off Skulk's wings."

Azerick sighed heavily. It was obvious neither Klaraxis nor the demons were going to let him get any peace until he made some kind of showing. He stood and followed Skulk down the black, depressing passageways that seemed to twist and turn randomly with no order or thought to their layout.

Azerick eventually stepped into the cavernous throne room belonging to Klaraxis. He seated himself upon the spacious granite and skull throne set atop a large dais of similar construction and looked down upon the demons waiting restlessly below. The opposing factions divided the room into two sides. On his left were nearly a dozen succubi, each glaring their hatred toward the toad-like balrogs to his right. Azerick was familiar with the succubi. He had fought some of them when he first came to this place, and they were commonly seen flying about the skies.

The balrogs tended to keep largely to themselves, living in colonies near the fringes of the realm. They looked like a cross between a toad and a gorilla. The creatures were covered in a pebbly hide the color of the dusky red landscape. Unlike toads, their front arms were a near match for their powerful hind legs in both size and strength. Their enormous mouth, which comprised a large portion of their entire head, opened to reveal rows upon rows of dagger-like teeth.

"What is it you want?" Azerick asked impatiently.

"The succubi invade our territory and steal what is ours," the balrog croaked. "We asked them to cease their encroachment but they refuse. We demanded and they still refuse."

"Yours is what you can defend. That is the law of the land," the succubus replied languidly.

"There are rules! You taunt and insult us. You hurl filth at us from the skies! Such insults will not be tolerated!"

"Or what?" the very feminine demon taunted. "If you and your pathetic ground-bound ilk cannot protect your hunting grounds, what do you think you are going to do to stop us?"

"Maybe make you ground-bound with us, harpy witch!"

Faster than Azerick thought possible, the balrog leapt at the succubus, grabbed her left wing near the base, and savagely tore it from her back. The room erupted into chaos. The grievously wounded succubus screeched in pain and rage and leapt away as her sisters took flight and began hurling balls of fire from their hands.

The Balrogs' warty hides were tough and resisted much of the damage the searing heat of the succubi's fireballs should have caused, so the winged demons changed tactics. They made swift, swooping dives at the ground-bound demons, hurling heavy objects they grabbed up from around the room and dove swiftly from the vaulted ceiling, slashing at the stouter demons' eyes with blades and claws. This tactic proved fatal in such a relatively confined area. Like a cat snatching a bird from the air, one balrog leapt thirty feet up, snatched a succubus from the air, twisted, and crushed its body, eliciting a series of sickening cracks until it ceased moving.

The flying demon women flapped their wings until the roof of the chamber prevented them from gaining any more altitude and focused their attacks on an individual balrog, pummeling it with stone and steel and striking it with dozens of fiery orbs. This concerted attack finally broke through the creature's skin and left it a battered and smoldering corpse upon the floor.

The balrogs retaliated by tearing head-sized stones from the floor and flinging them with the power and accuracy of a catapult. One stone caught a succubus in the chest, and it spiraled down like a struck bird. The two sides continued hurling stones, fire, and insults, and the casualties were slowly mounting, as well as the damage being done to the audience chamber.

You need to put an end to this. Your ambivalence appears as weakness. To allow this kind of conduct within my great hall is unacceptable!

"I find it rather amusing. The gods know I need some entertainment," Azerick retorted.

You will not find it amusing when they turn on you. The only thing keeping these creatures from each other's throats, as well as yours, is fear.

"Fine." Azerick stood and looked at both sides of the warring factions. "Enough!" Azerick had to duck as a stone the size of his head came whizzing past. "I said enough!"

Azerick raised his arms and extended his will. He thrust outward and sent every demon in the vast chamber crashing into the far wall hard enough to crack bones and stun the senses. He thrust his arms down, yanked the succubi from the air, and crushed all the demons to the floor.

Both sides turned their hateful glares toward Azerick. "You succubi stop poaching kills from the balrogs. If you see them hunting in an area, leave them be. Balrogs, the succubi are free to hunt wherever they wish, as are all of you, as long as they do not prevent you from doing the same."

"What of my wing!" the injured demon demanded. "He has ruined me!"

"You provoked him and it will grow back." *It will grow back, right?* Azerick silently asked Klaraxis.

It will, but to be flightless for even a moment is torture for one such as they.

Azerick shrugged, unconcerned for the succubus's plight. "Now, get out of my hall."

The injured succubus gave Azerick a hate-filled glare as she looked back and shuffled from the chamber, dripping black ichor from her ruined stump. Azerick practically collapsed upon the throne as he sat down. His use of power had exhausted him. There would be no more searching for a way out of this dismal place today.

You need to feed. If you will not devour the soul of one of the offerings locked below, at least consume a shade or draw from the power stored within my citadel.

Azerick knew of the humans who had been sent as offerings or who had foolishly come here of their own accord. They were wretched creatures, and he would have nothing to do with them. They were all evil people or thoroughly insane, driven mad from their captivity and torture. Neither could he destroy a shade. Such an act would prove he was no longer human and truly a denizen of this realm. Azerick could not bring himself to let go of the remaining vestige of his humanity.

However, he could not ignore Klaraxis's advice or his own hunger and ebbing strength. For centuries, the greater shades of this realm fed their energy into the stones of the massive fortress, turning them as black as their souls. The power was there for Klaraxis to draw upon for additional strength should he ever need to defend himself from an all-out attack from one of the lesser realm lords who desired to attain a loftier position. Three times in nearly two millennia, the demon lord had to defend himself from such an attack, and each time he had defeated his foes.

Azerick sought out the demonic source of power much as he did the Source and found it waiting for his call within the black stones of the mountainous ziggurat. Unlike the Source, the power here held traces of consciousness, and it cried out as Azerick consumed it. As loathsome as those cries were, it fed him and fueled his weary body. He felt his strength revitalized, if only partially. It was sufficient to go on, and that was enough for Azerick.

"Well, I think I handled that rather well, don't you?" Azerick asked Klaraxis.

Is that what you humans call a joke? You could hardly have performed worse. Your ineptness will surely destroy us both.

"You told me to make them stop and I did. I fail to see why you are still complaining. What would you have done?" Azerick asked.

I would have destroyed them all for daring to defile my hall. You gave them leave to act however they wished by not acting swiftly and decisively. You have shown weakness.

"You worry too much, Klaraxis. The issue is settled, and I have better things to do than to worry about the endless petty squabbles of demons."

Probably not for long, foolish human.

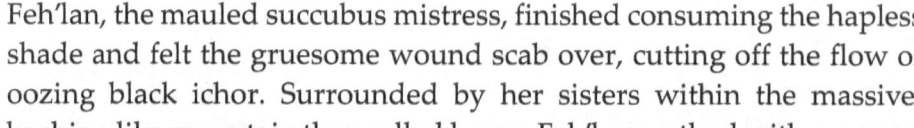

Feh'lan, the mauled succubus mistress, finished consuming the hapless shade and felt the gruesome wound scab over, cutting off the flow of oozing black ichor. Surrounded by her sisters within the massive, beehive-like mountain they called home, Feh'lan seethed with rage and thoughts of vengeance.

"Sisters, it is time we consider a change," Feh'lan declared as she consumed the shade's last wispy essence.

"What kind of change, sister?" Shree'la, the second-ranked succubus, asked.

"A change in leadership. Klaraxis is unfit for his position, and it is time for us to enact change."

Feathered wings ruffled nervously. "Feh'lan, Klaraxis has been lord of this realm for nearly two millennia. The only one who would even have a chance of supplanting him is Drak'kar, but even his power is a distant second to that of our master."

Feh'lan smiled, showing her two rows of needle-sharp teeth. "But Klaraxis is no longer in charge. We all know the human possessing his body has subverted him, yet another sign of his weakness. Did not any of you see him falter after striking us down?" Several of the succubi nodded. "Klaraxis is weak and no longer fit to rule. In his current state, I believe Drak'kar can easily destroy him. And we will help—for a price."

"If Drak'kar fails…" Shree'la began.

"Then we will all beg for death long before Klaraxis becomes bored enough to kill us, assuming he has any say in our fates whatsoever. Personally, I think the human is in complete control and lacks the stomach for such brutality. It is why our realm is in a shambles now. Even if my assertion proves wrong, is it not better than living upon the scraps of the ground-born?"

There was little debating as greed and frustration won out over potential torture and death. It took several more souls to repair Feh'lan's injury enough for her to travel and, even then, her sisters had to carry her in a sling. For succubi, or any flying creature, such humiliation only fueled their fury and desire to see the human-infected Klaraxis cast down from his lofty perch as overlord of the Fifth Circle.

A dozen succubi made up the treasonous diplomatic party. It took what could be called days in this timeless dimension to reach the border. Endless miles of red rock passed below the demons in a sea of otherwise featureless terrain. Eventually, twin spars of stone appeared far on the horizon. Distance was impossible to gauge for there was no curvature to the landscape in this world, only expansive flat plains of stone occasionally broken up by vast crevasses and spires of rock like the broken teeth of some enormous giant.

The first creatures to come into view were the colossal behemoths. The behemoths were practically mobile mountains. Standing thirty feet tall, the creatures formed the front line of defense against any hostile demons opening the gate from the Fourth Circle. The behemoths created a massive, shaggy wall of muscle and claws that made even the largest sword look pathetic in both size and sharpness.

As the succubi drew nearer, the smaller demons took shape. Other succubi on gate duty provided constant aerial surveillance while balrogs, jikin, kamaris, and an army of other demonic forces provided the bulwark against the constant threat of invasion. This was not the only gate separating the two demonic realms, but its commander was the stupidest and most likely to let them pass. Nor was this the only way to cross between realms. Far out into the wastelands lay a few shadow crossings. These were uncontrolled, but they were chaotic and extremely dangerous to use. Their denizens recognized no allegiance and considered anything stepping into its shadowy demesne as food.

Feh'lan and her sisters landed near the base of one of the two conical mountains that buttressed the gate as well as being the living quarters for those who guarded it. A tall and imposing figure strode out of the tower and approached. Feh'lan had dealt with the kamaris demon before. Halphis was typical of his kind if slightly more impressive than average. His skin was red, twin spiraling horns jutted up and lightly forward from his long-faced head, and his muscular legs ended in cloven hooves. A long barbed tail trailed several feet behind him, whipping back and forth like a cat ready to pounce.

"Feh'lan, it has been a long time. What brings you to the gate? Did you miss me?" Halphis asked.

"Hardly, but I will admit a certain happy coincidence," Feh'lan replied. She pushed her chest out and swayed seductively, drawing the commander's eyes to her breasts. Not that he needed such encouragement.

Halphis leaned to his left and gawked at the succubus's missing wing. "Who has brutalized you? Tell me and I shall eat his guts!"

"You say the sweetest things, Halphis. Some revolting balrog, but as much as I would enjoy seeing you dine upon his entrails, I am afraid I have more pressing duties at the moment."

Halphis grinned perversely. "I too have some matters of *pressing* to which I would like to attend."

"Singularly thinking as always, I see. My sisters and I need to go through the gate."

Halphis's face turned serious. "Feh'lan, you know I cannot let just anyone through. Why must you pass?"

"Klaraxis has returned, as I am certain you are aware, and has sent me and my sisters on a sort of diplomatic mission to inform Drak'kar that he is back."

Abyssal law held that no demon could wage war on another while the lord of the circle was on the material plane. Such rare occurrences benefitted the abyssal realm as a whole by spreading terror and gaining sacrifices from those who would seek demonic aid.

"Hmm, why would our prince bother?" Halphis asked.

Feh'lan twitched her shoulders, the lack of weight on the left side furiously reminding her of her loss. "How should I know? I am given to understand things did not go well. Perhaps Klaraxis is hoping Drak'kar is looking for a fight. Nothing soothes a battered ego like beating your archrival bloody."

"Hardly. Drak'kar is ambitious, but he is not stupid enough to think he can challenge Klaraxis." Halphis looked at the succubus shrewdly. "I suppose I would be remiss in my duties if I did not send a messenger to verify your claim."

Feh'lan knew the kind of game the gate commander was playing. She had counted on it. "Aw, you know how impatient I am. I would not visit that dreadful Fourth Circle if I could avoid it. Surely there is some way I could convince you to let us through without having to wait upon some slow messenger?"

"Sometimes I think you can read my mind, temptress." Halphis turned and led the succubus toward the interior of the monolithic structure.

Feh'lan returned almost an hour later, her mission an unabashed success. Such actions might make most creatures feel debased and filthy, but a succubus's feminine wiles were their most potent weapon, and they had no qualms about using them to get what they wanted.

"Come, sisters, it is time," Feh'lan informed her companions.

As the envoys approached the point between the two conical spires, runes flared all along their surface, and a shimmering screen leapt between them like the wavy distortion created by the sun beating down upon the desert sand. The distortion cleared, and a new vista appeared in the space between the two structures. Although the land beyond was equally as barren, there was a change in the hue and shape of the landscape. The stone was more grey and the terrain more rugged.

Immediately on the other side of the gate, a company of Klaraxis's demons stood at the ready. Beyond them, and just within visual range, stood the garrison of Fourth Circle demons who controlled another gate allowing access to their realm. The half-mile of land stretching out between the two gates was simply called the neutral grounds.

The Fifth Circle demons paid Feh'lan and her sisters little heed as they stepped through and cautiously crossed the neutral ground. The demons guarding the gate at the far end went on alert as the succubi approached, formed into ranks, and prepared themselves for treachery. Feh'lan snorted at the ridiculousness of their posturing. She and her sisters numbered a dozen while the demons guarding the neutral ground numbered at least a hundred.

Feh'lan kept them all on the ground as they approached while Fourth Circle succubi and other flying demons circled and swooped overhead. She and her sisters were in enemy territory now, and they needed to avoid doing anything considered hostile. A jikin demon stepped slightly to the fore of the front rank and stopped the approaching interlopers. The jikin was similar in appearance to the kamaris but shorter and broader. His legs were so short, the knuckles of his long, thick arms nearly dragged on the ground, and his horns jutted back instead of forward.

"Stop, Fifth Circle scum, and explain why you intrude upon my post."

Feh'lan dipped her head and stared at the demon's feet in a show of proper supplication. "Gate Commander, Klaraxis has returned to rule over his realm. We are here to deliver that information to Drak'kar."

"Consider it delivered and be gone from my sight."

Feh'lan dipped a fraction further. "It is Klaraxis's will that we pass on our message to your lord personally."

The jikin, Belgor, narrowed his eyes at the succubus. "Why would you need to do such a thing, and why should I allow you anywhere near our prince?"

"Truly I do not pretend to know the mind of our lord and master. Do you propose to know yours? I have information Drak'kar will almost certainly want to hear. I would not want to be the one who thought they knew better and kept the message from reaching him."

Belgor appeared to think for several moments before deciding the risk to himself if he kept these creatures and their information from reaching Drak'kar was far greater than allowing the succubi through the gate. "I will provide you with an escort. Attempt to deviate from their instructions or provide them the slightest sign of hostility and they will tear you apart."

"Of course, Gate Commander. I think Drak'kar will reward your wisdom when he hears what we have to say."

Belgor whistled shrilly and made several complex gestures with his hand. A squadron of nearly a score of succubi and another demon type looking like a giant bat only slightly more humanoid, called a grackin, converged overhead. Ten harunden beasts, which looked like a mutated hybrid of a mastiff and an alligator, raced through the formed ranks of demons and circled the succubi, snarling, drooling, and pawing at the ground in barely suppressed aggression.

"You will stay on the ground," Belgor told Feh'lan. "If you try to fly off, the harunden beasts will either tear you apart before you have the chance, or the flyers will bring you down and feed you to them. Do not stray, and obey all instructions, or you will not live to deliver your message, I promise you."

Feh'lan fought to control the impulse to comment on the gate commander's hospitality. Fortunately, wisdom won, if only just. "Of course, Commander, we will be on our best behavior."

Belgor scoffed, "It had best be better than that, or you'll never make it."

Feh'lan was forced to leave her sling behind, likely as an incentive to keep all of the succubi on the ground. As shrewd and self-serving as the succubi were, they possessed a fierce constancy to their own kind. The pillars of the gate flared and the squad of flying demons and their hounds escorted the entourage through.

The landscape made another abrupt if subtle change as they stepped through the gate and into the realm of the Fourth Circle. The term circle was misleading, and it had long confused almost everyone except for the few scholars who had studied the abyssal realm. Most people imagined the abyss as a series of rings with the goddess of death in the center acting as the hub. In reality, the abyssal realm looked more like a stack of plates with the Dark Queen at the bottom. There was no physical connection between circles, and the only way to move between them was by using the gates or a shadow way. Shadow ways were essentially rifts in the dimension one could use to travel between circles, but they were chaotic places, often shifting locations, and were host to some very unpleasant creatures.

Feh'lan and her sisters marched across the barren land, constantly surrounded by the harunden and watched from overhead by the Fourth Circle succubi and grackins. Walking was not only tedious, it was a serious blow to the pride of a succubus. Their kind considered such a mode of locomotion to be reserved for the lesser creatures. The group had traveled quite far, probably a mortal day or two, before one of the Fourth Circle succubi made a lazy spiral downward and fell into step with Feh'lan.

"I am surprised to meet a sister from the Fifth Circle. I am Kra'la," the succubus said.

Feh'lan paused before answering, but she decided there was little or no harm in being cordial. "I am Feh'lan."

"What would force you to risk an audience with Drak'kar? Does it have something to do with your wing?"

Feh'lan's stump of a wing made an involuntary twitch at the reminder. "It is not unrelated."

"I hope the one who damaged you has paid for its transgression," Kra'la said, seemingly sincere.

Feh'lan smiled. "Not yet, but he will."

"I hope Drak'kar finds whatever you have to tell him entertaining. It would not be unlike him to tear off your other wing simply for amusement should your words prove boring."

"I am certain he will be very interested in what I offer. Tell me, Kra'la, is Drak'kar a creature of his word?"

Kra'la paused before speaking. "If the gain is worth his time, he will treat you fairly. He is as quick to reward personal gain as he is to punish loss or failure. He will only betray someone if the gains of doing so outweigh keeping his word. So, Klaraxis has returned. Did his foray into the mortal realm go well?"

"It did not," Feh'lan responded darkly.

Kra'la continued to engage the Fifth Circle delegation in idle chatter, which made the passing time and miles almost bearable. The group eventually reached the lord of the Fourth Circle's monolithic, black pyramid. Although not as large as Klaraxis's colossal fortress, its simple, six-sided shape made it seem even more imposing. The top was shorn off about three-quarters of the way up. From each of the six corners, black claw-like protuberances sprouted up like the prongs of a ring used to hold a giant gem in place. If the huge setting had ever held such a jewel, someone had stolen it. The only thing adorning the massive claws now were bolts of lightning arcing between them.

Feh'lan and her group's escorts led them to the base of the ziggurat where a large opening flanked by massive columns stood under the watchful eyes of a mixed group of demons. Kra'la halted the procession a hundred yards from the entrance and flew to the alert guards. After a few minutes of conversation, the escort leader flew back and ordered them to proceed toward the entrance. Several demons, palace guards Feh'lan surmised, poured out from the entrance and took up the responsibility of leading the delegation inside. Only Kra'la and two of the harunden followed the party beyond the doors.

The inside of the pyramid was just as black as the outside. The walls of the passages they navigated for seemingly miles were all triangular, coming to a peak no less than twenty feet overhead and sometimes as much as fifty. Feh'lan's group and her guards came to a halt outside a set of massive doors where they waited nearly as long as it had taken to walk from the gate to the lord's seat of power. Feh'lan endured it, but she thought it a colossally stupid show of power. Especially considering what she had to offer. Organizing a demonic horde for something as great as assaulting a rival lord took time, and every minute Drak'kar wasted making her wait was time he could be using to organize his coup.

The doors finally opened and the procession marched inside. Beyond the doors was a cavernous chamber not unlike the one belonging to Klaraxis. The vaulted cathedral ceiling rose a hundred feet overhead where dozens of winged demons roosted and watched the happenings going on below. All around the massive chamber, demons stood by acting as guards and sycophants vying for favoritism.

Feh'lan hazarded a glance upward as they came to a halt before the expansive dais where Drak'kar reclined upon his throne. He was an ugly brute of a creature, four-armed and even taller than Klaraxis but sporting less mass. Another difference was his being wingless, but Feh'lan imagined the fact posed little hindrance for him. His four powerful arms and thick, muscular legs likely provided him with extraordinary speed and agility. His horns were straighter and more slender than Klaraxis's oxen-like protuberances. Thick olive-green skin covered his burly body.

"Explain their presence," Drak'kar boomed from atop his dais.

Kra'la stepped forward and dropped to her knees at the edge of the lowest step. "My Prince, they claim to bring a message you will wish to hear. They say it will please you greatly."

"Hmm, and what say you, Kra'la? Do you think it will please me?" the demon lord grumbled like an avalanche.

The succubus looked from the floor to Feh'lan and her sisters. "I do, My Prince."

"You had best hope so, or you will suffer a worse fate than the one with only a single wing for wasting my time and inflicting upon me the presence of Fifth Circle filth." Drak'kar's gaze fell upon Feh'lan with such intensity it was almost a physical weight bearing her down to the floor. "You have been mutilated. Such mutilation makes you weak. To be weak is to be devoured."

Feh'lan fought past the fear in her throat and responded, "It has made my body weak for a time, but it has made my resolve strong, Prince Drak'kar."

"The resolve to do what, harpy?"

Feh'lan knew Drak'kar was trying to bait her, to see if her resolve was strong enough to weather one of the greatest insults one could hurl at a succubus. Harpies were grotesque mortal creatures barely ranking above animals.

"To provide you with the means of destroying Klaraxis and ascending to the Fifth Circle."

"You will regret wasting my time. Klaraxis is a formidable opponent, and I will not expend the resources needed to take him down." Drak'kar looked to several hulking demons standing against the walls. "Tear off their wings and deliver them to the gate."

"Drak'kar, Klaraxis is weak! He failed miserably in his sojourn to the mortal world and is afflicted with the possession of a mortal sorcerer!"

Drak'kar raised two of his long, powerful arms, and the approaching demons stopped. "What kind of trick is Klaraxis playing? Did he send you to lure me into a trap?"

"No, My Prince! The sorcerer, whose body he was supposed to possess so he could walk the mortal realm, defeated him. When the body was later destroyed, both souls returned to Klaraxis's body, but the human sorcerer remained dominant. He either cannot or will not make full use of Klaraxis's power. My sisters and I all saw him falter after a damnable ground crawler tore off my wing."

Drak'kar stroked his thick, bony chin as he thought. "If the human did remain dominant, it is possible he cannot use Klaraxis's power without risking his demonic parasite taking control. Fellspawn!" One of the black shadows seemed to detach itself from the wall and glided toward the dais. "What do your kin know of this?"

"Master, we have seen signs. Klaraxis is not himself. He argues constantly with someone unseen. None have seen him feed."

"Why was this not reported to me?" Drak'kar quietly demanded.

"We were uncertain of the extent of the affliction or its source. We wished to have more facts before troubling you, master."

Drak'kar used all six limbs to propel himself off his throne and down the side of the dais to land atop the hapless shadow creature with unbelievable speed and ferocity. The demon prince tore the creature to shreds and shoved the shadowy bits into his mouth like a starving man. The carnage lasted only seconds before Drak'kar casually returned to his throne, leaving only tiny bits of black on the floor.

"Fellspawn!" he roared.

Another shadow glided forward and awaited its fate atop the remains of its brethren.

"Remind my spies it is I who decide what is important. They will not withhold information from me again for any reason."

"It will be so, My Prince."

Drak'kar returned his attention to his visitors who were nervously awaiting his response. "You shall remain here as my guests while I make further inquiries. Should this information prove true, and I become master of the Fifth Circle, I shall reward you as none has ever been rewarded before. Now go."

"You are as gracious as you are powerful, My Prince and soon-to-be-worthy master," Feh'lan crooned as she and her retinue backed out of the vast hall.

Once almost everyone had left the great hall, another shadow detached itself from a dark, recessed corner. Twin sparks of blue fire blazed as rage burned within it. *The sorcerer is mine! I cannot allow him to die by another's hand. I had hoped to grow stronger before I moved, but perhaps what I have gained is sufficient. It is an arduous journey and fraught with peril, particularly while I am in this form. I must assume another.*

As if the goddess of death and murder had been listening and answered his prayer, a grackin swooped down from the high ceiling. "You do not belong here, shade. That makes you open to be my dinner!"

The demon expected the shade to moan pitifully and anticipated the joy the creature's terror-filled suffering would bring. However, it did not wail, and it did not shrink away and quaver in fright of its imminent demise. The grackin lunged at the shade and the Rook vanished into a deep crack between the stones of the floor like water down a drain.

The demon cast about for the impossibly swift shade and tried to understand what was happening. That realization came in the form of a shadow blade piercing his back just below where the right wing joined the body. Instead of pulling the life force through the black blade, the Rook forced his own existence through the knife's ethereal form and into the demon's body. The grackin let out a short bark as the two souls warred for control of the demon's physical form.

The battle was short, and the Rook devoured the demon's essence from within. His glowing blue eyes replaced the red orbs of the grackin, and he stretched out his arms and wings and appreciated the solid if hideously ugly form.

"Yes, this will do most excellently," the Rook whispered.

The Rook soared over the desolate grey landscape, keeping a watchful eye out for other demons. The creatures were notoriously territorial and were quick to kill outsiders. Not just for food, but also for the entertainment such wanton murder and torture brought. The

Rook found it vile. Murder and death were things of necessity, vengeance, and business. It should be orderly and conducted with forethought. Murder was a means to an end—a final end.

CHAPTER 4

The school's masters were sitting around the large dining table in the old tower after the day's classes discussing the various activities and happenings while they waited for dinner. The tension caused by the Academy wizards' intrusion several months ago had lessened, as there appeared to be no further threats or inquiries. However, Magus Allister was far from feeling at ease.

"Franklin, has Ellyssa been missing classes again lately?" the old wizard asked.

"Yes, she has. At first, it was just a few here and there, but these last several months her truancy has gotten steadily worse. I would have brought it up, but the work she shows in class is excellent when she comes. Her focus and understanding have increased dramatically. She is really beginning to pull away from the other students, and I think we will have to put her in a more advanced class soon if she keeps going the way she is."

Allister nodded but was still troubled. "It is the same with the classes she has with me."

"Mine as well," Aggie piped in. "I believe she is still practicing a great deal outside of school. She is especially spending a lot of time in the laboratory with Azerick's tome."

"She is, and it concerns me more than her attitude or truancy," Allister admitted.

"Do you think she is overreaching herself?" Rusty asked.

Allister shook his head. "It does not appear she is. I'll admit that I am apprehensive with someone of her youth and inexperience having unfettered access to such a book. There is some rather advanced magic in there, which could be very dangerous. As you said though, it does not appear that she is overreaching herself. She has matured remarkably, and if the book gives her something other than her grief upon which to focus, I do not want to take it away without good cause. I will have to look into the matter in greater detail."

Daebian broke the seriousness of the table conversation as he bounced through the door, singing a song in his rich, high-pitched, and remarkably in-tune voice for someone so young. Even after nearly three years, his rapid growth and mental development astounded everyone. Were he the six-year-old he appeared to be, he would still be a prodigy in reading, mathematics, and any other academic subject thrown at him. He had not yet shown any inclination toward magic, but he had recently begun practicing with wooden swords with the martial students and had taken to it like a duck to water.

"Mother, look!" he shouted as he thrust a handful of flowers at Miranda.

Miranda's smile was so bright and loving it lit up the room and made everyone forget the pain she still held for her husband. "They are beautiful. Did you wash your hands?"

"Yep!" Daebian answered, thrusting out his hands open-palmed for inspection. "I made up a poem while I was picking them. Do you want to hear it?"

"Of course I do. We all love to hear your poems."

With encouragement from the adults at the table, Daebian straightened, and cleared his throat.

"Lying at peace and feeling lazy,
I sit within this field of daisies,
I look upon this glen of beauty,
And begin gathering them all to me,
I pluck one bloom after another,
But not a single one is as beautiful as Mother."

The adults clapped and Miranda pulled her son close. "Thank you. That was lovely."

"Did you see me at sword practice today?"

"I did. You did very well," Miranda said.

"Alex says I could be the best swordsman he's ever seen if I practice really hard," Daebian said excitedly.

"Then I am certain you shall be."

Allister cleared his throat. "Speaking of practicing hard, and returning to our original subject, has anyone seen Ellyssa today?"

"I know she spent most of the day in the laboratory," Colleen answered. "I think I spotted her leaving the grounds a couple of hours ago."

"I think she does some of her practicing in the woods to the east," Rusty added.

Ellyssa studied the dozen or so dummies spread throughout the clearing and hidden in the trees from her vantage point atop a rocky outcropping some twenty feet above the ground. It was obvious she had been using the clearing for some time given the amount of damage evident. The ground was bare and scorched. The surrounding trees all showed serious signs of abuse from large chunks of missing bark, stripped limbs, burn marks, and smaller trees ripped in half or completely uprooted.

Satisfied, Ellyssa took a deep breath then pulled the Source into her body and shaped it into a spell. Powerful azure streaks of light sped out and struck down three of the mannequins, blasting them apart and setting some of the straw and cotton stuffing aflame. She formed another spell, leapt off her rocky perch, and hurtled toward the ground.

She disappeared into the magical gate and instantly reappeared at its exit point high in the treetops at the opposite end of the clearing. This was her most dangerous move as the gate travel made her dizzy and queasy, which was a bad condition to be in when flying through the air thirty feet above the ground. Ellyssa fed a trickle of the Source into the length of rope looped around her waist. The stout cord snaked out as if alive and wrapped around a thick limb ahead of her. Ellyssa held onto the knotted end as the rope guided her onto another limb several feet below its anchor point.

Another thought and trickle of power made the rope release its grip on the branch overhead and return to its home encircling her narrow waist. Shaping the Source into another spell, thick frost covered everything around two more of the dummies. The cold was so intense, loud pops echoed across the clearing as the trees caught within the icy spell split and cracked.

Ellyssa opened another gate and practically ran along the tree limb like a squirrel before disappearing into the glimmering portal and depositing herself back atop her rocky bluff. The young mage turned her attention to several fist-sized stones scattered around her. They floated up and began orbiting the girl with increasing speed. The rocks became little more than a blur until Ellyssa redirected their force outward and sent them hurling one after another into the effigies. She innervated the stones with the Source so they struck with more than simple kinetic force. Each rock exploded violently and sent shards in every direction, decimating whatever it hit.

"Hey, watch it!" a voice cried out from the nearby woods.

There was no hesitation and little thought as Ellyssa lashed out at the unexpected voice. With a flick of her hand, the rope uncoiled and slashed across the clearing. The voice came again in a startled yelp as the rope yanked him from the foliage, hoisted him into a tree, and left him dangling by one foot.

"What are you doing out here, Roger?" Ellyssa shouted crossly across the field.

Roger wriggled around until he faced Ellyssa's direction. "Oh, you know, just hanging around."

Ellyssa stepped off the ledge and used the Source to lower herself gently to the ground. She stalked across the clearing and looked the upside-down Roger in the eyes.

"You could have gotten yourself killed."

"Yeah well, hanging around you has always posed a certain amount of danger."

Ellyssa stumbled back and nearly doubled over. Roger's words caught her like a punch to the stomach, but she recovered quickly and silently commanded the rope to release. Roger crashed onto the ground and looked abashed as he got to his feet and dusted himself off.

"Sorry. I didn't mean it like that."

"What are you doing here?" Ellyssa reiterated.

"You haven't been coming to class, so I wanted to see what you were up to."

"What I'm up to is called practicing," Ellyssa responded waspishly. "Is there something wrong with that?"

Roger looked around at the oft-abused clearing. "It looks like practice with intent."

"So what if it is?"

"So, do you remember what happened last time you got yourself into trouble? A lot of people died coming for you, Wolf, and Sandy. It's something you need to think about before you do something stupid—again."

Ellyssa's face reddened in conflicting states of shame and anger. "I'll tell you what I told Allister: I don't want anyone's help. Whatever problems I find, I will deal with on my own."

"You can pretty much bet that won't be a problem."

"Good!"

Roger let out an exasperated sigh. "I didn't mean it like that. It's just that you've become so unpleasant to be around."

A thunderous roar cut off Ellyssa's response, and the small glen grew darker as an enormous shadow partially blotted out the sun. Sandy raced by overhead and released a clap of lightning into her own clearing half a mile away. Even from where Ellyssa and Roger stood, they both felt the shockwaves as the dragon released spells of elemental fury.

Sandy had undergone a breaking very similar to Ellyssa's. They had beaten her with chains and forced her to kill. Like Ellyssa, they had stolen her innocence and replaced it with determination born of fear of ever being another victim. Since regaining her freedom, Sandy devoted her time to learning the magic of her draconic heritage, flight, and fighting. She was big now, nearly the size of a draft horse in the body alone. Her neck and tail easily doubled her length.

Using the knowledge she attained from delving into her egg memories and from what Allister was able to find in Azerick's big book, Sandy frequently practiced in a larger clearing to the east. The level of destruction there was far greater than what Ellyssa had inflicted upon hers. Sandy had torn entire trees from the ground, set large swaths of forest aflame only to extinguish them by summoning torrential storms.

Roger looked toward the flashes of lightning and fire. "She's almost as bad as you when it comes to obsessive practice."

"Maybe she wants to make sure anyone who tries to hurt her again will regret it. Maybe she wants to be strong enough so they can never hurt anyone else ever again." Ellyssa's visage grew dark, and she began walking in the direction of North Haven.

"What are you talking about, Ellyssa?" Roger called after her in frustration. "You sound like you mean to do something preemptive. Didn't you learn anything from your capture?"

Ellyssa shouted back without looking. "Yes. I learned to kill!" She ducked her head and whispered, "Without remorse."

It was a long walk to the city, but Ellyssa's legs had gotten used to it. She had made the trek many times to scout out the streets in search of slavers and those with whom they cavorted. It was a lot harder these days as the entire operation had been forced to go deep underground ever since King Jarvin required all officials to enforce the law against abductions and slavery. It did little to lessen the cases of abduction and made it more profitable for those willing to risk imprisonment and even death if caught trafficking humans. The king even had a sizeable navy now patrolling the seas to combat the worsening pirate situation, but they rarely caught slavers. The slavers simply tossed their precious cargo overboard and let the chains carry them to the sea floor long before the king's marines could board and investigate.

They were still here though, and Ellyssa knew how to find them. It was not difficult for a lone girl to find a slaver if she knew where to look. All too often, a girl found them without looking. Ellyssa's plan was simple. Walk the streets where she had spotted several suspicious characters. It was not hard for her to pass herself off as a homeless girl just looking for a doorway to protect her from the rain.

The slavers were getting wary as well. It was why she had been wandering around these parts every night for the past several weeks. New faces were looked upon with suspicion. Twice she had been accosted by thugs and degenerates, but neither had been slavers, and she had sent them on their way with some painful lessons regarding the treatment of women.

Once she formulated her plan and began practicing with purpose, her nightmares had lessened substantially. This fact alone convinced her she was on the right course in her life. As long as slavers, Captain Jake and Sonjay in particular, stalked the streets, Ellyssa would never find peace. The solution was simple; she would kill them all.

Ellyssa huddled under an awning outside of a shop missing so many cedar shingles it only kept off about half of the falling rain. She used a tattered canvas sack, like one a sailor may have discarded in favor of one in better shape, to ward off the chill and the rain that inevitably found its way through the leaky roof. She looked sick and half-asleep, but the reality was that she was very healthy and alert. Her diligence looked to have finally paid off as several men, maybe five in all, approached her from two different directions.

Ellyssa stood up and nervously cast her eyes between the two groups of men. She looked like a frightened rabbit, too terrified to run from the wolves closing in on her. However, the emotion coursing through her veins was not fear, but hatred and rage. The eyes of these men were indistinguishable from the ones who had taken her. Perhaps they were even the same men. They would know where Captain Jake was, and she would make them tell her.

"Easy there, girl," one of the slavers called out as if to coax a stray dog toward them. "We ain't gonna hurt ya. We just want to take ya to a nice place out of the rain and maybe get some food in ya. Wouldn't ya like that?"

When the men approached close enough for her to smell them, Ellyssa bolted between the only opening the two groups left her. The false kindness of the men vanished, and they all began shouting orders to each other and hurling curses at the girl for making them chase her. Three stayed on her tail while two others split off to get ahead of her.

Ellyssa ran down the alleys and narrow streets but made sure she did not lose her pursuers. The slavers probably thought she was running blind, but she was leading them to exactly where she wanted.

Several exhausting minutes of running ended with the girl trapped in an alley dead-ending in a solid wall of stone. She stood huddling against the wall, shielding her face with her arms as she pleaded for mercy.

"Please, sirs, please leave me be!"

All five slavers shared a laugh at the girl's helpless pleadings as they casually approached, one holding a large sack, another with a belaying pin ready and willing to knock her senseless at the first sign of a struggle.

"Keep your trap shut and there'll be no problems. There's no place left to run."

All five men stopped as the girl started laughing, stood up straight, and faced them without the slightest hint of the fear she displayed a moment ago. "Congratulations, you caught me, but I am afraid all you will find here tonight is your death. Whether your death is quick or painful is up to you."

"Shouldn'a made this difficult, girl," the man with the belaying pin said.

He took two swift steps forward and hurled the small club. The pin passed right through the space between her eyebrows and struck the wall with a sharp crack. As disconcerting as that was, the true panic set in when the laughing girl simply vanished.

"She's a ghost!" one man shouted. Several of them turned around to run only to find Ellyssa blocking the end of the alley.

"Oh, I'm far worse than that," Ellyssa said, cackling with delight.

Two of the slavers looked at each other and rushed the girl, drawing blades as they ran. This earned them the opportunity to die first. Ellyssa's laughter was lost in her fury as she pulled at the Source, commanding it to do her bidding. Errant energy caused her hair to stand on end and limned her in an ethereal light making her look positively terrifying, like some avenging spirit come to punish the men who had led such wicked lives and caused so much pain.

Twin bolts of azure energy lanced out from her hands, catching each one of the men rushing toward her. The force of the strikes crushed ribs, scorched flesh, and hurled them back even farther than they had run forward. The other three men looked about frantically, desperately searching for a way out. Their desperate searching was short-lived as ropes snaked down from the rooftops, wrapped around the men's chests and necks, and hoisted them several feet up the wall.

The slavers gagged and kicked wildly as the ropes threatened to cut off their airways. The men looked at Ellyssa with terrified eyes as she strode forward.

She looked up at the nearest dangling slaver. "Where is Captain Jake?"

The man gasped loudly when the rope loosened enough for him to speak. "I don't know, I swear! I don't know Captain Jake!"

"Wrong answer," Ellyssa said without emotion.

The rope retightened its grip, hoisted him several feet farther up the wall, and then dropped him. The rope snapped taut three feet short of the man's feet touching the ground. The crack of his neck was audible in the dark alley, and his struggles ceased. Ellyssa looked at the next hanging man and repeated the question.

"H-he ships out of the Isles of Ash ever since he got himself a whole lot of gold. Bought himself a new ship and everything. I don't sail with him. Never have! I don't know where he is now, I swear!"

"Do you know how he got his gold?"

"N-no, I don't," the man croaked.

"He got it by selling me," Ellyssa informed the slaver. "But he hasn't been paid in full, and I need to make sure he gets everything he has coming to him. What is the name of your ship, scum?"

The slaver whined pitifully. "S-sea Phoenix!"

"Is it at the dock now?"

"P-please, I can't say nothin'!"

With a twitch of her finger, the rope hauled the man a couple of feet higher up the wall.

"Dock three! Please, I don't wanna die!"

"How many of your captives begged for their lives, slaver? How many begged for their freedom? How many did you let go?"

The man dropped and ceased his struggles and pleading. Ellyssa stepped toward the last man still alive. The aroma of his soiling himself was almost overpowering, but Ellyssa refused to balk.

"Please, I'll tell you anything you want to know," the man said.

"I want to know where Captain Jake is," Ellyssa said once again.

"T-the Isles of Ash! Black Harbor!"

"You know for certain he is there now?"

"Yes! Yes, he's there now! You can get him!"

Ellyssa flashed a humorless smile. "You're lying to me, aren't you? You don't know Captain Jake or where he's at."

The slaver tried to think through his panic and grasped at any straw to save his pitiful life. "*Sea Phoenix*! Our ship is the *Sea Phoenix*!"

"He already told me that. You have no useful information for me, do you?"

Ellyssa turned away and proceeded to walk out of the alley, the slaver's pleas for mercy following her out until they abruptly cut off with the punctuating snap of the rope. "No remorse," she whispered into the night.

It did not take Ellyssa long to reach the docks since slavers rarely travelled far from their ship. Carrying trussed-up and bundled captives through the city was a tricky endeavor, especially with the Watch actually enforcing the king's law. It was not a great hindrance since most work in the city was found near the dock ward. Many of the desperate called it home even if that home was in an alley or wooden crate.

Given the small size of North Haven's harbor, finding the slave ship was quite easy. It sat moored at the end of the long pier where several men stood guard, watching for the City Guard and the rival thieves' guild. Ellyssa did not understand why the slavers and the thieves' guild were unable or unwilling to work together, but she was thankful for it. Slavers were largely thugs and brutes with little skill beyond sailing and preying upon the helpless. The thieves were far better organized and employed a host of skills that would have made Ellyssa's job much harder and much more dangerous.

Ellyssa was furious these scum operated right in the open with no shame and little fear. Whatever plan or tactic she had thought up vanished as she watched the men on the dock and crawling about the ship. All she saw was Captain Jake, Sonjay, and the rest of the slaver crew who had captured her, tormented her, and delivered her into the hands of those sadistic wizards in Bakhtaran.

The men on the dock guarding the ship went on alert as Ellyssa approached. When they saw it was a young woman, their tension turned to amusement. The men struck an easy pose, leaning against a coil of rope or a pier pillar but made ready to spring on the girl as she drew near. Their first thought was that she was a prostitute looking to make some quick coin. If she was, she was stupid, for she would find nothing here but a boat ride to hell.

"Hey, girl," one of the men called out as Ellyssa drew near, "you out here looking for a good time?"

Ellyssa smiled. "I guess you could say I am."

The man who spoke to her and one other were leaning against coils of stout rope used to tie off ships to the dock. The ends of those coils snaked up with a flick of Ellyssa's wrist, wrapped around the men's chests and throats, and flung them out over the harbor where the ropes dragged them to the bottom until the bubbles stopped. Two of the three remaining guards drew cutlasses and charged, only to be hurled back with a pair of magical strikes, crushing their chests and depositing one into the harbor and another twenty feet into the ship's rigging. The last man looked around in terror and jumped into the water before Ellyssa could deal with him.

The brief but terrified shouts of the men and the displays of magic caused an immediate uproar aboard the ship. The crew began shouting orders, a bell clanged loudly in alarm, and they began forming a defense. Several men lowered crossbows, and the twang of their strings accompanied the buzzing of deadly quarrels. The bolts flew by or dropped to the dock with a clatter as they met Ellyssa's magical shield.

Ellyssa countered by raking lightning through their ranks, striking down those she hit and sending the others ducking behind masts, crates, and anything affording a measure of concealment. Her strike started several small fires, which only added to the mayhem as she stepped across the gangplank and boarded the ship.

Seeing that their crossbows were useless, a dozen or more sailors rushed forward in hopes of overwhelming her by sheer numbers. Ellyssa struck out with bolts of energy then an entire wall of force as the men nearly trampled her underfoot. The wall blew most of them back but, forced to spread it out over such a large area, it did little except buy her a few moments of time. She used that time to open a gate to the far side of the ship where only a handful of men stood at the ready. One nearly succeeded in cleaving her skull with a hand axe before Ellyssa was able to shake off the disorientation of using her gate.

She spotted the man lunging for her out of the corner of her eye and struck out almost blindly. She clipped her attacker in the shoulder with a bolt of energy, spinning him around and over the nearby railing. Three others converged upon her with cutlasses held high. Ellyssa sent tendrils of power into the ropes crisscrossing the rigging overhead and pulled them down to her. She directed them against the three men and hurled them far out into the inky black water of the harbor.

Ellyssa allowed herself a moment to gloat as she turned back to face the rest of the crew and deliver unto them her furious judgment. It was nearly the last thing she did in this life. Her eyes went wide as she stared at the heavy ballista set amidships and aiming its lethal payload squarely at her. Before she could finish processing what was about to happen, the ballista crew triggered its massive weapon with a loud clatter.

An iron ball the size of a grapefruit struck Ellyssa in the chest and hurled her back where she fetched up painfully against the gunwale near the prow of the ship. Had her shield not blunted most of the force, she would likely have been spread out all over the deck in a great bloody mess. She tasted copper as blood filled her mouth, and she tried to get to her feet. A second artillery piece on the other side of the deck was about to finish what the first had failed to do. Her shield gone, strength failing, and bleeding from somewhere within her body, Ellyssa fell back and over the low railing just as the crew loosed several feet of heavy chain, tearing through the space she had been occupying.

Ellyssa struck the black water poorly, and the impact nearly pulled her into unconsciousness. Dazed and in enormous pain, she fought against the blackness of the water and the void within her own mind as she sank toward the sea floor. Hanging tenaciously onto consciousness with all of her strength, she willed her shield back into place, forcing the bitterly cold water away from her. She then directed the Source to push against the water, slowly propelling her toward the shore and away from the slavers who now crowded along the rail of the ship, ready to fire crossbows into her body should she surface.

The battered and defeated young wizard was able to get nearly a hundred yards from the ship before having to reach the surface and pull in some much-needed air. Forcing the water away from her body with her shield created little more than an empty space, leaving virtually nothing to breathe. Fortunately, it was a cloudy night and she made it beyond the slavers' range of vision before breaching the top of the water.

Ellyssa looked behind her and saw the crew had hacked away the mooring lines and was pushing out to sea. Already she could hear the whistles and the pounding feet of the Watch as they bore down on what must have been quite a racket. Coughing up a mouthful of blood, Ellyssa pushed painfully for shore, dreading the long walk back to the tower.

CHAPTER 5

"Have you had any luck finding that for which you have been searching, Magus?" the old librarian asked.

Allister looked up from the books piled in stacks all around him. "Not much more than I already knew, which is largely folklore and fairytales." Allister looked at the master librarian standing nearby in nightclothes. "Forgive me, Morvin, I let the hours slip past me once again."

Allister had been spending his days and most of his nights within the walls of North Haven's impressive library in hopes of finding more information about the book that had always held Azerick's, and now his apprentice's, attention.

Morvin waved his swollen-knuckled, liver-spotted hand dismissively. "Nonsense. It pleases me to see my library delved into so thoroughly. I was growing rather bored here until young Master Azerick opened his school up there. May the gods keep his soul. Now I have dozens of studious young minds all devouring my books as they were meant to be. Shall I expect you in the morning, Magus?"

Allister sighed heavily and rubbed his exhausted eyes. "No, Morvin, I think I have discovered all I can here. As great as your library is, I think what I am looking for is only to be found in the Academy archives."

"You do not sound eager to go back there."

"No, I am not. There are those who look upon what Azerick created as an affront to the Academy and its laws. We had a run-in with an Academy delegation a few months ago, and it did not end on a pleasant note."

"Surely they would not reject you?"

"Not as a body I don't think, but there are a few who will seek to make my visit unpleasant. Well, there's no helping it, and I'll be damned if I'm going to let a few rabble-rousers keep me from what I damn well earned."

The front doors of the library crashed open and several men wearing the uniform of the Watch burst in. Morvin jumped and nearly dropped the small oil lamp he was carrying. The squad of guardsmen crossed the library and stopped just before the table where Allister was sitting.

"Magus, I am so glad you are still here," the lead guardsman said. He was visibly agitated.

"Is there a problem, guardsman…?"

"Cruthers, Magus, Lieutenant Cruthers. There has been an incident at the docks and Inspector Orson requests your assistance. He feels there is a magical element involved."

A chill spread down Allister's spine. "I see. Please lead the way, Lieutenant."

Allister followed the Watch lieutenant out of the library and into a waiting coach along with three of his guardsmen. Allister was glad of the transport as it was a long walk to the docks and it had started to drizzle. All was silent inside the coach except for the clopping of horse hooves upon the cobbles and the pattering of the light rain as it struck the roof of the carriage. It took about ten minutes to get to the docks thanks to the empty streets of the late hour.

A man held an umbrella for the magus as he stepped from the coach and onto the dockside street. The old wizard nodded his appreciation and followed the umbrella to where several more men loomed over what appeared to be four bodies laid out side by side. A short, portly man of perhaps fifty years detached himself from the group as the newcomer approached.

"Magus Allister, I'm very glad you accepted my plea for assistance. I am Inspector Orson," the man said as he extended his hand.

Allister gripped the man's hand. "It sounded urgent. What was it you wished to show me?"

Inspector Orson turned to the four bodies. "My men heard a great racket about an hour ago. Several say they heard thunder and even spotted a bright flash they took to be lightning. Only it was low and these aren't thunderheads. By the time the Watch arrived, whatever had happened was over. Some witnesses say they saw a ship depart with what looked like a few small fires on her deck, but I guess the crew got them put out. We fished these four out of the harbor. At first, I figured there was a big row between some sailors or our more nefarious citizens, but then I took a closer look at the bodies. Three look as though they were run over by a wagon and this one is burnt all across his chest, but not by fire. Three of his toes exploded and blew the nails right off."

Allister nodded and knelt to examine the bodies. A guardsman held a lamp but the mage conjured his own light, which did a far better job of illuminating the area. Inspector Orson was right. Three of the men had suffered severe damage resulting in most of their ribs being smashed, which likely punctured several organs. The fourth man had a jagged burn line across his chest and down his left leg. A great deal of electricity had obviously exited from his foot.

The old mage cast an enchantment that picked up the residual emanations of magic sticking to all four men and detected trace bits of it still floating around the area. Someone had cast a great deal of magic here not long ago. A chill not born of the foul weather ran down his spine once again. He refused to believe that Ellyssa was capable of such a thing. She was angry, hurt, and distraught, but to come out here and do this was hard for him to accept.

"Do you know who these men were, Inspector?" Allister asked somberly.

"Sailors, not locals though. I'm guessing they belonged to the ship that took off. Two of them bear tattoos marking them as affiliated with smugglers and likely slavers. I don't think too many people are going to mourn their passing, but such violence, particularly if it is magical in nature, gives me great cause for concern. If that is the case, I figured you would want to know about it. That school of yours is the only place I know of where people practice such things."

"You think someone from the school is responsible?"

Orson shrugged his shoulders. "I don't know. Whether they are or not, you people will have far more luck deciphering what happened here than I will. So was it magic that killed them?"

"Unfortunately, yes. Did anyone say if they saw the person who did it?"

"Not yet. It'll take a couple of days to talk to everyone that may have seen what happened. It's likely we'll get more just by listening to the tavern gossip. People talk to their barkeep more than the Watch."

"I will look into it, but I must travel to Southport immediately. Should you need any assistance while I am away, Magus Aggie Sharpe or Magus Cossington can help you."

Inspector Orson thanked the magus for his help. Allister used all of his, and a fair amount of Lady Miranda's, authority to commission a courier ship to Southport. The crew did an excellent job of suppressing their displeasure at being roused in the middle of the night. Allister was under sail and headed south just over an hour after parting company with the inspector. He wondered if Ellyssa was capable of such a thing and realized he was trying to convince himself she was not, despite knowing better.

His first instinct was to rush back to the school and take away the book, but he discarded the idea. It was important to her and one of the few links she had to Azerick. Azerick wanted her to have access to it, and Allister could not take it away without knowing for certain if his fears were valid or not. It was almost inconceivable that they were.

It was a swift ship and the journey took just under three days. His heart felt the burden of duty with every step. The arduousness of his task did nothing to alleviate the pressing weight of responsibility. The Academy library was even vaster than North Haven's, but he dared not ask for help. Even a rumor of what he sought would throw the entire magic community into turmoil.

Allister was unable to accept even the possibility that the book could be what he sought: the Codex Arcana, the entire repository of all magic that ever existed. Created by the gods to help overthrow the dragon overlords, the codex was more than just a book, it was an archive of every spell and technique any creature of magic ever inscribed. Its existence was almost mythical. No one had even heard so much as a hint of its whereabouts in centuries. Now it could be in the hands of an angry child.

He knew little about the book, few if anyone living did, but the book's true power could not be accessed without the codex choosing the individual possessing it. At least, so he thought. He certainly hoped that was the case. There was just too much he did not know. The more he gnawed on his worries the more he doubted his choice in not securing the tome before he left. Why had he not taken the book? Allister told himself it was to respect Ellyssa's sole source of succor in these times of emotional turmoil, but he could not shake the feeling that it was something more.

Allister pushed his dark thoughts aside and focused on his task. What was done was done, and the only thing to do now was to find out what was really happening and deal with whatever the resulting facts revealed. He did not relish the task ahead of him. He knew that any real information on the Codex Arcana would be located in the archives, but the archives were sealed and only opened after a wizard provided significant proof that what he or she needed was located within and was of intrinsic value. That likely meant weeks of scouring the library and possibly begging access to private books and scrolls from some of the most prestigious members of the Academy.

He had been gone several years and few of the students recognized him, but the established wizards nodded and called out short greetings. A few looked at him with partially veiled hostility. Obviously, Magus Parkes and his two associates were not the only ones who disliked the concept of the orphans' academy. Allister had traveled over half the sparsely populated hallways on the way to the library before someone finally accosted him.

"Have you come to surrender your student, Allister?" Magus Harvey called out as he stepped from a side passage.

Allister paused and took a deep breath. "I have not. She has done nothing to warrant the disciplinary attentions of the Academy. I had thought the matter settled when you departed my school."

The wizard sneered contemptuously. "I departed under duress. You are in my halls now, Allister. I am watching you and your school, and when that little rogue of yours steps out of line, I will be there to hold both of you accountable."

Allister had gotten little sleep on the trip over and his exhaustion destroyed what little sufferance he had for fools. He called up the Source and lashed out at the upstart mage, lifting him from the floor and pinning him to the wall with enough force that he could not take a breath.

"You listen to me, *Wizard* Harvey!" Allister said with a dangerous tone. "Like it or not, I am a senior archmage of this academy and you will do well to remember it. Threaten or disrespect me again at your peril!"

The furious archmage released his hold on the Source and let the man crumple to the floor, gasping for breath. "This is precisely the conduct I would expect from that haven of miscreants!" Harvey shouted after the retreating magus.

Allister regretted letting the man get under his skin, but he was tired and torn between his duty and protecting Azerick's legacy, even when it appeared that his prodigy was heading down a dark path and threatened to bring the full weight of the Academy down upon them all.

CHAPTER 6

Sharrellan, dark goddess of the abyss, sat upon her alabaster throne strumming her long, black nails against its pristine white armrest. Drak'kar awaited her presence just beyond the doors, and she was in no mood to hear his petition. She knew what he wanted. She knew everything that happened within her realm. However, she had left Drak'kar fuming out in the antechamber for what were several mortal weeks, and she could not ignore him any longer without risking the demon lord doing something foolish.

"Krade, show Drak'kar in," she commanded her devil attendant.

Krade, tall, lean, and horned with coal-grey skin, bowed deep enough that his pointed beard nearly brushed the floor. "At once, mistress."

The devil practically glided across the white marble floor and threw open the tall doors. Only Krade's amazing agility kept Drak'kar from bowling him over as the demon lord bolted into the room and threw himself prostrate onto the floor in front of his queen.

"Speak quickly, Drak'kar. I have little time and less patience for nonsense," Sharrellan told the demon.

"Mistress, Klaraxis has returned in failure," Drak'kar said hurriedly.

Sharrellan looked down at the demon in annoyance. "Are you wasting my time with pointless updates? I know Klaraxis has returned, and I know he did not accomplish his goals."

"Mistress, he is weak! He is infected with the soul of a pitiful human. I beg you, give me leave to cast him down and take over the rule of the Fifth Circle."

"Such actions would interfere with my goals, Drak'kar. Now is not a time for division," the goddess told her minion.

Drak'kar rocked back on his heels in surprise. Never had a petition for advancement been denied when a lord had shown such weakness and failure. "Mistress, it is my right! It is the law."

Drak'kar did not have time to register his brash misconduct before Sharrellan sent him flying the full length of the enormous hall, smashing into the far wall with so much force even cruel Krade winced sympathetically at the sound of breaking bones.

"Do not presume to lecture me about the law!" Sharrellan seethed. "I made the laws! I made those laws to bring order to this chaotic place before you all destroyed each other, and you never enjoyed such strength before the law!"

"Mistress, forgive me," Drak'kar pleaded. "I only wish what is mine by your own divine providence."

Sharrellan released the magic pinning the demon in place and sat back down upon her throne. Drak'kar lay where he fell, not daring to move or utter a sound as his goddess sat in contemplation. Sharrellan closed her eyes and used her godly powers to look upon the weave of fate guiding all living things. In the span of a few breaths, she scanned and weighed hundreds, thousands, of possible outcomes and the forks each of those choices created within the timeline.

"Very well, Drak'kar. I grant you your right to ascend—if you can take it."

Drak'kar pressed himself against the floor in supplication. "I will not fail, mistress."

Azerick had spent the past several days painstakingly etching complex sigils on the walls, floor, and ceiling of the chamber. The room looked a great deal like the laboratory he created beneath the old tower of his school. Only a few bookcases jammed with books, scrolls, and loose parchment upon which various topics of lore were written adorned the room. A large alchemy bench sat against one wall, along with a cabinet full of various parts and liquids.

The largest sigil was a complex web of runes meticulously drawn in demon blood in the center of one otherwise bare wall. This is where Azerick hoped to tear open a rift between the abyss and his home realm. He had grown amazingly adept at tuning out Klaraxis's unending stream of complaints, but it did not keep the demon from voicing them in the least.

What do you hope to gain from this nonsense other than wasting time better spent administering your realm?

"You know what I hope to gain. Why do you continue asking?"

I hope that it will eventually make you realize you are an idiot.

"I know full well I am an idiot, but it will never keep me from trying. Now, if you are not going to help me, at least do not interfere."

Oh, I won't interfere. I want you to feel the full responsibility for your failure, after which I will tell you I told you so and hope you will then stop wasting both our time and start ruling, as you should, instead of chasing shadows.

"Fine, just shut up and let me do this."

Azerick examined his sigils one more time and then bent his entire focus into drawing and shaping the Source. He fed the energy into the sigils along with his new abyssal power. He knew this undertaking would require an enormous amount of power and again wondered if he possessed enough. Moreover, could he bring that power to bear without giving Klaraxis the opening he needed to wrest control of their shared body. Azerick had little doubt that if the demon ever got control it was highly unlikely that he could win it back. This was Klaraxis's body and that gave the demon an enormous advantage when it came to possession.

The sigils scrawled along the walls glowed while the massive, intricate rune flared with the brilliance of the sun. Cracks began to form in the wall along the scrollwork painted upon its surface. Bright rays of white light streaked across the room, bursting through the fissures. Azerick closed his eyes against the impossible brilliance, but the light was still bright enough to be painful. Not needing to see in order to direct the magical energy, Azerick turned his head away, which gave him some relief from the searing aura.

The room began to tremor as Azerick tore a hole through space, cutting through dimensions in his bid to go home. The rays of light dimmed, but the shaking increased until it felt as though the entire citadel would come crashing down. Somewhere in the back of his mind, he thought he could hear Klaraxis screaming. Whether it was in fear or anger he could not tell, nor could he expend the attention needed to determine which.

Able to see once again, Azerick looked at the wall and the spiderweb of deep fissures decorating its surface. Inside those cracks, he spied blackness punctuated with the twinkling of what looked like stars. Azerick knew this was the way out. He expended more power and forced the cracks to become major breaches, not just in the physical structure of the wall, but the metaphysical reality of intradimensional space. The rifts widened and Azerick thought he saw movement within, but it was difficult to tell with the entire room shaking.

...you damn idiot! he half-heard Klaraxis scream.

"What did you say?" Azerick shouted back.

Before the demon could answer, half a dozen tentacles bearing small mouths with razor-sharp teeth burst through the wall. The appendages were enormous, at least as thick as his body where they erupted from the wall, and Azerick had a powerful notion that what were flailing around the room were just the tips of a far larger creature.

One tentacle slammed into Azerick and hurled him against the wall with bone-jarring force as others writhed around the room, smashing cabinets and alchemy equipment, and sending books and papers everywhere. A tentacle wrapped around an overturned bookcase, crushed it to splinters, and then dashed the pieces against the floor and walls until it was little more than pulp.

Azerick tried to close the portal, but he had lost control of it to whatever it was on the other side desperately fighting to come through. Unable to close the rift, Azerick tried to drive the creature back into its own dimension. The sorcerer summoned his power and lashed out at the nearest tentacle with a beam of intense yellow light. The ray burned into the oily black appendage with a hiss like hot steel dipped into water for tempering.

The reaction was instantaneous. What had been random destruction became a concerted effort to crush the source of pain. All six rubbery arms lashed out at Azerick. Azerick leapt away and sent an arc lightning into one of the limbs questing for him. More black smoke and an acrid smell roiled off the struck tentacle, but it did little to slow or weaken it. Distracted by his target, he failed to see two other tentacles coming at him from opposite sides before they coiled around his body. Azerick nearly disappeared within the creature's grip as it tried to tear him apart.

Despite wearing the guise of his human form, Azerick still possessed Klaraxis's strength and resilience. Azerick gripped the tentacle with both hands and sent electricity coursing into it while the creature tried to tear the sorcerer in half. When that failed, the monster tried to pull him through the wall and into the maw of whatever waited beyond the rift. Azerick's body was repeatedly abused as the monster smashed him against the wall in its attempt to pull him through.

Azerick fought the creature as best he could, but with the repeated battering and flailing about, it was difficult to bring his magic to bear. He even tried to tear the tentacle apart with his bare hands, but the muscle was incredibly strong and refused to yield to his abuse.

You must free me or we are going to die! Klaraxis shouted inside Azerick's head.

"Then we'll die! I will never free you, Klaraxis, even if it means my own destruction."

You are an even greater fool than I thought, human!

Unable to pull its captured prey through the rift, the creature flung Azerick at the far wall. He struck the unyielding stone hard enough to crack its surface and send a spray of shards across the room. Azerick was dazed and struggled to get back to his feet. He braced himself as the tentacles streaked across the room at him. The appendages slapped against the wall around him, dropped to the floor, and lay still.

"What in the world have you been up to?" a sultry voice asked. Sharrellan let out a lilting laugh.

Azerick struggled to his feet and faced the goddess. "I was trying to go home."

"Foolish boy, you are home. Surely Klaraxis told you such a thing is not possible?"

"Impossible simply means one has not tried hard enough," Azerick responded defiantly.

The goddess smiled at her prince's stubbornness. "You always were a contrary child. It is what drew me to you. In this case however, your stubbornness will not see you to success as it did in the past."

"Are you saying no one has ever escaped this abyssal prison?" Azerick asked angrily.

"No one who belongs here," Sharrellan said.

"I do not belong here!"

"I disagree, as do the powers guiding the universe. Argue all you want with either of us, neither will avail you. You would be better served focusing your efforts on running your realm instead of toying with things you know nothing about."

I have told him, mistress!

"Of course you have, Klaraxis, and of course he does not listen. He is completely irrational, yet claims he does not belong here."

"I don't belong here!" Azerick heatedly insisted. "This is a world of pain, death, and selfishness. It is where these demons and the shades of evil men belong, not me."

"Not you?" Sharrellan asked incredulously. "My dear child, so many of these shades are here because of you. You have sent more souls pouring into my kingdom than anyone else since, well, a very, very long time."

"What are you talking about?" Azerick asked. "I have been forced to kill a few, several when my school was attacked, but that hardly makes me comparable to these monsters."

Sharrellan laughed deeply. "Oh, you poor child, you really don't know, do you?"

Azerick felt a sense of deep foreboding. Anything bringing the dark goddess such pleasure was sure to be bad. "Know what?"

"Do you not recall your final act before escaping the psyling city?"

Azerick thought back to that horrible day, the day he lost his first true love and unborn child. Revisiting the memory of Delinda brought on a fresh wave of pain even after all these years. He had escaped to the artifact room in Xornan's tower and used a malevolently evil staff to bar the door. He then used his sunder spell to weaken the structure of the staff so it would break and unleash its power, destroying the tower where so many painful memories lived, when the psylings managed to breach the door.

"I trapped the door in hopes of killing the psylings and the guards who were after us," Azerick said. "That hardly makes me a monster."

"My boy, that chamber contained more objects of power than almost any single place in your world. Other psyling lords also possessed their own hoards they stockpiled for their plans of conquest. When your little trap went off, it destroyed everything in the chamber, including the device that created gateways between worlds, which was nearly as powerful in its destruction as all the artifacts in the room combined. The explosion was strong enough to create a chain reaction, destroying the entire city and everyone in it. Child, you singlehandedly destroyed an entire species, and you don't think you belong here?"

Sharrellan laughed again. "You personally sent nearly a hundred thousand souls straight to the abyss. Do you think they all deserved to die? How many slaves were in the city, those poor wretches who were simply unfortunate enough to be caught up by those vile creatures just as you were? You are the best Hand I ever had."

Azerick reeled from the revelation. Was it true? Could he have killed all those people? He would not shed a tear or waste a single thought of remorse for the psylings, but all those people who were slaves just as he was were dead. All because he wanted to punish his captors. He could have simply escaped through the gate. But was leaving those people to suffer the indignity of slavery better than a swift death? Not to him, but that was not for him to decide. It was too much to process right now.

"Everyone died?" Azerick asked. He thought about Braunlen and some of the other decent people he had known.

"All but one. The abyssal elf managed to escape. The point is, my Hand, you have made a great many enemies serving me; most of whom are now here and looking for revenge."

"I didn't know. I never meant to do so much damage, especially to the ones who did not deserve it," Azerick said numbly.

"Do you think they care any more than I do if you meant to slaughter them or not? No need to answer. It was a rhetorical question. Even you certainly know the answer to that. The fact remains you have enemies here, and you have better things to do than bash your head against a wall trying to leave."

"You say I am the best Hand you have ever had. Why not send me back?" Azerick asked. "Obviously I am no good here."

"Your single line of thought is becoming tedious," the goddess replied darkly. "As I have told you, I cannot."

"You cannot or you will not?" Azerick challenged the goddess.

"Take your pick. They both end with the same result. I cannot because I do not possess the ability. I will not because there are greater things than you or even I in the making and those things require you to be here."

"What things require me to rot in the abyss?"

"Things I cannot tell you."

"Cannot or will not?"

Sharrellan smiled at Azerick, amused once again by his contrariness. "Will not."

"Why not? If I am needed to effect some greater scheme of yours, would I not be able to do more if I knew what it was I was supposed to be doing?"

"It is no scheme of mine, child. I do not know what you are to do, and if I told you what you faced then I would risk disrupting the strands of fate and you may not do what you need to do."

Azerick gave Sharrellan a perplexed look. "I don't understand. How would knowing what I need to do keep me from doing what I need to do? If I knew what I needed to do then I would do it, and far more efficiently than if I didn't know. Your argument is counterintuitive to me."

"That is because you are a child. Let us say you are a farmer and are about to take several of your cattle to town for slaughter. I come and tell you a highwayman will rob you of your coin and cows if you travel. What would you do?"

"I would not travel to the city, of course," Azerick replied. "I would at least delay my trip."

"Because you chose to avoid the robber, one of the cows selected for slaughter kicks over a lamp in the barn. The fire spreads from the barn to the house and the field of wheat. You and your family burn to death and the loss of all those cattle and the fields around your home cause a food shortage resulting in hardship for hundreds of people. Another scenario is one of the cows you were to slaughter contracts a disease, it spreads to your other cows, and to several herds around your farm. All of the cows die off or are culled because it causes a deadly illness to any human who eats them. This causes starvation and an economic collapse as beef becomes hard to get, making it too expensive for all but the wealthy to purchase. All this because you knew what was going to happen to you and you wanted to change your fate."

"But couldn't you tell me about the fire or the disease?"

"No, because any interference in free will can disrupt the strands of fate. I could not even tell you about the robber. I cannot see what will happen on the strands, only the placement of people and certain events. I know you are supposed to be here, but I cannot tell you what you must do or not do because I simply do not know. Not even the Sisters of Fate know what you are to do, only that you are here and your being here plays a significant role in what is happening or going to happen."

"I think I see. Have you seen me out of here?" Azerick asked hopefully.

Sharrellan smiled. "Goodbye, my Hand. Remember, you are surrounded by enemies."

The goddess vanished before Azerick's eyes. There was no puff of smoke, no flash of light, nor shimmering of a gate; she was just gone. Azerick looked at the destruction the creature had caused and sighed.

"Well, back to the drawing board."

What do you mean? Weren't you listening? She said you could not escape this place. Are you still going to pursue this idiot quest?

"Of course."

She told you it was a waste of time! She told you there were creatures here out for revenge! Why are you going to ignore our goddess's warning?

"She is your goddess, not mine, and I am going to continue to look for a way out because that is what I would normally be doing. If I stopped doing what I would normally do, then my barn burns down."

Your logic is annoyingly human! Fine, ignore the fact she told you that you are an idiot and wasting your time.

"She never said I was an idiot or wasting my time."

It was implied. You cannot ignore her warning of imminent threat. You need to reestablish your dominance to secure your authority. You continue to show weakness, and it invites covetous creatures to attack you.

"She never said there was an imminent threat."

Of course not! That would jeopardize free will and the strands of fate. Do you think she simply came here for a social call? She all but said someone was coming for you.

"So what would you have me do?"

I once called every demon under my command and slaughtered a thousand of them with contemptuous ease just to show the others I could do it.

"Not really my style. Either way, I can only do what I would normally do, and what I would normally do is not give a damn. Besides, I'm inside this ridiculously large fortress located in my own realm and surrounded by tens of thousands of demons. What could happen?"

***

The Rook flew across the barren landscape in his stolen form. It had taken a great deal of time to locate a shadow crossing. Three times he had lost a body in a fight with demons and other creatures of the realm, but they had been unprepared for him, and he dispatched them with relative ease. After absorbing their souls, he took the bodies of those who could fly.

He spotted blackness against the grey landscape and swooped down for a closer inspection. The Rook lit upon an overhang of jutting rock and peered into the inky black cleft in the stone beneath him. He knew this was what he sought and was no mere trick of shadow or simple crevice.

There was a coldness emanating from within not present in this world of nothingness. His breath came out in thick plumes of white vapor as if giving a visual warning of the forbidden place. The Rook slipped into the crevice and the darkness instantly swallowed him whole.

The Rook allowed his eyes to adjust to the unnatural darkness within the rift, but even his demon-enhanced vision had trouble piercing the gloom beyond a few yards. He lightly brushed the cavern walls with his hands and wings to help guide him through the twisting and often narrow fissure. It was slow going, but there appeared to be few divergent paths and even fewer that would accommodate his form. He was unconcerned with this. If the passage ever became too tight to navigate, he could abandon his stolen body and easily glide through. It would certainly allow him to travel faster, but he did not know if another host would be readily available on the other side. His shade form was also especially vulnerable to the attacks of the demons, who looked upon his kind as food.

The Rook's eyes continually darted toward flickers of movement that looked like nothing more than a shift in the shadows that highlighted the already black surfaces of the cavern. Almost anyone would simply have ignored this as a trick of the light, but the Rook's assassin-trained mind knew something was watching and following. Whatever they were, he knew there were several, it was impossible for him to capture more than a flutter of them out of the corner of his eye.

He was about to discount the creatures as being little more than shadowy cave lizards when they decided to strike. There was no change in movement to warn him of the impending danger. The black walls of the passage seemed to come alive and wrapped around his hands and wings as they brushed the surface. They continued to flow over his body until the shadows engulfed him.

Despite their insubstantial nature, the shadows tore at his physical body. He heard and felt his joints popping. The Rook detached himself from his host's nervous system as the shadows began tearing him apart. As his physical vessel died, he tried to escape in his true form. He had barely gotten out of his body when the shadows grabbed and held onto his shade form.

"Tressspassserrr," the shadows whispered menacingly.

The shadows began to pull him apart just as they had his physical body and he cried out.

"Waaait. Killlerrr."

"Yesss! Killlerrr."

"Ssshaaadowww brrrotherrr."

The shadows stopped pulling and began caressing his form, even sending ethereal tendrils through his body.

"Yesss, ssshaaadowww brrrotherrr."

"You seeek passsaaage, ssshaaadowww brrrotherrr?"

It took a moment for the Rook to understand. He had always been a creature of the shadows. Born in a dark alley and left to die. Raised in the dark confines of an abbey where he learned to worship Sharrellan. The shadows had always comforted him as a blanket comforts a child.

"Yes. I seek passage to the Fifth Circle."

"Come, ssshaaadowww brrrotherrr, we willl ssshow youuu the waaay."

The shadows still held him, but now their touch was light and they carried him swiftly through the passage. The black walls raced by faster than if he were on the swiftest mount. The feeling was exhilarating and terrifying. Even after all this time, his mind held on to some of his physical limitations. The shadows chased him through twisting turns, up vertical fissures, and down shafts that must have plummeted thousands of feet.

The Rook spotted a brightening in the surrounding tunnel. It was at that moment his shadow brothers stopped and released their hold on him. The spectral assassin looked closer and saw that the passage ahead definitely grew more luminous. The faint light had a reddish cast to it, and he knew that he was now within the Fifth Circle. The Rook glided toward the light, but his journey was far from over. There was a great expanse of land to cross full of hostile demons, and just getting into Klaraxis's citadel was likely going to pose its own challenges.

"Goood huuuntiiing, ssshaaadowww brrrotherrr."

CHAPTER 7

Olivia raced down the street, her worn and battered sandals slapping against the cobblestones as she ran, their rhythmic staccato broken every time a puddle or pile of horse droppings forced her to evade the obstacle. Running while clutching the parcel in her arms was difficult enough without having to dodge such hazards, but it was how she earned her keep.

One of many orphans populating North Haven, she had been lucky enough to get work at the courier service where they allowed her to live in the back room. What little coin she earned was from the occasional tip of a generous client. The promise of a large tip and note of urgency were the only reasons she was working past dark. Normally, she would never be on the streets this late, but sometimes an order came in that needed to be filled no matter the hour.

She was well known by now, having been doing her rounds for the last two years, and no one really bothered her. Her bright smile and friendly demeanor made her popular and welcome almost anywhere her deliveries took her. However, even with the Witch of North Haven putting the fear of the gods into the slavers these days, a lone, ten-year-old girl was still in danger traveling the streets after dark. The witch may have the slavers scared, but there were still those willing to risk her wrath. She could not be everywhere after all.

Olivia finally reached her destination and hesitated at the front of the building. She was in the industrial ward, and the streets were practically deserted since almost everyone was done working for the day and were probably sitting in their homes or enjoying a drink at one of the numerous inns and taverns throughout the city. She tried the door and, after discovering it open, stepped into the gloomy interior.

"H-hello?" she called out hesitantly.

A voice answered from farther back in the shop. "Back here."

Olivia followed the voice and spotted the faint glow of a lamp or candle through a doorway at the far end of the large building. She was still cautious but relieved to be nearly finished with this job. It was late and she was hungry. Of course, she still had to make it back home.

She stepped through the doorway and into a room dimly lit by a small lamp. A man in his fifties, or maybe sixties, was sitting on a high stool examining something on a workbench. He did not turn when Olivia entered, so she cleared her throat and spoke.

"Sir, I have your package."

The man turned on his stool and smiled. "It seems we have a bit of a problem. That is not the package I want." Olivia glanced down at the paper-wrapped parcel in her hands in confusion. "I'm afraid you are the package."

Before she could ask what he meant, someone grabbed her from behind. Olivia was young, but she was no fool. Fools did not live long on the streets. She let loose an ear-piercing shriek, grabbed the small knife she always wore at her hip, and was able to move her arm enough to stab the forearm of the man holding her.

"Ow, the little rat stuck me!" the slaver cried as he watched the girl break free and run.

Olivia put her feet in motion the instant the man let go of her. He stood between her and the door, so she ran for the only other possible route of escape she saw. The room she was in was large, almost like a small warehouse. It stood three stories tall but was mostly open at the top. Large crates and various tools and machinery filled much of the room and the partial floors above. She ran up the stairs and looked for a way out.

She heard several men clomping up the rickety stairs after her as she ducked around and under crates and large, dusty objects of which she could not decipher their use. Unable to find a ladder to the roof, Olivia crawled beneath something that looked like a big loom with massive rollers. She curled up in a dark corner and listened as the men searched and cursed as they fumbled around in the darkness.

Her heart was beating so hard she was sure the men would hear it if they got close enough. Olivia wondered if the men would eventually give up. She doubted it. They knew she was here and would likely not leave until they got her. Maybe the Watch heard her scream and was already coming to investigate? She doubted that as well. There were few residents and little to steal in the district, so the Watch made very few rounds this far in.

Olivia bit her lip and tried to quiet her breathing as the glow of a lamp drew closer. Her body shook as she stared wide-eyed at the pair of feet visible beneath the machine. They turned and a grinning face replaced them.

"Found ya, ya little rat!"

Olivia screamed and slashed at the grasping hand. The man, down on all fours, managed to grab her wrist, wrested the knife from her small hand, and dragged her out. Olivia tried scratching and biting until the man slammed her against the machine.

"Stop squirming or I'll club ya senseless," the slaver said. He stuffed a wad of cloth deep into her mouth when she tried to scream again.

Olivia fought back the urge to gag on the filthy cloth and ceased her struggling. There was little she could accomplish by continuing to fight other than being beaten. The slaver carried her downstairs draped over his shoulder. Once at the bottom, he dropped Olivia onto a carpet spread out on the floor. A hundred things ran through Olivia's mind, each of them more horrifying than the last. She was almost relieved when her captor simply rolled her up into a bundle and hoisted her back onto his shoulder.

"Damn, for a stray, she sure eats well," the slaver said as he adjusted his burden to accommodate the unexpected weight. "Remember what I said, ya start to struggle or cry out and we'll club ya senseless."

Olivia did as she was told and tried to ignore the discomfort and queasiness caused by being draped over the man's shoulder and the bobbing motion. At least the carpet provided some protection from the man's shoulder digging into her ribs. From the number of twists and turns they made, Olivia assumed they were taking a surreptitious route along the back alleys and narrow, unused byways between buildings.

The odor of the port became strong enough for Olivia to detect it even over the smell of the carpet. She heard the lapping of water against the docks and the creaking of the moored ships nearby. The sickening motion stopped and a new voice spoke.

"Here are your papers clearing your cargo. You shouldn't have any problems with customs, as usual."

Olivia heard the telltale clink of coins exchanging hands and they began to move again. The sound of her captors' feet became hollow as they stepped onto the dock and boarded their ship. The man carrying her dropped her unceremoniously onto the deck and used his foot none too gently to unroll her.

One of the slavers opened a hatch from where at least a dozen frightened faces looked up. "Climb on down there. You're on our ship and there's no place to run."

Olivia stood up and smiled. "You're right. There is no place to run," she said, kicking the hatch shut.

The three slavers stood immobile, unsure of what to make of the girl's sudden change in behavior. Even as their slow-processing brains formulated a response, the girl's form began to shift. She grew taller and aged several years right before their eyes. Her short brown hair lengthened and became a dark blond with a lock of white framing each side of her face.

"The witch!" one of the men called out.

Ellyssa had been locating and killing pirates for weeks, but she was never able to board one of their ships. The slavers had begun staying out at sea after her failed attempt to destroy the ship and crew. Now they dropped their men off and returned at a prearranged time or when someone signaled them with a lantern.

She had been playing Olivia for almost a week after extracting information out of some of the slavers she brought to justice. It was just a matter of time before they struck at the easy target she created for them. The real Olivia was living in Ellyssa's room as one of the newest students to attend the orphans' academy. It had not taken much to persuade the girl she was better off there than working for the courier service.

One man turned to run, but Ellyssa reached over her head, grabbed one of the lines strung through the rigging with the Source, and gave him a gallows death. The closest slavers to her drew blades and charged, eliciting a hue and cry of alarm. An evil smile formed on

Ellyssa's face as she sent them sprawling with a wave of arcane power. The deck of the ship came alive with the chaotic activity of a kicked anthill. Slavers raced around the deck, cranked the windlasses of the heavy ballistas, charged her with drawn swords, and aimed crossbows.

Ellyssa opened a magical gate just as more than a dozen crossbows twanged and two ballista bolts tore through the air where she had been standing. She stepped out onto a yardarm, gripped the mast to steady herself, and laughed maniacally as she looked down and saw several slavers struck by quarrels meant for her. A heavy spear launched by one of the ballistae tore through two slavers and buried itself in the mizzenmast.

Stepping out onto the narrow spar was a dangerous maneuver even without the vertigo-inducing effects of the gate spell, but Ellyssa had spent a great deal of time practicing just such a feat. She had learned from her first shipboard battle that the sheer numbers and heavy weapons were capable of overwhelming her, so she formulated a plan to mitigate those threats.

Out of range of everything but the crossbows, Ellyssa destroyed the heavy weapons with explosive balls of fire, incinerating weapons and crew, and setting parts of the deck aflame. Not wanting to burn the ship to the waterline with captives aboard, she channeled the Source down into the sea and brought forth a wall of water flooding over the deck, extinguishing the flames and washing the slavers off their feet.

The effort it took to move such a large volume of water was very taxing, and Ellyssa felt herself fatiguing. Before the slavers could regain their feet, the young mage reached out to the mile of cordage making up the rigging. Ellyssa's magic severed lines and sent them after the panicked men. Like snagging tuna out of the water, Ellyssa savagely jerked the men from the deck one after another until the only things moving were the writhing slavers suspended twenty and thirty feet in the air.

Ellyssa brought one of the struggling men near. "Where is Captain Jake?"

The man kicked his feet and grasped the rope coiled around his chest and neck. "I-I don't know!"

"Too bad for you then," Ellyssa replied.

The man dropped several feet and his struggles ended. She drew another man near, asked the same question, and received the same response. Man after man begged for mercy and claimed to know little or nothing. Some began spinning tales and offering guesses in hopes of placating her, but Ellyssa saw through the lies and deceptions.

"All you have to do is tell me where Captain Jake is and I will let you go free! Is it too much to ask in exchange for your miserable lives?" Ellyssa demanded, then brought another man to her. "Where is he?"

"P-please! I don't know!" the slaver sputtered.

"Useless!" Ellyssa spat, then prepared to dispose of this scum just as she had the others.

"Sonjay!" the man yelled just as he began to plummet.

Ellyssa halted the man's fall. "What of Sonjay?"

"H-he might know where he is!"

"Where is Sonjay?"

"I don't know for sure, but I know he has his own ship now and runs black market cargo between Lazuul, Southport, and here. He usually makes his run north around this time of year. Please, that's all I know!"

"Finally, one amongst you is actually worth something," Ellyssa said, smiling.

The wizard grabbed a rope and used her magic to lower herself down to the deck. Her work here was done and she could hear the whistles and shouts of the Watch growing nearer as they came to investigate the commotion.

"Wait!" the dangling slaver said as she turned to leave. "You said you would free me!"

Ellyssa looked up at the terrified man. "So I did." With a flick of her wrist, the man dropped, the rope reached its end, and his neck audibly snapped. "Now you are the freest person on this ship."

Ellyssa strode from the ship and, with her back turned, released the rest of the crew with a thought and left their corpses dangling like the ornaments of some macabre winterfest tree. She was exhausted, but her work was not yet over.

The harbormaster peered through the door of his small cabin on the dock at the slave ship moored at the farthest pier. He watched in horror as the fireballs erupted on the ship and the screams of men reached his ears. He knew what had happened. The Witch of North Haven had found them and punished them for their evil ways. He had heard the rumors, and he knew the slavers were operating at a high level of alert. These ones gambled and lost.

There had been no more commotion from the ship for several minutes now, and he could hear the Watch arriving. The last thing he wanted was to talk to the Watch. He guessed there was no avoiding it, however. As the harbormaster, they were certain to want to speak with him about anything happening on the docks. He shouldn't fret over it. There was nothing tying him to the slavers other than the gold stashed in his wall, and that was plain gold crowns. Some might wonder where he got so much gold, if it came up, but bribes and kickbacks were a long tradition for his position. Of course, those were generally for simple black market goods, not human trafficking.

The harbormaster started with a gasp when he turned and looked into the angry eyes of a young woman. He had no idea how she had gained entry. There was only the one door to his cabin. His first thought was that she was a thief and his eyes automatically shifted to the hidden panel in his wall.

"Looking for this, Harbormaster?" Ellyssa asked, holding up a large pouch full of coins.

"Who are you? What are you doing in here, and what do you think you are doing with my gold?" the man demanded.

Ellyssa conjured a small light so the man could see her clearly inside the unlit interior of the cabin. The harbormaster's face paled and sweat beaded on his brow as he realized who, or what, had come for him. His cabin was built atop the pier and so was situated several feet above the water. He looked at the trapdoor leading to a small rowboat tied up directly below.

Ellyssa followed his eyes to the trapdoor. "Go ahead. Open it."

The harbormaster looked to see if the witch was trying to trick him. When she did not move, he edged toward the trapdoor. When the girl did nothing but smile at him, he opened the panel and bent down toward the ladder leading to his boat.

"Harbormaster," Ellyssa said, making the man jump up, "don't forget your gold."

He turned and felt his entire body go rigid and an invisible hand force open his mouth as if locked in mid-scream. His eyes bulged as he watched the gold inside his bag slither out of the top like a snake from a hole. The gold was no longer in coins. It looked as if it were molten and no longer solid. The gold serpent twisted and writhed toward his open mouth, slithered down his throat, and into his stomach. Ellyssa gave the man a push with her magic, and he disappeared into the opening in the floor with a splash.

Ellyssa was exhausted, but at least her work was complete—for tonight. It was a long walk back to the school, but getting rid of so much human filth lent her strength as she left her gruesome work for the Watch to clean up.

Inspector Orson stood by as the Watch cut down the last of the slavers. So far, they had found thirty-three dead crew members, most of them hanging from yardarms and rigging. They found eleven young boys, girls, and women chained inside the hold, a testament to this ship's purpose.

"Inspector," Lieutenant John Cruthers called out, "we have located the harbormaster."

"It's about damn time. Bring him here," the inspector ordered.

"Yes, sir. They are hoisting him up now."

Inspector Orson turned. "What do you mean they are hoisting him up?"

Lieutenant Cruthers cleared his throat. "We found him in the water beneath his cabin, sir."

"What kind of new hell is this?"

The inspector stormed off toward the harbormaster's cabin, making the lieutenant quicken his pace to keep up. These murders had been going on for nearly a year, and he was no closer to solving them. The fact they identified most of the victims as slavers, and the rest were suspected of being such, did little to mollify his or the duchess's frustration at having a vigilante running amok in North Haven. The two men reached the cabin just as a pair of watchmen hoisted the body of the harbormaster out of the portal in the cabin floor.

"What made you think to search the water for him?" Inspector Orson asked.

"We found the trapdoor open and I spotted a bit of blood on the edge where he probably hit his head when he fell." Lieutenant Cruthers pointed to the spot of blood.

"Good work." The inspector knelt down and looked at the body. "There appears to be something in his mouth. Get me some damn light over here!"

Several watchmen turned up the wicks on their oil lamps and brought them closer. Inspector Orson reached into the harbormaster's mouth with two fingers and tried to extract the metal, but it barely moved under his touch.

"Open his shirt."

The lieutenant hastened to obey and tore the fabric down the middle, exposing the man's front. The inspector applied more force to the object and the harbormaster's stomach moved. Several of the Watch jumped back with looks of surprise or disgust.

"What do you think it is?" The Watch lieutenant asked.

"I'm not certain, but I have an idea. How strong is your stomach?"

"As strong as any man's, I'll wager."

"Good. Open him up. Whatever this is, it goes all the way to his gullet."

John Cruthers made as neat an incision as he could with his dagger and exposed the stomach cavity. The lieutenant and his fellow guards flinched at the smell that assaulted them.

"Now reach in there, find the end of this thing, and pull it out. The benefit of being in charge," the inspector explained when John balked at the order.

Lieutenant Cruthers looked at one of the guardsmen and jerked his head toward the harbormaster's body. Not outranking anyone else present, the man muttered a curse and knelt next to the body. Turning his head away, he reached into the cavity and fumbled around for a moment before extracting a large, gore-covered object.

"Someone get something to clean this off," Cruthers ordered.

Another guard found a bucket, filled it with the water beneath the trapdoor, and poured it over the item and the grateful guard's hands. The object was clearly gold and looked almost like a club. It had a handle running the length of the harbormaster's throat down to his stomach where it ended in a globulus mass.

"By the gods," John exclaimed. "What do you make of it, Inspector?"

Inspector Orson looked thoughtful a moment. "The northern barbarians had a method of execution reserved strictly for those who betrayed the tribe out of greed. They stuffed whatever the man or woman received as payment for their betrayal down the throat of the accused. If it was land, the chief rammed soil down the offender's throat until he was stuffed full and suffocated. If it was coin or steel, they melted the metal down and poured it into them. A horrible way to go."

"You think that's what happened here?"

"Not exactly, but close. There are no burn marks in or around the mouth. Neither are his insides seared, which would be the case if the gold had been molten."

"You think it is magic again," the lieutenant said.

"Undoubtedly. I recall something similar to this happening in Southport nearly a decade ago. As I heard it, there was a man being held in a cell awaiting interrogation by the king's magistrate. When the magistrate arrived, they found the stone around the door melted as if it were wax and resolidified. They found the prisoner suspended from the ceiling, his hands and feet meshed within the stone."

"Sounds horrible."

"Indeed. Would you like to hazard a guess as to the man's name?" the inspector asked.

"I would hardly know where to begin," John replied.

"Darius Giles." The lieutenant furrowed his brow. "That's right, the father of our own Lord Giles."

"Do you think this is the work of the same assassin?"

"I don't know, but if he has come for the son, he is a couple years too late." Inspector Orson sighed. "I believe it is time I sent a report to Southport. This is the second major use of magic in committing these crimes, and our local magicians seem disinclined to provide much help.

Have your men clean up this mess while I pen a letter to Inspector Lazlo in Southport. I pray he can convince the Academy to send help."

Allister leaned back in his chair and rubbed his eyes. From the mark of the candle, he knew he had been poring over these ancient manuscripts for nine hours straight. He glanced at the half-eaten meal at the end of the small table, but he had no appetite. He had been in the lore vault for nearly five days and only after almost a month of research in the Grand Library. Only his rank within the Academy and calling in nearly every favor owed him got him access without divulging specifically what it was he was looking for.

He had found out very little, as he had expected, but what he did find was very disturbing. It was mostly rumors about powerful wizards and sorcerers who may have possessed the Codex Arcana and used the lore it contained to carve out their own little empires. All fell from power for one reason or another. Some speculated that the book itself was the reason. Either someone else discovered its existence and took it, or the book fell silent, perhaps in its desire to find a better master.

There were scant descriptions upon which to judge whether the book Azerick had brought back was the codex, seeing as how very few people had ever seen it. Those who had almost invariably coveted it, and they were not inclined to share any information about it whatsoever.

The greatest bit of information he had found was a fragile scroll written in elvish, but his familiarity with the language was poor, and his was the best in the Academy. He was currently going over a journal once belonging to one of the first headmasters of the Academy. She was one of only two people in human history to preside over the school while the Codex Arcana was counted amongst its artifacts.

The journal was nearly six hundred years old, and Magus Keller's handwriting suggested she suffered from a mild palsy of some kind. She wrote extensively of trying to unravel the codex's secrets for decades, but to no avail. The book refused to share anything beyond its basic store of lore to her or anyone else at the Academy. She went on to say she and the council believed the tome did eventually speak to a young sorcerer, ironically enough, but the man managed to vanish and no one had seen either one since.

The woman detailed so much about trying to unlock the codex's secrets, but never once thought to describe the blasted thing so someone else might know what to look for should it ever reappear! Frustrated, Allister slammed the book closed, creasing the last page. With a sigh of admonishment, he opened the back cover and did his best to smooth out the wrinkle. He gasped, for on the inside of the back cover was a small drawing in exquisite detail of the book now sitting on a podium in the laboratory back home.

There was also a small note neatly written beneath the picture. He closed the book, gently this time, and let out the breath he had been holding for some time. Allister scratched at his beard as he thought of his next course of action. The old mage knew he was really just stalling, having determined there was only one real option open to him other than going home and pretending none of this had happened.

With a heart heavy from the weight of duty, Allister reset the wards upon the steel door to the lore vault. The lore keeper was not around, so Allister would need to inform him his work was finished so the keeper could ensure the wards were properly set. It was early evening, so the headmaster might still be in her office. He walked dully up the stairs until he stood outside her door.

The headmaster beckoned Allister to come in after he knocked. "Allister, did you finally find what you were looking for?"

Allister sat heavily in one of the padded chairs. "Unfortunately, Headmaster."

"Headmaster? Come now, Allister, you and I have been friends far too long to be so formal," she said.

"Perhaps not for much longer, Maureen. I need to borrow the Bekkin stone," Allister said solemnly.

The headmaster's hand absently touched the stone hanging around her neck beneath her robes. "How in the world do you even know of such a thing? I did not know of its existence until after becoming headmaster."

"Headmaster Keller mentioned it in a journal I found in the lore vault."

Maureen pierced her old friend with a steely look. "The fact you ask for it means you know what it is for. Are you telling me you have found the Codex Arcana?"

Allister looked at the ceiling and breathed out a slow breath. "I cannot know for certain until I use the stone, but the evidence is rather damning."

"Allister, you know if you find the Codex Arcana, you must bring it to the Academy. That book must be safeguarded and its knowledge made available to all who are willing to follow Academy law."

"I do, Maureen. I do wonder if it would really be available to all. The council has not been terribly inclusive for some time."

"The council is old and headstrong, but so am I. The codex could advance our understanding of magic severalfold, and in order for that to happen it must be available to those with the strength, experience, and discipline to use it. Obviously, we cannot let just anyone plumb its depths. Imagine the damage if someone of an inexperienced or foolish nature were allowed to use it."

Allister buried his troubled expression inside his ample white beard. "I can well imagine. Will you give me the stone?"

From around her neck, Maureen lifted a simple leather cord from which dangled a faceted amber crystal the size of a petite woman's pinky finger. "You must promise me you will bring the codex back here. I'll have your word on it."

"You have my word, Headmaster," the sorrowful old wizard answered as he took the crystal.

Allister had to wait a full day before he found a ship to take him north. The winds were not as favorable, nor was the ship as swift as the courier vessel he had used to come south. Every hour dragged on like an eternity and it set his nerves on edge. The crew learned to avoid the dour archmage.

It was five stressful days before the ship finally reached North Haven's port. Allister was so angry and impatient by this time he set the customs official's hat on fire when the man tried to keep him from debarking before he had made his customs inspections. No doubt,

Allister would receive a stern rebuke from Duchess Mellina in the following days for his behavior.

He did not stop to speak with anyone when the coach deposited him upon the steps of the old tower. Despite his travel-induced exhaustion, Allister went to the lab where the tome was always located. He found it perched upon the podium as always. He let out a sigh of relief as he half-expected it to be gone. Allister pulled the crystal from his pocket and stepped toward the book. If this were truly the Codex Arcana, the crystal would glow with a silvery light.

The old archmage held the crystal out and approached as if he expected the book to strike out at him. He mentally berated himself and dangled the crystal directly over the open pages and—nothing. Neither a glow nor any other sign the crystal recognized the tome as the codex. Allister felt such relief he did not even mind having wasted a month of his life researching this fool's errand.

That was when he detected a slight vibration in the crystal. The tremor increased and the stone began to dance wildly on its cord. It took Allister only a moment to realize what was happening. The codex had tried to suppress the power of the crystal, and now the two forces were warring. The book did not want to be found. The crystal exploded in a flash and a spray of shards, cutting into Allister's face and hand.

The archmage looked at the tome lying upon the podium. "Dear gods. You are why I did not return immediately and take you to the Academy." The book lay silent upon the podium. "If you are able to influence my actions, what have you done to the girl?"

Ellyssa was in Azerick's vault, searching for something to help her in her quest to eradicate the slavers and find Captain Jake. She had made several forays to the vault since her first battle on the slave ship, but she always turned around, unable to bring herself to take what she needed. It had to be done. The things she had learned over the past weeks required more power. She had exhausted herself on the ship, and if dealing with Sonjay meant another battle like that one, she needed to be able to channel more of the Source with more efficiency.

She stood in front of the rack holding an assortment of objects, but she had been staring at two in particular for at least the last twenty minutes. Azerick's silver ring and bracelets rested in a felt-lined box side by side. Just looking at the two objects that had been such a part of him caused a wave of anguish to crash down upon her. They were his, every bit as much as his staff was, and she did not deserve to have them. But she needed them. She needed them in order to be strong, like him.

Steeling her resolve, Ellyssa slipped the ring onto her finger and snapped the bracelets around her wrists. The shame of wearing what was his burned as if they were fresh from the forge. She shuddered as the tingle of magic washed over her. Ellyssa instantly felt her connection to the Source grow significantly stronger as the ring created a magical link between her and it.

She had just steadied herself when a sound came from down the hall in the direction of the laboratory. Ellyssa ran from the vault and raced down the short passage to the lab. Through the open door, she spied Allister standing over the book and wiping at his face with his hands. All over the floor, tiny bits of what looked like glass sparkled under the glow of the lamps.

"What are you doing with my book?" Ellyssa asked.

Allister turned at the sudden intrusion. "Your book? When did it become your book? The book is here for all of us to use," the old mage said. The look in Ellyssa's eyes made him speak calmly.

Ellyssa sidled around as if Allister were a dangerous animal that might attack. "I need it to make me stronger. You said yourself I needed to be strong. The book makes me strong."

"Oh, my dear girl, you mistake power for strength," Allister said. He shook his head sadly. "Power gives us the ability to destroy, but strength comes from within. Strength allows us to make the right decisions when the right thing is so very difficult to choose."

Ellyssa positioned herself so the book was between her and Allister. "For my purposes, power suits me just fine."

"Ellyssa, the men you have killed are not the ones who took you. They are not the ones who killed Azerick. What you are doing makes you no better than the slavers."

"They will lead me to Captain Jake. I don't need to be better, only more dangerous."

Allister realized Ellyssa was beyond reason. The innocent, precocious little girl was gone. In her place stood a young woman so full of hate and grief, she would not stop until she was dead.

"Ellyssa, I don't think you understand what the book is or what it is doing to you. It is dangerous and it is using you. You are not yourself right now. You must be strong and let go."

Ellyssa sneered. "I know exactly what it is, and we use each other. The codex wants to be used. It needs someone who is willing to use it and possesses the strength to wield what it shows. That is why it picked Azerick. That is why it picked me."

"I'm sorry, but it is too powerful and too dangerous to stay here. I am taking it to the Academy where access to it can be controlled and its use properly monitored," Allister said with finality.

"I cannot let you take the codex, Allister."

"You cannot let me?" Allister shouted, his patience finally having reached their limit. "You listen to me, child, I…"

Ellyssa struck so fast and with such power, Allister barely had time to register the attack and bring a ward to bear before the wave of force struck him full on, hurling him through the open doorway and dashing him painfully against the wall. Another spell slammed the door shut, and runes of warding flared all around it, sealing the portal closed.

Ellyssa grabbed the book from the podium and clutched it to her chest. She could hear Allister pounding at the door and trying to unravel the wards keeping it sealed. The book had shown her how to improve the ones Azerick had made years ago, but she knew even those would not keep the archmage out for long.

"I need to get out of here!" Ellyssa cried out in panic. "How? Show me."

A section of wall slid into the floor, exposing a long, dark passageway appearing to extend far beneath the school grounds. Ellyssa did not hesitate. Clutching the book to her chest, she ran across the lab and into the gloomy passageway. The tunnel went completely black when the section of wall returned to its previous place and sealed her in.

Ellyssa conjured a light and ran. The passage extended hundreds of yards and opened out into a cleft in the mountainside. The book urged her to keep running east along the base of the mountains. Once, she thought she spotted Sandy flying far to the south and hoped she did not turn her way. The dragon's keen eyesight could easily pick her out from miles away.

The book guided her eastward for several miles. As the night grew long, Ellyssa began to feel the chill of the evening air. Her legs ached and her lungs burned from the punishing pace she set, but still the book pushed her to keep moving. When she could go no farther, she spotted a narrow split in the face of the mountain. Under the codex's guidance, she squeezed into the fissure and discovered a cave. When she brightened her light, she saw it had once been occupied, but not for a very long time. The rotted remnants of a table, chair, and crude bed indicated someone had once lived here.

Following the sound of running water, Ellyssa found a natural spring feeding a shallow pool. The pool disappeared in a crack in the rocks where it constantly drained off as the spring continually filled it. A flat slab of rock jutting from the wall made the perfect place on which to set the book. As soon as Ellyssa put the book down, it flipped open and the words crawled around the page.

Ellyssa read what appeared to be a sort of journal written by a wizard hundreds of years ago. He had come into possession of the Codex Arcana and retreated to this hideout when the Academy seemed bent on taking it away from him. There was more, but Ellyssa was too tired to read anything else. Lacking a bed, she managed to strip the limbs from several young pine trees and made a pallet that would suffice until she could get something better.

Daebian spotted the black silhouette against the grey backdrop of the mountains from his perch atop the school wall. He watched Ellyssa run off into the night-shrouded forest, and his face split into a wry smile.

"Into the trees,
Ellyssa flees,
Trying to put her past behind her.
How many tears must she cry,
How many more men must die,

Before she soothes her anger?"

CHAPTER 8

The Rook glided silently down the passages of Klaraxis's gigantic citadel. Gaining entry had proven to be rather simple once he shed the body of his last host and traveled once more as a shade. His ethereal body was an advantage when it came to the ease with which he could move about and hide in the shadows, but it also put him lowest on the food chain. He would need to get another host soon.

His shade form allowed him to blend into and become one with any of the numerous shadows cast by the flames continually burning in the small stone basins sporadically attached to the walls. It was by sticking to and blending into those shadows that the Rook was able to traverse the labyrinthine corridors undetected. Ahead, he spotted the movement of a pair of demons and ducked down a narrower and darker side passage. The Rook thought himself safe until a form stepped out of the deepest shadows.

"You must be lost, shade," the impossibly black creature said as it climbed down the wall toward the assassin. "Why aren't you down in the warrens feeding your essence into the fortress like a good little shade?"

The demon was humanoid, but its limbs were unusually long and slender. Its skin was the blackest black the Rook could conceive of, and it glistened like the scales of a freshly shed viper. The Rook tried to escape into a nearby shadow but his former sanctuary seemed to reject his presence.

"You will find no safety there, little shade. These shadows belong to me. As a full shade, I would normally take you back down to the warrens, but seeing as how our prince no longer involves himself in our affairs, I think I shall simply devour you."

The demon lunged with startling swiftness and sank its black claws into the Rook as if he were solid flesh. Pain flared from his wounds, but he was a veteran of combat and did not panic. The demon snapped at the Rook's face, but the assassin thrust one of his spectral arms into its gaping maw, saving himself from a swift death.

Shades did not usually fight back, and this unexpected defense caused the demon to falter in its attack. It tried to pull back, but the shade's arm sprouted thorns and lodged its appendage inside the demon's mouth. The Rook extended his hand into a blade, thrust it into the creature's heart, and forced his essence into the demon's body.

Although the demon flailed about madly, the true battle was being waged inside its own body. Unfortunately, this was a battleground well suited to the Rook, for the mind was full of shadows in which to hide and launch unexpected assaults against the host. All of those places where even demons did not like to go: doubt, fear, weakness, and shame, were pools of darkness from which to strike. Even the Rook had these, but he had explored them, embraced them, and so they afforded his enemies no advantage. The demon never stood a chance once the assassin gained access to its soul.

The Rook liked this new body. The way it commanded the shadows made him feel as if it had belonged to him the entire time. He was able to move about and hide with exceptional ease, watching the denizens of the fortress going about their business from high along the top of the wall where shadows cast the ceiling in perpetual darkness.

Several times, he spotted his quarry walking the halls, usually to or from the chamber containing an assortment of books and artifacts. From the ramblings of what he assumed were conversations with his host, the sorcerer seemed bent on finding a way out of the abyss. The Rook was unsure if such a thing were possible, but if it were, he would need to strike before that happened. It was a fine balancing act of not letting the sorcerer slip through his fingers and not moving with undue haste.

Despite his outward appearance, this was still the lord of the Fifth Circle, and short of the goddess, he was arguably the most powerful creature in this realm. How much having the human in control affected his strength and abilities was an unknown, so for now he would have to wait and study his prey.

Azerick slammed the book shut with a curse. "Are there no more books in this accursed realm?"

None to advance your pointless quest, Klaraxis replied shortly. There are disturbances in my realm. I can feel it. You must stop wasting time with this futile endeavor and accept your position!

"You have been singing that same song since I got here, and it is not improving with repetition," Azerick replied dismissively. "How long have you lorded over this place?"

Nearly two thousand of your years.

"In all that time, no one has ever escaped? No one ever found a way out?"

No.

"You hesitated. Why did you hesitate when you answered?" Azerick demanded.

I did not hesitate.

"Yes you did, demon. Now, tell me the truth. Who got out? How?"

An elf foolishly found his way here and later escaped. It was a different situation and does not apply to you.

"Tell me how he did it!"

No!

Azerick delved into his mind and attacked Klaraxis with his will. When he was in his own body, it was a simple matter to force the demon to obey, but here, in Klaraxis's body and his seat of power, the demon was a formidable opponent. Azerick struck at the demon and Klaraxis fought back, each engaging in a sort of mental wrestling match, trying to make the other submit.

"Tell me about how he got out!"

There is nothing to tell, now stop this!

Azerick had the demon "pinned" but was unable to hurt him enough to make him reveal whatever secret he was holding back. Azerick had one more card to play, but he was unsure what effect it would have, given his and Klaraxis's close bond. Deciding it was the only way to get what he wanted, Azerick used the demon's soul name—and immediately regretted it. Azerick and Klaraxis both cried out as agony coursed through their shared body and soul.

You incredible idiot! I hope that teaches you a lesson, Klaraxis seethed.

"Nope. Now tell me what you know, or I will do it again," Azerick threatened through clenched teeth as he gasped in pain.

Not even you would be that stupid or hardheaded." Klaraxis scoffed, calling the human's bluff.

"Wrong again. You should know me better than that by now."

Both creatures screamed once again as the fiery whip of Klaraxis's soul name scourged their entwined spirits. The Rook watched the human form of the demon lord fall into some sort of fit. The assassin surmised there was some internal battle being waged between the two creatures. This was probably the best chance he had at delivering a mortal blow. He would not attempt a possession, despite how much the thought of owning such a powerful body pleased him. Both were creatures of extraordinary will and either of them would likely tear the Rook to pieces. No, this would have to be swift and decisive.

The Rook crept along the dark ceiling and down the wall to get near the preoccupied human's back. He pulled the shadows around him and wore them like a great, voluminous cloak. The assassin formed his shadow blade and infused it with a substantial amount of his life force, innervating it into something far more deadly than a simple knife. He locked his eyes on his target's back where the heart lay beating beneath a few inches of bone and muscle. The Rook launched himself from the wall like a coiled spring, arm cocked back and ready to strike.

The room filled with the smell of brimstone as Skulk popped into existence only a few feet away. "Great Master, faithful Skulk has brought you urgent—" the demog began then screeched when he saw the black demon flying toward his master's back.

Azerick turned the instant Skulk apparated into the room. He twisted and leapt away at the last instant. Icy pain flared across his chest as the Rook's ghostly blade cut through his body, narrowly missing his heart. Azerick ignored the searing pain and grabbed the attacking demon by the wrist before he could finish bringing his weapon around. The Rook flung a glob of shadows at his prey's face and blinded him as it wrapped around his head like a wet towel.

Unfortunately for the Rook, Azerick's human form belied the demonic strength he possessed, and the momentary loss of vision did little to hamper his reply to the assault. Azerick whipped the Rook around by his arm, smashing him against the floor and wall like a washerwoman beating her laundry against a rock. Fury filled Azerick at the demon's audacity. When the creature ceased its struggling, Azerick placed his hand against his attacker's chest and poured black energy into it long after there was no further sign of life.

Klaraxis felt the accursed human's control slip the more he channeled his rage and unleashed his abyssal power. The demon subtly added fuel to that rage, teasing it from a fire into a raging inferno. The more anger Azerick felt and used to energize his magic, the more his control slipped and the closer Klaraxis came to gaining possession of his body. Fear and anger were to demons like air and water were to most other forms of life. They ate and drank it in, gaining sustenance from its consumption. Azerick felt this as well and forced himself to return to a sense of calm. He shuddered as he shook off the demon's influence.

Sensing his host's imminent demise, the Rook fled his physical form just as the black fire tore through it. He willed his shade into the dark cleft between the floor's stones and escaped, though not without feeling the scourge of the human's abyssal power as it destroyed the demon's black body.

You see! Even your own minions turn against you!

"Shut up, demon!" Azerick turned to the demog. "What urgent news do you bring, Skulk?"

The little demog looked at the body of the demon then up at Azerick. "Glorious Master, Fourth Circle demons invade through the Omega Gate. Messenger says horrible succubi betray you and let them through."

I told you something was wrong, and you did not believe me!

"I never said I did not believe you. I said I did not care."

Klaraxis screamed his fury at the obstinate human. *You must do something—now! Drak'kar will be heading this invasion, and when he gets here, he will take this realm for his own.*

"So let him have it. I have no interest in it." Azerick dismissed the demon's complaining.

You cannot be this stupid. Drak'kar is the lord of the Fourth Circle and very powerful. He will seek to destroy us both or, if he is truly foolish, enslave us long enough to consume our souls.

"You cannot defeat him?"

I can, of course. It is you who cannot. If we are to survive, you must give me the freedom to battle him. You must give up control of this body.

"That will never happen," Azerick said.

Obstinate human! At least summon my minions. Right now, they are likely being destroyed. You must reach out to them and gather them into a fighting force to slow Drak'kar's advance and weaken him.

"How do I do that?"

I can do it, but they need us to lead them into battle. Even your pathetically limited power is formidable and will make a substantial impact upon the battlefield.

Azerick did his best to determine if the demon was trying to trick him, but he did not detect any treachery. That did not mean there was none. Both of them were able to keep things from the other and hide their motives behind half-truths and veils of secrecy.

"Very well, Klaraxis, summon your horde."

We must go to my throne so I can see where to send my warriors.

Azerick made his way to the enormous throne and sat down upon the stone and bone construction. He relaxed his mental lockdown and allowed Klaraxis a small measure of freedom to act. Klaraxis gazed into the shallow bowl cut into the arm of the throne. The pool of blood filling the bowl reflected an image of a battlefield. The disproportionate numbers made it more of a bloodbath than a battle. Azerick could not tell one demon from another, but it was apparent a vastly superior force was tearing apart another.

Klaraxis pulled the image closer and Azerick saw a massive four-armed demon look up and smile, somehow knowing his foe was watching him. The sorcerer felt more than heard the summons Klaraxis sent out to the farthest reaches of his substantial domain. Hundreds of thousands of demons heeded their master's call and raced with all speed to intercept the invading force.

That will slow them, but you neglecting your duties and failing to listen to me will cost tens of thousands of lives.

"As if I care. Now, tell me of the person who escaped," Azerick demanded.

If I tell you, you will take an active role in defending my realm?

"Of course, if for no other reason than self-preservation."

It was nearly a thousand of your years ago. The foolish elves sought to remove themselves from this world by shifting their northern kingdom to a pocket universe where they could live without threat of the encroaching humans. They made a grievous error and brushed against my realm. I was able to shift the focus of their spell enough to rip a hole between our worlds.

"So you managed to create an opening between here and my world? If you did it once, why not again?"

The elven kingdom was no longer in your world. It was between worlds and, even then, had they not done most of the work, I could never have done even that. The barrier between us was tissue-thin.

"But you said an elf came over and later escaped. So another rift or gate must have been created to do that," Azerick persisted.

I am getting to that. You have no patience.

"And you have no sense of urgency. Get on with it."

Klaraxis sighed heavily at the frustration he always felt when dealing directly with the human sorcerer. *The elf wizard who orchestrated their near demise came through the rift so he could close it. There was no other way as I was holding it open so my minions could enjoy punishing the foolish creatures. It was a glorious day, full of carnage. The elf managed to close the rift, but there was no way for him to escape back through before it sealed forever. I spent one of your decades causing the greatest amount of suffering I could devise.*

"After ten years he escaped? How?"

I do not know.

Azerick snarled, "You are lying, demon. Tell me or I will torture you with your soul name until one of us goes completely mad."

Klaraxis laughed. *It would be such an ironic end. By the time I was through with the elf, he too was thoroughly insane. But such a threat will only result in both our suffering. I do not know how he escaped. I returned for his daily torture and found him gone.*

"How do you know he escaped the abyss and did not simply flee?"

There was a powerful but strange magic in the air. It was without a doubt transdimensional, but who or what cast it I cannot say. I have never sensed such magic before or since.

"Would Sharrellan know?" Azerick asked anxiously.

Of course. The goddess knows everything happening in her realm.

"Well then, I suppose it is time to pay her a visit."

You do not simply drop in when you feel like it and disturb our dark queen! You swore to engage in the battle for our kingdom and very lives!

"I lied," Azerick responded lightly. He stepped toward the rune-inscribed circle set in the floor behind his throne.

Cursed, vile, lying human! Never have I hated another creature as I do you! Should I ever regain control of this body, somehow, someway, I will make the torture I inflicted upon the elf look like a mild spring rain!

"You should be pleased your influence is rubbing off on me. Now, how does this thing work?" Azerick mused as he studied the glyphs. "Ah, I think I see."

Klaraxis tried to control Azerick's legs, and when that failed, he attempted to interfere with his channeling power into the transportation glyphs. Azerick shoved the demon aside and activated the gate. His stomach leapt into his throat as he felt his body plummet through space only to have it drop into his boots a moment later. The experience was similar to his gate spell but far more pronounced. His new form handled this kind of translocation far better than his human one, and he shuddered to think what that would have been like.

Azerick found himself in a surprisingly pleasant chamber of white marble. Soft music echoed through the room from some unknown source. A set of tall doors set in one end of the room displayed the only visible entrance or exit.

Listen to me well, human. You shall be in the presence of our queen. Never forget she is the sole authority here, and her word is everything. Conduct yourself properly or risk her wrath.

"You have so little faith in me, Klaraxis."

Incorrect. I have absolutely no faith in you. There are protocols here to which you must adhere. Her seneschal, a devil named Krade, will soon come and inform us Sharrellan is aware of our presence and we shall await her pleasure. Do not insult him. Krade is our goddess's personal attendant and best not trifled with.

"You sound as though you are afraid of him. Is he truly that powerful?" Azerick enjoyed poking at the demon lord's pride.

He is a power within his own right, but it is the patient, manipulative subtlety of his kind that makes him dangerous. You will never see him. Even as the world around you grows chaotic, he will remain in the shadows as you struggle to maintain control.

"I see. So what else must I know so I do not embarrass myself?"

Sharrellan will make us await her pleasure, but I do not think it will be long, perhaps one of your days at most. She knows everything in her realm and is aware of our urgency. All you have to do is sit and wait. When you address her, you will do so with absolute deference and humility. She is not some trumped-up noble whose authority is nothing more than a virtue of birth. She is the ultimate power, and her rule is absolute. Even the other gods tread lightly for fear of incurring her wrath.

"Be patient, be polite, and be deferential. Is that all?"

Yes, it is so simple even you should have no trouble following it.

Azerick looked at the doors. "I have a better idea."

Before Klaraxis could convey his feeling of dread into words, Azerick unleashed his magic upon the doors. The doors crashed inward on their hinges with a resounding boom, sending Krade tumbling when the heavy wood struck him full in the face just as he was about to open them.

Azerick strode confidently into the enormous chamber. "Sharrellan, you lied to me!"

Azerick's rage nearly faltered as he took in the beauty of Sharrellan's palatial throne room. He had expected it to be as dark, dismal, and disturbing as Klaraxis's abode. However, it was the exact opposite. Every surface was of white marble with brilliant silver veins. Fruit trees and flowering bushes and shrubs filled the air with their pleasant aroma. The dark goddess herself sat upon a throne of crystal, or possibly diamond, her flowing black gown of spider silk standing out in stark contrast. It was a place more befitting Ellanee, goddess of nature, than the queen of death.

Krade leapt to his feet with a hiss, ready to tear the upstart apart.

"Leave him, Krade. His manners are still terribly human," the goddess ordered.

The devil gave Azerick a look promising terrible retribution and stepped to the side of the room.

"Why are you here instead of defending yourself from Drak'kar's invasion?"

"You lied to me about it being impossible to get home. There was an elf here and he did it. I demand to know how!"

"Child, you demand nothing from me. I told you no one who belonged here has ever left. It was a true statement then, and it still is. Why you insist upon wasting your time trying to go home is beyond me. Your former wife and son are doing just fine without you. It is this home that is in desperate need of your attention." Sharrellan smiled cruelly.

Azerick had gone to great lengths to avoid thinking about Miranda and his child. The emotional pain was a distraction he could not afford. He needed his full attention focused on getting home. Hearing the goddess speak so lightly of the pain he tried hardest to avoid was staggering.

"I-I have a son?" Azerick almost choked on the words, fighting back tears of both sorrow and joy. "How is he? Is he well?"

"He is—healthy."

"Why do you hedge? What is wrong with him?"

"Nothing is *wrong* with him. He is exceptionally bright and creative. I assume he gets that from you. He does mature at a rapid pace, which I attribute to his other father."

Klaraxis laughed smugly. I told you, human. Your son is as much mine as yours. How that must stick in your craw!

"Shut up, demon; he is my son and mine alone. You have no influence over him and you never will!" Azerick turned his attention back to the goddess. "You still hedge. What are you not telling me?"

Sharrellan pursed her red, perfect lips and paused. "He is complicated."

"Complicated how?"

"We are all but blind to his existence."

Azerick tried to understand what the goddess was saying. "Who is blind, how?"

"We, the gods, and even the Sisters of Fate are unable to see him within the weave. Such a thing has never happened before. The Sisters are quite upset about it."

Azerick swallowed, trying to digest this new information. "What does that mean?"

The goddess shrugged. "It means he could be the solution to saving your world or be the source of its destruction. The Sisters have been able to spot just a glimmer, for the briefest of instances, of his involvement on both strands. If it were up to me, I would simply drown the brat. I think his existence is a far greater threat than the possibility of his being a benefit."

"You will stay away from my son!" Azerick screamed in fury and fear for his child.

"There you go making demands again. I must tell you, I do not find your complete lack of obeisance endearing." Sharrellan gave Azerick's anger a dismissive wave of her hand.

Hearing about his son made Azerick even more anxious to return home. His son needed a father to help guide him into manhood, especially since he was so different from other children. He knew what could happen to the spirit and character of a person who was peculiar. The hardships of being different or strange affected people and seldom in a good way. Azerick only needed to look at himself to see that and desperately wanted better for his son.

"Tell me how the elf got out or so help me I'll...!" Azerick warned.

Sharrellan stood up, her patience at an end. "You'll what? Your obstinacy was amusing for a time, but that time is over! This is where you belong now, and you will act in accordance to your..."

Before Sharrellan could finish her rebuke, Azerick pulled from the Source and wrapped it around his abyssal power, creating a spell of enormous power. His fury was so raw and primal, had Klaraxis not been stunned by the swiftness of the unexpected assault, he likely could have seized control and dominated the human parasite. As it was, the demon was unable to react to Azerick's incomprehensible action before he lashed out.

A black ray of abyssal power wrapped in silver arcs of lightning erupted from Azerick's hands and streaked out toward the goddess. Her look of utter disbelief that anyone would dare strike at her was so profound it was almost comical. The ray struck her with astonishing power, knocking the goddess of death backward over her crystal throne.

You complete, utter fool! You have destroyed us both!

Before Azerick could form a single thought in response, Sharrellan flew into the air, a billowing, black-shrouded form of pure fury. "You ungrateful, impudent, little shit!"

Azerick had barely had time to brace himself when an invisible mountain of force slammed into his body. The blow sent him flying backward at a frightening rate. Azerick tried to prepare himself for the inevitable impact with the unyielding wall a few score feet behind him, but it never came. The sorcerer opened his eyes and watched the blur of the alien landscape fly by as he continued his uncontrollable flight. Seconds and then minutes passed and still he did not stop.

Just as he began to wonder if he would fly forever, he struck something so hard he was certain his body would shatter into a thousand pieces. Azerick lay upon the floor back in his citadel, languishing in the pain caused by his abrupt impact with the wall.

"I think I could have handled that a little better," Azerick quipped.

You are such an idiot that you make idiots look brilliant by comparison.

Azerick bit back a cry of pain as he rolled into a sitting position. "Come on, you can't tell me you never wanted to do that. Admit it, it felt good, didn't it?"

Azerick could feel Klaraxis's smile. *I will never admit such a thing.*

CHAPTER 9

Allister answered the insistent knocking coming from the main door. He grumbled to himself about being interrupted on his way to the dining room and then grumbled aloud when he saw who it was.

"I would ask what you three idiots want, but I already have a pretty good idea." Allister glowered at the three Academy wizards.

"Allister!" Colleen admonished from behind him. "Such behavior is not appropriate. It sets a bad example for the children."

"You're right, my dear. I only know one of them as an idiot. I simply assumed the same for the other two based upon the company they keep."

"It is still no way to speak to guests, no matter your personal conflicts," Colleen insisted.

"They are not guests until someone invites them in. Until then, they are unwanted intruders whom I am legally entitled to blast to smithereens if I feel the least bit threatened."

"I assure you, Magus, we have no intention of threatening anyone," Magus Harvey responded.

"You see. We were about to have supper. Would you all join us?" Colleen said.

"And now they're guests," Allister grumbled as he stalked off to the dining room.

Colleen appeared in the dining hall a moment later, towing the three wizards behind her. "Allister, since you seem to know our guests, would you please make the introductions?"

Allister tried to glare at Rusty's wife, but her ever-present smile crushed his attempts to be cross with her. "Everyone, this is Magus Robert Harvey, Oliver Parkes, and Melanie Brown."

"Where would you like us to sit, Lady Colleen?" Magus Harvey asked.

"The bottom of the harbor has ample seating. I hear the fish is especially fresh," Allister said.

"Allister, if you continue to behave this way, you can eat in the living room with the dog!" Colleen admonished. "Anywhere is fine."

"I must take the blame for Magus Allister's brusque behavior, Lady Colleen," Magus Harvey explained. "I'm afraid I did not act as politely as I should have on our previous meetings."

Colleen fixed the archmage with a look. "You see, Allister, he has apologized, so there is no need for further rudeness."

Allister sank into his beard. "That was no apology. An apology is admitting you were a pompous ass."

"And I accept your apology, Magus." His guest suppressed a smile. "And who is this young man?"

"That is my son, Daebian, Magus," Miranda said.

"Azerick's son?"

"Yes."

Robert looked at the boy quizzically. "Forgive me, My Lady, I had thought he was not yet born when Magus Giles passed. Am I in error?"

Miranda smiled to cover her discomfort about talking of her son's unusual maturity. "You are correct, Magus. Daebian is quite special."

Daebian smiled as he shifted his gaze between the Academy wizard and his mother.

"It certainly appears so, My Lady. Has he displayed any other unique traits?"

"Other than his enjoyment of music and poetry, no." Miranda looked at her son. "Do you have a new poem for us tonight, sweetheart?"

Daebian smiled, showing his tiny white teeth. "Yes, Mother.
Three hounds chase after a rabbit,
Hoping to track her to her lair.
But just when they think they have her,
They discover a badger,
And the battle is more than they can bear.
They thought their prey was weak,
And backed her against a wall.

The hounds picked a fight,
In the dead of night,
But it was not the rabbit who would fall."

Wizard Harvey cleared his throat. "An interesting verse."

Miranda smiled uncomfortably at her guests. "I admit we do not always understand them. Sometimes boys just enjoy being silly."

Allister thought this a good time to return to the purpose of the wizards' visit. "I assume you are here because of Ellyssa."

"You assume correctly."

"If you expect any help from us you can forget it," Allister said. "As far as I am concerned, she has done nothing but take out the trash the Watch either cannot or will not deal with, and I won't hand her over for inquisition for that."

Magus Harvey hid any slight he may have felt behind his smile. "On the contrary, we are here to request that you not to interfere in any way. We do ask for you to answer any questions we might have, but expect you not to involve yourselves directly in either the rogue's defense or apprehension. Conflicts of interest and all that and, before you ask, I do possess a writ of apprehension and inquisition signed by the council. I have already taken the liberty of providing Duchess Mellina with a copy to avoid conflicts with the local authority. I also possess an order instructing all those who fall under the authority of the Academy to be honest and forthright when answering any questions we ask in regards to resolving this situation. Failure to comply with the order is considered harboring a rogue wizard and punishable by Academy law."

"Oh good, for a while there I was beginning to think I was wrong in regards to my initial assessment of your putrid character," Allister responded.

"Perhaps, perhaps not. I can only attest to doing my duty. Judgment of my character is for others to decide. Do you know the location of Ms. Jensen?"

Allister answered reluctantly but honestly. "No, and Aggie has been scrying every day for the past month looking for her. Wherever she is, it is either well warded or she discovered how to hide herself. The latter is the most probable since she has the book."

"Well, if Magus Sharpe is unable to divine her location, it is no wonder we have had no luck. Her divination skills are still regarded as the best in the Academy," Magus Brown said.

"Thank you, dear. It is nice to know I am still appreciated," Aggie replied.

"Are you saying you positively identified the Codex Arcana and the girl is in possession of it?" Magus Harvey asked anxiously.

"Yes on both counts, I'm afraid," Allister rumbled, feeling rather embarrassed at having to admit it.

"I still don't understand why the book is so important," Rusty said. "I've used it and, although there is certainly some great information in it, I don't see what would make her so desperate to keep it; certainly not so much she would attack you for it."

"You have not told your people about the codex?" Magus Brown asked.

"No. I thought the fewer people involved the better, but I suppose the time has come to explain everything." Allister directed his words at Rusty and the other young wizards at the table. "The codex is more than just a book—when it wants to be. It is a magical tome, which contains far more than what most people see upon its pages. Some say that it was created by the gods and contains all knowledge of every type of magic that ever existed."

Rusty looked at Allister quizzically. "You said when it chooses. Are you saying this thing is sentient?"

"Not in a way as to be alive, not how we perceive such things. When a magical artifact is created with that much power, it gains a sense of purpose, mostly from those who handle it extensively. It does not think per se, but it comprehends the purpose for which it was created. The Codex Arcana is an enormously powerful artifact, and it has been in the hands of some of the mightiest wizards and other creatures in existence. When it senses a possessor has the power and the willingness to use it to its full potential, only then will the book reveal itself for what it is and what it can give."

Rusty's eyes widened and his jaw dropped. "All known magic?"

"That is one theory. There are many unknowns as the codex inexplicably vanishes before anyone has the time to study it fully. Usually in the hands of someone who wants to possess it for themselves. The few decades it was in the possession of the Academy, it revealed very little. The first person it 'spoke' to disappeared along with it."

Rusty blew out a long breath. "And now Ellyssa has it. This cannot be good."

"Do you know if the book speaks to her?" Magus Harvey asked.

Allister thought a moment. "I strongly believe so. It is one reason why I do not hold her entirely to blame for her actions. She was frightened, and I believe the codex is having an undue influence on her."

Aggie snorted. "I think you're just an old softy and a sucker for a pretty face. If I get my hands on her, I'll beat her bloody."

"I do not think the codex will be much of a mitigating factor at her trial," Magus Harvey explained. "The codex offers itself to those already of the disposition to use it. How they choose to use it is entirely of their own making. What little influence the book may have is going to be a poor defense."

"As far as you know," Allister countered. "I spent the better part of a month digging through the Academy archives, and our knowledge of it is poor at best. It also actively tried to prevent me from discovering its identity."

"We shall see. I believe it is time we were leaving. Nearly all of her attacks have been in the evening, and we must be prepared to intercept her. Lady Colleen, fellow mages, it has been a pleasure to dine with you this evening."

Allister hurried to his feet. "Allow me to show you out."

"No need to trouble yourself; we know the way," Magus Harvey said cordially.

"Trust me; it will be the highlight of my evening."

Allister showed the three Academy wizards to the door, glad to part company with them. Magus Harvey turned as Allister was gently shoving them out the tower.

"I do not want to leave you with the wrong impression of me, Magus. I will see this school brought fully under the auspices of the Academy, and when I bring this rogue to trial, I will have all I need to convince the council to act. It's nothing personal, mind you. As I said, it is my duty."

"You're wrong, Harvey; it is quite personal."

Allister closed the door more gently than his anger demanded. Robert Harvey's assertion was more than just an idle threat. Between Ellyssa's antics, the codex, and Azerick's previous run-in with the Academy, the school was without a doubt in serious jeopardy, and not even his standing would likely save it.

Ellyssa, wearing the magical guise of a young man, helped shuttle the heavy cargo crates from the recently docked ship onto the waiting wagons. She had been working on the docks in this form for nearly two weeks. It was exhausting work, but it was the best way to get a close look at any ship and crew sailing into port. It also helped build her physical strength. Azerick had always said strong muscles were as important as a strong mind and were the foundation of a strong body, so she willingly suffered the strain.

She found the physical exertion of working on the docks provided an excellent means of mental and emotional diversion. As long as Ellyssa focused on her work and her muscles constantly protested their exertion, her mind was distracted from much of her inner turmoil. Ever since she began actively hunting Captain Jake and the slavers, her night terrors and hallucinations had diminished substantially. It was all the encouragement she needed to know she was doing the right thing.

Ellyssa began working on the docks shortly after one of the slavers told her Sonjay was moving black market cargo aboard his own ship and was likely to make a port call to North Haven soon. Her suspicion peaked the moment the ship made dock. The ship moored right before the port closed for the night, which meant the customs crew and harbormaster would likely be hasty in their inspection.

It was very unlikely there were slaves aboard or that it would be taking any on. Ellyssa had not seen so much as a hint of a slave ship since she had made an example out of the last one that docked. Word got around about how the previous harbormaster also met his grisly demise for associating with slavers. The lack of a friendly harbormaster and the threat of a very unpleasant death at the hands of the Witch of North Haven made it too risky for slavers to bring their ships in.

Ellyssa had caught a few of the scum lurking about the streets and discovered they had dropped anchor in a natural cove two days to the south. She had gotten to the slavers before they could bundle up any captives and carry them out of the city. She thought about acquiring a horse and going after their ship, but there was no way of knowing if it would be there or if she could even find it. Besides, she had a more important target to watch for.

Although she was still new to the profession, the amount of cargo she and her fellow dock workers unloaded seemed a little light. It was not unheard of for a ship to sail without a fully laden vessel, but it was rare. Her suspicions were borne out when the crew began unloading smaller crates and individual items by hand a couple of hours later. Ellyssa watched the goings-on for more than an hour before the crew finished loading their illegal wares into a wagon.

Ellyssa spotted a large man debark with the bulk of his crew once the wagon left. She was uncertain if it was Sonjay, given the darkness, until he passed by a streetlamp close to where she was hiding. She unconsciously pulled the Source into her but let it go. She needed more than simple revenge. She needed information. She needed Captain Jake.

She let the group of men pass and shadowed them through the streets. It did not take long for the group of sailors to reach their destination: a seedy tavern just a few blocks from the docks. The noise from inside hit Ellyssa like a strong wind the moment she opened the door. The smell of alcohol and unwashed bodies nearly completed the job of shoving her back outside as thoroughly as a bouncer.

It took several minutes to find Sonjay and his crew despite his size and unique appearance. The owner of the establishment did not spend much on lighting, and smoke filled the room like the morning fog on Blackmoore Swamp. The acrid smoke from pipes and other smoldering, dried vegetation made her eyes water and burned her throat. Ellyssa fought back the urge to gag, a sure sign she was an outsider here.

Ellyssa ordered a pitcher of ale and threaded her way through the crowded tavern, deftly dodging patrons milling around. She admired the serving women for their ability to avoid the jostling, shoving, and ofttimes groping men, all without ever spilling a drop. She approached Sonjay's table and shouted to be heard over the din of the boisterous crowd.

"Captain, mind if I join you?" Ellyssa asked.

The ship's captain looked about to tell her to go jump in the harbor until Ellyssa raised the pitcher of ale and grinned. "I suppose there's room for you and your friend, especially if you've a mind to have more join you later."

Ellyssa sat down when several of the men scooted over enough to make room for her on the bench. The sailors drained the last drop of ale from the pitcher as they passed it around, so Ellyssa raised the empty vessel overhead, indicating the need for another to be brought over.

"So what brings a boy like you to my table with gifts I doubt you can afford?" The dark-skinned man asked.

"I consider it more of an investment than a gift," Ellyssa replied. "I'm looking for work."

Sonjay narrowed his eyes at the illusion-shrouded young woman. "You look familiar."

"I helped unload some of your cargo today."

"Sounds like you have a job then."

"I'm looking for something steadier and better paying. I think maybe if I sailed with you I could do a lot better," Ellyssa told the captain.

The serving woman brought the requested pitcher over and set it on the table. Ellyssa dropped a few coins into her palm and poured Sonjay another mug, deftly dribbling in the contents of a small glass vial as she did so. The hilt of a knife at Sonjay's side drew her eyes. The captain saw her looking and pulled it from his hip.

"You like that, do you?" He held it up and showed it off. "My former captain gave me that when I left his ship to captain my own.

Ellyssa studied the ivory handle with its elaborate scrimshaw. "You must have been good friends. Why did you leave his ship?"

Sonjay smiled, revealing a mouthful of white teeth standing out in stark contrast to his nearly black skin. "We'd made the delivery of a lifetime. Got so much gold I bought his old ship with my share and he bought himself a brand new one. I took on a new crew and started working for myself. No matter how good your job is or who you work for, second is still second and Sonjay is a man destined to be first."

"It sounds like I found the right man to work for," Ellyssa said.

"How do I know you have the barnacles to do what we do? Some of our business requires a certain willingness to overlook some of the oppressive laws of the kingdom, particularly those of taxation."

"I watched you unload your additional cargo after the port authorities left." Ellyssa tried to whisper conspiratorially while still allowing Sonjay to hear her.

Sonjay's jovial smile vanished like the sun behind an ominous black cloud. "You risk your life just mentioning that fact."

Ellyssa could not help but look at the huge hand now tightly gripping the fine hilt of that knife. "I just wanted to confirm my hunch was right. Fact is, honest work is fine when you can get it, but it don't come along often and it don't pay nearly as well. You don't need to worry about my stomach. It's tasted enough foulness to build up a pretty powerful tolerance to just about anything I need to do."

The big man appeared to think while his now silent crew waited to react to his response. Ellyssa was certain the men would grab her and make her disappear with just the slightest indication from their captain. Everyone, including Ellyssa, seemed to relax when the big man's smile returned.

"You come to my ship tomorrow night. I have some cargo to pick up and take south. You seem smart if not very big. I can use smart people to…" Sonjay cut off his words as a cramp brought his hand to his stomach.

"You all right, Cap'n?" one of his crewmen asked.

Sonjay's face contorted in discomfort. "I think I got a bad clam in that chowder. I need to hit the privy and bilge my hull."

A few of the men snickered at the comment as Sonjay pushed through the crowd with the grace of a bull. Ellyssa watched him exit out a door set in the back of the tavern.

"I'm going to go get another pitcher," Ellyssa said.

She vanished into the crowd and made her way outside. The door led to the alley where a crude outdoor privy had been erected. She could hear Sonjay as the mild poison she spiked his ale with violently purged his system.

Ellyssa dropped the illusion so the former slaver could see her for who she was before he died. She jerked open the door to the privy and coldly stared at the man who was little more than a slightly blacker silhouette in the darkness.

"Hey! The damn thing's in use! Go use the wall!" Sonjay glared at the figure standing in the open door.

Ellyssa conjured a light and let its luminescence wash over her face. Sonjay narrowed his eyes at her, trying to place the face. She smiled as she watched those eyes go round with recognition and fear.

"You!"

"I'm glad you remember who I am. Do you remember what I am as well?" Ellyssa asked.

Sonjay tried to leap to his feet, but Ellyssa wove a spell and forced him to sit back down. "Where is Captain Jake?"

"How in the abyss should I know?" The fear he felt was evident in his voice.

"You were his closest friend, Sonjay. He gave you this knife." Ellyssa pulled the blade free from the scabbard near his feet.

"I've only crossed his path twice in the years since I struck out on my own, I swear! I don't know where he is right now or his route. He likes to run between the Black Sand Isles and the shipping lanes whenever the mood strikes him, picking off stray merchant ships. Half the year he lives like a prince in a villa on one of the islands. That's all I know!"

Ellyssa tucked the knife into the leather belt encircling her slender waist. "If that's all you know, then I guess it will have to do."

Ellyssa summoned the Source, and the boards upon which Sonjay sat creaked ominously. The big man gasped and splayed his hands out wide to brace himself. Twin columns of human filth burst through the wood, wrapped around his chest and face, and pulled him head first into the muck. Only Sonjay's feet were visible as they stuck up out of the ruined seat and futilely kicked the air until he drowned in the most horrible manner imaginable. Ellyssa smiled at the irony.

Magus Brown started in surprise when the crystal in her hand glowed with lavender light. "Robert, look at this. Someone nearby is channeling the Source."

Magus Harvey looked over at his fellow mage. "Excellent, Melanie. Can you determine the direction and distance?"

The wizard studied her crystal, slowly directing it left and right. "That way, perhaps four or five blocks."

"Near the docks. I knew she would return eventually! We must intercept her before she ceases her casting and we lose her."

The three Academy wizards broke into a jog, following the pulsing light of Magus Brown's crystal. They came to a side street and she pointed left with her glowing talisman. The hearts of all three wizards raced as they neared the rogue mage. None of them were battle trained. There was a special branch of the Academy trained for combat and dealing with hostile wizards, but the inquisitors were stationed in the desert city of Argoth to act as a defense against Sumaran invasion. The far more numerous Academy wizards dealt with any attack coming from the southern passage nearest Southport. Magus Harvey was not too concerned. They were three full wizards from the Academy and they could certainly handle one girl.

"She is just ahead and drawing nearer," Melanie whispered urgently.

Magus Harvey scanned the area. "Melanie, hide in the alley to the right. Oliver, to the side street on our left."

Ellyssa hastened down the dark street in search of the nearest gate leading out of the city. She had perfected the permanent gate that had been such an utter failure a few years ago. In a small cave just a mile north of the city, she had created a stable portal to her new home. She was extremely grateful, as it saved her nearly a ten-mile walk to reach the city. Her nerves went on alert as a man stepped from the shadows of a nearby building and planted himself in the middle of the street.

"That is close enough," the man said.

Ellyssa stopped, turned her head from side to side, and saw two more figures emerge from behind and to each side of her. "I know you.

You are the man from the Academy who threatened to close down the school."

"I'm glad you know that, so you know I have the authority and duty to apprehend you for unlawful use of magic. You are also in illegal possession of a magical artifact, which shall be turned over to the Academy at once."

Ellyssa slowly shook her head. "You are not my enemy, Magus. Do not become so."

"You are surrounded by three Academy wizards. Resisting will only result in far more severe punishment. Come quietly and hand over the Codex Arcana, and things will go much better for you," Magus Harvey assured her.

Beneath her calm façade, Ellyssa seethed. These people did not understand what she did! They could never understand. And they wanted her book. She could not allow that to happen. The codex was too important. The wizard was still talking, but Ellyssa stopped listening and broke into a sprint directly toward him. Magus Harvey stopped his pointless attempts at persuasion mid-sentence when she unexpectedly charged him.

Ellyssa sensed the other two wizards begin casting before she heard their rhythmic chanting. Thanks to Azerick's ring, she cut through the ether and grabbed hold of the Source almost as if it were an extension of herself. The young mage ripped open a portal and instantly closed the hundred feet of open ground between her and Wizard Harvey.

Robert's eyes flew wide as the girl instantly appeared only a few feet in front of him. He deduced what the girl had done and was amazed she was not only able to maintain her sprint with only a bit of wobbling, but also to form another spell so quickly after gating. Such means of travel were very disorienting, even if for only a few moments.

Further pondering was impossible as a powerful force struck him hard enough to launch him several feet through the air. The spells of Melanie and Oliver passed harmlessly through the space Ellyssa had been occupying. One bright orb of light struck an awning support and sent the porch crashing to the ground.

Magus Harvey rolled to his feet holding his ribs and watched the girl race down a side street. "You two go that way and try to cut her off, and be careful! We need her alive to get the codex."

Robert took a few stumbling steps then chased after Ellyssa. Melanie and Oliver ran down the street parallel to the one Ellyssa had fled down. Robert emerged at an intersection and spotted the girl as she burst into the open from the street ahead of him. Their eyes locked, but before the girl could strike at him, Magus Harvey released the energy he had been holding at the ready.

The magical bolt lit up the street like a small sun as it streaked toward its target. The girl's eyes flared as she tried to bring up a ward but was too slow. The strike sent her careening into the wall of a building where she lay moaning but unable to muster the strength to move. Magus Harvey strode toward the incapacitated girl with a smile on his lips and a spell at the ready. Magus Parkes burst from the alley just a moment later.

"What have you done?" Oliver asked his fellow wizard.

Magus Harvey appeared confused a moment then looked at the form huddled on the ground. He conjured a light and saw that he had struck down Magus Brown.

"Blast it all! The girl must have dropped an illusion on Melanie when she came out of the alley. She's clever, I'll give her that."

"There!" Oliver pointed when he spotted movement from down the street.

"Come, we cannot allow her to escape!"

"What about Melanie?" Magus Parkes asked.

Robert looked down at their comrade who was slowly regaining consciousness. "Leave her, Oliver. She will be fine for now."

The two men hastened after the fleeing girl. The pair drew nearer until the single figure split into two and went in separate directions upon reaching the next cross street.

"Damn her and her illusions!" Magus Harvey shouted. "We'll have to split up, but be careful."

Robert turned right while Oliver sprinted after the figure running to the left. Both men continued to catch glimpses of the girl as she raced down the street and darted around corners. Magus Parkes nearly ran into the rogue wizard when she apparently found the alley blocked and tried to double back. Oliver did not hesitate to lash out with a force strike. Ellyssa dove to the ground and tried to roll out of its path, but the spell caught her a glancing blow and turned her roll into a tumble.

She released a stream of brilliant bolts, but the wizard's shield absorbed most of it.

She tried to run again but another assault took her in the back. The spell lifted her from the ground and slammed her into the wall of a small shop. Ellyssa lay on the ground gasping for breath and quietly weeping as the wizard cautiously approached. When Magus Parkes looked down at the girl, he could see she really was little more than a girl, a girl who may never see full womanhood if her trial went poorly.

"Stop fighting now. It's over," Oliver said softly.

"No, it's just beginning," Ellyssa said as she stepped up behind him.

Magus Parkes saw the girl on the ground vanish and spun around to face the voice at his back. He had just a moment to capture the cold determination in the girl's eyes before she hit him hard enough to send him through the wall of the shop. He looked up just in time to erect a ward as Ellyssa brought half the roof down on top of him.

Robert Harvey heard the exchange of magical attacks echoing through the night-shrouded streets. He realized he was the one chasing the phantasm while Oliver had obviously found the girl. He ran back toward the sound of battle with a curse and hoped he got there before it was over. Given their level of success thus far, he had less than high hopes of Parkes defeating the girl on his own. Even that tiny bit of optimism was smashed when he reached the ruined store.

Magus Parkes's muffled shout came from under the destroyed timbers. "She ran toward the docks!"

Magus Harvey refused to allow the girl to slip away. He knew her tricks now, and her illusions would not fool him again. He spotted Ellyssa as she darted down another alley. Robert took a small gamble by using the Source to coax more speed from his fatiguing legs and began closing the distance separating them.

Ellyssa found her path blocked by a low wall of cracked and warped boards. She demanded more speed from her muscles, leapt up, and grasped the top of the boards. She ignored the splinters digging into her hands as she pulled herself up. The flash of light practically blinded her and pain shot across her leg from the lightning bolt the Academy wizard unleashed upon her.

Ellyssa winced when her injured leg struck the ground. She staggered slightly as she ran, blinking away the brilliant motes of light swimming crazily before her eyes. Magus Harvey did not bother trying to scale the wall. Instead, he simply unleashed a ball of fire and obliterated the flimsy structure. His spell had the added effect of illuminating the dark street and showed Ellyssa racing for the docks.

Magus Harvey saw the girl flee down another narrow street before bursting out into the open ground of the dock front. Crates, nets, and crab pots exploded as Magus Harvey launched a series of simple force strikes at the fleeing mage in an attempt to trip her up and stun her long enough to subdue her.

Ellyssa raised an arm to shield her face from the flying splinters of wood despite the protection her ward offered. She felt several strikes glance off her hasty shield and knew it was only a matter of seconds before the wizard realized he would have to expend more power to take her down.

Robert saw the girl rapidly approaching the end of the dockfront. The girl looked panicked as she realized there was no place to go. A large fish-processing factory blocked her egress to the right and only the long dock and an endless ocean offered an option other than turning and fighting. The girl chose flight until she reached the end of the dock.

"It is a long swim to anywhere," Magus Harvey told the girl who was looking from him to the water like a trapped animal. "You are stronger and more skilled than I had anticipated. It is a shame you chose the path of a criminal. The Academy is lacking in true talent like yours these days."

Ellyssa glared at the wizard. "You let slavers take people away, you ignore the suffering of the common people knowing you have the power to make a difference, and you call me the criminal?"

"Had you attended a proper school, you would know the history of our order and why we must remain separate from the daily running of the kingdom."

"Your order would never have allowed me in. I came from a poor home with no titles or wealthy benefactors. I am one of those people you would have watched sold into slavery or worse. You people are the criminals for ignoring what you have the power to stop! I have the power, and I will not ignore the suffering!"

"You may have stopped the suffering of a few faceless commoners," Robert said, "but how much suffering have you caused to those you know in the process? Has all the pain and tragedy your actions caused been worth your vaunted ideals? Was it a fair exchange? I had dinner with a lovely woman and bright young boy who would certainly say it was not."

Ellyssa intentionally kept the man talking so she could distract him so he would not notice the small tendril of power she directed at one of the thick coils of rope behind him. Despite this, his words burned her like fire down to her soul with their truthfulness. No, it was not a fair exchange. Not yet. Not until Captain Jake was dead, and not even then. Probably never.

"You are exhausted and out of room to run," Robert continued. "Tell me where the Codex Arcana is and surrender to me. It is time to end this pointless crusade."

Ellyssa coaxed the rope toward the wizard and struck. Magus Harvey let out a yelp as the animated cord constricted around his ankle and jerked him into the ocean. Ellyssa channeled her power into the rope until she could no longer affect it. By the time she had reached the limit of her power, Magus Harvey was treading water and shedding his heavy clothing half a mile from the docks.

After a rapid sprint out of the city, Ellyssa practically fell through the magical gate and stumbled into the dark chamber of the cave now serving as her home. Despite her exhaustion, she went to the codex where it lay open upon the natural shelf of stone protruding from the wall. Or perhaps not so natural. Many of the features within the cave looked to have been molded by human hands wielding magic. She was not sure what she could do with the dagger, but she was certain the book would.

"I need to find Captain Jake. I have his dagger." A smile played across Ellyssa's lips. "Show me."

The pages fanned as if blown by a strong breeze or an invisible hand. The sheets ceased their turning and words formed upon them, each perfectly penned character glowing faintly with a silver light.

"Yes, this will work. I need to kill him when I find him, and I want him to see my face. I want him to look upon me with terror in his eyes so great it follows him to the abyss where it will be the thing of his nightmares for all eternity. Show me."

Again, the pages fanned before her eyes and the glow of the letters shone off her sweat-dotted face. Another smile found its way onto her face, darker and more sinister than any before. The spell the book showed was perfect, as were they all, but it was very complex and it would require a great deal of study. Ellyssa had never heard of such a spell or dreamt such a thing was possible. It would take her to the edge of her strength and very possibly beyond.

Having recovered from their arcane beatings, Oliver and Melanie raced toward the docks. By the time they arrived, Magus Harvey was calling out to them only a few hundred feet from shore.

"Throw me a rope!" Robert gasped out, obviously very fatigued.

With help from his associates, Magus Harvey soon stood on the docks, shivering. He had shed almost everything except his underclothes to keep from drowning. A simple spell dried him out and warded off the cold.

"It appears that we have underestimated the girl," Magus Harvey declared. "Her innate strength and access to the codex make her more than a simple journeyman mage."

"So what do we do now? Seek her out or lay in wait again?" Melanie asked.

Robert pursed his lips in thought. "No. We shall return to the Academy and hand this over to the inquisitors. Given her actions this night, I have no doubt the council will agree that their involvement is warranted."

Magus Parkes frowned his displeasure. "You do not think we three can take down a child? You want to go back to the Academy empty-handed?"

"I have no doubt we could overpower her regardless of the codex or her abilities. She is just a novice after all. The problem lies in taking her alive so we can recover the Codex Arcana. Its acquisition is paramount. The inquisitors are trained for this sort of thing. We are not, and I will not allow even my great arrogance to jeopardize the recovery of the codex."

Magus Harvey spent the several days of travel back to Southport preparing to address the council. He and the other two members of his ill-fated expedition soon stood before the assembly. At least two dozen wizards sat upon the benches behind them.

"Magus Harvey, I presume you and your colleagues called this council to session regarding the mage, Ellyssa Jensen, and the disposition of the Codex Arcana," Headmaster Florent stated bluntly. "Since you have not handed over either of those two things, I can also assume your mission was not a success."

Magus Harvey took a step forward and ducked his head. "It was not, Headmaster. The girl was much stronger than expected. Even taking that and the fact she possessed the Codex Arcana, I believe much of the difficulty in capturing her was her obvious militant training."

A great deal of murmuring arose. "You confirmed the book in question is the codex?" the headmaster asked.

"As much as I was able. Magus Allister was convinced it was. When he attempted to secure it, the girl attacked him and fled. Neither they nor we were able to locate where she is hiding."

"Ms. Jensen attacked the archmage? Successfully?" Magus Sorenson asked.

"So the archmage says. He claims the girl took him by surprise and was able to secure the room in which the book was located. By the time he was able to unravel the wards securing the room, she had vanished with the book."

Magus Mason King, the councilmember to the right of the headmaster asked, "Do you believe this account?"

"I cannot say with certainty, but I have no reason to doubt his claim," Robert answered.

Magus Douglas spoke up. "I believe with this new information we must revisit the debate of what to do with this girl and that school."

"Magus Harvey," Headmaster Florent asked, "what is you and your team's assessment of this situation?"

"Councilmembers, I believe we must file a formal request of inquisition to bring this rogue mage to heel and recover the codex. I believe her obvious militant training requires the expertise of the inquisitors in order to capture her alive and extract the location of the codex. I also feel this training with an obvious combative bent is the reason this situation is as complex as it is. Because of the unlawful and unregulated training, I once again recommend the school be shut down."

Several wizards in the gallery seconded this motion. The council began debating, which devolved into outright arguing and shouting. The headmaster and Magus Morgarum were the only two who strongly voted against the recommendation. It took all of Headmaster Florent's maneuvering and calling in favors, but the council finally reached a solution.

The headmaster banged the butt of her staff on the floor to restore order. "I will personally contact the inquisitors and give them all of the information we have on the subject of Ellyssa Jensen. In five days, a contingent of two score full wizards and archmages, along with one thousand mounted soldiers from the Martial Academy will take ships to North Haven and place the school under the control of the Academy. This is not a siege! The members of the Magus Academy are there to augment the teaching staff already in place and to ensure Academy laws and curriculum are followed to the highest standard. The soldiers are merely a show of force to discourage any resistance to the order. I hope this meets with your approval, Magus Harvey?"

"It does, Headmaster. I think the council has made a wise decision, given the circumstances."

Headmaster Florent turned to her other councilors. "That contingent will gut our already meager staff. I move we recall several wizards to return to the Academy to avoid disrupting classes."

"Agreed." Magus Sorenson nodded her approval along with several of the others. "I shall contact the Office of Inquisition after adjourning this council."

CHAPTER 10

*W*e must act now. We have no more time to gather our forces, Klaraxis told Azerick. Drak'kar is drawing nearer and thousands of our minions are dying with every delay.

"All right. I'll take what I have and order those still coming to converge here," Azerick responded. "From there I can order them forward or create a second line of defense."

I am glad to see you are not a complete idiot when it comes to tactics. If only you had shown such wisdom in the rest of your life, this all might have been avoided.

"It's just one criticism after another with you."

Azerick stepped to the ledge of the tallest tower of the citadel and looked out over the amassed throng of demons anxiously milling about below and up at the hundreds flying overhead. With a wordless call, he ordered them to mobilize as he shed his human form and took on Klaraxis's fearsome visage. Azerick leapt from the tower precipice, unfurled his enormous, bat-like wings, and soared over the heads of those on the ground.

The succubi and other flying demons formed ranks around him while those on the ground raced across the barren landscape. Azerick was forced to slow himself and his flyers to keep from outdistancing the horde below, but not by much. The flightless demons possessed nearly inexhaustible stamina on their home plane and swiftly ate up the miles.

Despite the progress of Drak'kar's juggernaut forces, Klaraxis's domain was vast, and it took a substantial amount of time to reach the site of the nearest battle. Azerick's incredibly keen eyes spotted the battle long before his host was near enough to engage it. There was no sign of Drak'kar, and the numbers involved suggested this was merely an advance party or perhaps a large group that had simply decided to strike out on its own to create havoc.

About a thousand Fourth Circle demons were tearing apart maybe a fifth that number of his people. Azerick felt a moment of emotional discomfort when he realized he considered the demons his people. He ignored Klaraxis's chuckling at his inner turmoil and led his flyers to engage the invaders without waiting for the bulk of his forces. The embattled demons below simply did not have that much time.

The enemy only had a few flyers, and their attention was so engaged on the battle raging on the ground they did not spot Azerick and his minions before he set upon them. Several of Azerick's grackin struck the flying enemy from above, sinking long talons and blades of black metal into the flesh of their foes. Succubi hurled small balls of fire whenever a target presented itself and occasionally dove in with claws and blades to stab and slash before swooping higher into the air.

One of the flying grackin, unnoticed in the ensuing chaos, glared down at the broad back of the demon lord with hateful blue eyes. The Rook made a few halfhearted swooping attacks against Drak'kar's forces, but he focused most of his attention on Azerick. He could not afford to miss a second time. It would put the powerful creature on too high an alert. He must bide his time and wait until he was vulnerable.

The fighting was so tightly packed Azerick gave up trying to use his magic, finding it easier to wade into the melee and use his enormous size and natural strength to crush and rip apart the smaller demons. Klaraxis cackled with glee at the carnage Azerick caused and used his influence to urge the human to even greater levels of violence. The demon lord's influence was so subtle Azerick found himself covered in gore and watching the remaining enemies retreating before he realized he had fallen fully within the joy the destruction brought him.

The demons made a terrible mistake by fleeing en masse. Their cohesive retreat allowed Azerick to bring his awesome magic to bear without fear of destroying his own forces. With a few powerful beats of his leathery wings, he looked down at the demons running away and hurled a massive ball of fire into the center of their ranks. The fireball erupted when it struck, and created a concussive blast of fiery death for a hundred yards in every direction, effectively destroying the remaining enemy. Succubi and grackins swooped down and easily finished off the few survivors.

Azerick clenched his fists and took several deep breaths in an attempt to slow his pounding heart and cool the fires of bloodlust and destruction burning within him. It was then he realized he had lost a measure of control and fallen into the unfolding chaos. Had he not noticed Klaraxis's influence and allowed the rage and ecstasy of the battle to continue, it might have consumed him and allowed the demon to regain control.

That was a glorious battle if short-lived. You have a fighting spirit for a human, Klaraxis said.

"I know what you tried to do, demon, and it will not work. I will not let you push me over the brink so you can take control."

It did not work this time, human, but perhaps the next time, or the time after that. Time is on my side, and I only have to win once where you must win every battle in which we engage.

"Then I will win every battle from here until the end of eternity."

We shall see. Drak'kar and his main host are near. I can sense it. That battle will be truly telling and will require everything you have just to survive, much less win. You will have to embrace all of your rage, pain, love, and hatred to access your full potential and tap the bulk of your power. Even then, I do not think you can defeat him yourself. You will need me. You will have to give me control or risk death.

"Then I'll die," Azerick swore. "I will never exist as your slave. Not yours or anyone's ever again."

So you say now, human, but there are far worse fates than death. If you allow Drak'kar to win, you may very well learn what those are.

Azerick tried to dismiss Klaraxis's words, but he could not help but wonder how much of the elation he felt at unleashing such violence was a result of the demon's influence, and how much of it came from some dark recess within him. The innocent, happy boy he had been died with his parents and friends, and in the ashes of those agonizing losses, Azerick was reborn and delivered by the hands of vengeance. His quest for vengeance was paved in blood, blood nothing could ever wash clean. Every time he thought he was free of his need for retribution, some other event arose to revitalize it. Would he ever be free of its compulsive, destructive influence? How long would it continue to drive him? Even in death, it burned within him.

He and his horde raced onward across the vast, desolate wasteland of his kingdom. Massive black fissures gave evidence of dark canyons and gulches that forced Azerick to maneuver his army and avoid them. Those gullies, crevasses, and craters were the only features of the otherwise barren landscape, with the exception of a few giant boulders that looked to have been casually tossed around.

I sense the battle unfolding not far beyond the Shattered Lands, Klaraxis said.

Azerick looked down as the last of the deep crevasses fell behind him and mentally nodded. He too could sense the battle being waged only a few minutes ahead of him. If he concentrated, he could hear the screams and cries of his people as they fought for their land and lives. Once again, it troubled him to think of these creatures not just as people but as *his* people. Azerick wanted to maintain his aloofness from them and even his perceived superiority over what he saw as a violent, evil, and despicable race, but he found it increasingly difficult to do so.

The first thing Azerick spotted from his lofty vantage point was a massive cloud of reddish dust rising a hundred feet into the air and stretching for at least a mile. As he and his army drew near, Azerick began picking out darker specks within the dust cloud. Some flew above and were punctuated by balls of fire and arcs of lightning. Far more ran and leapt about on the ground as they raked, bit, and clawed one another to shreds.

Azerick felt the presence of Drak'kar before he saw him. It did not take long for Azerick to spot the hulking demon lord amongst the throng. The four-armed brute picked up and smashed two or three of the smaller demons at a time. Occasionally, Drak'kar would unleash powerful magic when a tightly bunched knot of defenders presented itself, incinerating and exploding dozens at once. He did not seem to care if he caught several of his own warriors in the blast.

Azerick summoned dozens of succubi and grackin to form a screen in front of him. He was unsure if Drak'kar could sense him as well or if he was too distracted by the battle to notice his presence, but he hoped to launch an attack that would take the powerful demon by surprise. Visually obscured by his allies, Azerick entered a steep dive while channeling the Source and lacing it with demonic power.

Scores of Fourth Circle demons flew toward the newcomers in an attempt to intercept them. The opposing forces clashed, clawing, slashing, and biting. Most creatures broke apart and circled in an attempt to gain the advantage of height while several stayed locked in combat until they hit the ground where most continued battling until they were lost in the general bedlam.

Drak'kar looked up and smiled just as Azerick burst through the aerial battle lines. That smile vanished when Azerick struck him with an orb of black energy wreathed in silver flames. The awesome power of the dual energies threw Drak'kar a hundred feet and left a large ring of open ground where he and a few dozen demons once fought. The oasis vanished almost instantly as the battling hordes rushed in to fill the void like rushing water.

Azerick leveled his flight with a flick of his powerful wings and sped toward the downed demon lord, readying a second powerful spell as he raced over the heads of the tens of thousands of demons. Azerick hurled another orb of arcane destruction at Drak'kar before the demon lord was able to halt his uncontrolled tumble.

Drak'kar rolled away impossibly fast an instant before Azerick's follow-up spell struck and cratered the ground. Azerick beat his wings and hovered just beyond the billowing cloud of red dust, trying to pierce the obscuring veil with his eyes. A swift-moving silhouette was the only warning Azerick got before Drak'kar burst from the cloud dozens of feet in the air, the feat accomplished by an amazing thrust of his powerful legs. Azerick was too slow to avoid the demon, and the pair plummeted to the ground with Drak'kar locking onto Azerick with his four incredibly strong arms.

The falling demon lords crushed several unlucky creatures when they struck the ground and began exchanging bone-jarring blows. A large, clear expanse of ground opened up as the lesser demons moved away from the two titanic princes without ever breaking away from their individual battles.

Azerick landed a heavy blow to Drak'kar's broad jaw and tried to follow it up with a second strike, but the demon lord caught his swinging fist in one of his hands and delivered a staggering blow to

Azerick's head. Azerick swung his left arm with all his considerable might, but Drak'kar trapped it as well and began raining a fusillade of punishing blows into Azerick's body with his two lower arms.

A swift head-butt staggered Azerick who then felt himself flying backward when Drak'kar leapt up and kicked him in the chest with both legs. Azerick regained his feet and struck out with his magic, knocking his foe back several staggering steps but failing to do any real harm. He launched himself into the air since he found himself at a severe disadvantage in a ground battle. He wished he had spent more time studying barehanded brawling techniques with Ewen and Alex instead of focusing just on his staff work. It was obvious Drak'kar's fighting skills outclassed his own.

Safely out of Drak'kar's reach, or so he hoped, Azerick launched a massive fireball at his opponent, but Drak'kar was not without his own magic. The lord of the Fourth Circle crossed his arms in front of his face and body and let the inferno wash over him. Drak'kar then grabbed several large stones from the ground, imbued them with an aura of fire, and threw them at Azerick who was hovering a hundred feet in the air. The small meteors flashed by far faster than even Drak'kar's muscles could possibly hurl them on their own.

The flaming missiles streaked past as Azerick swooped and dodged. Several came near enough to burn his flesh, and one managed to punch a hole in the leathery lower portion of his right wing. Azerick raked lightning across the battlefield, slaying dozens of lesser demons, but the powerful stroke elicited little more than a grimace of pain from Drak'kar.

Azerick was so focused on his battle with Drak'kar and evading those hellish stones, he completely disregarded the larger battle. He realized his fatal error when at least half a dozen succubi and grackin broke free from their aerial fights and struck him from behind. Claws and knives slashed at the vulnerable membrane of his wings, making them useless. Azerick rolled and tried to put some of the attacking demons beneath him to cushion his impact with the ground. The cracking of bone not belonging to him gave evidence to at least a moderately successful maneuver.

Azerick unleashed a burst of arcane power that exploded outward from his body and sent demons and parts of demons flying in every direction. He turned to face Drak'kar only to find the demon lord barreling at him like an ape, using his four arms to help propel his body at a fantastic speed. In less than a second, Drak'kar struck his rival with the force of a rockslide.

Azerick looked up at the bland sky and tried to focus his wavering vision on the swooping, wheeling aerial acrobatics taking place overhead. He knew he needed to regain his feet, but his muscles were slow to respond. He had just gotten his feet beneath him when Drak'kar grabbed him by one leg and began smashing him against the ground as if he were a broom being used to swat mice.

You are too weak! I told you this, Klaraxis raged, *true fear evident in his thoughts. You must escape and recover or we will both surely die!*

Azerick was beyond attempting to respond as he gathered his will and the last of his flagging strength. At the apex of Drak'kar's next swing, Azerick crunched himself into a sit-up and grabbed one of the powerful arms being used to bash him against the ground with both hands. He braced himself for the next punishing impact with the ground. Azerick struck the ground once more, but not nearly as hard as with the previous assaults thanks to a better position. He then sent a tremendously powerful jolt coursing through Drak'kar's body.

Drak'kar released his hold on Azerick and let out a bestial howl of true pain. Azerick kicked the injured demon lord in the leg from where he lay on the ground and managed to topple him. He then sent a mental order to his minions and several hundred demons broke away from the battle and leapt upon Drak'kar.

The Fourth Circle prince ripped the limbs from the attacking horde, smashed them with his fists, and destroyed them with magic by the score, but still the demons piled onto him, heedless of their own survival. Azerick knew his lesser creatures could do little more than slow the powerful demon lord, but that was all he needed them to do.

Azerick conjured a gate and stumbled through it to deposit himself nearly a mile from his previous position. Even this tremendously long step barely got him past the farthest lines of battle. A multitude of enemies spotted him and leapt to finish him off, but a second gate took him safely out of reach. A third portal took him to the edge of the Shattered Lands. Lacking the strength to summon another gate,

Azerick picked the nearest great crevasse and ran shakily for its concealing depths.

He looked up from the shadowy canyon and spotted several flying demons furtively seeking him and certainly relaying anything they saw to Drak'kar. The deep gullies possessed several overhanging slabs of rock affording Azerick some concealment, but there were also many open stretches leaving him exposed. Several times, an aerial scout spotted him and swooped nearer, but the demon never attempted to engage him. Even in his brutally battered condition, a lone demon, or even several, was no match for the power he could still bring to bear.

Azerick knew he was not safe, however. Those grackin and succubi were certainly informing their master of his moves, and Drak'kar would not be far behind. He stuck to the shadows as best he could and even created some using his demonic power, but the keen eyesight of the demons searching for him could pierce such veils if they were alert enough.

The area of the Shattered Lands was vast, and the crevasses and canyons constantly branched off like a colossal, dried-up lakebed. Dead ends constantly forced Azerick to double back and take another route, each time putting him closer to discovery and the questing arms of Drak'kar who desperately wanted to tear him apart.

"Where are you, Klaraxis?" The booming question echoed off the walls of the canyons. "You are weak! You allowed a pathetic human to subvert you. Yes, I know of your affliction. Let me end what must be a humiliating torture for you."

Azerick pressed his back against the unyielding stone behind him as he drew in several deep breaths. He poked his head out from under the ledge he was hiding beneath and saw three demons flying overhead looking for him. Several avenues afforded him a way out from his hiding spot, but any one of them could take him right to Drak'kar. The way the canyons reflected sound made it impossible to tell from which direction the voice came.

"Come out and fight me some more," Drak'kar taunted. "You are strong for a human out of your element, and our battle amuses me. Fight well, and I will reward you with a quick death."

Azerick could tell Drak'kar was getting closer, but how close and from what direction he could not ascertain. He could feel his home, his bastion of power, far in the distance. It lay in the opposite direction of the battle and was his best chance at defense. He chose a chasm appearing to go in that direction and bolted. Azerick glanced up and saw the flyers overhead change the pattern of their flight. He knew they had spotted him.

"Run, little human. I enjoy the hunt! Know that your efforts are futile. There are few ways out of the Shattered Lands and no way for you to escape your fate!"

Azerick gave up on trying to avoid the watchful eyes of the scouts and focused on putting distance between him and his hunter. Drak'kar's laughter echoed off the walls as his minions kept him informed of his prey's location. Azerick ran for all he was worth, but even had he not suffered a brutal beating at Drak'kar's many hands, he knew he could not possibly outrun the demon on the ground. The thought made him glance remorsefully at his shredded wings.

The taunting voice chased Azerick through the maze of stony fissures as he ran a zigzag slalom through the towering, confining walls. He skidded to a stop in the red sand carpeting the canyon floor. The passage came to another dead end a few yards away. Azerick made a quick search for another way out, but there was none. As he prepared to run the quarter mile or so back to the last place the chasm branched, a large shape blotted out the light just before it bore him to the ground.

Drak'kar lifted Azerick's huge body with one hand wrapped around his neck and pummeled Azerick several times before hurling him against the wall of rock. Azerick's vision swam as he tried to focus on Drak'kar's grinning face. With no escape in sight and his strength insufficient to defeat the demon lord, Azerick tried to prepare his mind for the true death that had been shadowing him for most of his life.

"It was a fun chase," Drak'kar said, "but not enjoyable enough for me to grant you the quick death I promised. I am afraid it is going to take quite some time. Were you still the Klaraxis I knew and almost respected, I probably would not risk keeping you around, no matter how much joy I would lose by choosing not to use you as my plaything. But in your present form, I now see I have nothing to fear."

"Master, there is a way out behind you," a voice whispered behind Azerick. "You must change shape, or you will not fit. Change, quickly, and come around the left side of the boulder."

Azerick did not acknowledge the voice. He did not even shift his eyes, instead keeping them trained on Drak'kar as he gloated over his victory. Azerick used Klaraxis's shape-shifting ability to resume his human form. Before he even completed the change, he rolled swiftly to his left and found there was indeed a narrow crevice behind the boulder he was fetched up against. Azerick wriggled into the cleft, and strong arms reached out, grabbed him by the wrists, and pulled him in.

He heard Drak'kar roar with rage and felt his powerful body crash against the boulder. Loud cracking sounds filled the air as Drak'kar continued to scream his outrage and tore at the rock with his hands, ripping off huge chunks of stone and hurling them behind him. Azerick kicked with his legs as the creature ahead of him pulled him in deeper. What started as a simple crack in the cliff face eventually became a cave large enough for him to stand erect in.

Even in his human guise, Azerick still possessed his demonic inheritance and was able to see in the darkness with great clarity. The creature was a balrog and looked much like a frog the size of a large man, with arms only slightly smaller than its powerful hind legs. Azerick caught his breath, turned, and used his magic to collapse the entire passage through which he had come. He was unsure if Drak'kar could also change shape, but he was going to take no chances.

"Who are you? What is this place?" Azerick asked.

"I am Fu'Marb," the demon explained. "This is a secret way, a way through the Shattered Lands. My home is not far, and I know the secret ways intimately. I serve my prince well, yes?"

"You do, Fu'Marb, but why are you not in the battle. How did you find me?"

The balrog licked his lips nervously with his enormous tongue. "I was in the battle, near the back. I saw My Prince, um, choose to leave the battle to his faithful minions. I saw many flyers and the horrible Drak'kar following you. I thought maybe I could be more help to my master here than fighting the unworthy. I did right, master?"

"You did, Fu'Marb. Is there a way out, preferably nearer the citadel?" Azerick asked.

The balrog bobbed his entire body up and down. "Yes, master! Through that passage, we can walk the entire length of the Shattered Lands."

"That is very good. Lead the way, Fu'Marb."

The balrog bobbed up and down twice before hurriedly leading the way down the tunnel. Fu'Marb often looked back to ensure his prince was following and did not fall far behind. Azerick let the demon precede him down the passage and never saw the sinister grin stretching across the creature's broad face or the blue glimmer occasionally emanating from his eyes.

The Rook had not lied, not entirely. The balrog had indeed lived nearby, but he never joined the battle. The assassin found the coward hiding amongst the rocks after he followed Azerick as he fled the battle. He then decided to abandon his flying form and use the balrog as his host. Instead of simply driving out Fu'Marb's soul, he consumed it, memories and all. He needed the balrog's knowledge of these twisting canyons and dark tunnels. When the time was right, he would plunge his ethereal blade into the sorcerer's back and finally complete his contract.

CHAPTER II

Ellyssa closed the Codex Arcana. Her hands trembled and her stomach fluttered, so she took a deep breath to steady her nerves. She had spent the past fortnight studying this spell, and she was as ready as her patience allowed. She stepped to the edge of the natural pool formed from the small stream of water running through a crack in the wall. The young mage began the complex incantation and weaving of mystical energy.

The weave was extremely complex and took all of her concentration. Ellyssa had practiced drawing it on paper and mimicked the somatic motions hundreds of times in the previous two weeks until she could repeat it flawlessly. Still her nerves warred with her concentration, trying their best to make her misstep and fail, or worse, create a destructive weave that could rage out of control and destroy her.

Ellyssa pulled at the Source, demanding it fuel her spell, and it answered her call. Her skin felt on fire as she channeled more and more power into her body and used it to energize her magical weave. She trembled from the pain and effort of channeling so much power, but her focus remained resolute as she neared the spell's completion.

Pulling out the blade once belonging to Captain Jake, Ellyssa slashed her hand then tossed the knife into the pool of water. Still holding onto the weave of her spell, she knelt beside the pool, thrust her bleeding hand into the water, and then plunged her head beneath the surface, screaming out the final word of her incantation.

Captain Jake stood near the open cargo hatch of his ship supervising the distribution of pirated cargo between his flagship and the other frigate with which he collaborated. They were both anchored far out at sea and had recently plundered a large cargo ship of her goods. His haul was in a bit of disarray as the cargo ship had been taking on water fast and did not offer them the option of an orderly transfer.

The battle had been a bloody affair. The cargo hauler possessed a large crew, half of whom were mercenaries for the explicit purpose of battling pirates. The king's new navy patrolled shipping lanes nearer land, so most pirates like him stuck to the deeper waters far from shore. Fortunately for him and his fellow pirates, there were still those merchants foolish or brave enough, or who thought they could hire enough muscle for protection, to risk the longer routes to acquire the rare luxury goods from Lazuul and other exotic places.

Only a few pirates like him had recently broken from tradition and worked as a consolidated team instead of going it alone. The new navy and better-armed merchant galleons made pirating a risky affair. Many of the other captains called him spineless and a poor excuse for a pirate. Jake thought himself pragmatic and smart enough to adapt to the changing winds.

"Captain, something coming toward us off the port rail," came the report from the crow's nest.

Captain Jake pulled the brass spyglass from his hip, extended it to its full length, and peered out into the ocean. From his lower vantage point, he failed to spot what his lookout had seen. Then, a minute later, a small distortion on the sea's surface appeared in his view. The swell appeared to grow larger as it approached his two ships.

The captain cupped his hands in front of his mouth and called up to the crow's nest. "What do you make it out to be?"

The lookout had a much larger spyglass and could mount it to the edge of the crow's nest. "Looks like a swell, maybe breaking into a wave."

Rogue waves were not unheard of, but the sea was almost glass smooth and the waters here were very deep. Those two conditions alone made the possibility of a rogue wave very unlikely. Jake continued to watch the swell, now definitely a wave as the white froth of water highlighted its apex and moved with unnatural speed. Its location and the speed of its approach were not the only things unusual about it. Any single wave like that, usually caused by some massive upheaval like an erupting volcano or earthquake, spanned miles. This one was, at most, a few hundred yards wide and heading directly for his ships.

"Batten the hatches and tie in!" Jake ordered.

"Captain, we ain't finished transferring the cargo," a crewman yelled back.

"Forget the cargo! Someone's set a spirit on us."

His crew scrambled about the deck, following the captain's orders. The men redoubled their efforts when the wave was close enough for them to see with their own eyes. It continued to grow as it got closer, and it now reached higher than the ship's deck. Captain Jake kept his spyglass trained on the strange wave and gasped as he made out a form beginning to take shape in the frothing cusp.

Captain's Jake's jaw began to tremble uncontrollably as a face, etched with fury, appeared. There was no longer any doubt this was an unnatural phenomenon, nor was he a random target. The Witch of North Haven had finally found him. He had heard of the deaths in the city and of the young woman who always asked for him by name before killing every slave runner she could get her hands on. Jake had long suspected her identity, but now there was no longer any doubt. The girl wizard he had captured and sold to the vila had escaped and was now hunting him down, just as she had promised.

He had learned of the vila's death at the hands of an army led by a sorcerer. He assumed it was the girl's master. She had warned him he was a very dangerous man and would come for her. However, he also heard that the sorcerer had died in the battle, so he thought himself reasonably safe. Jake still avoided the mainland ports, especially after hearing about the witch looking for him. Apparently, he had underestimated the girl's determination and ability.

An awful keening like the wail of a banshee coupled with the force of a hurricane filled his ears and turned his guts to water. Every man aboard stopped what they were doing, clasped their hands over their ears, and looked out in horror at the wave as it grew until it towered over the top of the mainmast. All could see the face of the witch, screaming her rage. Deep within her briny eyes, her hatred promised death for every man aboard.

The witch wave formed two fists the size of large wagons and the entire form crashed down upon his ship, crushing everything and everyone beneath its thousands of gallons of liquid mass. Wood splintered and shattered under the assault and crushed or washed men from the deck. The ensorcelled wave tore Captain Jake's ship apart and pulled it beneath the briny surface. The second ship fared better as it was not the witch's focus, but it too was brutalized by the terrifying construct. The outer edge of the wave snapped all three masts, stripped it of sails, and nearly capsized it. The wave swept at least two dozen men overboard, half of whom never returned to the surface. The terrifying assault passed as swiftly as it struck.

Ellyssa awoke sore, exhausted, and in a great deal of pain. She was lying next to the pool, how long she had been there was anyone's guess. Given how hungry she was, probably at least a day if not two or even three. She was lucky to have apparently rolled over and out of the pool at some point, or she probably would have drowned.

Movement in the darkness alerted her to the fact she was not alone. Ellyssa drew a tendril of power from the Source and created a soft light. Even that small feat made her head swim and ache with a dull throbbing. At the edge of her pale blue light, she saw Wolf sitting at her small rickety table with Ghost practically attached to his hip as usual.

"How long have I been laying here?" Ellyssa asked, staring up at the ceiling.

"I found you about a day and a half ago," Wolf replied. "A rough guess is that you were lying in that puddle for almost a day already."

"How did you find me?"

Wolf let out a laugh that sounded closer to a bark. "It was easy, Ghost could smell you a mile away. Once I got within a hundred yards, I could smell you too. Just because you want to hunt pirates and slavers doesn't mean you have to match them in hygiene."

Ellyssa knew she had let herself go and accepted Wolf's criticism. When her entire life turned to hunting down Captain Jake and killing slavers, grooming fell far down the list of importance. After she left the school, it stopped mattering at all. She wanted to snap back that he was not one to talk about hygiene, but he had stopped being that filthy, wild boy a long time ago. He was eighteen now and every inch a man, a man who knew most of the girls at the school liked to look at him and giggled whenever he came around.

Wolf had shed the dirty, stringy boy look practically overnight a couple of years ago. He was now a young man with a body chiseled from a life of living in the woods and doing everything himself. He kept his long black hair in a tight braid and enjoyed showing off his fit body for the local girls by refusing to wear a shirt until winter forced everyone else into parkas. Technically, it was not a new behavior; it was just no one really noticed until recently.

"You know, with running water inside your cave, it wouldn't kill you to use it once in a while."

Ellyssa felt disgusting. Dried blood caked her face where it had run from her ears and nose. Her clothes had been sodden and then dried on her body, and they had been nowhere near clean to begin with.

"Fine, turn around," Ellyssa ordered.

Surprise flashed across Wolf's face. "Whoa, I didn't mean right this instant!"

"Doesn't matter. These clothes are ruined, and I'm not putting a clean set on over a filthy body. Not again, anyway. Now, turn around."

Wolf quirked his mouth in a smirk and faced away. He casually let his hand fall onto the wolf's head pommel of the shortsword Azerick had given him years ago. The blade was magical, and he discovered with it he could see through Ghost's eyes. It wasn't as if he wanted to leer at Ellyssa, he saw her as a sister and he was sure she looked at him as a brother, but it could make for some really good jokes later on.

Ellyssa started to peel off her clothes then spotted Ghost looking at her with what she could swear was a grin. "Ghost, you turn around too! I don't know what you are up to, but I know it's something. I can feel it."

Wolf barked out another laugh, and Ghost joined him at the far end of the chamber. Ellyssa found the remnants of the dagger at the bottom of the pool, now nothing more than a charred lump of slag, and tossed it out. She wadded up her shirt and used it to scrub most of the sweat, blood, and crud from her body. She made sure Wolf and Ghost were behaving themselves before briskly crossing the room and retrieving one of her few spare sets of clothing.

"Okay, you two creeps can turn around now."

"I brought you some food. I figured you would be hungry when you woke up," Wolf said. He brought two plates laden with edibles over to the small table.

"I'm starving!"

Wolf picked at his plate while Ellyssa scarfed down everything on her plate and then began picking morsels off his. Wolf let the famished girl eat without interruption until she relieved nearly half of his plate of its contents.

"So what did you do?" Wolf asked once Ellyssa's chewing slowed enough for her to talk between bites.

Ellyssa swallowed and took a breath. "I found Captain Jake."

"In North Haven?" Wolf asked.

Ellyssa shook her head as she chased down another bite of food with a drink of water. "He was out at sea. I found him by using a type of scrying spell." Ellyssa explained how she had found Sonjay, taken his knife, and was then attacked by Academy wizards. "I found another spell in the book enabling me to send a huge wave at his ship, and I crushed it."

Wolf's eyes widened. "Wow. So did you kill him?"

Ellyssa's shoulders slumped and she looked down at her empty plate. "I don't think so. The last thing I saw was Captain Jake clinging onto a piece of wood. Some men were trying to get to him and there was another ship I didn't sink."

"What are you going to do now?"

"I don't know. Still look for him, but now I don't have any leads and he knows I'm after him."

"People are really upset about the book you took," Wolf said with a glance at the tome open on the stone shelf.

Ellyssa followed his eyes and took on a distant look. "I don't care. They don't know how to use it properly, and the book wants me, not them."

"The book wants you? It talks to you?"

Ellyssa brought her attention back to the table. "Not really, not with words. It's more like a feeling, emotions. No, not emotion, more like an urge or desire. I just know the book wants me and not them."

Wolf looked troubled by her explanation. "Whatever it is, it doesn't sound good. How do you know this thing isn't affecting you, making you do things? Allister said the Academy would stop at nothing to get their hands on that book. If you keep doing what you are doing, they will catch you eventually."

"The book is not making me do anything!" Ellyssa snapped. "It doesn't care what I do, it doesn't have any wants or designs other than to be used, and it wants to be used by me. Maybe they will get me one day and take the book. It won't do them any good unless it decides to talk to them, and I don't think it wants to. I don't want to talk about the book. I won't give it up."

It was Wolf's turn to shrug. "Fine, then what do you want to talk about?"

"I don't want to talk about anything," Ellyssa responded. She crossed her arms and looked away petulantly.

"You need to talk to someone, otherwise you'll start talking to yourself and go mad."

"You talk to a wolf and you think I'm the one going mad?"

Wolf smiled. "Ghost is a good listener and has never given me bad advice."

"Fine, I'll get a pet. Go catch me a squirrel and I'll talk to it."

"Squirrels are horrible listeners and even worse at giving good advice because they're all nuts," Wolf replied, then burst out laughing.

"Yeah, I'm the one going crazy in this room," Ellyssa mumbled dryly. "How long have you known where I was?"

Wolf reined in his laughter and wiped his eyes. "We found you a couple weeks after you left the school."

"It took you that long?"

"I didn't care to look."

"So why did you?"

"Roger was worried about you. He likes you. A lot I think," Wolf told her.

Ellyssa looked down at the table. "He's better off forgetting about me."

"Yeah, that's what I told him. So what are you going to do now?"

Ellyssa looked around the cave. "I think the first thing I need to do is get some new clothes, but I'm too tired and sore to go into town."

"I can sneak some of your old stuff out of your room if you want. No one pays any real attention to me, except in the kitchens and some of the girls, and they aren't interested in what I'm carrying." Wolf burst out into another fit of laughter.

"Thank you, Wolf. Some food would be nice too if you can get it."

"If? I'm Wolf of the wild. There are no ifs."

Ellyssa could not help but smile. The expression and the sentiment it caused felt alien to her. She could not remember the last time a smile adorned her face that was not driven by a sadistic glee for revenge. Wolf and Ghost disappeared out of the cleft making up her doorway and jogged west in the direction of the school. Despite having been unconscious for a couple of days, Ellyssa was exhausted and lay down on her makeshift bed for a nap.

It was an easy task to jog the few miles to the school, but Ghost seemed particularly eager to make the trip back. As they drew nearer the school, Wolf could sense Ghost's anxiety increasing, which caused a spike in his own. The two forest creatures stopped at the edge of the woods nearest the school. Wolf and Ghost stayed within the tree line as they made their way to the southern end of the school.

Arrayed outside the main gates were at least two thousand soldiers and what appeared to be something close to two dozen wizards, all almost certainly from the Academy. Nearly an equal number of forces stood along the tops of the walls and the roofs of buildings. There did not appear to have been any hostile actions as of yet, but there was a definite tension in the air.

"Ghost, creep closer so I can hear," Wolf told his companion.

The big wolf crouched and crept across the open expanse of land as if he were stalking prey. Wolf touched the pommel of his sword and merged his vision and hearing with Ghost's. Ghost padded forward, his ears pitched toward the people on the ground exchanging words with those on the wall. Wolf guessed this army must have come by ship, as there was no way they would have gotten within a day of the school by land without him knowing.

"Harvey," Allister shouted down, "what is the meaning of this?"

"I think you know, Allister," Magus Harvey answered. "I told you I would either shut this school down or bring it under the control of the Academy."

"You bring armed men and wizards to a school full of children, my home?" the old archmage shouted in righteous fury.

"This contingent is only to ensure no one acts rashly. It shall come to nothing as long as you comply with Academy edicts."

Miranda laid a restraining hand on Allister's forearm. "Wait, look out there."

Allister looked to where Miranda pointed and saw a mass of cavalry flying Duchess Mellina's standard galloping toward the school. From the dust farther down the road, he assumed an equally large number of footmen followed. The clarion calls of a dozen horns preceded the cavalry's arrival, likely in an attempt to preempt any hostile actions by either side.

Duchess Mellina reined her horse in hard with General Brague at her immediate right. She glared fiercely from under her open helm. "Who is in charge here?"

Magus Harvey bowed at the waist. "I am in charge of this task force, Your Grace. I am Magus Robert Harvey, appointed by the Academy to carry out its instructions."

"I don't give a damn if Solarian himself appointed you. How dare you bring an armed contingent into my duchy and threaten not just my citizens, but my own daughter and grandson! You will leave my territory immediately."

"Your Grace, your daughter and grandson are free to leave at any time," the wizard said smoothly, "but this school unlawfully teaches magic and therefore falls under the jurisdiction of Academy law, not that of the state or the crown."

"Academy autonomy does not allow you to bring armed troops through my city without notice or permission. I have half a mind to clap you in irons for that!"

Magus Harvey continued to smile in his annoyingly ingratiating manner. "You did not receive my notice? I apologize, Your Grace, I must have forgotten to file it with your staff. I would ask that you refrain from carrying out your threat of incarceration. Interfering with the legal execution of Academy law is against the king's law and could have rather serious repercussions."

Mellina took several controlled breaths to keep the scowl from her face, and General Brague looked as though he was just waiting for a signal to cut this wizard's head off. "I will speak with my daughter and Magus Allister. General, keep to my side."

"Always, Your Grace," the general replied.

"Thank you, Your Grace," Magus Harvey said, thinking he had cowed the duchess.

"It is not for your benefit, you little dung heap!" the duchess snapped in a rare show of vulgarity, nearly trampling the annoying mage with her horse. "Open a gate for myself and the general," Mellina called out.

A sally gate opened, and the duchess and her general guided their mounts through. The inside of the school compound was prepared for battle. The students of the orphans' academy had erected multiple barricades and defensive positions in what must have been very short order. Mellina and General Brague gave an invisible nod to the students' training and discipline.

The duchess and her general dismounted near the wall and ascended the ramp to its top where they located Magus Allister and Miranda along with several other senior staff members of the school.

"Miranda, Magus, please tell me what is transpiring here," Duchess Mellina said. "If I must listen to that arrogant little twit down there, I may very well ask the general to cut him down."

"I still can if you would like, Your Grace," Brague mumbled.

"You are sweet to offer, but let us try a diplomatic approach first. What is this all about?"

Allister answered, "He first came last year ago looking for Ellyssa and threatened to shut down the school. From what I can tell, he failed to get Ellyssa and is now trying to accomplish his secondary task."

"And his claim of legal authority?"

"I assume the Academy council has issued an edict of some sort. He did wave a piece of parchment at me," Allister said.

Mellina gave the archmage a disapproving look. "You did not bother to read it? What exactly is his intent?"

Allister looked abashed. "I am not certain, Your Grace."

Mellina rolled her eyes. "I expect such verbal impairment from men, but I thought I had trained you better, Miranda." The duchess looked down at the people below. "You there, annoying little man, what are your intentions here?"

"Magus Harvey, Your Grace," the wizard clarified.

"Oh, as if I care; now, answer my question."

Magus Harvey's ingratiating smile slipped to a scowl at being so readily dismissed. "I have an order from the Academy to place this school under its direct control and supervision. Several Academy staff will stay on as instructors and council members to ensure Academy law, guidelines, and curriculum are strictly adhered to. Were it up to me, I would shut it down completely, but there are those who have chosen to keep it open as long as it complies with Academy standards."

Mellina turned to Allister and Miranda. "What is your decision? My infantry are nearly here. I will support your decision, king's or Academy law be damned. I will deal with that when it comes."

"They are talking about taking over my home, Mother," Miranda said forlornly.

Rusty took a step forward and spoke. "Will it really be that much different than what we do now? Our curriculum is a little more advanced and faster-paced than at the Academy, but our classes are already overflowing. More instructors could help a great deal, even if it means we give up some control."

"It's not about keeping control, Franklin," Allister said. "It's about surrendering Azerick's legacy to a bunch of elitist snobs. Many of these new wizards, Harvey in particular, support the Academy's exclusivity in regards to attendance. I will not allow this jumped-up jackanapes to dictate our enrollment."

"Perhaps an agreement can be reached in regards to shared authority," the duchess suggested.

Allister considered it and called down to the assembled forces. "The current administrators of the school will have equal authority and positions on the council, and any admissions, expulsions, or punishments will follow Academy rules regardless of social standing or wealth."

"Allister, you are hardly in a position to make demands. The Academy has given me authority in this matter, and I am under no requirements to make concessions."

"I strongly suggest you take note of the two thousand men approaching and rethink your position, annoying little man," Mellina recommended loudly. "You may wish to confer with your soldiers' officers regarding tactics when trapped between a fortified wall and numerically superior forces. I think he will recommend you to consider concessions."

Magus Harvey's face burned with such intensity its discoloring was evident even to those atop the wall. "You would dare violate the laws of the king as well as the Academy?"

A devious smile played across the duchess's lips. "Are you referring to the same king whom my forces and members of this school personally returned to the throne? Would you also be referring to the same Academy whose two most senior archmages are now standing atop this wall? I believe you are, and I will take my chances with the political fallout."

Magus Harvey stewed over the unexpected turn of events. He had planned on cowing the stubborn Allister into submission. He had not expected the duchess to be so intractable and quick to rise to the school's defense. It was poor planning on his part, and he accepted it. He could still achieve victory even if not wholly as planned. He could not eject most of the low-class trash if he agreed to the archmage's terms, but he would still have control over the curriculum. He would agree, but the applied magic course currently being taught would come to a glacial crawl.

"All right, I will agree to the terms, but know the Academy has appointed me as headmaster, and I will not tolerate dissension from the staff or students."

Allister internally railed against the thought of this man acting as headmaster and feared for his school under his control, but the only other option was to fight, and fighting meant people dying. This school had seen too many of its students and staff perish in the battles with Ulric's mercenaries and the undead terror on that dreadful night. It would be different, uncomfortable even, but the school would survive.

"Very well, Harvey. I will comply with the Academy's order as long as you honor your agreement as well."

"I will keep my word, Magus Allister, and it is Headmaster Harvey, if you please.

"Headlessmaster Harvey would please me more," Allister grumbled. "Open the gates."

Magus Harvey, his fellow wizards, and several score of soldiers passed through the gates. Magus Allister ordered everyone to stand down and return to duties or dorms. He, Miranda, and the duchess then met Magus Harvey's contingent on the ground.

"I am glad you chose to be reasonable, Magus Allister," the new headmaster said with a self-satisfied smile.

"Same for you, Harvey," Allister retorted shortly.

"Headmaster Harvey, Magus Allister. We do not want your lack of protocol to be seen as disrespect. Such a thing could rub off on the impressionable young minds of our students, which could foment dissent and cause them to act in a manner resulting in expulsion. We would not want that to happen, would we?"

"No..." The old mage choked back the bile that rose in his throat. "...Headmaster."

Headmaster Harvey smiled in a way that made it look more like a sneer. "Excellent. I shall have my quarters and office set up at the top of one of the towers. The larger one will do nicely."

"The hell it will!" Miranda shouted. "Those towers are my home, built by my husband. They are not part of the school and you shall not step foot inside of either of them without my leave. You can find housing in one of the dormitories or in the city. I am sure we can create a suitable office in one of the outbuildings."

"What? This is unacceptable!" Harvey railed. "I am the headmaster, and I require suitable accommodations on the grounds."

"Then file a construction request with the Academy so they can agree on building and budget plans. I am certain it should not take more than six months for such a request to go through all the proper channels," Allister said.

The new headmaster looked as if he wanted to continue his protests and demands, but a look at Duchess Mellina's face clearly indicated this was a nonnegotiable issue. As the ruler of this region, she could simply recall the property and structures and reclaim them as her own. The fact she had the forces to evict him and his contingent convinced him to cease his protests.

The headmaster fumed. "You may all think you have won this little battle, but I won the war and don't you ever forget it!"

"I will never forget it, Headmaster," Allister responded. "You can count on it."

Wolf eased the tension on his bowstring and lowered it when it appeared there was not going to be a battle. He had the back of the wizard doing all the talking dead to rights. It was a long shot, but with the longbow he completed last year, he knew he could make it. He was not sure what was going on, but he knew none of it could be good.

"C'mon, Ghost, let's sneak around to the east side and cut through the kitchens. We'll need to grab some food anyway."

The odd pair skirted the woods and dashed across the open ground until they reached the wall. Wolf and Ghost edged along the wall until they found a small door set in the thick stone walls. These egresses were usually open to allow people to go freely to and from the school, but the heightened alert status saw them all tightly shut.

"Hey," Wolf called up to the sentry standing guard atop the wall, "open up. I need to get some food from the kitchens."

The young man looked down and smiled at them. "Now's probably a good time while everyone's pretty much distracted. You can probably get in and out without Agnes putting a skillet upside your head."

It had been more than a year since any of the cooking staff did more than give Wolf a scowl for filching food, which perturbed him. He thought it extremely rude of Agnes to deprive him of one of his favorite games by not trying to crack his skull whenever he snuck into her kitchen during one of his "urban foraging" expeditions. Wolf was certain she stopped trying to brain him just to be mean.

Wolf and Ghost stepped through the gate and crossed the grounds to the kitchen located in the old tower. The two stuck close to the buildings and did their best to remain unseen despite the fact nearly everyone's attention was focused toward the main gates and the apparent intruders. Wolf found the door leading into the kitchen, open as always to let out the extreme heat from the stoves.

The kitchen was bustling, mostly from boiling water in nearly every available pot to clean wounds and sterilize bandages in case a battle had erupted, but there were also a couple of large stew pots to keep the bellies of the defenders fed. The other kitchens were certain to be in a similar state of controlled chaos.

"There's some cured meat and dry foodstuffs over there," Agnes said sternly, pointing with her overly large wooden spoon. "Take what you want; just stay out of the way!"

Wolf was disappointed once again. The old woman did not even have the decency to take a swipe at him as he threaded his way through the kitchen to fill his sack. He wondered what he had done wrong to make the woman so hateful. Oh well, now was not the time to dwell on such things. The new developments he had seen at the gates instilled a greater sense of urgency.

Wolf and Ghost ran from the kitchen, through the dining room, and up the stairs of the tower to Ellyssa's old room. Wolf entered the room without knocking, startling the young girl inside who was watching the goings-on outside from the small window of her room. Wolf had forgotten about the girl, Olivia, who Ellyssa put in her room while she disguised herself as the delivery girl. When Ellyssa left, no one bothered to move her to the dormitories, so she just stayed here.

"Wolf, you scared me," Olivia declared as she pressed a hand to her pounding heart. "Do you know what's going on down there?"

"I don't know. Something about some new wizards taking over the school or something," Wolf said. "I need to get some of Ellyssa's clothes. Do you know where they are?"

Olivia nodded and pointed at the big wardrobe. "They're still in there, most of them. I never bothered to move them since I didn't know when she would come back, and I don't need that many clothes anyway."

Wolf opened the double doors and found a knapsack sitting on the bottom next to several pairs of footwear. He grabbed the newest pair of shoes and boots and stuffed them in the knapsack. He then selected several practical articles of clothing. Ellyssa had a few nice dresses, but he doubted she would be attending very many social events, so he left those hanging up.

With the pack now full and strapped to his back, Wolf and Ghost padded softly back down the stairs. They both stopped as several voices echoed up the spiraling staircase. Wolf recognized Allister and Miranda talking, along with Rusty and a couple of others. He waited until the dining room door muffled their voices before resuming his escape. He had just reached the bottom of the stairs when Allister's booming voice startled him.

"Wolf, what do you have there?"

Wolf shot Ghost an accusatory look for letting an old man—even if he was a wizard—catch them off guard. "Just some food and things."

"Stuff from Ellyssa's room perhaps?" Wolf tried to formulate an excuse, but his mind felt like a rabbit caught in a snare. "You know the Academy is very serious about discovering her whereabouts. Should you happen to cross paths, let her know this is a very bad place for her to be right now."

"Um, okay."

Allister disappeared back into the dining room and Wolf darted out the front doors. The crowd of people was slowly dispersing and the martial students began taking down the barricades. No one paid any attention to Wolf or Ghost amongst the hustle and bustle of the Academy's intrusion.

Wolf kept up an impressive pace back to Ellyssa's sanctuary despite his burden. Rarely encumbered by anything more than his bow and quiver, the knapsack and bag of food made him feel unbalanced and as clumsy as an ogre. Normally able to move as quietly through the woods as a gentle breeze, he cringed every time a twig snapped or a pinecone crunched under his soft leather-soled feet. Still, his unflagging stride ate up the miles and brought him to the entrance of the cave in short order.

"Ellyssa, wake up!" Wolf shouted when he ran into the cave and saw Ellyssa asleep on her pallet.

Ellyssa turned her head and cracked open one eye. "Thanks, but you didn't have to wake me. You can just leave it on the floor."

"No, you have to get up and leave right now," Wolf insisted.

Ellyssa forced herself to sit up. "Leave? Why? I can't even stay awake much less take a vacation somewhere."

"Well, you need to find the strength. The school's been taken over by a bunch of wizards and soldiers from the Academy."

Ellyssa shook her head to try and clear away some of the fog. "Allister would never let that happen."

"Well, he did and he is no longer in charge. Some guy named Harvey or something is calling himself headmaster. I thought they were going to fight when the duchess showed up with half her army, but Allister and the others decided to give in."

"Why are they here? What are they doing?" Ellyssa asked, now coming fully awake.

Wolf wagged his head. "I don't know. I couldn't hear everything, but it sounded like the Academy didn't like the idea of people learning magic without them being in charge."

Ellyssa felt her face heat. "It's because Azerick isn't here. He would have fought them. It wasn't worth the conflict between us and the Academy as long as nothing bad happened. This is my fault, because I killed those slavers."

"I'm not sure. That Harvey guy sounded like he didn't like the school regardless of what you did. Azerick had a title and the king's friendship. He was a hero. I think that, more than anything, kept the Academy from butting in. That and the fact he would have blasted anyone who messed with his school."

Ellyssa smiled as she thought of how Azerick would have dealt with the Academy. "Do you think they are after me?"

"I don't know, but there are a lot of new wizards there now, and it would be a good place to create a base from which to look for you. Allister caught me coming down the stairs from your room and told me I should tell you it wasn't safe around there. I think he may have meant all of North Haven, not just the school."

"Do you think he suspected you knew where I was?" Ellyssa grew nervous, wondering if Allister still cared enough about her to neglect his duty to the Academy.

"I'm pretty sure he knew I was getting stuff for you."

"I need to leave then. It's not going to be easy. I still feel weak as a babe."

"I can help get you nearer to Southport."

"What makes you think I'm going to Southport?" Ellyssa snapped.

Wolf crooked an eyebrow. "Well, there's not many slavers in Brelland or Brightridge, and Southport has the largest port in the kingdom, hence the largest slaver activity as well. I suppose you could go to Langdon's Crossing, but they are nearly as fanatical about killing slavers as you are. I hear they nail them to ships' masts stuck in the ground facing the sea as a warning to other slavers and pirates. Come on, Ellyssa, you know you can trust me. I'm not going to tell anyone where you are."

"I know, and I'm sorry." Ellyssa's shoulders slumped. "I just felt abandoned after I came back, and I have a hard time trusting anyone. I've felt on my own for so long now."

"You haven't exactly made it easy to get close to you."

"I know. I didn't want anyone to get close to me. I didn't want anyone else to get hurt because of me."

"But you're still going to hunt slavers?"

"Until I kill the man who took me, yes," she responded resolutely.

"You're going into the same city where the people who want to capture you live. Do you think that's a good idea?"

Ellyssa snorted derisively. "If this Harvey guy is the best they can come up with to catch me, I'm not too worried. Besides, from what I have heard about the number of wizards at the Academy, it looks like most of them are now here. Plus, there are a lot more places for me to hide in Southport."

"But you don't know the city like you do North Haven," Wolf pointed out.

"I'll learn. Adapting is the one thing I am good at."

"Can you travel? We should leave as soon as possible."

The thought of traveling did not sound pleasant at all. She was tempted to ask Wolf to talk Peck out of one of his horses, but then she would have to get it back to him, and Wolf did not like to ride. A horse also meant taking the roads, and she did not like that idea much either. Despite soundly beating Magus Harvey and his cohorts, Ellyssa seriously doubted the Academy had given up trying to find her or the book. Despite her bravado, she was not looking forward to another conflict with them.

"I guess I'll have to be. Do you think Sandy would be willing to help, at least part of the way?"

Wolf's face hardened and his eyes turned serious. "I don't know. She's been as fanatical about practicing and getting stronger as you have been, and about as friendly too. I suppose we can ask."

Wolf shouldered the knapsack, and Ellyssa slung the sack of food over one shoulder by a strap. She dropped the Codex Arcana into an oiled leather satchel and draped it across her other shoulder before following behind Wolf and Ghost. She cast her small but cozy cave a final regretful glance as they left it behind.

It was slow going as Ellyssa's fatigue forced them to a snail's pace. Ghost constantly raced ahead of them, ranging back and forth to relieve the boredom of having to wait on her. It was mid-afternoon when she had discovered Wolf and Ghost watching over her in her cave, and it did not take long before the sun dipped below the horizon, plunging the forest into darkness.

"We should stop for the night," Wolf suggested. "Hopefully you will recover some strength by morning."

Ellyssa needed no encouragement and dropped down on the deer trail they were following. "I hope so. It'll take a month at this pace if I have to walk the entire way there. Do you know where Sandy is? I have hardly seen her near the school since we came back."

"She been going farther away from the school as her magic gets stronger. I don't know if it's because she is afraid of causing any damage nearby or if she just feels more confident being alone. The last place I saw her was in a big clearing about a day's walk southeast of the school."

"A day's walk for you or for me?" Ellyssa asked with a groan.

Wolf grinned. "Best make it a day and a half, assuming you can pick up the pace a bit tomorrow."

Wolf cut small branches from several different pine trees, so as not to harm the trees, and made a bed of them for her. Ellyssa laid a blanket over the matting and climbed between the folds. Wolf's only concession to comfort was his own bed of pine boughs upon which he curled up with Ghost for warmth.

Despite her exhaustion, Ellyssa had a hard time falling asleep. She wondered what the Academy takeover of the school meant for those who depended on the home and education it provided. What did it mean for her? She finally fell asleep after deciding it did not matter. Nothing would stop her from reaching her goal, whatever it was.

Wolf woke her at least an hour before sunrise. He already had a pan of oatmeal boiled soft enough to eat. Ghost was nowhere to be seen. Even though he could be standing just a few yards away, his black coat made him invisible in the darkness, Ellyssa figured he was out finding his own breakfast.

The morning air was brisk and Ellyssa kept her blanket wrapped around her shoulders as she ate her breakfast. Her body felt as though she had slept on a bed of rocks instead of pine boughs. Her muscles protested with every movement and she felt like one giant bruise. Her battle with the Academy wizards had not left her feeling this exhausted and battered. She was now realizing how close she had come to letting the Source consume her.

One of the first things the magus students were taught was not to exceed their ability to channel the Source, or it could easily destroy them. The spell she had used was extremely advanced and far exceeded her experience and ability to cast safely. Even now, when she tried to touch the Source, it felt as if she were trying to tie her shoes with numb fingers.

"Do you think we will be able to find Sandy today?" Ellyssa asked, a little puff of fog giving a physical presence to each word.

"Probably. The real question is whether she will talk to us much less fly you close enough to Southport to walk there on your own."

"You don't think she will talk to us?"

Wolf shrugged. "Probably, even though she has gotten as moody and antisocial as you since we got back. The hard part will be getting her to stop destroying everything around her long enough to talk. She trains all day long, calling lightning, hurling boulders, and shredding everything she can get her claws on, including the boulders."

"It really changed us all, didn't it?"

"Do you mean the breaking or Azerick's death?"

Ellyssa doodled in the dirt with a small stick. "Both, I guess."

"Yeah, it did," Wolf said solemnly.

Ellyssa mentally staunched the tears that came unbidden to her eyes. "Does that mean they won? Are we truly broken then?"

"No," Wolf said decisively, "they hurt us, they tortured us, and they certainly changed us, but they did not break us. We are all stronger now. Are we damaged? Maybe, depending on how you look at it, but the vila and his ilk ultimately failed. We lost Azerick, and that loss can never be replaced, but we are the winners because we go on. We still fight. That is what Azerick always did no matter what. He said we can never lose as long as we still fight."

"Do you think he's still fighting, wherever he is now?" Ellyssa sniffled, then wiped her nose with her sleeve.

Wolf's face lit up in a huge grin. "Oh yeah. He's still fighting, and I feel sorry for whoever gets in his way. Even the gods."

CHAPTER 12

Fu'Marb skittered along the cavern passage ahead of Azerick as they negotiated the dark, twisting passages. The balrog spoke very little, which was fine with Azerick since he had little attention for anything except the aches radiating through his abused body.

Azerick kept a wary eye on the toad-like demon. Perhaps it was his general distrust of his kind, or simply years of dealing with people and creatures who meant him harm, but he could not shake the feeling there was something off about Fu'Marb. Azerick had long abandoned the concept of pure coincidence, and the demon's sudden appearance was a big one.

He had already been the target of assassination once. Just because he killed his attempted killer did not eliminate the possibility of another assassin, possibly several. There could be an entire movement collaborating for his overthrow. Fu'Marb had yet to do anything overt, even suspicious, but Azerick was intent on staying vigilant for any sign of treachery.

The Rook continued to look back at his target, but the sorcerer refused to drop his guard and never took any of the opportunities to take the lead the assassin presented. He was unsure if the human was suspicious of him or simply cautious.

His failed attempt at killing him definitely made his task that much more difficult, but the Rook enjoyed a challenge. He possessed infinite patience, and time was the one thing he had plenty of as long as Drak'kar did not kill him first. Should that happen, the Rook would have no choice but to seek retribution against the demon lord. One did not steal the Rook's kills.

"My Prince, you lag behind," the Rook said. "Do you wish to rest?"

There was little else Azerick would like to do than rest, but he needed to get back to his citadel to recover and prepare his last line of defense. "No, Fu'Marb, I am able to carry on. Continue leading the way."

"As you wish, My Prince."

The passage was completely dark. Not a single mote of light found its way down the endless expanse of twisting blackness. Mile after mile, the pair trekked through the abyssal catacombs, following the winding path like pieces of food through the digestive system of some massive beast. Azerick could not help but feel exactly like that, as if the abyss were one enormous creature that had swallowed him whole.

"Fu'Marb, you said you saw me in the battle and followed me?" Azerick asked.

"Yes, My Prince."

"How exactly did you manage that?" Azerick asked, knowing a flightless demon could never keep him in view while he was gating.

"With great difficulty and this." The Rook tapped on his snout with a long finger. "I knew you were headed for the Shattered Lands. Even so, I lost track many times. Then I heard the invader shouting and the sound of battle. Sound carries far in the rifts. Few can tell from whence a sound comes, but Fu'Marb can."

It was a reasonable explanation, but Azerick was still wary. He could not shake the feeling Fu'Marb's appearance was not purely happenstance. It seemed like an awful lot of initiative for a demon. One thing he had learned in this place was never to drop his guard.

Azerick's vigilance was frustrating and his questions reeked of suspicion. The Rook sensed the sorcerer accepted his explanation but was not entirely duped. He could still feel a tension between them, whether it was specifically directed at him or from a general distrust, he could not be sure. What he did know was that he was running out of time. His best chances for success were while he led him through these passages. Once outside, it would be nearly impossible for him to gain an advantage.

"Ssshaaadowww brothhherrr."

The Rook flinched inwardly when he felt something caress his pebbly skin and whisper in his ear. He looked back at the human, but he did not appear to have heard the breeze-like whisper.

"Murderrr isss in yourrr hearrrt. Youuu huuunt?"

The Rook lowered his voice as much as possible. "Yes."

"Why doesss yourrr prey liiive?"

"He is powerful. I must time my kill perfectly or risk losing him again."

"Yesss, we senssse hisss powerrr. Weee can help youuu, Ssshaaadowww brothhherrr. Eeembraccce the ssshaaadowsss."

The Rook slowly began putting more distance between him and the sorcerer. He soon spotted a fork in the path ahead and a sharp turn. The Rook darted around the corner and wrapped himself in shadows so thick even demonic eyes could not easily pierce them.

"Fu'Marb, where are you?" Azerick called.

"Here, My Prince," the Rook answered from around the bend. "We are getting near."

Azerick made the turn and felt an icy pain stab through his chest. Azerick spun with a sharp gasp, a ball of fire clutched in his upturned palm, ready to unleash fiery death upon whatever was attacking him. Another icy slash cut him across his left calf. He spun around again and hurled his fire into the darkness.

Out of the corner of his eye, Azerick spotted an indistinct dark blur skitter across the wall of the cave and vanish into deeper shadows. More shadowy figures leapt from every surface and cranny, slashing at him with the cold, spectral touch of death. Azerick's body felt as though it had just plunged through the ice of a frozen lake. His mind raced, but his body was slow to respond.

He raked the walls with lightning and filled the tunnel with fire. The shadow creatures fled his onslaught, but they returned in an instant, slashing with their insubstantial weapons that passed through clothing and magical wards as easily as they did flesh and bone.

Rage mixed with fear as Azerick tried to figure out how to battle something that did not fully exist. They seemed to fear his fire and lightning, but still they returned and harried him. The shade creatures fled again as he filled the passageway with fire. When they returned to attack, Azerick was struck with inspiration. It was not the fire or the lightning they feared, but the light those spells produced. The way to destroy a shadow was with light!

Azerick summoned the power of the Source and filled his hand with a miniature sun. The shadow creatures howled in pain and fled into the deepest cracks and fissures they could find before the dreadful light destroyed them. Motion caught Azerick's attention and he turned and lashed out with a strike of pure force. The spell caught the Rook full in the chest just as he lowered himself from the roof of the cave to strike Azerick in the back.

"Treacherous creature!" Azerick snarled, summoning the power to crush the demon.

The Rook scuttled backward and pressed himself to the floor. "No, My Prince, Fu'Marb would never attempt treachery! I wandered too far ahead, eager to fulfill my great master's desire to be free of these caves. I heard the battle and returned as fast as I could! I came to protect you from the horrible shadow spawn, as feeble as my help would be."

Crush him now! Klaraxis seethed.

"Now you want to supply some input?" Azerick asked. "You have been joyfully silent this entire time."

If you are too stupid to give me control, I thought it best not to distract you. A wasted effort since you failed miserably anyway. I do not like this creature. You should kill him and take strength from his life essence.

"I don't like him either, but I still need him to get me out." Azerick returned his attention to Fu'Marb. "You said we are getting close to the way out?"

The demon's entire body bobbed up and down. "Yes, Glorious Prince! I will lead you out. I will not fail you again."

"Go, but do not stray from my sight," Azerick ordered.

Fu'Marb waggled his entire body once more and carefully picked his way down the passage, constantly stopping to ensure Azerick was following. Azerick allowed a shudder to reverberate through his body only after the demon turned away. The icy pain the shadow spawn's attacks caused was agonizing, but he could not allow himself to show how badly they hurt him. Keeping his brilliant light blazing in his palm, Azerick followed the demon at a close but wary distance.

The Rook fumed at yet another failed attempt. The luck of this creature was beyond anything he had dealt with before. He focused on stilling his anger and summoning his patience. Luck, no matter how potent, eventually ran out. It was the law of the cosmos, and when that happened, he would strike.

The passage continued to cut a winding path through the red stone without any discernible indication they were getting nearer to finding a way out. Azerick was beginning to think Fu'Marb was intentionally leading him astray in hopes of creating another ambush. He still was not certain the demon was not responsible for the first. Just as his suspicions began to nag him to the point he could no longer ignore them, Azerick noticed a slight diffusing of the darkness that was not due to his magical light.

"See, master, I have found the way for you!" Fu'Marb croaked excitedly.

A few minutes later, the tunnel ended at what appeared to be a large red eye. The landscape beyond shone at the end of the passageway with the usual dreary redness and wan light of the Fifth Circle, but it looked as glorious as the first sunrise he had seen after escaping the psylings. Fu'Marb darted ahead just outside the tunnel's iris as Azerick followed him out.

The Rook pressed his body against the ground in his supplicating manner, summoned his ethereal, soul-rending blade, and hid it beneath his body. He watched the sorcerer step from the tunnel and look up at the featureless sky. Now was the time to strike, while his guard was down.

Azerick stepped from the tunnel and looked up. He found himself in some sort of canyon. Red stone cliffs stretched what must have been a thousand feet over his head in every direction but straight ahead. He glanced back at the supplicating balrog then looked back up at the towering cliffs and the only apparent way out.

"I would ask where to from here, but it looks like there is only one direction that does not require wings," Azerick said.

The Rook crept silently closer on his belly. "Yes, My Prince. Through the gorge you will find your way."

"You sound like you do not intend to go with me."

"I should return to the battle. Where you must go is no place for Fu'Marb," the demon explained.

Azerick squinted into the distance but failed to see anything other than the red cliffs. "Where exactly am I going?"

The Rook tensed his legs beneath him, their incredible strength more than sufficient to carry him the thirty feet separating him from his prey. The assassin leapt with his black blade held high.

"Straight into the heart of oblivion!"

Azerick spun, and although wary of the demon, his speed and the suddenness of the attack caught him by surprise. Fu'Marb had covered half the distance between them by the time Azerick was able to turn far enough to see him. He saw the shadowy blade gripped in the assassin's hand and knew if it was the same type of weapon as the shadow spawn in the tunnel then his wards were useless.

Azerick tried to backpedal and raised his arm in a futile defense. Another, much larger shape dropped from the sky and crushed Fu'Marb to the ground hard enough to raise a cloud of dust. Azerick heard bones crunch with the impact. Drak'kar grabbed the balrog by the leg, slammed him into the ground twice, and then hurled him against the cliff with a sickening smack of more broken bones and a splatter of black viscous blood.

Drak'kar must have been clinging to one of the cliff sides, probably directly above the cave opening, and been hiding in a dark cleft of rock. Azerick had little time to ponder his fortune, both good and bad, as the demon lord lunged with his impossible speed and kicked him in the chest. Azerick flew back and struck the wall not far from the very dead Fu'Marb.

"You see how pathetic you are? Even your own turn against you," Drak'kar said.

Azerick had not recovered from their previous battle, but he was not nearly as weak as he had been. He knew he would have only one chance and drew upon the Source. He laced his spell with abyssal power and unleashed it against his foe. Drak'kar actually smiled even as the strike blasted him from his feet and smashed him against the solid stone near the cave entrance.

"I was hoping you were not just going to let me kill you without a fight." Drak'kar laughingly grumbled as he regained his feet.

"I will never go down without a fight!" Azerick shouted, tearing at the two disparate sources of magic with wild abandon.

Azerick shaped the spell similar to the one he had used to undermine the boulder that killed the dragon years ago. Only he fueled this one with the power of abyssal corruption on a scale he could never have achieved in his human body. Azerick struck not at Drak'kar, but the cliffs behind and to both sides of the demon lord. A deafening rumble filled the canyon as the stone shattered and fell in a hail of massive boulders so great it looked as though the world were imploding.

Drak'kar roared furiously and tried to leap at the sorcerer bent in concentration. A boulder the size of a small cottage caught the demon prince in the back and crushed him to the ground much as he had done to Fu'Marb. Drak'kar continued to scream in pain and outrage until hundreds of feet of rock entombed him beneath their crushing embrace. Azerick stumbled back, gasping and avoiding the occasional tumbling rock not satisfied with burying just one demon.

Azerick felt like passing out, but he knew if he gave into his weakness, he might never get up again. He took several steadying breaths and focused on the small mountain of fallen stones. Deep beneath its wasted surface, Azerick sensed Drak'kar's presence, alive, in pain, and very angry. He knew the demon lord was probably already calling to his minions for aid. Azerick needed to leave this area as fast as his exhausted body would allow.

Azerick thought of the many battles he had faced in his life, and the only one he recalled putting him in this much pain and leaving him feeling this weak was when the abyssal elf, Teraneshala, had nearly killed him. If it were not for the awesome strength and durability of Klaraxis's body, he certainly would not be capable of pressing on or possibly surviving such a beating.

The walls of the canyon continued to tower over him, looking down like gods, ready to crush him like an insect at the slightest misstep. The divide narrowed as if the canyon walls were the hands of a god closing in to swat him. As the towering walls continued to contract, Azerick began to fear the fissure would close completely and he would have to climb the thousand or so feet of sheer rock face to escape this chasm.

Just when he thought he had reached the inevitable end where the walls were close enough to touch with his outstretched arms, the fissure opened into a wide valley just a short distance ahead. Azerick escaped the narrow confines of the cleft and breathed a sigh of relief as he stepped into the much wider canyon. He jumped when a voice spoke right into his ear.

"I am so glad you finally made it," Krade said silkily.

Azerick spun and lashed out with a pathetic display of magic at whoever had spoken. Even that small effort made his head reel. He saw the speaker vanish in a puff of pink smoke, leaving behind only a vaporous silhouette and the stench of brimstone.

"So hostile," Sharrellan's seneschal said.

"What do you want, Krade," Azerick demanded as he turned and faced the devil.

The devil smiled. "I told you I would make you pay for your impertinence. Now is the time to collect."

Azerick replied with far more menace than he thought he could actually deliver. "I have faced Drak'kar twice and survived. Do not think that I am afraid of anything you can do."

"Me? I'm not going to do anything. It is much more satisfying to watch you torture yourself."

"If you expect me to torture myself you are in for a long wait."

"Nonsense. You have been torturing yourself from the time you got here, but like an amateur. I will show you what true pain is." Krade waved at the expanse beyond. "What you see before you is the Valley of Lies. I am the Master of Lies and shall be your guide as you pass through it."

"Why would you think lies could torment me?" Azerick asked.

"Because, as we examine and accept our lies, we discover truth, and the truth can be a very painful thing to behold."

"Why should I listen to the Keeper of Lies? Doesn't that mean everything you say is a lie?"

"Of course."

Azerick looked up at the cliffs reaching into the bland sky. "I refuse to dance to your tune, devil."

Azerick exchanged his soft human fingernails for Klaraxis's iron-like talons and began scaling the cliff face. Although severely weakened, Klaraxis's incredible strength allowed Azerick to pull his body up the sheer, expansive escarpment. Even with his demonic strength, the climb was arduous, and his already debilitated body soon began to flag.

He looked up and saw hundreds of feet of rock rising above him and a nearly equal distance beneath him when he looked down. Azerick took a minute to rest and then continued his ascent. Thrusting hands into cracks and claws into solid stone when no handholds presented themselves, Azerick continued to pull himself up the wall. Minutes stretched into hours and every movement became agony, but he refused to relent.

"Why do you continue to punish yourself?" Krade asked. "This physical self-torture became boring hours ago."

Azerick looked over his left shoulder and saw the devil perched on an outcropping of rock he swore was not there before. He looked past Krade's grinning face and down at the ground, which still seemed the exact same distance away as the last time he looked despite at least two hours of constant climbing.

"Why am I no nearer the top?" Azerick demanded. He suspected the devil was involved in some sort of trickery.

"The top is a lie, of course," Krade replied gleefully. "Now I get to ask a question. Why are you so afraid to face your lies? Do you fear the truth so much you willingly put yourself in this physical agony to avoid the assault to your conscience?"

"I have no lies from which to hide!"

"That is a lie. See how easily they fly from your lips, like bees from a hive. That is okay, for within the lie rests the truth, if one has the courage to open one's eyes and see it. Do you have the courage to look upon your lies and see the truth, or do you prefer to keep brute-forcing your way past it like you are doing now; like you have always done?"

"I have no lies, you damnable devil! I have always lived my life as one of truth. I have faced more truths than you can imagine!"

Krade tilted his head back and laughed. "Yet here you are, clinging to this crag, this towering wall of lies, like an insect, instead of simply walking the valley. If you have nothing to hide then the valley holds no fear for you."

"Fine, I will walk your Valley of Lies and show you I speak only the truth, as I always have. Now help me off this damnable wall."

"No."

Azerick's face burned. "Why not? If you are so eager to have me walk your valley, then help me down so we can get on with it."

"You chose to ascend this wall despite it being monumentally more taxing. The ground is where you will find the truth, and you must reach it yourself."

Azerick gathered up the Source and tried to blast the arrogant devil from his perch. Krade vanished in a puff of pink smoke with a laugh as Azerick's spell shattered the rock ledge. Pieces of stone rained down on his head and Azerick felt himself falling. The ruddy stone of the cliff flashed by as the wind rushed past his ears with an eerie howl.

The sorcerer struck the ground and his vision went black. Azerick was certain he now stood at the precipice marking the final end to his life. He almost welcomed it. Light flooded his senses when he opened his eyes and gasped in a great lungful of air to replace what his impact had violently expelled. Azerick knew he should be dead now; even in this demonic body, such a fall should be at the very least crippling, if not lethal. He reasoned this to be another effect of this peculiar place.

Krade's long face filled his vision as he looked up at the mauve sky. "Ouch. I did not expect you to be in such a hurry to face your lies."

Azerick rolled painfully to his feet. "I have no lies. I am not like you, Klaraxis, or these other wretched creatures."

"When it comes to honesty, you fall far short of Klaraxis. He, like most of us here, is far more honest than you have ever been. Klaraxis has no delusions as to his motives, desires, or actions. You, a murderer, and at such a young age when you started upon the path of slaughter, have lived your entire life wrapped in lies; your every motive a lie to justify your bloodlust."

"I killed only those who tried to hurt me or to avenge my family's murder," Azerick said through clenched teeth.

"You lie," Krade countered. "You say you hunted and killed all these men to avenge your parents and friends. What good does a dead man do another dead man, or woman? Your desire to kill those people had nothing to do with helping your mother, father, Jon Locke, or any of the others. It was all about making yourself feel better. It was about reclaiming power so you did not feel helpless. It was about punishing those who took from you. Go on, deny it."

Azerick opened his mouth to do just that, but the words would not come. The lies that had come so easily to mind clogged his windpipe and refused to become words. He knew the truth. He wanted revenge, he wanted to punish everyone who had wronged him and caused him pain, not for those he lost, but to ease his own conscience, to relieve the burden of his failure to protect them. Every man or woman he killed, every drop of spilled blood was a balm meant to soothe the pain of his own fear, anger, and guilt.

"Ah, I see in the watery pools of your eyes you now accept the truth you hid even from yourself. The greatest lies ever told never pass our lips."

Azerick took a shuddering breath. "Fine, I killed those people because I wanted to punish them for what they had done. I did it for me, but the people I killed were horrible people who enjoyed causing grief and deserved to die. But I am not like you and these other creatures who kill simply for the joy of it! I am still better than that!"

Krade's chiseled face split with a pointy-toothed grin. "Really? Everyone was evil and deserved to die? You know this for a fact? Did you know everyone in the guild house you burned to the ground? Is it impossible to believe some of those men, some of those children, who were inside were not monsters and threw their lot in with the thieves out of necessity? Have you never been placed in a situation where you had to act out of necessity even when such actions went against your basic nature? What about all of those who died when you destroyed the psyling city? Were they all evil? I would say not even a majority would fall under what you consider evil, and they numbered in the tens of thousands."

"I never meant to destroy the city! Their deaths were an accident." Azerick felt a fresh wave of remorse wash over him.

"I'm sure knowing that makes them feel better about dying."

"So what do you want from me? Do you want me to say I'm no better than Klaraxis?" Azerick demanded.

"I want you to acknowledge the truth."

"What truth is that?"

"The truth that not only are you no better than Klaraxis, you fall rather short," Krade answered.

Rage suffused Azerick's body. How dare this creature condemn him for doing what he was forced to do? He never asked someone to murder his parents. He never asked to be taken a slave and forced to kill. And he never asked Ulric or Jarvin to drag him into their political intrigues and problems. To condemn his entire existence, to claim it was all one expansive lie was beyond untenable.

"Who are you to judge me or my actions?" Azerick demanded. "You, Klaraxis, and these other monstrosities exist only to destroy and cause pain. I may have done some things I am not proud of, but at least I have the capacity for regret and remorse. I gave hundreds of children a home and taught them the skills they needed to survive and flourish. What have you and your ilk ever done to help anyone?"

Krade clapped his hands and practically squealed in delight. "I love how quickly you jump to your greatest lies. All lies, every one of them."

"What do you mean? I did those things, and nothing you say can take them away from me!"

"Of course you did those things, but your assertion of altruism is the lie. You claim to have saved these children. You say that you empowered them by teaching them to fight, but whom were you really saving? Was it really the nameless, faceless, little wretches of North Haven, or was it the frightened little boy, homeless, parentless and huddling in the cold, dark corner of an abandoned building in Southport? Yes, you see it now. You thought by creating that silly school of yours you could paddle up the stream of time and save poor little Azerick, show him he was strong and that you could save him. But you cannot, and his fearful weeping still fills your ears, a weeping so intense all the misguided attempts at heroics cannot stifle it."

Azerick wanted to shout his denial, lash out and destroy this creature and his lies, but part of him questioned who the true liar was. What were his true motivations? How many of those children he professed to have saved died because of him? Dozens fell during the siege and the night the dead rose from their graves. He did not save them, yet he took in more knowing the gods and fates still toyed with him, used him as a piece in some greater game that put them all at risk. What was the real purpose of teaching all these children to kill?

The sound of soft weeping reached his ears and interrupted his self-recriminating thoughts. A chill ran through him as he imagined it was the terrified child within him as Krade said, but he realized the sound came from outside his head and could discern the direction from whence it came. Azerick followed the sound deeper into the canyon, pausing several times to cock an ear in order to maintain his bearing.

Azerick soon came upon a large boulder butted up against the canyon wall to his right. The crying was coming from behind its monolithic mass. He carefully skirted around the rock, keeping his distance. There he found a young boy, huddled in the corner created by the cliff wall and the stone. He looked up and stared at Azerick. It was almost like looking in a mirror, a mirror reflecting an image from years past.

The terrified face could have been his, and for a moment, he thought it was. He thought it was some illusion cast by the devil to torment him, but then he spied the differences in the boy's features. The eyes were much darker than his own were, almost black, and the chin and cheekbones reminded him of Miranda.

Azerick released a shuddering breath. "What evil is this, Krade?"

The devil beamed as if Azerick had just paid him the highest compliment. "What a perfectly formed question. This is your son Daebian."

Azerick felt sick to the point of vomiting. "You lie. He cannot be here."

"He most definitely is, and I do not lie."

Azerick spun toward Krade. "You lie! You said you always lie."

Krade twitched his shoulders. "I lied. I am the Keeper of Lies, it is what I do."

"F-father, is that you?" Daebian asked.

Azerick looked at the boy skeptically even as his heart was torn asunder. "How would you know me?"

"Mother talks about you all the time. She said we look alike. Sometimes when I dream, I see you, and yours is the face I see." Daebian shook his head and wiped the tears from his eyes with his sleeve. "I have this feeling I know you, that we share some kind of connection. I don't know. I'm scared. Are you my father?"

Azerick's heart pounded a syncopated rhythm that made him think it would surely burst. He looked upon Daebian and wanted to deny him, wanted desperately to shout down the cruel lie Krade placed before him, but he too felt a connection, a bond with the boy.

"Yes, if you are truly Daebian, my Daebian, then I am your father," Azerick answered in a quiet voice.

"But you died. Have I died? Please, Father, I am so scared! Where am I?"

Azerick could take no more. Lie or not, he knew this to be his son. He rushed forward and scooped the boy into his arms, each of them soaking the other's shoulder with tears.

"No, you are not dead. It's okay, I'm here, Daebian. I will protect you," Azerick swore.

Azerick wept harder as the boy tightened his grip around his neck. He could feel the warmth of his breath and the pressure of his arms around him. No illusion he knew of could produce such physical sensations. Tears continued to flow unbidden as Azerick did what he never thought he would have the chance to do—hold his son.

Azerick finally found the strength to pull his head away and look beseechingly at Krade. "How have you done this terrible thing? Send him back home, please."

"I cannot for I did not bring him here. You brought him here with your lies. The Valley of Lies forces you to face yourself in your entirety. The boy is part of you, part of your lies. He will only find his way home when you find yours."

"Tell me what I have to do! How do I find my way out of here?"

"By finding and accepting the truth about yourself. Truth, not the truth you use to make your existence bearable, but the real truth, is the only way to escape your lies."

"Father, what is that man?" Daebian asked, his voice muffled by the cloth of Azerick's shirt. "He frightens me."

Azerick stroked his son's head. "You do not have to be afraid. He is nothing. I will not let anyone harm you."

"Nothing? You are so hurtful," Krade said. "Come, we must proceed if we are to ever leave this place."

Azerick set Daebian down and took him by the hand. "Lead the way. I will do whatever it takes to get my son out of here."

"So you say, but few have the courage or honesty to do so."

Daebian looked up at Azerick. "Are we going home, Father?"

"Yes, I am taking you home. Just stay close to me and everything will be fine."

"Oh, I seriously doubt that, liar," Krade said.

As they continued their march through the valley, the scenery never changed. It almost felt as though they were not making any progress despite the moving of their feet. Small eddies of wind spun tiny clouds of dust, but no breeze ever touched them. It was neither hot nor cold, light nor dark. There was nothing to give the slightest hint of life in this place.

"Why do you hold onto the boy so adamantly?" Krade asked.

"What do you mean? He is my son. Maybe your kind does not understand such a concept."

Krade lifted one of his thin black eyebrows. "What concept is that?"

"Love," Azerick supplied.

"Oh yes, love." the devil cackled. "The greatest lie of all! Finally, we get to the heart of everything."

Azerick snorted derisively. "I would not expect your kind to understand. You are incapable of love. No matter what you say or show me, I love my son and my wife and I will do anything to protect them. That is the truth and I dare you to try to show me otherwise."

"You really should not tempt a devil so."

Vicious snarling and the snapping of enormous jaws mixed with a woman's screams filled the valley. Another set of screams joined the first and sent a rush of dread surging through Azerick's body. He raced ahead as fast as Daebian's small legs allowed. When that proved too slow, Azerick scooped the boy up in his arms and sprinted.

Azerick slid to a halt as he rounded a corner and saw two women chained to the cliff wall on opposite sides of the gorge. He let his son slip from his arms and doubled over from the awful ache filling his gut. Chained to the stone on his left was Miranda. On the right side of the canyon, Delinda was similarly restrained. Only inches away from each of them, a slavering, snarling harunden lunged and struggled at the end of a chain, desperately trying to reach the women and tear them to shreds.

"This is not real," Azerick declared as he shook his head. "Delinda is dead and Miranda is safe at home."

Krade sidled up beside him. "On the contrary, the abyss is open to all, alive or dead. You have but to look upon your son to know that."

"What purpose could this possibly serve other than to cause me pain?" Azerick demanded.

"I want you to see the truth of your professed love. I want you to choose the one you truly love."

"I cannot choose!"

"You must, and before you think it, you cannot save them both. If you try, both will die. If you refuse, both will die. You claim to love. I say it is a lie. Your choice will decide who is right."

"How can I choose when I love them both?"

"You claim love prevents you from choosing. I say this is a lie. It is not love making the choice difficult but guilt. Guilt over doing what you know you must do, guilt over finally admitting your love is a lie."

"Love is never a lie!" Azerick raged.

"Of course it is," Krade insisted, "especially yours. You do not love for the sake of love. You love for how it makes you feel, the security and sense of normality it bestows. Pure love is an illusion, a lie. It is like a strong drink; if it did not bring the pleasure of intoxication, you would never suffer the vile taste of it. Love is all about you and the pleasure it brings, and for that you suffer the inevitable pain and bitterness it causes. Your first love is long dead and cannot bring you any pleasure by reciprocating your fallacious love, so that leaves guilt as your only true motivation. Guilt will trump love every time because guilt is a true emotion unlike the wispy intangibility of love."

"Azerick, save me!" Miranda pleaded. "I am your wife and the mother of your son. Will you allow me to die in front of his eyes?"

"No, Azerick, save me!" Delinda cried. "I am your first true love. Our love was real. You let me die once; will you do it again?"

Azerick's eyes shifted back and forth between the two women, his heart tearing in two, each half trying to escape his chest and fly to the women he loved. To choose one would deny the love he held for the other and prove the devil right. It would prove that love was conditional and subject to degradation. Azerick was damned no matter how he chose.

"Father, why are you not saving Mother?" Daebian's small voice begged.

Azerick tore his eyes away from the nightmare ahead of him. "Why are you doing this to me? You wanted to hurt me for my behavior. You have done so. Let them go."

"I am doing nothing except holding the mirror. What you see is your own reflection in all its truth. You must choose, human."

"I cannot choose, devil!"

"Then you have already chosen, just as I knew you would."

The chains holding back the two harunden snapped, ringing out with the chime of a bell sounding out a death knell. The enormous demonic dogs tore into the two helpless humans with stomach-turning brutality. Azerick screamed with a savage fury matching the snarls of the harunden. Inky black flames shot out of Azerick's hands and enveloped the demon savaging Miranda's corpse, incinerating the creature in an instant.

The second demon dog ceased its attack on Delinda and charged, its four powerful legs devouring the ground between them. Azerick lashed out with black flames once more, but the creature dodged nimbly to the side and continued its charge. Before he could follow up with another spell, the harunden launched itself into the air and clamped its powerful jaws around the forearm Azerick brought up to protect himself. He transformed into Klaraxis's massive frame to give him more leverage and to prevent the harunden from tossing his small human body about.

As he formed a spell to strike down the demon, Azerick heard Daebian's soft chanting.

"Torn between truth and lie,

Father faced a problem,

He could not choose between them,

And so now we all must die."

A knife appeared in Daebian's small hand and he plunged it low into Azerick's side. Pain shot through his body and suffused his soul. The pain went far beyond what simple steel could produce. It was agony born of a blade crafted from guilt, betrayal, and failure. It cut with the razor sharpness of truth, a truth that cut deeper than mere flesh.

Crying out, blinded by the composite amalgamation of all those agonizing emotions, Azerick unleashed his abyssal fury. The harunden barked out a short but ear-piercing yelp as the spell blasted it off Azerick's arm and left it a smoking husk of a corpse. Spinning, he backhanded Daebian away with enough force to send him careening into the wall of stone where he crumpled into a heap.

Shocked out of his rage, Azerick shifted back into his human body and raced over to his fallen son. He dropped to his knees, cradled Daebian's small body in his arms, and wept. Great shuddering sobs wracked his body as he gently rocked the boy in his arms.

"Now you see," Krade said. "You chose guilt over so-called love. When put to the test, your love failed."

"Have you not tortured me enough?" Azerick sobbed.

"You torture yourself. As long as you cling to your lies, your soul will always be in a state of torment."

Azerick shook his head, rubbing his face into his son's shoulder. "Fine, you win. Maybe my love is not altruistic and selfless. Maybe no one's is. Maybe the choices I made in my life were not always for someone else's benefit or welfare but for my own. But I made my choices, I did what I did because I thought it was right, consequences be damned! I don't care if they were right or wrong. I don't care if it was for my benefit or someone else's. They were my choices, I made them as my conscience dictated, and I will not apologize for any of it!"

"Finally, you see the truth of yourself," Krade intoned.

Daebian's body turned into the red sand of the valley floor and ran through Azerick's fingers to form a pile in front of him. Azerick rolled the grains in his palms with his thumbs, mixing it with the tears rolling off his face.

"Damn you," he whispered.

"I was damned at the moment of my conception, as were you."

Azerick ran his hands through the mound of sand that was his son before standing and turning to face the devil. Krade was gone, as he expected, but so too was the valley. The impossibly high walls had vanished, and only the unchanging vista of this hellish place filled his vision.

Turning a slow circle, Azerick spotted a black, uniform shape in the distance. Anger slowly replaced sorrow as he processed what Krade had done to him. He was furious. The valley had been a lie. His son, wife, and love were all lies. Worst of all was the realization that he was nothing but a lie.

Azerick extended his hand toward his citadel and curled his fingers as if to pluck it from the horizon. With a snarl, he jerked his arm toward his chest and found himself standing in front of the enormous doors. The two insectoid-looking demons standing sentry flinched at their master's sudden arrival.

"Prepare yourselves. We shall soon be under siege." Azerick pushed past his minions and disappeared inside.

CHAPTER 13

Ellyssa lagged behind Wolf and Ghost as she gingerly picked her way through the forest, ducking branches and untangling every manner of thorny vegetation from her clothes and hair. She had been born and raised in the city and had never felt comfortable in the woods. Watching Wolf easily thread his way through even the densest undergrowth, she now understood why he chose a minimalistic approach to fashion.

After nearly another full day of traipsing through the woods, Ellyssa heard a thunderous crash and saw a flash of lightning. A moment later, another low boom reached her ears but without the telltale flash. She scanned the skies and soon spotted Sandy silhouetted against the light grey clouds high overhead. Even in the wan light of the cloudy, early evening sun, her brilliant scales found enough light to gleam like a tight cluster of stars.

The trio dropped into a trough created by two low but steep hills. When they emerged from the depression, Sandy was nowhere to be seen. The forest was silent, no longer wracked by the crack of lightning and splitting of trees. Ellyssa began to worry Sandy had flown off and she would be forced to walk or hitch a ride on a merchant wagon to reach Southport.

They had just dropped down the other side of the hill when the woods to Ellyssa's left practically exploded. Ellyssa performed a backpedaling leap away and promptly fell on her backside. Despite the surprise ambush, Ellyssa's constant training allowed her to have a spell ready on her lips by the time she struck the ground. She let the energy drain away when she spotted Sandy's enormous head and looked at Wolf's grinning face.

"Dang it, Sandy, you scared the crap out of me!" Ellyssa shouted.

Sandy displayed a double row of sharp white teeth. "That was the intent."

"You're lucky I didn't blast you!"

Sandy snorted. "With what? I felt you call upon the Source, and it answered with a feeble response."

Ellyssa's stomach fluttered and her face heated. Sandy was right. Drawing upon the Source felt like trying to tie her shoes with fingers numbed by the cold, and it terrified her. She wondered if she had permanently damaged herself. The thought was more frightening than the idea of Academy wizards getting their hands on her. Her magic was all she had. It was all she was.

Ellyssa got up and brushed at the detritus clinging to her clothes. "I will never understand how something the size of a house can be so sneaky."

Sandy let Ellyssa's exaggeration pass. She was only about the size of a large draft horse, her tail and neck slightly doubling her overall length. Even so, she was a fearsome sight to behold, particularly when taken unawares.

"She didn't surprise me or Ghost," Wolf said.

Sandy swiveled her big wedge-shaped head toward the half-elf. "That's because you're a pointy-eared little freak."

"You knew she was there the whole time? Why didn't you warn me?"

Wolf pulled his tongue back in from sticking it out at Sandy. "Because it wouldn't have been any fun. Besides, someone needs to knock you on your butt once in a while to keep your head from swelling up too much."

Ellyssa bit off her retort and shrugged. "You're probably right."

"So what are you doing this far from the school?"

Sandy asked the question openly, but Ellyssa knew it was directed at her. "Wolf says something happened at the school. Some Academy wizards and soldiers showed up and took over."

A low rumble filled the air as Sandy growled her displeasure. Despite remaining aloof since their return from Sumara, Sandy saw the school as her home and everyone in it her family.

"What do they want?" Sandy asked.

Ellyssa answered. "The Academy does not like the school not being under their control. I overheard Allister arguing with another man from the Academy about it when they came looking for me."

Sandy slowly bobbed her head. "And with Azerick gone, they felt confident about forcing their assertions without provoking open conflict. It would seem the ripples caused by your monumental stupidity continue to disrupt the placidity of the waters that are our lives."

Ellyssa flinched at the harshness of Sandy's softly spoken words. "I'm sorry, but you don't understand."

"I understand all too well. We were all hurt and damaged during our captivity. Few people can pinpoint the exact moment their childhood ended, but we can, all three of us. My tormentors are all dead or of no consequence, so I must take out my rage, pain, and frustrations upon the land. I do this to become stronger so no one can ever hurt me again. But some of yours are still out there, and as long as they live, your soul can never be at peace, can never feel truly safe. Until they are dead, part of you will still be a captive in Sumara."

"So you do understand. I'm glad someone does."

"I understand why you are hunting slavers. What I don't understand is what you are doing here. If you think to enlist me in throwing those Academy idiots out of the school, you had better have a good plan. Those kids have all seen too much fighting in their lives. We all have."

Ellyssa shook her head. "No, I'm not going to fight them. From what I overheard and what Wolf told me, it sounds like things won't change too much except for who's in charge. I need to get to Southport and the sooner the better. I don't think the Academy is done looking for me, and I was hoping you would fly me there."

Sandy's body tensed then relaxed. "The last time I carried someone on my back things went badly, but I can see why you would want to get away from these wizards. I imagine they are very eager to get their hands on that book."

Ellyssa took a defensive step back. "How do you know about the book?"

"I can sense it. It is very powerful. Most any wizard would do whatever it takes to recover it. I have to fight my instincts to covet it for myself. I would do anything to keep it for myself, except betray a friend."

"So we're still friends?" Ellyssa asked, nervously shuffling her feet.

"We are. Some of the strongest friendships are bound by a shared pain. We all made our choices and, in the end, no one suffered for any reason other than their own."

Ellyssa visibly swallowed. "That's what Allister told me right after Azerick died. I didn't believe him. I didn't want to. I wanted to hurt, to suffer for what I did. Every time someone told me it wasn't my fault, I wanted to punish myself even more for their refusal to do so. I guess I thought it was easier that way, for everyone. I know they wanted to blame me. They wanted to yell at me and tell me how angry they were, but they couldn't. For Azerick's sake, they couldn't. So I did it for them, and for myself."

"I think you underestimate their ability for forgiveness," Sandy said.

"Maybe, but I don't underestimate mine," Ellyssa replied. "Will you take me to Southport?"

Sandy sighed as she overcame her disinclination to be used as a mode of transportation. "I will take you a day's walk from the walls but no closer."

Ellyssa nodded her understanding. "Thank you, Sandy. When do you want to leave?"

Sandy looked at the setting sun. "Now is a good time. It allows me to make most of the flight at night and deliver you by morning."

"Wow, that's fast," Ellyssa exclaimed. "So how does this work?"

Wolf pulled a coil of rope out of his pack and looped it once around Sandy's neck and then under her forelegs. "Sandy, if you get any bigger I'll need to get a longer rope."

The dragon glared at Wolf. "You speak as though this will become a recurring thing. I assure you, it will not."

"You have all the humor of a porcupine," Wolf scoffed. "You two are a perfect pair."

Sandy snorted hard enough to make Wolf's ponytail dance as he tightened the makeshift saddle and tied Ellyssa's satchel of clothes and sack of food to the dragon's harness. He then lifted Ellyssa up onto

Sandy's broad back and instructed her how to secure her legs beneath the two loops of rope.

"You can lean back between her wing joints and actually sleep," Wolf told her.

"Thanks, if I'm not terrified out of my wits I will certainly try," Ellyssa said.

Wolf looked up at Ellyssa. "I hope you can come back some day. This place gets kind of boring without you."

Ellyssa smiled down at him. "When I come back, it will be to toss these Academy idiots out on their collective asses."

Sandy gave an approving growl. "Be careful. You are going to be in their backyard, you know."

"When's the last time a wizard ever left his lab to tend to his yard?" Ellyssa's face adopted a more serious look. "Wolf, thank you for everything you have done." Ghost let out a sharp sneeze. "You too, Ghost. Keep an eye on those Academy goons. I don't want them to feel too comfortable here."

"We will, you can count on it," Wolf assured her. "Do what Sandy says and be careful. Wizards may not go outside much, but if you set one of their houses on fire, you can bet they're going to come out for a look."

Ellyssa simply waved and urged Sandy to take flight. Twice as big and significantly stronger, the young dragon had none of the troubles getting off the ground and into the air that she had when she and Wolf had made those first few flights. Her powerful muscles worked her wings with enough force that Wolf had to brace himself to keep from being blown off his feet by the strong wind.

Ellyssa's stomach sank as the ground dropped away. It then jumped into her throat when she looked down and saw miles of verdant forest stretching out to a horizon that had never looked so far away. She looked behind her and it seemed like she was almost at eye level with the northern mountain peaks. Looking to her right, her vision was able to encompass the entire city of North Haven.

Terror held her firmly in its grasp until the frigid air of the high altitude forced her to overcome her fear and act. Ellyssa managed to conjure a weak ward. Although unlikely to stop an arrow, it was sufficient to keep out some of the chill and enough of the wind to keep her eyes from streaming tears the entire way. Ellyssa's fear soon abated as she accepted that Sandy's broad back and Wolf's makeshift harness provided a secure position. She allowed herself to lean back and let exhaustion pull her into a much-needed slumber.

Ellyssa dreamed she was a dragon, flying over the blue swells of an endless sea. In the distance, she spotted the white sails of a ship and tilted her wings to fly closer. Even from more than a mile away, her keen eyes picked out Captain Jake at the helm. Their eyes locked: Ellyssa's radiating hate, Jake's full of terror.

Ellyssa slammed down onto the ship's deck, ripping sail from the lines and snapping the mizzenmast. Captain Jake tried to run, but the rocking of the ship threw him from his feet. Ellyssa pounced and pinned him to the deck with one of her talons. She slowly dragged her claw from Captain Jake's chest to his waist, opening the slaver up like a fish being prepared for cooking.

Crossbow bolts, knives, and belaying pins bounced off her hard scales as the crew tried desperately to drive her away. Ellyssa's foot slipped in the blood pooling around Jake's corpse as she turned to face the minor threat. Filling her giant lungs with air, she breathed a jet of fire stretching to the very front of the ship, immolating dozens of men and setting the ship aflame.

The ship rocked beneath her and she could feel it sinking. Ellyssa tried to take to the air, but several ropes tangled her wings. She used her dexterous paws and their sharp claws to untangle and slice at the bindings. More ropes found their way around her as if they were serpents constricting around her body and wings. The sinking ship pulled her down as it slid beneath the surface. She thrust her head up and extended her neck in a desperate attempt to keep from drowning. The ship lurched again, hard this time as if it had struck a reef.

"Ellyssa," Sandy's voice cut through the ether of her dream, "we are here, wake up."

Ellyssa peeled her eyes open and squinted at the early morning light. She sat up and saw the sun was maybe an hour above the horizon. They rested in a clearing Sandy had chosen as a place to set down. Ellyssa heard the sound of running water and spotted the stream running nearby. She slipped her legs out from under the ropes, slid off

Sandy's back, and fell on her backside when her legs refused to support her.

"It's okay," Sandy told her, "Wolf did the same thing the first time too."

Ellyssa gave Sandy a small, embarrassed smile and struggled to get her legs to respond. After several attempts, she finally got her appendages to cooperate enough to carry her to the stream so she could appease her parched throat. Sandy thrust her muzzle into the water next to Ellyssa and drank deeply.

Sandy finally quenched her thirst and found Ellyssa pacing the clearing to restore normal function to her legs. "We're about a half-day's walk from Southport. Head southeast and you should reach the gates before sundown. I could have gotten you a little closer, but you looked like you were trying to untie yourself and jump off my back."

"Yeah, I was having a dream," Ellyssa replied sheepishly. "Sorry about that."

"How are you feeling?"

"My legs are still rubbery, but I'm okay."

"I was referring more to your magic," Sandy clarified.

Ellyssa beckoned forth a small tendril of magic. "It feels better. Not a hundred percent, but better than yesterday."

"Remember what I said about being careful. Wizards are a patient bunch. Just because they have not chased you recently does not mean they have given up. They want your book, and I bet they want it pretty bad."

"Well, that wizard, Harvey, looks like he is tied up in North Haven now. If he is still looking for me, he's looking in the wrong city."

"What if the Academy found someone else to look for you and the book?" Sandy asked.

"Unless they're saving their best for last, I am not too worried. He was an idiot."

"They underestimated you before. Do not expect them to do so again," Sandy warned.

"I won't," Ellyssa replied.

"Can you make it to the city okay?"

Ellyssa hefted her rucksack and slung the sack of food over her shoulder by its cord. "I'll make it. Thank you, Sandy."

Sandy simply nodded and lifted into the air with a gust of wind and cloud of dust. Ellyssa looked toward the sun, oriented herself southeast, and began walking.

Allister stood to the left of Headmaster Harvey's desk facing four wizards in black clothing and hooded black cloaks trimmed in deep scarlet. Three were men and one was a woman, each shrouded in the heavy folds of their cloaks. They were all standing, with the exception of the headmaster who was seated, in Harvey's temporary office while workers constructed a suitable building. The four wizards were inquisitors, specially trained in battling other mages. They were as aloof as they were haughty, their status and combative specialty instilling an almost universal sense of arrogance and superiority.

"Inquisitors," Headmaster Harvey greeted them with a nod, "I presume you are here in regard to our rogue problem."

"We are," Inquisitor Fennrick replied. "We have been monitoring the city for a few months now and have yet to detect a trace of magical activity outside the walls of this school."

"That is hardly surprising," the headmaster responded. "She has shown herself to be adept at hiding. Even Magus Sharpe was unable to locate her, and she is considered one of the best augurists known to the Academy."

"Yes, I am sure she is quite competent by academic standards," Inquisitor Fennrick said, "but my people and I specialize in this sort of thing. No, I believe the girl is no longer in the city, and that is why I requested this meeting. Magus Allister, I understand you probably know her best. Have you seen or heard anything about her or her whereabouts?"

"No," Allister replied shortly.

"Magus, I would remind you that withholding any information regarding the activities of any suspected rogue mages can result in severe punishment."

"Are you threatening me, boy?" the archmage bristled.

"Not at all. I just would not want to see such an esteemed member of our order brought down because of misplaced sentimentality."

Harvey cut in before Allister could respond. "I believe it is more natural obstinacy than sentimentality. He was equally unhelpful in my investigation. Had he been willing to work with me, this may well have been resolved by now."

"That hardly seems likely," the inquisitor said. "It is my understanding you did manage to locate the child and she humiliated the lot of you."

Harvey's face flushed and anger spread through him like the heat of the desert sun. "This young woman has the Codex Arcana. Were it a simple matter of execution, I assure you, my people and I would have had little difficulty taking her to task. My orders were clear, and that was to recover the codex. To do that, we needed the girl alive. Under those parameters, she had a distinct advantage."

"Your excuse has some merit, I suppose. Fortunately, my people and I are able to perform even under such strictures, but that is neither here nor there. The issue at hand is locating the girl. I have reason to believe others may be aiding her by providing her with necessities such as food. I will need to question several of your students who know her best. I understand there is a wildling living in the forest near here who often pilfers food from your larders and is a friend of hers. I will need to interrogate him as well."

Allister's fury boiled over at the wizard's audacity. "The hell you will! You will not interrogate any child in this school, especially that boy!"

Inquisitor Fennrick looked unmoved by the archmage's outburst. "I remind you again of the penalties of interfering with inquisitor business."

"If you think I am interfering now, try interrogating that boy or these students and see what happens."

The three inquisitors standing with Fennrick shifted their posture as tension filled the room. Harvey stood up from behind his desk and tried to calm everyone before a battle broke out between the formidable archmage and four highly lethal inquisitors.

"Please, let us all remain rational. Magus Allister, need I remind you I am now in charge here, and I will decide what will and will not happen on these grounds as it pertains to *my* students."

Allister wheeled on the headmaster. "Like you have done to their education? You have them repeating things they learned their first year! You are intentionally blocking their access to higher-level magic. Try to deny it!"

"I deny nothing. Until I am comfortable with their knowledge and discipline, our curriculum will focus on the basics, which have been largely ignored under your and the deceased sorcerer's guidance. The goals of the Academy are primarily scholarly, not militant. Those who show a desire and adeptness for this can apply for further training with the inquisitors when the time comes."

A knock at the door interrupted further argument. Harvey's personal aide cautiously entered after receiving permission to intrude.

"Excuse me, Headmaster. A courier just arrived with a missive for Inquisitor Fennrick. He said it was urgent."

With a nod from Harvey, the aide handed a folded and wax-sealed document to the lead inquisitor and vanished into the small reception room outside. A slight grin played across Fennrick's face as he read.

"It would seem our young rogue has indeed left this region and is now stirring up trouble in Southport."

"Southport?" Harvey exclaimed. "Why would the girl do something so incredibly foolish right under the Academy's nose? Surely they have already apprehended her?"

"It appears they tried, and with as much success as you. You should feel more at ease with their failure having diluted your own. It is apparent the fault is not just yours, but with the institution in which you were educated."

"It is the same institution as yours," Harvey forced through clenched jaws.

Fennrick smiled arrogantly at the headmaster. "I exceeded their training a long time ago, Headmaster."

Harvey waited for the inquisitors to leave the room before exploding. "What an infuriating man! I have never seen such arrogance!"

"I recommend you look closer at the mirror next time you shave or you might cut yourself," Allister said, then left the headmaster to fume in his office.

CHAPTER 14

Fall was well entrenched and Ellyssa pulled the tattered blanket draped over her shoulders tighter. Although sheathed in the magical guise of a crippled beggar, she wore some of her warmest clothes beneath her illusion, having to remain stationary still allowed the cold to seep through and bite at her flesh. It likely would have been unbearable were it not for a subtle ward used to protect her from the elements.

She had been in Southport for nearly three months. Her magic had slowly returned to her, and within a week, she had recovered the full use of it. It was fortunate it had. Barely two weeks ago, a pair of wizards found her lurking in the Squatters' Quarter in search of slavers on the hunt. She now understood why Azerick pushed his students to learn combative magic with which to defend themselves. The wizards she fought probably knew a great deal more than she did about magic, but their study was obviously geared toward the academic. Despite their greater knowledge, and even power, they did not have the mindset to use it properly in a down and dirty street fight.

Finding slavers in Southport turned out to be rather easy, but word circulated that the Witch of North Haven now hunted the hunters, and they were running scared. It had been days since she spotted anything more than some fencing and black marketing, but those people were not her concern. Not one of the slavers or pirates she got hold of claimed to know anything of Captain Jake other than he kept near the Black Sand Isles and their various pirate ports. Ellyssa figured he must have limped his way to a shipyard there instead of the nearer Southport. She did not like the idea of becoming part of a pirate crew so she could search for him in the isles, but if things did not change soon, that was exactly what she would have to do.

It was late and Ellyssa was cold, bored, and tired. She made a show of struggling to her feet, so as not to break character, and hobbled on a crutch down the dockside street. Not until she rounded a second corner and ducked into the concealing darkness of a building's shadow did she drop her illusive disguise.

Ellyssa was surprised by how much she missed Sandy, Wolf, Roger, and the others. Despite her aloofness and desire for solitude, having a physical distance between them made her feel alone. Likely it was the knowledge they were always there at the ready should she need them. She wondered if there would ever be a way for her to go home after all this was over. She doubted it.

She stepped out of the shadow and back onto the walkway, tapping her crutch on the wooden footpath. Ellyssa did not pause to ponder what danger approached when the hairs on her arm stood up. She ripped open a gate and dove through the same instant the storefront exploded.

"Tamara, please keep in mind we need her alive," Inquisitor Fennrick cautioned.

"Of course, Fennrick," the woman responded with a smile.

"Did you see where she went?"

Tamara looked up and down the dark street. "I think she gated away. She cannot be far. One of the others should spot her in a moment."

Fennrick cocked an ear. "Do you hear that?"

The strange rhythmical whumping sound grew louder until a large stick or branch struck Fennrick's ward and clattered to the ground. Had he not had his ward raised, it would have hit him right between the eyes. The inquisitor reached down and picked it up.

"What is it?" Tamara asked.

Fennrick grinned. "The crutch the girl was using in her disguise. Cute."

A feeling of electricity tingled across his hand and spread up his arm. He hurled the crutch away and it exploded just as it left his hand, knocking him and Tamara to the ground.

"When is the Academy going to learn to stop sending fools after me?" Ellyssa's voice echoed down the deserted street.

The two inquisitors regained their feet and faced the direction of the voice. "They have learned, girl, which is why they sent for us. Why don't you save yourself a great deal of pain and come peacefully?" Fennrick asked.

"So you can execute me after a sham trial? I think not."

Another explosion rocked the block. "Fennrick, she's over here!" Inquisitor Mills shouted.

"You and Forrest try to get ahead of her, and we will trap her between us," Fennrick shouted back.

Ellyssa spotted the wizard standing on the rooftop just as he tried to crush her with a blast of force. She dove into the alley next to her as pieces of wood and chunks of dirt and stone rained onto her back. She found the wizard on another roof across the street while still hidden in the dark alleyway. She called on the Source and wrapped the alley's shadows around her body before creeping forward.

Looking behind her, Ellyssa created a web of magic that would wrap an illusion of herself around the wizard she could hear running after her. Like a spider web, the spell clung to the walls and waited for the wizard to run through it. She then turned her attention to the man standing on the rooftop and waited until she could hear the one from the alley getting closer. Just as the wizard in the alley ran through her web, Ellyssa cast an illusion of her image onto the man on the roof.

Inquisitor Forrest looked toward the alley and spotted the girl running out of it. Inquisitor Mills ran out of the alley and saw the girl on the roof. Both wizards began forming their spells, but Forrest was faster. Mills saw he was not going to get his spell off before the girl did and tried to dive away, but his realization came too late and the spell struck him in the side. His ward flared brightly as it tried to protect him. His shield saved him from severe injury, but the force of the impact left him dazed.

Inquisitor Forrest cursed when he saw the illusion wrapped around Mills come unraveled by his assault. "Beware your shots; the girl is using illusions against us!" Forrest spotted the girl when she moved, and launched another, even more powerful force strike.

Ellyssa recognized the spell and prepared to counter it. Instead of expending the energy to dodge it or block it with a spell of equal power, she simply opened a gate directly in front of her with the entrance and exit pointed toward the caster. Inquisitor Mills cursed once again as he realized what the clever girl had just done. He threw himself backward as his own spell obliterated the entire corner of the building upon which he was standing.

Motion out of the corner of her eye saved her life as Ellyssa dodged aside. Despite her quick actions, Inquisitor Tamara's spell clipped her hard and spun her into the street. Ellyssa kept tumbling even as she formed a spell. It was thankfully simple and she hoped it would buy her enough time to get to her feet. She rolled onto her side facing the inquisitor and cast her spell. The road in front of Tamara erupted upward in a wave of dust, soil, and cobblestones. The wizard hunched down and poured power into her ward as the wave of earth matter cascaded over her.

Ellyssa leapt to her feet only to have the wizard on the roof blast her back off them. Rolling with the impact, Ellyssa stood, lurched drunkenly, and took off running, fueling the muscles of her legs with magic. She could hear the shouts and footfalls of the two mages racing after her. Ellyssa stretched her arms out to her sides and unleashed her arcane power.

The building fronts exploded into the street where a fierce wind created a vortex of swirling timber and stone. Every home and building front exploded inward, torn from the main structure by the massive vacuum, and followed in her wake like rushing water. The fury of the tempest forced Inquisitors Forrest and Tamara to end their chase and reinforce their wards before the flying materials shredded them.

When the massive assault stopped, the two inquisitors found themselves near the end of the street facing the brick wall of a large building. The buildings and homes along the street were in ruins, their entire street-side walls lying scattered across the avenue. The two wizards looked in the only two directions the girl could have run.

"Well, she had to go left or right," Inquisitor Tamara said.

"Unless I gated in behind you," came Ellyssa's cold voice directly to their rear.

Ellyssa struck before the two mages could turn around, the force of her strike hurling them through the air to smash into the brick wall a full thirty feet from where she was standing. Seeing both inquisitors dazed beyond coherency, Ellyssa left the pair twitching and moaning as she ran down the street to her right.

She had barely taken half a dozen steps when something struck her from behind and sent electricity coursing through her body, numbing her limbs and senses. Ellyssa cursed through the pain and surprise at her own stupidity. She had made a fundamental error in any battle, losing count of the number of enemies she faced. There had been another man with the woman in the first contest and the two men in the street whom she tricked into striking at each other for a total of four not three.

Ellyssa felt the ground lift up from beneath her and begin folding itself around her body in an earthen and quarried stone cocoon. She thought fast. She needed to keep an arm free if she was going to have any chance of defending herself. The swelling earth raised her from the ground and pressed her against the side of a building. The dark silhouette of a man slowly resolved into Inquisitor Fennrick as he sauntered closer.

"I will give you credit. You are a very clever girl. A shame you wasted your talents on murder," he said, stopping perhaps a score of feet away.

Ellyssa glared down at the man. "It was not murder! Every man I killed was a pirate or a slaver, and both warrant immediate execution under the king's law!"

"As do your actions under Academy law. The difference is you will get the trial denied those men."

"They chose their fate when they chose their profession, just as you chose yours when you attacked me."

Ellyssa cast her spell with a final flick of the wrist of her free hand. She opened a gate directly beneath Fennrick's feet and placed the exit less than twenty feet over his head. The inquisitor let out a short bark of surprise as he fell, and fell, and continued to fall, picking up speed as he dropped through the portals. Within seconds, he was traveling at such a rate he had to close his eyes against the wind.

Without Fennrick focusing on the spell holding her against the wall, Ellyssa was able to dispel it. Her earthen shackles crumbled into loose dirt and stone and deposited her onto the street. She stepped toward the falling wizard and shouted so he could hear her over the wind blasting past his ears.

"I will tell you what I told those other fools: leave me alone before someone gets hurt."

She then used her magic to give the inquisitor a nudge, making him spin on every axis imaginable. Ellyssa conjured another gate and disappeared onto a nearby roof.

Tamara and Forrest reached the scene a moment before Inquisitor Mills stumbled in, still trying to shake off his bludgeoning. All three looked upon the scene in amazed wonderment.

"By the gods, I never would have thought of that," Inquisitor Tamara gasped.

Inquisitor Mills stifled a smile. "The girl is clever, I'll grant her that."

"If you all are finished gawking, get me out of this before I sick up all over myself!" Fennrick shouted then clamped his jaws shut.

He was far more concerned with what would happen to him when the spell expired and he struck the cobblestones at a speed no man has likely ever before traveled. The other three inquisitors looked at their comrade and each other, trying to decipher the riddle before them.

"Need I remind you speed is of paramount importance here?" Fennrick called out between clenched teeth.

"I have an idea," Inquisitor Tamara declared. "You two be ready to catch him."

The lady mage conjured her own gate and slipped it between the ones cast by the rogue wizard. Fennrick fell into the new gate entrance and launched skyward as he rocketed straight up out of Tamara's exit portal. He could not help but open his eyes and marvel at the expansive black vista hundreds of feet below him. Miles of street lamps outlined the avenues of the wealthier districts, and he could take them all in with a single glance from his terrifying height. Then he once again plummeted toward the ground.

It was all too much and he released a shrill scream lasting several seconds until he felt magic envelop him like a gentle hand. Fennrick let out several ragged gasps as he felt himself slow until he came to a near halt a few tens of feet above the cobblestone street. Mills and Forrest then guided him the rest of the way down where Fennrick promptly staggered to the nearest wall and sank into a sitting position.

"I never would have thought to use a simple gate spell in such an offensive manner," Forrest remarked as Fennrick regained his composure.

Mills nodded in agreement. "Such a clever girl. She would have made a fantastic inquisitor."

Fennrick stood up on shaky legs. "She is not clever; she is brilliant, too brilliant and too strong for us to take by force with the restriction of taking her alive."

"Yes, particularly when she is under no such restraint," Tamara agreed.

"She could have killed Fennrick," Forrest pointed out.

"Indeed, yet she did not, and I plan to make her regret her decision," Fennrick hissed.

Ellyssa ran along the roofs as far as she could before climbing down and fleeing through the streets. She kept to the shadows and alleys, and took a circuitous route back to the inn where she had rented a room. She thought of the buildings she had damaged and wondered if she should go back and make restitution to the owners. Let the Academy pay for it! It was their fault anyway.

She snuck in through the inn's kitchen. Pain flared across her back and reminded Ellyssa of the injury she had taken in the battle. Herbalism and alchemy were never her strong suits, but she knew enough to treat some minor wounds. She rooted around the kitchen and found an onion and some chamomile. She chopped up the onion with a knife then crushed it with a rolling pin.

Ellyssa scooped the mix into a clean cloth and quietly made her way up the stairs to her room. She paused outside her door and examined her wards. From what she could tell, no one had passed through them while she was out. She fished the small key from her pocket, unlocked the door, and stepped into its dark interior. The oil lamp on the table flared to life with the snap of her fingers.

She winced when she pulled her shirt off over her head and it rubbed against the throbbing welt and blister raised across her back.

Ellyssa laid the towel on her bed, spread the onion and chamomile concoction on it, and lay atop it. She then tied the compress in place and breathed a sigh of relief as it extinguished the searing, throbbing heat.

Ellyssa replayed the battle in her mind. This group was different from the others. They seemed to know how to fight. She was certain they too had underestimated her and made mistakes, but it was not for lack of skill. The fact they apparently wanted her alive, wanted the book more likely, was the only reason she probably emerged victorious.

She was not sure what to do now. They also seemed to be wearing some kind of uniform as well. The Academy must have sent a more capable group. This was going to make her job more difficult. She wondered if she could avoid them. She also wondered how they had found her. It was obvious they had set themselves up to ambush her, so they must have known where she was.

If they were adept at capturing wizards, they probably had a way to detect latent magical signatures. She had been cloaking herself in an illusion all day. She had been doing that for almost the entire time she had been in Southport. She had also used magic to deal with some people and interrogate them for information about Captain Jake. Ellyssa reasoned she had been leaving a magical scent throughout the city for weeks, especially around the docks, and like bloodhounds, they had sniffed her out.

Fear shot through her as she thought about the wards on her room. Ellyssa relaxed, knowing many of the wards cast on her room were specifically crafted to prevent detection from all manner of inquiry. The book had given them to her and she knew they were strong. It was a good thing she was exhausted; otherwise, the stress of having to deal with this new threat would have kept her awake. Ellyssa's injury forced her to sleep on her stomach, which was something else to irritate her no end, but even that could not keep her awake for long.

Morning came with the intrusiveness of a siege. The sun breached her consciousness as it poured through the window and was about as welcome as enemy infantry. Ellyssa was determined to continue to fight to the bitter end, but the rumbling in her stomach forced her to accept the sun's terms of surrender. She was still dressed in yesterday's clothes with the exception of her ruined shirt, so she donned a new one and followed the smell of food downstairs with one last hateful look at the sun, promising resumption of hostilities later.

"Hey, girl, rough night?" the innkeeper asked with far too much exuberance.

"Food!" Ellyssa demanded as she found an empty table, which she promptly dropped her head onto with a dull thud.

Frank, the innkeeper, showed up a minute later with a plate of food, setting it in front of the sleeping girl hard enough to wake her. Ellyssa looked up and tried to glare her displeasure, but Frank was a kindly man who always smiled at her. He probably thought she was a prostitute since he made a point of informing her, shortly after she rented the room, that he ran a clean inn and did not tolerate any sordid activities. Ellyssa promised there would be nothing of the sort and let the man think what he wanted.

"You're looking especially radiant today," Frank said. "Sleep well?"

"Ha-ha," Ellyssa replied dryly. "I hear the duke is looking for a new jester. Perhaps you should go apply."

"I think a smart girl like you can find better work that won't keep you out so late."

"I think you should...oh, I'm too tired to play this game today," Ellyssa mumbled.

Concern shot through her as she realized she really was too tired to engage in their usual banter. In fact, Ellyssa could barely force her eyes open and was rapidly losing that battle as well. The last thing she saw before the world went black was Frank's apologetic eyes.

"Oh, Frank, you bast..." Ellyssa mumbled before she blacked out.

Frank slid the plate of food away so Ellyssa would not land face-first into its remains. He gently guided her head down as two dark-garbed men got up from a nearby table and took hold of the girl.

"Your cooperation is greatly appreciated," said one of the men.

Frank's face flushed with a mixture of anger and shame. "Just get out of my inn."

The two men smiled as they lifted Ellyssa from her chair and disappeared with their burden through the back door. Frank hated his part in this sordid business, but there were some folks you just did not want to run afoul of.

Ellyssa opened her eyes and discovered her hands tied and her mouth gagged. She fought down the rising panic of, once again, being held captive. She looked around the room and saw she was in a chamber of stone walls weeping with excess moisture. A single door looked to be the only way out. She sat in a plain chair across from a slightly larger chair with a felt-padded seat. Ellyssa suspected she would be having company soon.

Within seconds of regaining consciousness, the door opened and two men strode in. One was large with a head so bald it shone in the lamplight. The other man was of average height and build, dark-haired with a thin, black mustache, and wore expensive clothing. In other circumstances, Ellyssa might have considered him handsome for an older man. She guessed him to be in charge. He confirmed her suspicions when he sat in the chair across from her.

"Look at the defiant, unbridled fury in her eyes, Braxis," Andrill said to the bald man standing over his shoulder. "Does it remind you of anyone?"

Braxis smiled. "It sure does. Best be careful if she espouses his other attributes as well."

"Indeed." The man in the chair faced Ellyssa again. "Hello, my dear. My name is Andrill, and this is my dear associate, Braxis. You must be wondering what causes me to bring you here, and under such rude circumstances. I will explain everything, but first we must come to an accord. First off, I mean you absolutely no harm. Now, I know this may be difficult to accept given the first impressions of your treatment, but please look at it from my point of view. So, if you promise not to harm my people, or me, I will untie you and remove that dreadful gag. Agreed?"

Ellyssa looked at the man as if he were insane.

"Oh, of course," Andrill responded with a flippant wave of his hand. "Any promises are certainly conditional upon the behavior of me and mine. Expecting you not to slaughter us all should we display violence is just silly."

Ellyssa glared daggers at the man for several heartbeats then nodded her head once. Braxis cut the cords binding her hands and removed the braided cloth from her mouth.

"You two purse-cutting dung eaters just signed your death warrants," Ellyssa spat but made no move to attack.

Andrill turned to look at Braxis again. "Azerick Sir was so much more polite."

Braxis nodded. "He was. Manners were obviously not part of her curriculum."

Ellyssa's heart skipped a beat at the mention of Azerick's name. These men knew him and they knew her, or at least enough about her to know they had a relationship. She assumed it must not be too bad since they were willing to talk and free her at her word.

"What do want, and why did you poison me?" Ellyssa demanded. "And how do you know Azerick?"

"Azerick was an old associate of mine before he left to join that Academy and promptly disappeared. My condolences on his passing."

"What does that have to do with me?"

Andrill pursed his lips as he mentally arranged his next words. "Azerick owed me a great favor, two actually, and due to his unfortunate death is unable to repay them."

"That still does not explain what you want with me," Ellyssa stated, already seeing where this was going.

"As his ward, and something of an heir, I was hoping to impress upon you the obligation of fulfilling those favors."

"That's not going to happen," Ellyssa informed him bluntly. "Anything between you and Azerick died with him, like so many other things did. Besides, I have my own debts to collect, and they are gaining interest every minute."

Andrill smiled and steepled his fingers under his chin. "Ah yes, Captain Jake, the terrible slaver."

Ellyssa narrowed her eyes. "You seem to know an awful lot about me."

"I know a lot about many things. It is my primary business. Oh sure, I dabble in the occasional robbery or fencing operation, but my true stock and trade is information. I really did not expect you to throw in your lot with me out of some sense of duty or obligation to your mentor just because you might find some easing of the guilt you may feel for your part in his death. Hmm, no? Oh well, it was worth a try. How about I offer you something you want in return for your help with my little problem?"

"What do you think you can give me I can't get on my own if I want it?" Ellyssa asked slowly.

Andrill leaned forward in his chair. "I can give you Captain Jake."

Ellyssa exploded from her chair and tore at the Source. Braxis and Andrill felt a crushing weight strike them in the chest and pin them to wall.

"Where is he? If you know you had best tell me now!" Ellyssa screamed in uncontrolled rage.

Andrill made a halting motion and then pointed to the floor with his index finger. Ellyssa looked around the room and spotted several black holes in the wall revealing the presence of hidden passages. She imagined men behind those openings pointing loaded crossbows at her. Ellyssa was certain she could protect herself from them, but listening might be a better course of action right now. Ellyssa let the two thieves drop to their feet and sat back down. Andrill and Braxis resumed their original positions, but only Andrill was still smiling.

"As I was saying," Andrill said, "information is my business, one at which I am very good. I do not know where Captain Jake is right this instant, but if you help me, I can find him."

"If you can find him so easily then why not find him before abducting me?" Ellyssa demanded to know. "Then you would have a bargaining chip in your hand, which is far more substantial than a promise you may or may not be able to keep after you get what you want."

"See how clever she is, Braxis? So much like our dear friend Azerick. Two reasons, child, one you just saw. Had I the information ahead of time, you could have extracted it from me without paying your fair share of the deal. Two, I cannot get that information until you help me."

"Why not?"

"What do you know of the thieves' guild?" Andrill asked.

"Nothing, other than you steal things."

Andrill clapped his hands once. "Oh good, I love to tell a good story. The thieves' guild was originally comprised of independent chapter houses, each led by a house master. I am the house master of the Night Ravens. Each chapter house had its own territory carved out in the city. There were, of course, the occasional battles for territory, but overall it was an equitable arrangement. That changed a few years ago when a newcomer by the name of Faralynn took over the leadership of one of the houses. Faralynn is a brutal expansionist, and I lost a little territory but only the bit I had gained when Azerick helped eliminate Daedric's Demons. Things seemed to even out over the next year or so, but then she began expanding again. Pretty soon, she declared herself the guild leader of all Southport and each chapter house either paid her to operate or she wiped them out to a man."

"So you work for her? If everyone hates this setup, why not just work together to kill her?"

"I do not work for her, which is why my house now resides here. Do you recognize it?" Andrill asked.

"No, why should I?"

"It used to belong to a much younger Azerick," Andrill explained. "I sort of bent one of our agreements about following him home. I have a terrible curiosity and felt it in my best interest to know where to find him should I need him. Discovering the boy was capable of using magic came as a bit of a shock to the first of my men to enter this place. Quite literally in fact. Azerick had placed some rather unpleasant surprises for uninvited guests, but we got that all taken care of. It was expensive, I can tell you."

"You still haven't told me why Faralynn is such a problem."

"The problem is that Faralynn has a wizard working for her, and a rather powerful one, if I am any sort of judge of such things. All who have tried to unseat her and break up her little monopoly have met with an exceedingly grisly demise. That is why I need you, the Witch of North Haven. I do love that little title they bestowed on you. It is quite catchy and very frightening—to slavers anyway."

"So, I take care of the wizard and help you remove this Faralynn woman and you promise me Captain Jake," Ellyssa clarified.

"Exactly. Once Faralynn is removed, I can call in my resources from the holes in which they are hiding, the ones still alive that is, and re-establish my intelligence network."

"How long? How long after I kill this wizard and thief will it take you to find Captain Jake?"

Andrill let out a long breath as he thought. "I will have to replace several people, but mostly just ears and laymen. My higher-ups were largely able to retreat into hiding and are just waiting for word to re-emerge. Give me six months, a year at the outset, and I promise to deliver Captain Jake into your hands."

"So long," Ellyssa whispered.

"Not as long as you have been searching. I understand the Academy is looking for you as well. By aiding me, you can get Captain Jake while lying low and away from the prying eyes of the Academy."

Ellyssa thought about the offer. She hated the idea of needing someone else's help, but the longer she tried and failed to find Captain Jake, the more likely those idiots from the Academy would finally catch her. She also did not know how much she could trust Andrill.

He was a thief and, in Ellyssa's opinion, one up from being a pirate. The man said he knew Azerick, but were they friends or enemies? He talked as if they were friends, but of course, he would if he wanted Ellyssa's help. Despite her misgivings, Ellyssa had to accept that if she wanted to kill Captain Jake, she was going to need help.

"All right, I'll help you."

Andrill clapped his hands together and stood. "Wonderful! I knew this would be a profitable venture."

"So when do we do this?"

"It will take a few days for me to find out where Faralynn is hiding," Andrill explained. "She moves constantly. That is the problem with behaving in a way that makes nearly everyone want to kill you; it breeds paranoia. A few of my men will show you out," Andrill said, gesturing toward the door. "I do hope you accept my apologies, but I must insist on blindfolding you until you reach street level."

"Fine, but don't think for a second to bind my hands again. By the way, if you cross me, I will hunt you down and kill you just like I did those slavers," Ellyssa warned as she stepped through the door.

Braxis looked at his boss. "I think you just made a deal with a devil."

"Such is the way of business sometimes. We just need to make doubly sure we hold up our end of the bargain."

Three men in drab clothing waited for her just outside the room. Most of the light within the long, stone corridor came from a few far-spaced oil lamps attached to the wall, but a faint blue light also emanated from some sort of phosphorescent lichen.

One of the men tied a silk cloth over her eyes and gently guided her by the elbow. The grating of stone on stone echoed through the dank corridor and the smell of sewage struck her like a physical blow. For a moment, Ellyssa feared she would be forced to trudge through the city's waste, but there appeared to be a raised walkway running along the sewer tunnel.

The thieves led her through at least two miles of twisting, reeking tunnels before she heard a sewer grate being lifted up. She ascended a ladder leading to the street above. Even the pervasive seaside aroma of Southport smelled sweet after traversing the sewers. She sucked in several lungfuls of air to clear out the stench.

Ellyssa blinked her eyes a few times and turned as soon as they lifted the blindfold, but the three thieves had already vanished back down the grate. The only thing she saw of them was the cover being seated back in place.

She gained her bearings and headed toward Frank's inn. She needed to have a word with him. Keeping a wary eye out for thieves, slavers, and wizards, Ellyssa navigated the streets crowded with afternoon traffic. Her stomach snarled loud enough to draw a few stares and served to remind her that she had not yet been allowed to finish a single meal today. A quick stop at a food booth fixed that.

Ellyssa stepped through the doors and locked eyes with the innkeeper. She read a bag of mixed emotions on the man's face. She saw shame, regret, and even a little fear before he dropped his eyes. Ellyssa walked to the bar where Frank continued to polish a glass long after it was clean.

"Andrill said he wouldn't hurt you. I'm glad he kept his word," the innkeeper said as Ellyssa sat down.

"Me too. I wouldn't want my death to weigh on your conscience."

"I'm real sorry for my part in this. If I thought he was going to hurt you, I like to think I would have warned you or something."

Ellyssa grunted an acknowledgement. "I guess it's probably a good thing you didn't do something stupid like that. What do you know of Andrill?"

Frank looked down at the glass he was scrubbing. "Not much. I don't consort with those types, but since I had to do business with one, I'm glad it was Andrill."

"So you think he's a man of his word?" Ellyssa asked.

Frank nodded. "From what I've heard, as best he can. Don't get me wrong. He's a thief, and no thief is successful by being a nice guy. He'll kill you quick as any man, but not without good reason. It's more than most will give you."

"That's good to know. It turns out we can be of mutual use to each other. The only problem is that I have to do my part before he can do his. I have enough enemies to deal with without adding him to the list for reneging."

Frank bit his lip and nodded. "He said you were dangerous. That was why he insisted we do it the way we did."

"He's right. Remember that the next time you think about betraying my trust. What do you know about a woman named Faralynn?"

"She is as bad as they come. I'd steer clear of her at any cost. Some people claim she's insane. I think she's just mean. I hear she has a wizard working for her too, as if she weren't bad enough by herself."

Ellyssa nodded, stood up, and turned toward the stairs as Frank scrubbed at an invisible speck of dirt on the glass.

"I'll send a bath up to your room. You stink something awful."

Ellyssa cracked a smile. "You sure know how to charm a girl, Frank."

She enjoyed a long soak in a hot bath with a liberal additive of scented salts. Maybe the luxurious bath salts were Frank's way of apologizing. Then again, maybe she just smelled so bad he was afraid she would drive away other customers. Still feeling the effects of her battle the previous night, as well as from the trace amounts of Andrill's poison creeping through her veins, Ellyssa retired early that night.

She awoke the next morning feeling far better than she did the previous day even before she was drugged and dragged down to the sewers. Andrill said he needed a few days to prepare, so Ellyssa decided to make some preparations of her own.

Ellyssa found a paper-wrapped bundle outside her door and knew it to be the clothes the washerwoman took yesterday. She tossed the parcel on her bed and descended the stairs to the common room. Frank gave her a nervous smile when he spotted her at the foot of the stairs.

"Breakfast?" the innkeeper asked.

"Definitely," Ellyssa responded.

Frank disappeared into the kitchen. As soon as he vanished beyond the door, Ellyssa darted across the room and stole down the stairs next to the bar leading to the cellar. Conjuring a tiny light in the palm of her hand, Ellyssa ducked behind a large wine cask and dropped to her knees. Using a bit of magic, she lifted one of the large flagstones from the floor and set it aside.

She reached into the cavity beneath and retrieved her precious book. Setting it on the floor, she told the book to show her what she needed. It flipped open at her command and displayed the desired pages with glowing text. Ellyssa committed the words to memory, replaced the book and flagstone, and double-checked her wards keeping it safe.

Ellyssa hurried back up the steps and looked for Frank before emerging from the stairs and finding a seat at her preferred table. Frank arrived from the kitchen not a moment later with a plate heaped with food. The innkeeper had learned early in Ellyssa's stay she possessed quite an appetite.

She finished her breakfast without leaving a bit of food for the hog trough Frank kept out back and left the inn. The sun had been up long enough for the majority of the populace to start their day, and the streets were crowded as she made the long walk to the merchants' district.

Ellyssa found the shop she was looking for and walked through the doors. A small bell dangling above the entrance chimed to announce her. A heavyset man wearing a red vest with gold embroidery, a matching conical hat with a gold tassel on top, and with a thick, black mustache greeted her as she entered.

"Welcome, pretty, young miss!" the man called out. "How can Azeel be of service to you?"

Ellyssa looked at the shelves full of glassware. "I need glass and was told you had a wide assortment."

"Yes! My worthless son-in-law blows almost everything you see," Azeel proclaimed with a wave. "I told him he could blow glass here or go back to Sumara without my daughter and blow sand out of his nostrils for the rest of his days. In a rare show of wisdom, he chose glass. If you do not see anything you like, I can take a custom order and have it to you within a week."

Ellyssa picked through the shelves of glass. She did not have a week to get exactly what the book had shown, but there was enough to choose from to suit her purpose. She selected four pieces as well as some accessories like tubing, oil burners, and rubber stoppers.

Azeel packed the assortment in a wooden box padded with straw. Ellyssa left Azeel's and found an herbalist's shop a short distance away. Buying the things she needed, she hurried back toward the inn. Only a few blocks away, a trio of men stepped in front of her as she hustled down a lesser-used passage between buildings.

"What's in the box, girl?" the largest of the three men asked.

"Nothing to interest you," Ellyssa said bluntly. "Now, clear out of my way before I make you regret it."

The tall thin one jabbed an elbow in the big one's ribs. "You better watch out, Hugo; she looks like a tough one."

Hugo returned his friend's grin. "Yeah, Carrot, she might just whoop all three of us. Maybe we should give her our money?"

"I'll settle for you getting out of my way, but if you annoy me, I might just take it," Ellyssa warned the thugs.

"Cute. Now, gimme what you got in the box," Hugo ordered, no longer pretending to be humorous.

Ellyssa took a step back to give herself a little more space. "I'm warning you, I don't want to have to thrash you right now."

Ellyssa really did not want to use her magic just in case those wizards were near enough to sense her. Luckily, she was still quite a distance from the inn, so even if they did detect her residual magic later it was unlikely they could follow it back to her.

Hugo let out an annoyed sigh. "Rolly, grab the damn box."

The dark-haired man made a halfhearted lunge. Ellyssa grabbed his outstretched arm and sent a jolt of electricity through it powerful enough to stun him and burn the flesh beneath her hand.

Hugo and Carrot froze in terror as a nightmare from years past unfolded before their eyes. A jet of flame from Ellyssa's outflung hand set Carrot's knit hat aflame, breaking him out of the spell he was in and sending him beating a screeching retreat.

Carrot's screaming also put motion into Hugo's legs, but not nearly enough. A force strike impacted his back and slammed him into the nearest wall. Ellyssa then shaped it around him and smashed him into the unyielding surface until his screams stopped.

She then reached down and plucked a small pouch of coins from Rolly's unconscious body. Ellyssa was about to search Hugo but stopped when she saw the dark stain expanding across the front of his trousers. She did not really need the coin, but she could not pass up the poetic justice of it all.

Ellyssa made it back to the inn without further incident. She climbed the stairs, breathing hard and sweating from racing across the district just in case someone detected her magic usage. She unpacked the box's contents on the small table and set up the pieces. She soon had water boiling and began adding the items from the herbalist shop just as the book told her to. Andrill had shown her her vulnerability to poisons and she meant to ensure she would not be taken easily again.

CHAPTER 15

Ellyssa spent the next few days laying low and keeping off the streets as much as possible. She managed to craft antidotes for lethal as well as tranquilizing poisons. Of course, they could not protect her from every type of poison imaginable, but it was something.

A knock at her door early in the morning startled her. With a spell on her lips, Ellyssa opened the door. Just beyond the doorway stood a man in nondescript clothing. The fluttering in her stomach hinted as to the man's purpose.

"We have located her," he said without preamble. "She will be staying in a manor house tonight in the upper merchants' district. Andrill wanted to inform you so you could prepare. Someone will come for you tonight when the time nears."

Ellyssa did not answer and the man did not wait for her to. He simply turned and vanished down the stairs as soon as he delivered his message. Ellyssa closed the door and sat back down on her bed. Her nerves warred within her, setting her flesh tingling.

Battle was nothing new to her, but this was the first time she would be deliberately fighting another wizard. Somehow, she doubted this man was an Academy rube like the others. Nor was he going to be concerned with her survival. She needed to be prepared to fight a very difficult battle. Scooting her back against the headboard, Ellyssa sat cross-legged with her spell book open on her lap and began preparing for tonight.

Ellyssa lost herself in her trance as she ran her list of spells over in her mind, memorizing each word and each weave in exacting detail so she could cast them almost without thought no matter what was happening around her. She replayed them all until they were as familiar to her as her own name.

Time became as indistinct as air as she delved into her magic. She was as startled by the knock on her door as by the darkness seeping through her small window. Her legs were stiff from remaining immobile for such a long time and protested each step she took toward the door.

"It is time," the thief said as soon as Ellyssa opened the door. "Are you prepared?"

Ellyssa nodded. "I just need to grab something to eat on the way out."

The man nodded in return and said, "Make it something quick. Timing is of the utmost importance."

He led the way down the stairs. Once in the common room, Ellyssa had Frank retrieve a biscuit with some meat and cheese slipped into the middle. She ate her simple fare as the thief led her through the streets toward the upper merchants' district.

Of course, the guild thief did not lead them in a direct route, instead navigating through a myriad of alleys and shops. The rough homes and buildings of the common quarter continually improved as they made their way north across the city. More homes were painted here and the streets were cleaner and better maintained. Clean but quaint homes became stately manors with stone and wrought-iron walls.

It was through the gates of one of these homes her guide led her. Ellyssa first thought the place abandoned, but then she noticed the thief making subtle but deliberate motions with his hand and occasionally clicking his tongue or letting out a short whistle. It was then Ellyssa felt numerous sets of eyes watching her from the shadows. Trees, hedges, and shrubbery decorated the fine lawn and provided an untold number of places for a skilled thief to find refuge.

They walked the stone path leading to the doors of the manor. Her guide rapped out an obvious code upon the glossy oak doors. Ellyssa heard several latches being thrown before the door opened, at first just a crack, then wide enough to permit them to pass.

A woman in leathers decorated with at least a dozen throwing knives took charge of the young wizard as soon as she stepped into the dimly lit foyer. Like the other two thieves she had met today, she did not waste time with words and simply expected Ellyssa to follow without question.

They passed through the foyer and emerged in a large living chamber adequately illuminated by several lamps and a pair of chandeliers. Leaning over a table set near the middle of the room were Andrill, Braxis, and four other men. The men pored over a map that appeared to Ellyssa to be a detailed plan of another mansion.

"Wonderful, our secret weapon has arrived," Andrill said. Ellyssa took a place next to the table.

Ellyssa looked at Andrill and Braxis and said, "It looks like you started the battle early," commenting on the cuts and bruises evident on both men's faces.

Andrill gave his usual charming smile. "Some people are reluctant to give information or provide assistance, but everyone has their breaking point."

"This is our secret weapon?" a large, thick-necked man asked as if Ellyssa's presence were a joke.

"I assure you, Trevor, she is quite formidable," Andrill replied. "Have you heard of the Witch of North Haven?"

Trevor looked at Ellyssa as if he were sizing up a horse before placing a bet. "This slip of a girl?"

"This slip of a girl has killed dozens of slavers, sunk their ships, and battled several Academy wizards at once and prevailed. If Faralynn has shown us anything, it is not to judge one's strength by simple body mass."

"I hope you are right," the house leader replied.

Andrill turned his attention back to her. "Ellyssa, this is Trevor, another house leader whom I trust enough to help in this endeavor. Understand this is going to be an enormous operation. We have hundreds of our members poised to strike at nearly every one of Faralynn's chapter houses. Our job is to take out Faralynn and her wizard. Our targets are always together and currently in a manor a few blocks from here. We know from experience the wizard is able to detect our presence the instant we come near any place in which they are residing. It is probably the biggest factor in our inability to bring Faralynn down."

"He would definitely have the place warded," Ellyssa confirmed.

"Precisely, and that is where you come in. We need you to get us past those wards so we can get close enough to strike before kicking the hornet's nest. Until now, any spies I sent anywhere Faralynn resided were killed before they got near the house. Can you get us closer?"

Ellyssa chewed her lip as she thought. "Most wizards cast wards in layers. A full block is stretching even an alarm ward thin, so it probably won't be that complex. Unless he is exceptionally masterful, I should be able to breach it without detection. The problem will be the inner wards. Those are bound to be harder, and even if I can dismantle them, doing so without his knowledge could be challenging."

Andrill nodded as he followed along. "If you can get us up to the doors, it should be sufficient to give us a chance. At that point, your job is to neutralize the wizard before he incinerates us all. Without his interference, we will have a much more level playing field."

"Faralynn will probably be thinking the same thing and send her wizard after me, so it shouldn't be too hard to separate the two of them."

"You have a good head for tactics," Andrill commended.

"I had a good teacher."

Trevor interjected, "Our people are in position and waiting on our signal. Best we get ourselves placed as well."

"Ready?" Andrill asked.

Ellyssa swallowed down her nervousness and twitched her head in an affirmative. Several men and a few women closed ranks behind them as they led the way out of the manor and onto the street. Ellyssa took the lead since no one knew precisely where the boundary to the wizard's wards lay.

Dark shapes flitted across rooftops and down alleys as the party moved toward Faralynn's redoubt with as much stealth as nearly a hundred bodies could make. Ellyssa sent very subtle tendrils of detection magic ahead of her in hopes of sensing the ward without alerting its creator.

Andrill warned her in a whisper they were drawing close to Faralynn's mansion. A moment later, Ellyssa held up a hand, stopping everyone in their tracks. It was a weak ward and easy to disassemble without alerting the wizard who created it. Andrill made a slight motion and a woman in her thirties appeared at his side.

"How many lookouts have we crossed?" Andrill asked the woman.

"Seven," she answered, "all neutralized."

They had already killed seven people? Ellyssa never heard a sound, nor had anyone around her given any indication they had known any hostiles were nearby. Yet the only person who appeared the least bit surprised by this information was Ellyssa.

"Ellyssa, we will need to move with a great deal of stealth from here on out," Andrill told her.

They weren't already? Ellyssa gained a newfound respect for these thieves. They obviously honed their skills every bit as much as she did to the point where their abilities were almost magical, to her thinking.

"Stick near to me and do exactly as I tell you."

Ellyssa nodded and moved as quietly as she could. Andrill directed her toward shadows looking no different to her from any other stretch of road or walkway. He pointed to where she should step and how to bend her body to conform to whatever they were currently using for concealment.

They stopped before reaching the end of the street, which opened in front of a long, stone and wrought-iron wall. Ellyssa stretched her probing magic out across the street and lightly brushed against the ward surrounding the entire complex.

"The wall is warded," she informed the thief leader.

"Can you take it down from here?"

Ellyssa swung her head from side to side. "I'll have to get closer, preferably right up against the wall."

Andrill gestured with his left hand and several thieves disappeared behind them. A moment later, Ellyssa heard the soft twang of a crossbow, padded to be especially quiet, from the roof of the building next to her. Three more muffled shots followed the first. Andrill then motioned for her to proceed to the wall, guiding her with a hand on her back.

Ellyssa stopped a few feet from the wall and used her magic to get a closer look at the ward. She chewed her lip as her magic revealed a ward significantly more complex than the first. She followed the strands comprising the weave of the spell with her mind before attempting to unravel it. It was extraordinarily difficult, like choosing a single thread in a tapestry, following it across the entire weave, and removing just that thread without disturbing any of the others.

Minutes passed and Ellyssa could feel Andrill's mounting anxiety. Only the shadow of the wall they crouched near provided any sort of concealment, and another guard could happen upon the ones killed a few minutes ago and raise the alarm.

Ellyssa pulled free one last thread and announced her success. "Got it."

"Does the wizard know you have disabled it?" Andrill asked.

"I don't think so, not unless he deliberately checks on it. Now what?"

"We get over the wall and hope there are no more of these damn things," Andrill said.

The rest of the thieves scurried across the street and pressed against the stone wall. Small grappling hooks trailing rope the same color as the stone arced over and attached to the wrought-iron spearheads. Men and women in dark clothes scaled the ropes and disappeared over the wall as swiftly as Ellyssa could have covered the same distance walking down the sidewalk. And with about as much ease.

Andrill helped Ellyssa up the rope and dropped down beside her on the other side of the wall. Most of their allies had already vanished into the shadows and shrubs, their existence occasionally punctuated by a muffled cry or soft thud of a body striking the ground.

"We are doing excellent so far,' Andrill whispered. "They have been relying on the wizard too much and have gotten lax. Can you feel any more wards?"

Ellyssa sent her magic forward, crawling along the ground and floating through the air, questing and probing with fingers as light as strands of spider silk. She soon discovered the complex wards cast all along the exterior of the mansion and withdrew from her magical inspection.

"As I thought, the entire outside of the house is protected," Ellyssa informed the thieves near her.

"Can you remove it?" Trevor asked.

Ellyssa replayed what she saw of the weaves in her mind. "I don't know. These are the primary defensive wards and are much stronger than the others were. They are as well crafted as any I have ever seen. I suggest we be prepared for discovery."

Trevor looked grim but Andrill gave her a reassuring smile. "We are far closer than we have been before and are in a good position from which to strike. Do your best, and we shall be ready to act, no matter the outcome."

"We need to get closer, but no one must get too near the house," Ellyssa said.

Andrill and Trevor whispered and gestured to their nearest cohorts and waited a few minutes for the affirmative replies of their people. The thief bosses received word that everyone understood and beckoned the assault group forward.

Ellyssa motioned for them to stop about ten feet from the mansion's wall and bent her mind to the task of unraveling the ward. Fresh sweat soon beaded on her brow and ran into her eyes. Ellyssa felt her body fatiguing under the enormous mental exertion she expended on the ward. She began to worry that if the wizard was as adept at fighting as he was at making wards, she could soon be facing a serious challenge.

"Now this is interesting," Rhys said, breaking the silence of the parlor.

Faralynn looked up from the glass of red wine she was enjoying. She looked at the wizard. The once horribly burned side of his face was locked in concentration. "What is that, Rhys?"

"Someone is trying to breach my house wards, as they have already succeeded in doing to the two outer ones."

Faralynn threw back the remains of the glass and stood abruptly. "Who is it?"

Rhys closed his eyes and looked into the ether. "I am not sure. A woman, a young one at that."

"Academy?"

"No, I think not. She shows a definite education, but her technique is not well honed. She almost feels like a hedge wizard, strong but informal and unstructured."

"Can you defeat her?"

"Of course," Rhys scoffed. "She is a child, no matter the evidence of her raw talent."

"I recall you saying something similar in regards to a boy who destroyed both your black tower and your face," the thief responded drolly.

"That was different and you know it," the wizard snapped. "That idiot Shakrill summoned a damn demon and lost control."

Faralynn thought for moment. "It must be that imbecile Andrill. It seems he found himself a wizard and thinks to unseat me. You say the wizard is young?"

"She appears to be, possibly only just out of girlhood."

"The arrogant fool probably latched onto the first person he found with talent and thinks he can challenge me. Come, Rhys, let us go take care of Andrill and his child wizard."

Rhys followed in Faralynn's angry wake as she shouted the alarm. All through the mansion, thieves relayed the warning and grabbed up their weapons.

"Bloody hell!" Ellyssa cursed, standing up. "I've been made. Stand back!"

The two guild bosses took several steps back, each removed a copper tube from their pocket, and pulled an attached cord dangling from one end. A bright orb of light streaked out of each of them and rocketed over a hundred feet in the air. Seconds later, several more balls of fire dotted the skies over the city.

Ellyssa drew in the Source and hurled it against the stone and stucco wall before her. The barrier shattered and blasted chunks of stone into the interior of the house, striking down several thieves who were already racing to the defensive. Dark shapes erupted from the shadows and poured through the breach, many leading with the twang of crossbows before pulling blades and diving headlong into the brutal melee.

By the time Ellyssa and Andrill pushed their way through the breach, the spacious ballroom beyond was a press of flashing, thrusting and slashing steel, and twisting bodies. Ellyssa briefly wondered how the combatants could tell friend from foe. Fortunately, that was little of her concern. Her job was to find the wizard and remove him from the battle.

Ellyssa had to wait only a moment for the wizard to appear. A slight tingling on the back of her neck was the only warning she got before the entire length of wall behind her and Andrill erupted into flames. Ellyssa managed to raise a protective shield an instant before the fire washed over her and the guild boss. Several thieves nearby were not as fortunate. Stepping clear of the flames and pulling Andrill along with her, Ellyssa dropped her shield and extinguished the flames trying to seal the breach in the wall.

"Up there!" Andrill shouted, pointing to a balcony on the second floor.

Ellyssa responded by launching a fat ball of fire from her hands that exploded in the alcove where the wizard had been standing. Ellyssa knew her strike had missed and looked around furtively for the wizard to reappear. Knowing the wizard had simply leapt away, she raked lightning along the second floor, sending chunks of stone and plaster raining down onto the ground floor and destroying an entire length of wall.

"You need to get that little witch out of here before she brings the entire building down on top of all of our heads!" Faralynn shouted at Rhys as they both sought cover around an upstairs corner.

"Are you all right to defend against Andrill's men on your own?" Rhys asked.

"Yes, just break their momentum and I can lead them through the tunnels below and bleed them out."

Rhys nodded and emerged at the edge of the gaping hole that had once been a wall. A dozen luminous orbs materialized in a line near the room's ceiling and streaked down into the melee below. It was not precisely a surgical strike, but most of those brought down by the magical assault were enemy.

Ellyssa spotted the wizard just as he unleashed his magic. She sent a stream of fiery orbs lancing back at him, but Rhys simply stepped off the ledge and vanished. Ellyssa knew he must have used a gate and looked frantically for him to reappear. Once again, the wizard did not keep her waiting.

Andrill shoved Ellyssa to the side and dove away in the opposite direction just as a green ray of light with the circumference of a large melon shot between them. The deadly beam burned through half a dozen fighters and several walls beyond them. Ellyssa rolled to her feet and spotted the wizard outside where he had gated in behind them.

"This is what you have been waiting for. Go get him," Andrill told her.

Ellyssa sprinted through the huge fissure in the wall as streaks of arcane power lanced from her hands out into the darkness. She did not expect to hit the wizard, only to keep him moving and on the defensive long enough for her to get clear of the building and outside.

Anticipating her foe's tactics, Ellyssa ripped open a gate and dove through just as she cleared the hole in the wall and emerged near the stone and wrought-iron fence surrounding the mansion.

A ball of fire exploded right where she would have emerged had she not leapt through her magical gate at the last instant. The wizard's fireball illuminated a massive swath of the grounds and revealed his position. Ellyssa released another powerful arc of lightning and shattered the tree behind Rhys.

Rhys saw the spell coming and dove aside, using his magic to help his legs launch him nearly thirty feet in a single leap. The wizard had another spell on his lips even as his feet touched the ground. Rhys spun toward the girl and curled his right hand into an upward grasping claw.

The soil beneath Ellyssa's feet began churning as if something enormous were burrowing its way out to devour her. She leapt away, but the ground burst beneath her in a spray of dark soil and detritus and wrapped around her body. The earthen fist raised her high off the ground. Wind blew her hair back as the hand tried to dash her against the manicured lawn.

Thinking fast, Ellyssa wrenched open another gate directly below her. Her and the fist vanished into the gate's entrance and spilled out into the street just beyond the mansion's surrounding wall. Severed from its magical point of origin, the earthen hand crumbled back into an inanimate pile of dirt, stones, and grass.

Reaching down and grabbing a double handful of small rocks, Ellyssa sent them streaking skyward. The rocks burst into flame and plummeted back down like small meteors, filling the majority of the front lawn with dozens of man-sized craters.

Ellyssa could not see the wizard past the wall, the devastation her spell had wrought, or if she had managed to strike him with one of the meteors. She sincerely doubted it and was not about to gamble her life by sitting still. She darted into the alley across the street just as a massive section of the wall next to her exploded.

Rhys was impressed with the girl's talent and imagination. She fought much more like a Black Tower wizard than any bookish Academy mage he had ever met. There was something in her determination and ferocity that reminded him of the way the sorcerer had fought in the days prior to that terrifying night when the demon brought the tower down.

Several orange streaks shooting up over the stone wall interrupted his recollections. Knowing what was coming, Rhys took off at a run as the world began exploding around him. He poured power into his magical shield and unconsciously raised an arm to protect his eyes from the dirt and rock blasting up from the ground. It felt as if the fusillade would never end despite its relative brevity. The moment the last meteor struck, Rhys spun toward the wall where he had seen the spell originate and hurled a massive sphere of pure force against it.

With any luck, the bricks of the wall had crushed the girl's skull, but he was not going to take any chances. She had already proven herself more than competent and fully capable of killing him. Rhys ran to the wall and jogged next to it until he was able to peek through the destroyed section. He snapped his head back as a stream of arcane bolts smashed into the wall and streaked past his face.

"You are very talented for one so young," Rhys shouted into the darkness. "There is no need for us to destroy each other."

Rhys made a slit in the air, passed through parallel dimensions, and stepped onto a roof overlooking the alley. A quiet incantation and a complex waving of his hands filled the alley with fire from one end to the other and high enough to force him to take a step back to avoid the flames.

"Are you still with me, little mage? I hope you didn't get singed."

Ellyssa sprinted toward the far end of the alley and emerged onto the street just as flames filled the narrow confines.

"The thieves are a nation unto themselves and they needed a leader, a queen. Faralynn brought order to a chaotic, disorganized society. We can use a girl of your strength and intelligence. You do not have to die tonight."

Rhys felt a slight tremor in the roof beneath his feet and leapt the span between buildings just as the entire surface collapsed into the interior of the structure. A billowing cloud of dust filled the air behind him as he sprinted to another nearby building.

"What did Andrill offer you, gold and sweet words? It is Andrill, is it not? I thought I saw him in that row within the mansion. Do not let his silver tongue fool you, girl. The man is every bit the thief, liar, and cutthroat Faralynn is."

Ellyssa tried to ignore the wizard's words except to discern his location, but still her mind weighed them. Andrill was a thief and had drugged her. He had made promises she had no way of ensuring he kept. She did not know if he even could keep them. Everything was based purely on trust, trust in a man she had only just met, a man who built his entire existence on deception and double-talk.

Whatever, she had made her choice and chosen her side. Andrill would give her what she wanted or he would pay. Ellyssa would uphold her end of the bargain and trust Andrill did the same. She would get Captain Jake, even if it meant making a deal with the dark goddess herself.

Ellyssa tracked the voice and responded with a punishing hailstorm that punched fist-sized holes through the roof and shattered against the stone cobbles of the streets. She saw the wizard leap from the building and run down another street, chunks of ice fragmenting and sizzling against his ward.

Ellyssa clung to the shadows next to the buildings and worked her way around toward the area where she saw the wizard disappear. She used her magic to pull the shadows in tighter and move with her. The streets were empty, partly because of the hour, but mainly from the ungodly destruction everyone within a quarter mile could feel or hear being wrought, and no one wanted to be caught up in that.

She spotted the wizard running out of the alley and racing toward another side street. Ellyssa broke from her concealment and sprinted after him, launching a barrage of arcane bolts. One of the bolts tore right through the man's body, but the only discernible effect was a large, smoking hole on the side of the building next to him.

Ellyssa knew what was happening and leapt with all her might, even using the Source to help propel her up and away. Her quick-thinking saved her life, but only just. A massive explosion rocked the entire block and blasted a hole spanning the entire width of the street all the way down to the sewers below.

The concussive blast struck Ellyssa in mid-leap and sent her crashing into the side of a nearby building. Her wards flared before shattering under the power of the blast and her body took the full brunt of her collision with the wall.

Ellyssa tried to get her feet beneath her and make a stand, but her mind reeled and her muscles refused to obey. She mentally cursed herself for falling for the same kind of illusion she herself had used several times in the past. Rhys stepped out of the side street and casually sauntered toward her, even pausing to peer into the black hole to admire the destruction of his handiwork.

"I would offer you a chance to live, but I can see by the look on your face you would not accept it, or if you did, I would have to watch my back for the rest of my probably short life. So I think it best for everyone, except you of course, that I kill you now."

The battle raged through the mansion as the opposing sides launched wave after wave of attacks. Andrill's people had the momentum and steadily repelled the attempts to push them back. Deeper into the house they fought, dodging surprise attacks, hurled daggers, and volleys of crossbow bolts.

Faralynn grabbed one of her lieutenants. "Pull everyone back and make toward the catacombs. We'll bleed them to death in the tunnels!"

The thief boss released her officer who darted down the halls, spreading word to make a tactical retreat. Faralynn hated to give up the house, but Andrill's people had penetrated too far in before she could form a cohesive defense. She had sent runners to several other houses, but none had yet come to the rescue. She figured Andrill and probably a few others displeased with the new hierarchy were at this moment launching separate attacks against those as well.

It was a bold move, but destined to fail. She was too well established and had more people. This battle would boil down to a war of maneuvering and attrition. Andrill and whatever fools he had convinced to gamble away their existence could not contend. All Faralynn needed to do was withdraw then strike from a position of strength.

Faralynn's people began to conglomerate around her as they fought their way into the basement and down into the catacombs below. As soon as Faralynn and her defenders made it to the dark maze of tunnels, they broke off to harry the attackers and make them pay in blood for every inch of ground they gained.

Andrill saw that Faralynn was making a concerted retreat to the lower levels of the house and called for Trevor and his people to converge on his position. After regrouping his people, Andrill led his thieves in an assault against those defending the stairs leading down. The stairwell filled with the hissing of crossbow bolts, forcing him and his attackers back.

Andrill's soldiers lobbed flash bombs made from ceramic spheres packed with some expensive alchemic powders down the stairs. The flash bombs burst with a concussive force and spray of ceramic shards, disorienting and injuring the thieves defending the stairs.

The attackers charged down the steps and into the basement, dispatching the thieves guarding their leader's retreat. The basement was huge and spanned nearly the length and width of the entire mansion above. It took several minutes to locate the hidden passage leading to the tunnels beneath the city.

Crossbows loosed from within the dark passageway took down the first men through the door. Flash bombs launched from slings and crossbow quarrels replied in kind, allowing them to charge into the dank aqueducts and meet Faralynn's people with steel.

Andrill's forces gained the tunnels where they were set upon with a series of hit and run strikes. The fighters on Andrill's flanks and rear fell prey to hidden assaults launched from the many labyrinthine side channels.

"Trevor," Andrill called out, "take some of our forces and secure our flanks before they bleed us dry!"

The big guild boss inclined his head once and motioned to several others nearby. Four groups set off down side passages to blunt Faralynn's ambush attacks while Andrill and the bulk of his forces continued down the main tunnel. Andrill and his people crept silently down the central passage along the narrow walkway running along the wall. Murky water of an unknown depth slowly flowed through the center giving off a distinctly unpleasant aroma.

A massive explosion shook the tunnel, causing Andrill to throw himself flat and knocking several thieves into the fetid water. Those on the ledges rescued their comrades from the wastewater.

"What in the abyss was that?" Braxis hissed from behind Andrill.

"My guess would be our fiery young lady," Andrill answered.

Faralynn watched the tunnel collapse ahead of her, burying at least a dozen of her people and sealing off the passage. "Damn it all to the abyss and back! We'll have to backtrack and find a way around this."

"We may run into Andrill's people if he has managed to follow," a lieutenant said.

"Then I will deal with him."

Faralynn led the bulk of her forces back down the blocked tunnel in search of another side passage that would lead to the main aquifer. Within minutes, a runner approached her.

"Faralynn, we spotted lanterns ahead."

"Are there any other passages that will allow us to avoid them?" the guild boss asked.

"No. There is a passage ahead that should take us around the area of the collapse, but we will not reach it before Andrill's people."

"All right, it is time for me to deal with this popinjay once and for all."

Faralynn stormed forward, forcing her people to follow in her furious wake. The guild boss stalked down the dank corridors, her progress lit only by a dim, shielded light. She spotted the wan illumination of a shuttered lamp ahead a few minutes later.

"Andrill, is that you?" she shouted at the dark shapes huddled around the lamp.

"It is. Have you decided to surrender and face the judgment of the houses?" Andrill asked.

"Hardly. The passage ahead has collapsed. We can battle here and cut each other to pieces, or you and I can settle this between ourselves."

Andrill pondered Faralynn's offer. They could battle it out here in a final stand, but it would be a bloody affair with no guarantee of success. Neither could he allow Faralynn and her people to withdraw since she had far greater forces to call upon than he did, which would make resumption of hostilities untenable.

"All right, you and I," Andrill responded, accepting the personal challenge. "Winner allows the loser's people to depart in peace with no promises made after that."

"Agreed."

Both guild bosses began slowly moving toward each other until Andrill suddenly stopped. "Oops, bootlace is untied."

Andrill knelt and grabbed the laces. Braxis' crossbow quarrel passed over his head so close it ruffled Andrill's hair. Faralynn cursed as she spun away and heard one of her men let out a grunt followed by the dull thud of his body striking the ground behind her.

"Always the treacherous snake, Andrill!" the woman shouted.

Andrill looked up from his boot. "Better a live snake than a dead bitch."

Faralynn made to hurl another insult but the blood welling up in her throat cut off her words. She pressed a hand to the minor cut on her hip and looked at the fresh blood on it. Faralynn spit out a gob of blood to curse the man, but the extraordinarily virulent poison had already set in and was rapidly dissolving her organs.

As Faralynn's corpse struck the ground, and before her followers could react, Andrill called out to them. "Think before you choose to throw your lives away for a dead woman. Did you hear the explosion a moment ago? That was the death of your wizard."

Andrill knew it was a bluff, but it was one he was willing to make to prevent more bloodshed—especially his own. "It's time to go back to the old guild ways where an industrious man or woman could rise to be the boss of their own house and not be pressed under the thumb of another. Go back down the passage and we will leave you to determine your own fates. Continue to fight us, and we will seal those same fates here and now."

There were mutterings and more than a few curses issuing from the darkness as the thieves debated a course of action. Valor in defeat won out as the thieves slunk back into the darkness of the passage from which they came. Andrill led his people to the side tunnel Faralynn was trying to gain in hopes of finding a way back to street level.

Ellyssa lay on the ground, pressed against the building, and watched as the wizard prepared a spell to snuff out the pathetic candle of her existence. There was little she could do to prevent it, no spell she could conjure strong enough to defeat the ward she could see glimmering like a soap bubble around his body before he unleashed arcane fury upon her.

Still, she refused to lie back and let death take her without fighting until the last breath left her body forever. Ellyssa reached into her jacket and pulled out one of the darts she had favored since hunting rats as a punishment when she was a little girl. She flicked the dart with expert aim and used a trickle of the Source to help speed its way despite knowing the futility of the gesture.

Rhys watched the dart leave her hand and smirked, knowing the pathetic thing would never breach his ward. Ellyssa watched as her dart seemed to fly as if it were taking a languid swim through water. The wizard made the final form of his weave and was about to unleash his spell when something appeared to distract him.

The mage turned his head with a look of surprise and confusion on his face. Ellyssa's dart slipped through the ward and stuck him in the side of his neck. Rhys grabbed the projectile and tore it from his flesh, eliciting a spray of blood from the severed artery. He collapsed before his confusion ever resolved itself into understanding the cause of his death.

Ellyssa did not attempt to move from where she lay. Her body demanded she stay still while her mind was engaged in trying to understand what had happened. Something had distracted the wizard enough to cause his ward to falter, but she had seen nothing or no one that could have done it. Wards required very little concentration to maintain. Unless something occurred to weaken it, her dart should never have been able to breach it.

She spotted movement at the massive crater in the street and tried to get on her feet as several dark shapes crawled out of it like roaches through a crack in the kitchen floor.

Andrill's voice hissed through the night like a passing arrow. "Ellyssa, is that you?"

Ellyssa waved and slumped back down against the wall. The figures ran toward her in a crouch born of habit. She recognized Andrill and Braxis first, then the wide face of Trevor as they came near.

"Looks like you got him good," Andrill remarked as he stepped past Rhys's body.

"Did you help?" Ellyssa asked shakily.

Andrill cocked his head to the side. "Help how? No, we just got here. Why do you ask?"

Ellyssa raised her arm for help getting up. "No reason," she said as Andrill pulled her to her feet.

"We need to clear off the streets. It will take some time for the power vacuum to gain equilibrium again. We can wait out the fighting in my hideout. The streets are not going to be safe for a few days."

Ellyssa could already see several orange halos dotting the sky, and the bitter smoke of burning wood assailed her senses. Andrill led her and his group of thieves one way while Trevor took another group in a separate direction. After traversing several blocks, Andrill decided it was best to travel the rest of the way underground. Whether it was because of the battles raging above, or he did not want her to see any street accesses near his lair, she did not know.

The smell of smoke lost the battle for supremacy to the fetid water of the sewers. Luckily, there were walkways built into the tunnels that kept them from having to slog through the waste. Ellyssa decided this would be a bad place to be during heavy rains as she figured the water level could easily rise high enough to drown the walkways and anyone unfortunate enough to find themselves in the dank waterways.

After what felt like an eternity of navigating the gloomy, rank tunnels, they stopped at what appeared to be a dead end. One of the thieves felt around the solid wall and Ellyssa heard a click. A section of the wall swung open and Andrill guided Ellyssa inside. Just as she crossed the threshold, she felt something sting her on the back of her neck. Ellyssa slapped at the irritant and pulled out a tiny dart.

Ellyssa felt a tingling rapidly spreading down her neck and across her back. Without hesitation, she reached into the small pocket inside her jacket and pulled out a steel vial filled with the antivenom she had cooked up in case of such treachery. She was exhausted, but with her anger at Andrill's betrayal fueling her magic, Ellyssa was certain she had more than enough strength to make him and his thieves pay dearly.

She flipped the cork out with her thumb, but before she could bring the contents to her lips, a powerful force slammed into her chest and crushed her against the wall. The stone melted, ran over her outflung hands and arms, and solidified. Four figures covered in black cloaks stepped out of the darkness.

"Very good, Andrill," Inquisitor Fennrick said. "I hope you were able to achieve your goals as well, not that I honestly care."

"Faralynn and her wizard are dead," Andrill replied flatly.

"Good for you. Do you have the other half of our arrangement?"

Andrill made a beckoning motion with his left hand and a thief stepped forward with a leather satchel. Andrill took the bag and passed it to the wizard. Ellyssa entered a new state of rage when she saw Fennrick slip her precious book out of the leather sleeve.

A thousand hateful things sprang to her mind and she was about to unleash them all upon Fennrick and Andrill. She looked at the thief's face, saw the scrapes and bruises that were not nearly as fresh as those from tonight's battle, and recalled his earlier words: *Some people are reluctant to give information or provide assistance, but everyone has their breaking point.*

Ellyssa realized the thief had not betrayed her willingly, but it was small comfort when she saw the codex in Fennrick's grasp. She was not even sure if it was enough for her to spare the thief's life if she managed to escape yet another capture. Andrill met her eyes and apparently read her thoughts.

"It may come as little comfort, but I will make good on my promise. I will give you Captain Jake, for whatever good it may do you wherever it is they are taking you."

"How nice," Fennrick drolled. "I see the honorable thief still keeps his word, whenever it is not too inconvenient to do so."

Andrill turned his eyes on the inquisitor. "Fennrick, you caught me in a time of weakness, but that state is not to be for much longer. I do not recommend you ever step foot in Southport again."

Fennrick responded with a smirk and stepped toward his captive. Extending a finger, he touched its tip to Ellyssa's forehead and spoke a word of magic. Ellyssa's head jerked back and the world fell into blackness.

CHAPTER 16

Azerick stood upon a parapet watching the chaos unfold all around him. Drak'kar's horde reached his citadel in what he could vaguely comprehend as about three days ago. His own demonic minions created a barrier on the ground thousands deep, but it was slowly eroding away like sand under the relentless pounding of ocean waves.

The cacophonic sound was as unimaginable as it was indescribable. Tens of thousands of demons clashed and shrieked as they clawed, bit, and tore each other to pieces. Flying demons wheeled in an aerial combat, clawing, slashing, and hurling magic and stones at each other as well as those on the ground.

Whenever a flyer managed to break through the defenders, it threw itself against the fortress's powerful wards, striking it like a bird flying into a gigantic window. The demons clawed and unleashed magic at the invisible barrier until attacked by defenders or Azerick incinerated them with his magic. Occasionally, Azerick launched powerful arcane spells into the masses of demons below, but it was as effective as swatting a plague of locusts with a broom.

Azerick could see the gigantic demon lord in the midst of the battle from his vantage point, tearing apart any lesser creature near him and unleashing devastating magic that slew his enemies by the score. Azerick struck at Drak'kar a few times, but the distance was too great and Drak'kar's defenses were too strong to do any good.

Never has anyone assaulted my fortress before, Klaraxis seethed. *Your ineptitude has brought us ruin.*

"Drak'kar will breach the wards?" Azerick asked.

Eventually, unless you allow me control so I can bring my full might to bear. I am strongest here in my seat of power and can yet turn the tide of this battle.

"That will never happen, demon."

Then you condemn us all.

Drak'kar moved back from the front lines of the battle, bored with slaughtering the lesser creatures who foolishly interposed themselves between him and his greatest desire. The demon lord longed to get his claws into Klaraxis's black flesh, no matter who was controlling the body. He would ascend to his rightful place as master of the Fifth Circle, the greatest of all demon lords. He spotted the mutilated succubus, pushed past his minions, and approached her.

Feh'lan's wing had mostly grown back, but she was not yet ready for flight. The constant reminder of her ultimate humiliation and violation served to fuel her hatred and thirst for vengeance.

Feh'lan spotted the hulking and temperamental demon lord striding toward her and bowed low. "My Prince, your battle goes well."

"My battle goes far too slowly! Klaraxis's defenses are stronger than I had anticipated."

"You will breach them and then destroy Klaraxis. None shall deny you what is rightfully yours."

"The delay is interminable. Search that pathetic harpy brain of yours and find me a way in," Drak'kar snapped. "Klaraxis is not as helpless as I thought, and it will do me no good to exhaust myself before confronting him."

Feh'lan had spent a great deal of time in the citadel and searched her memories for anything that would help Drak'kar. She had thrown in her lot with him, and her survival necessitated his victory.

"My Prince, if you could reach the fortress's barrier you could weaken a small portion of it enough to get inside," Feh'lan offered.

"I could, but there are as yet a sea of vermin in my path, and I do not wish to have them nibbling at my ankles as I do so."

"Could we not burrow beneath the surface?" Feh'lan suggested. "We could come out at the wailing pits deep beneath the citadel. There you could take your time creating your breach. By the time Klaraxis or the human detect your presence, you and your chosen forces will be inside."

"Yes." Drak'kar scratched his chin as he considered her idea. "Your plan has merit. I will need to create a screen so we can work undetected."

Drak'kar summoned three enormous demons with wide, squat bodies supported on four legs, each bearing long, diamond-hard claws designed to cut through stone as easily as a sharp knife through soft cheese. Bony plates covered the demons' backs, each one punctuated with a knobby spike.

The demon lord conjured a large vortex of swirling dust, masking the activity of the huge diggers as they began excavating. Drak'kar enlisted a small army of demons to haul away the loose dirt and rubble kicked back by the burrowing behemoths. Just an hour after they started, the diggers had already managed to create an impressive tunnel. It would take little time for them to dig beneath the battle raging above and reach the lower levels of the citadel.

It was a good thing Azerick no longer needed sleep, because the racket outside would never have permitted it. As it was, it was all he could do to focus his attention on the books in front of him. Finding himself largely useless to the fight raging outside, Azerick spent time going back through the tomes and scrolls Klaraxis possessed in hopes of uncovering something he had missed.

Again, you spend hours pointlessly toiling over these useless books as if you expect to find the answers to all your problems. You have but one solution: allow me to take control and destroy Drak'kar.

"I had a book once that was very good at answering nearly all my questions," Azerick replied distractedly as he turned another page.

Ah yes, the Codex Arcana. I do not believe even you understood the full import of what you possessed, Klaraxis said with a chuckle. There may have been an answer to your dilemma in it, but you do not have it now, and nothing I possess comes close to containing what you seek.

The sound of Skulk's fluttering wings preceded the small demon's entrance. Azerick had forbidden the demon from simply popping in and out since it took hours for the smell to dissipate due to this realm's complete lack of fresh air to clear out the sulfurous stench.

"Glorious Master," Skulk said obsequiously, "there are strange happenings on the battlefield."

Azerick looked up from his book. "What kind of strange happenings?"

"Skulk does not know, Great Master."

Azerick stood with a sigh and walked briskly down the dark halls of his fortress. There were several thousand demons inside, anxiously maintaining vigilance in case the enemy breached the walls. Despite the numbers, the vastness of the structure prevented the feeling of overcrowding.

He climbed the stairs of one of the primary towers and looked out across the battlefield from the vantage point of the parapet.

"What is he up to?" Azerick asked semi-rhetorically as he stared at the large dust cloud billowing in the distance.

I could not guess, but I know it is something deliberate and foreboding, Klaraxis answered.

Azerick summoned his magic and attempted to cast his sight into the cloud, but Drak'kar's magic would not allow him to spy on whatever nefarious plot he was enacting. Using one of Klaraxis's demonic powers, Azerick grabbed the sight of a nearby succubus and directed her to fly toward the cloud, but before she could do more than brush the edge, an arcane bolt struck her down and demons tore her body to shreds. Azerick instantly withdrew, not wanting to share in the pain of the creature's demise. Whatever plot Drak'kar was hatching, the demon lord was ensuring it remained a secret.

"Skulk!" Azerick shouted.

The little demog instantly appeared in a rotten-egg scented puff of yellow smoke. Azerick let it go since they were outside and his summons required some urgency.

"Yes, Great One," Skulk intoned.

"Send word to everyone inside to be on alert. I don't know what Drak'kar is up to, but I have a feeling we will soon find out."

Drak'kar watched as a steady stream of demons carted out armloads of dirt and rock torn loose by the burrowing beldgar demons. Hour after meaningless hour, demons excavated and cleared the tunnel, clawing inexorably closer to their goal. Several times, Drak'kar sensed the human who dominated his arch-foe trying to spy on his operation. The human was clumsy, and it was easy to drive him away or destroy his spies.

"Great Prince, we are beneath the citadel and near the wall of the wailing pits," a balrog demon said as he dumped an armload of dirt.

"Excellent. Lead a contingent in after me," Drak'kar ordered, then entered the tunnel.

The beldgar demons were excellent diggers and the tunnel ran straight and true at a downward slope until leveling out about thirty feet below the surface. There it continued for nearly a mile. The diameter of the tunnel was more than sufficient to accommodate Drak'kar's huge form, until it ended at an earthen wall near the outermost edge of the fortress above.

Drak'kar pushed past scores of demons already crowding the far end of the passage. He spotted a ranking succubus near the wall standing between the two beldgar. The succubus bowed deeply as Drak'kar stepped near.

"My Lord Drak'kar, we are as close as we dare go while the citadel's wards are intact," the demon reported.

"How close are we to the interior?" the demon lord asked.

"Just over a hundred feet of earth separates us from one of the wailing pits. From there, we will have full access to the interior of the citadel proper," the succubus answered, smiling eagerly.

"Very well, have the beldgar be at the ready. I do not know if I can pierce Klaraxis's wards without his knowing, so they will need to be ready to tear through the last of the physical impediment with great haste."

"They await your command, My Prince."

Drak'kar knelt and bent his focus outward, gently probing the massive, ancient wards. As he expected, they were supremely formidable. Klaraxis was a master of magic, even more so than he was, and the demon lord had spent an eon building and reinforcing the wards enveloping his citadel.

Drak'kar turned to the succubus standing a respectful distance behind him. "Krasha, I will require assistance. Bring me the mutilated traitor and her cohorts."

"At once, My Prince," Krasha replied with a bow.

Krasha returned several minutes later with Feh'lan and her sisters following dutifully behind her. Feh'lan stepped slightly ahead of the others and all knelt before the powerful Drak'kar.

"Feh'lan," Drak'kar rumbled, "your assistance has provided me with a great opportunity, but I must ask yet again for your aid."

"I am yours to command, My Lord," the succubus intoned obediently. "Anything I can do to see you to your rightful place I put at your disposal."

Drak'kar's spreading smile held not a hint of amusement. "I am glad you feel that way."

Faster than the eye could track, Drak'kar reached out with his four powerful arms, gripped the succubus tightly, and promptly twisted her head all the way around. The sickening crack of bone echoed down the passageway and Feh'lan's sisters shrieked in terror and outrage. Before they could attempt to flee, several demons leapt upon them and pinned them to the ground.

Still grasping Feh'lan's corpse in two of his hands, the demon lord plunged a claw into her body and began slinging her black blood across the walls of the cavern. To the untrained eye, the ropy spatters looked like nothing more than random gore, but they began to form a pattern and created a complex weave.

Succubi were amongst the more magically gifted of the lesser demons, and their blood provided additional strength to the arcane sigil. The fact these creatures were familiar with the fortress and frequently passed through its powerful wards made them the optimal agents to bring the magical defenses down. Even so, it would take a highly complex sigil and a lot of blood. It was fortunate Drak'kar had such assets at hand.

Despite the seemingly haphazard way Drak'kar slung the viscous blood on the wall, it was a painstaking activity and the immeasurable minutes rolled into hours. The death of another succubus marked each passing segment of time with the accuracy of a well-made clock. Drak'kar eventually stepped back to admire his work and declared it suitable.

He looked at the last remaining succubus. "It would appear I have no need of your blood."

The demon felt a small measure of relief intersperse with the stark terror she had undergone for the past several hours.

"However," Drak'kar continued, "you may yet be of use." He turned to the minions holding the succubus. "Take her and these corpses and make them an example of how I tolerate betrayal."

Drak'kar was already too engrossed in the next stage of his work to hear the terror-driven pleadings as the succubus was led out of the tunnel to meet her fate. The demon lord returned his focus on the gruesome sigils painted on every surface around him. The creation of the runes was the easy part. Now he would have to use all his skill to breach the wards without alerting Klaraxis before he was ready.

Even with the sigil he created, the task of penetrating the citadel's wards was a monumental challenge. Klaraxis was more adept at magic than he was, and it took all his focus and power just to make the attempt. Demons brought shades to Drak'kar for him to consume as the strain left him famished and in need of sustenance.

Only the iron discipline Drak'kar employed in his fighting skills allowed him to make progress and maintain the focus he needed. He sensed his resolve was slowly but steadily defeating the fortress's defenses as he chipped away at the arcane barrier's intangible existence.

Drak'kar finally felt the wards surrender their vigilance and stepped back to collect himself. He commanded another shade be brought, which he consumed, and felt its life force replenish him.

"It is done," Drak'kar proclaimed. "Have the beldgar complete the excavation and ensure the soldiers are prepared to infiltrate the fortress."

"Your will be done, Great Master," the succubus answered.

Minutes later, Drak'kar's minions informed him only a thin shell of stone stood between them and the wailing pits. The demon lord commanded his forces to gather behind him as he approached the final, feeble barrier standing between him and his nemesis. Drak'kar used his magic to smash through the rock and stepped into the wailing pits. Shades, whose sole existence was to feed their soul energy into the black stones of the citadel, moaned as the invading demons tore into them.

Azerick looked up from his book as a chill ran through him. "Something is wrong."

Klaraxis sent his limited presence into the stone of his fortress. *Our enemy has infiltrated my fortress! They come from the wailing pits and will soon reach the upper levels.*

With a deep, shuddering breath, Azerick adopted Klaraxis's powerful form and set out to do battle.

Drak'kar sent his minions to wreak havoc inside the halls of the citadel. He sought a very specific target and ignored the defending demons, allowing his small army to deal with the defenders unless they got in his way. He could sense Klaraxis's presence still within the citadel's ebony confines. It was only a matter of time before he tracked his archrival down and destroyed him.

The demon lord gleefully tore apart any demon foolish enough to attack him or unlucky enough to simply come within his view. Drak'kar let the corpse of an unfortunate balrog slip from his grasp as he felt Klaraxis's presence grow nearer. The continued distraction of these insects began to wear on Drak'kar's patience. He cast his eyes and senses about in an effort to locate his nemesis.

The wall next to him exploded as Klaraxis scanned the dim hallway, sending him, along with several tons of cut and shattered stone, crashing through the opposite wall. Drak'kar leapt to his feet and hurled a thousand-pound block of stone back through the gaping hole in both walls. Azerick ripped a hole through the dimensions, stepped through, and landed a solid kick into Drak'kar's back, sending the hulking demon on a trajectory almost identical to his thrown stone block.

Azerick charged through the crumbling apertures after Drak'kar and searched the room for his foe. Drak'kar dropped from the shadows of the high ceiling and landed heavily onto Azerick's back. Azerick tried to throw the demon off as the weight made his knees buckle, but he felt himself lifted in the air before he could plant his feet.

Drak'kar hoisted Azerick from the ground with his two upper arms and mercilessly pounded his body with a series of blows from his lower ones. The blows landed so fast it was like a solid, agonizing pulse. The demon prince held Azerick at arm's length, raised a powerful leg, and kicked him in the chest, enlarging the hole in the wall as his body plowed through the stone.

"Yes, fight me, weakling!" Drak'kar roared gleefully as he stepped through the wall after Azerick.

Azerick did not even bother to stand before retaliating. Sending his arcane power through the stones of the citadel, he conjured a pillar of stone beneath Drak'kar and slammed him into the ceiling. Another pillar of stone crushed the demon lord back into the floor, shattering the rock into rubble and casting out a spiderweb of cracks beneath him.

Drak'kar stood up, chuckling. "That hurt, gloriously. I might grant you a quick death after all."

"If you liked that, then you'll really enjoy this," Azerick replied.

The entire section of wall at the end of the passageway raced down the hall with the speed of an arrow. Wind, created by the displacement of the air filling the hall struck the sorcerer in the face as Drak'kar vanished from sight, carried away by the speeding section of stone. The room trembled when the wall and its demonic cargo abruptly reached the end of the corridor with a deafening crash.

Azerick stepped into the corridor and held his breath against the obscuring, choking dust as it slowly settled to the floor. Even his demonic eyes struggled to pierce the grey haze veiling the passage. Azerick had only a fraction of a second's warning when he spotted the slightly darker shape of a hurled block of stone before it struck him in the chest, knocking him back over a dozen feet.

He barely returned to a crouch before a crimson beam of arcane power sent him reeling farther down the hallway. Drak'kar burst out of the diminishing dust cloud and landed a solid punch to Azerick's head at a dead sprint. Azerick was airborne once again until the distant wall arrested his brief flight.

Drak'kar launched himself at Azerick before he could fully recover, planting both feet into his chest and sending the sorcerer the rest of the way through the already damaged wall. The Fourth Circle demon was in a fighting frenzy now and wasted no time on mocking words or glib retorts.

Drak'kar waded through the rubble, grabbed up Azerick by his arm and leg near the hip and shoulder, and began mercilessly bashing him into the floor until the stone yielded and crumbled beneath him. The sudden lack of resistance caused Drak'kar to fumble his grip and Azerick fell through the void to land heavily onto the floor of the chamber below.

Azerick did not pause to give his enemy another chance to brutalize him. He fought past the pain and did his best to shake off the effect of his stunned senses as he rolled to his feet and made a stumbling run for the room's exit. He had barely made it out of the room when the ceiling caved in on top of him, the huge stone blocks pummeling him onto the floor.

Drak'kar leapt through the newest hole in Klaraxis's citadel and pulled Azerick from the rubble by the throat. The demon lord smashed him against the wall several times before flinging him back into the room. He reached into the chamber with invisible hands of magic, grasped the edges of the hole in the ceiling, and tore down another large section of the floor above.

Azerick reeled under the pummeling of falling stone as it threatened to bury him. Seeing his foe stunned, Drak'kar paused to allow himself a gloating chortle as he felt his ultimate victory near at hand.

You must give me control! Klaraxis screamed inside Azerick's head.

Azerick fought to clear the cobwebs from his mind. "No! I will not give in to you! I will not become your slave!"

Then you doom us both! Will you give in to death? Are you so willing to admit defeat and accept an end to everything? If you do not give me control, you are surrendering to Drak'kar and giving up everything you are or will ever be.

Azerick wanted to deny the demon, wanted to convince himself it was just another ploy of Klaraxis to assert his dominance over this body, but the demon was right. Azerick had no problem accepting death. What he could not accept was giving up and letting it take him without knowing he did *everything* he could to deny it.

To simply give up was anathema to him and a far worse fate than death could bring. Even if Klaraxis took control, Azerick knew the demon could not banish his existence, just as Azerick could not banish the demon. As long as he existed, he could fight. If he could fight, he could one day win again.

"All right, demon. I give you this body, but know I will fight you for it every minute for the remainder of our shared existence."

Azerick released his mental grip on their body and Klaraxis practically hurled him into the recesses of his mind as he leapt to the fore with a scream of primal fury and exultation. Klaraxis's clawed fingers dug into the black stone and drank in the power stored there over the centuries by the shades in the wailing pits. Klaraxis stood upon his powerful ebony legs and the blocks of stone rose with him.

"Oh good, there is still some fight left in you, pathetic little human parasite." Drak'kar smiled.

Klaraxis grinned evilly. "Not human, not anymore and never again."

Drak'kar took a step back as he realized his victory was no longer near at hand. Klaraxis was the most powerful demon in the abyss by a significant margin. Only the human's weakness had convinced him to challenge his rival. However, not all was lost. Klaraxis had taken a thrashing, and he was nowhere near his full strength despite his return. Even as Drak'kar took a brutal beating from the stones Klaraxis sent hurling at him, he felt they were equal at the least, and Drak'kar was in far better shape.

The Fourth Circle demon lord climbed to his feet and willed bone-like swords to grow from each of his forearms. He tensed his muscles, ready to hurl himself at Klaraxis and engage him in a decisive melee. Before Drak'kar could close the distance, a black figure detached itself from the shadows and plunged a shadowy blade into Klaraxis's lower back.

Klaraxis released a roar as an indescribable pain lanced through his back. The ethereal blade cut not with the pain of steel but with the agony of rage, remorse, betrayal, and hatred. It was a thing of emotion and it cut deeper than any steel could.

The Rook plunged his shadow blade into the demon's back as he clung to him like a wasp, twisting his black stinger into the sorcerer's flesh. The assassin allowed the warmth of success to wash through him as his blade finally found its target.

Satisfaction filled the Rook as he redeemed himself for his greatest and only failure. Complacency born of overconfidence had allowed a lowly goblin to kill him. The humiliation added another layer to his failure so unbearable it followed him even into the afterlife. His mission accomplished, his failure redeemed, he could find peace even in this hellish place.

Without warning, a strange silver beam shot through the hole in the ceiling. It appeared to continue upward through the highest reaches of the fortress and into the sky. A shimmering rainbow limned the silver ray that looked and felt far more substantial than simple light.

The Rook and Drak'kar both screamed in rage and denial as their mutual enemy began floating upward. Drak'kar broke into a sprint, desperate to plunge his bone swords into Klaraxis before he could escape. The Rook refused to surrender his prey and dug the claws of his demonic hand into Klaraxis's black flesh even as he felt himself lifted from the ground and torn apart.

Drak'kar skidded to a stop and roared his outrage as he saw his prey escaping. The enraged demon spun on the figure emerging from the shadows.

"You did this!" the demon lord seethed.

"I provided a needed assist," Sharrellan clarified.

"You said he was mine!"

"I said you could challenge him and ascend his position if you were successful, and so you have. I also told you that this little coup of yours threatened to disrupt my plans. Now you have what you want, and I have what I want."

Drak'kar clenched and unclenched his fists—all four of them. "I wanted to destroy him."

"The fates are fickle and uncertain, my dear Drak'kar, you may yet get your chance."

Klaraxis looked down and saw the black-skinned demon clinging to him like a leech as both their bodies stretched far beyond physical reality. Both creatures' torsos stretched beyond the fortress while their legs remained inside it. The pain was unimaginable as the liquid silver pulled them continually upward.

The abyss finally relented its hold, and the two creatures' lower bodies snapped upward to rejoin their uppers, easing some of the torment afflicting them. The beam expanded and Klaraxis and the Rook soared through a silver tube shimmering with a myriad of hues like oil on the surface of water, twisting, rising, plummeting through the dimensions separating the untold number of realms and realities.

A sudden turn and twist sent the Rook flying from Klaraxis's back and careening through the void. With the assassin and his dreadful blade gone, much of the pain still afflicting Klaraxis vanished with him. He found himself unable to focus as his mind fought to comprehend what was happening. It was a battle he was destined to lose. Klaraxis and Azerick both felt their consciousness finally surrender its grip and tear away from their body like a shirt being violently ripped from their back and casually tossed into the corner of the great void.

CHAPTER 17

Ellyssa awoke in a small cell with a solid steel door. A cot, waste bucket, and the sigils marking nearly every inch of every surface were the only things decorating the ten foot by ten foot room. She did not know how long she had been unconscious, but given the generally horrible way her body felt and the incredible emptiness of her stomach, she suspected the time was measured in days.

At least she was no longer wearing her shackles. Ellyssa tried to reach the Source but could not sense even a trace of its existence. She looked at the runes deeply etched into the walls and deduced their purpose. Some were designed to fortify the physical structure of the walls and prevent scrying, but the majority prevented anyone in this cell from wielding magic.

It was Bakhtaran all over again, and the thought terrified her. But she was no longer a little girl, and her experiences at the hands of her chain mistress, Misha, had made her stronger. Whatever they were going to do to her, Ellyssa swore they would not break her.

Inquisitor Fennrick stepped through the doors of Duchess Paullina's private study and bowed deeply at the waist. Senior Inquisitor Elias was already present and seated, sipping a glass of what appeared to be brandy.

"What news, Fennrick?" the duchess asked without preamble.

"About what we expected, Your Grace," the inquisitor replied. "No one is able to use the codex beyond its mundane purpose."

Duchess Paullina curled her lip in annoyance. "That is very inconvenient. With the girl being the only known key to the book, we cannot execute her." The duchess paused for thought. "This could work to our benefit as well. The Academy is not pleased you left Southport without handing over the codex."

Elias nodded. "I have been receiving messages daily from Headmaster Florent. She is becoming increasingly impatient with me."

"Yes. I just received a letter from Duchess Mellina hinting at significant political fallout should harm come to this brat of a child. The last thing I need is for her to involve Jarvin. It was pure luck I did not swing with those other fools after Ulric and Caalendor's successive failures."

"I am sure it was due as much to your brilliance as luck, Your Grace," Senior Inquisitor Elias said.

"Shut up, Elias," Paullina snapped. "You know I cannot stand a sycophant. You are right, however. Ulric was a buffoon, and I gave him even odds of pulling off his coup. Fortunately, I had the good sense to err on the side of caution and was able to distance myself enough to get away with my head attached. Still, Jarvin knows I do not care for him, and it will not do to provoke him or his friends. So, we shall appease North Haven and the king by not executing the girl, and we shall stave off the Academy's demands for the Codex Arcana by reminding them that without the girl the codex is useless to them. I expect they will make some pilgrimage here to see if the book will speak to any of them. Do you see that as a possibility, Fennrick?"

"It is certainly all but imminent, but it is nothing for which to be concerned. Historically, the codex is very particular and, as far as I have been able to learn, has never spoken to more than one person at any one time. Even if we executed the girl, I sincerely doubt it would choose another from the stock available here or at the Academy. It is always a possibility, but it is more likely we would have to wait a few hundred years for another wizard to come along that the book deems suitable."

"That settles it then. Elias, remind the Academy ours is the only place suitable to imprison a wizard of her talent and, since she is the only way we have of utilizing the full potential of the codex, the book must logically stay here as well."

"The Academy will not like it," Elias said gravely.

Paullina brushed away his concern with a flick of her wrist. "As if I care a whit what those bookworms like. Fennrick, have you checked on our young charge?"

"I was going to awaken her after our meeting if she has not already regained consciousness."

"Do that. I cannot imagine sleeping for a fortnight is terribly healthy," the duchess replied offhandedly. "We will schedule her trial for tomorrow where we will certainly arrive at execution as her punishment."

Elias cleared his throat. "Your Grace, was it not your idea to not execute her?"

"Of course, you idiot, but obviously we will not tell her that. We will offer to commute her sentence in lieu of her cooperation. I swear, I do not know whose boots you licked to achieve your position, but they should be beaten with a stick. Fennrick, you understand what is happening, do you not?"

Fennrick ducked his head. "Implicitly, Your Grace. If there is nothing else, I shall attend to our prisoner and set things in motion."

Paullina nodded to the wizard who then made to leave. Upon opening the door, a page stood just on the other side, apparently deliberating whether to knock. Catching the duchess's eye, the page stepped into the room and bowed deeply after Fennrick pushed past.

"What is it?" Paullina asked waspishly.

"Your Grace, your husband wishes to see you at your earliest convenience." the page said with a pronounced tremor in his voice.

"Did he say it was urgent?"

"He did, Your Grace."

The duchess smiled. "Tell him I will see him tomorrow after breakfast. Then reschedule his appointment for later that afternoon first thing tomorrow morning." Paullina looked at Elias. "I had his favorite horse put down after it came in third in yesterday's race and he probably wants to complain. Ugh, he's probably miffed enough to whine incessantly through dinner over it." She turned back to the page. "Best fit him in this afternoon before dinner. I will not have my meal spoiled by his pouting. I swear that man is as stupid as you are, Elias, and twice as irritating."

"Indeed, Your Grace," Elias intoned.

"Oh and, boy," the duchess called after the departing page, "inform my chef I am in the mood for horsemeat kebobs with sweet and sour apples tonight."

Ellyssa stood and clenched her fists when she heard the door opening. She launched herself at Fennrick the instant she recognized his face. The wizard pointed his palm at her as if to tell her to stop and a force struck her in the chest hard enough to throw her back onto her cot.

"That's hardly any way to greet the man who saved your life," Fennrick said casually.

Ellyssa gripped the rail of her cot hard enough to whiten her knuckles. "What are you talking about?"

"I think you know," Fennrick said with a wry grin.

Ellyssa thought back to the final moments of her fight with the thief wizard. "It was you. You weakened his ward and distracted him."

"I couldn't have him kill you. It would be inconvenient for us."

Ellyssa did not bother to stand again. She was powerless to harm the wizard and was not sure if she had the strength to hurt him if she could. Her head ached and her body felt like a sack of mush.

"Where am I? What do you want with me?" She gave Fennrick a defiant scowl.

"You are in a holding cell beneath the Hall of Inquisition. I am sure you have already discovered your inability to channel the Source?" Ellyssa responded with a sour look. "Tomorrow, you will be tried for a multitude of crimes involving the illegal use of magic, most of which carry the mandatory sentence of execution."

Ellyssa's head slunk dejectedly. Not from the threat of death, but because she would not be able to destroy Captain Jake and scour every slave ship and crew from the face of the planet. Perhaps her spirit would continue in this world like the banshee at the school. Then she could haunt Jake and his ilk for all eternity.

Fennrick watched her lips turn upward. "Not many people smile when they learn of their impending death."

"Most people probably put more value on their lives."

Of all the responses the inquisitor had prepared for, eager acceptance was not one of them. He began to wonder if the girl really was insane. If she sought to use this as a defense, it would not do her any good. Insane wizards were executed for the safety of the public no matter their crimes.

Fennrick continued unabated. "We can however accept certain mitigating circumstances which could commute your execution to a term of imprisonment. I can likely get your cell upgraded to one a bit more accommodating as well."

Ellyssa smirked and let out a small laugh. "You can't read the book. Not one of you high and mighty inquisitors, or probably Academy snobs either, can get the book to talk to you."

Fennrick's face showed his displeasure despite his neutral tone. "As of yet, you are correct. However, the Academy is certainly going to be sending delegations to inspect the codex. All it takes is for one of them to be chosen, and then you are no longer necessary."

Ellyssa mulled over her options and responses then nodded. "I want it in writing that if I help you use the book you will not execute me when I am no longer needed."

"I am certain I can get that assurance from the duchess and the inquisition council."

Fennrick kept stone-faced but inside he was elated. His ability to plumb the depths of the Codex Arcana would increase his knowledge considerably and guarantee him the highest position within the order, even if it did require going through the girl.

"There is a ritual to complete, but I will need you to get a few things," Ellyssa continued.

"I will ensure you have everything you need."

"First, you need to get a rough-hewn staff. Length is not as important as girth. Then bend over at the waist and, you may need assistance with this next part…"

The inquisitor turned red-faced with indignation. "We will see how amusing and defiant you are after your trial!"

Inquisitor Fennrick stormed from the cell and Ellyssa listened to the thick bolt clack securely closed. A myriad of emotions warred within her as she pondered what appeared to be her imminent demise. First was fear, followed by a sort of numb acceptance. The most surprising emotion finally achieving dominance was relief and even some anticipation.

Ellyssa had not realized how exhausting holding on to so much hate, guilt, and fear had been. Her entire body seemed to melt as her muscles relaxed for the first time in years. No more pain of abandonment, no more guilt for Azerick's death, and no more hateful eyes stabbing her with blame. Finally, there would be an end. Ellyssa slept more soundly that night than any other since her enslavement.

Despite her peaceful sleep, strangely bereft of the usual nightmares, Ellyssa snapped awake the instant she heard the key fitted to the lock of her cell. As she expected, Fennrick emerged from the open door, but this time with two other wizards at his side.

"I hope you had plenty of time to consider your situation last night," the inquisitor stated.

"I did." Ellyssa met his look from where she sat on the edge of the cot.

"You can save yourself this unpleasantness by cooperating," Fennrick said once more. "My offer still stands."

A wry grin tugged at the corner of Ellyssa's mouth. "So does mine."

Fennrick's expression soured. "Stand up and extend your arms."

Ellyssa complied and the man snapped on the rune-etched shackles preventing her from reaching the Source. Fennrick grabbed her roughly by the elbow and pushed her into the dim passageway beyond her door. Ellyssa was not very familiar with dungeons, but this one seemed much cleaner than she imagined them to be.

Fennrick guided her up a narrow, winding staircase while the other two wizards kept pace several feet to her front and back. After ascending perhaps twenty feet, the party came to a landing. The inquisitor guided her through a door, but the stairs continued upward into what Ellyssa assumed was a tower.

The plain stone of the dungeon became polished red marble. The palatial décor of the place made Ellyssa wonder if she were in the duchess's palace. Wherever she was, it was large and heavily populated with wizards, nearly all of whom gave her stern looks in passing. The group finally arrived at what appeared to be an antechamber where one of her escorts detached from the group and vanished through a second set of doors.

Despite her earlier acceptance of death, Ellyssa found the wait interminable. No one spoke or even allowed her to sit upon one of the padded benches stretching along the two opposing walls. Apparently, those inside were nearly as eager to finish this as she was because it was barely an hour before her missing guard returned and motioned them inside.

Ellyssa felt the first pangs of fear, even panic, the instant she stepped into the room. It was a circular room made of multiple tiers of white marble, contrasting sharply with the three or four score of black-clad inquisitors seated within. Ellyssa's heart hammered in her chest as Fennrick forced her to the center of a room that felt far too much like the training pits of Bakhtaran. Had the floor been comprised of sand instead of marble, Ellyssa was certain she would have lost her mind.

She took several deep, shuddering breaths and summoned her focus as she had been taught to do when working magic under stressful circumstances. It took several moments, but her head finally cleared and her heart returned to a more normal if still elevated rate. She met the eyes of the stern woman directly ahead of her and the only one seated on a throne instead of the endless circular benches ringing the arena-like chamber.

"Ellyssa Jensen," Duchess Paullina called down from her lofty seat, "I am Duchess Paullina, hereto referred to as Your Grace. As the head of state, I preside over all court trials whose significance warrants my attention within my demesne."

"Did you preside over your own trial when King Jarvin was hanging the rest of the traitors as well?" Ellyssa boldly countered.

Several wizards shifted in agitation and faces burned red at Ellyssa's effrontery. "Miss Jensen, such disrespect will not bode well for you during this trial. I strongly suggest you take this very seriously."

"I fail to see how it could *bode* any worse. I was already told I would be executed after this farce of a trial, so why don't we just skip all this pointless posturing and get on with it?"

"Very well, Miss Jensen. You are accused of pursuing magic without the lawful guidance of an approved member of the Academy. On numerous occasions, you used magic during criminal activity that included assault, destruction of property, and murder. You also used magic to assault several members of the Academy and the Office of Inquisition while dutifully assigned to your apprehension. How do you plead?"

"Guilty, and if you remove these shackles I'll give you a firsthand account of a few of those bogus charges!"

The duchess set her jaw and steeled herself against Ellyssa's blatant disrespect. This was the point in a trial where nearly all the convicted begged for mercy. The girl's fearless hostility left her a bit off balance.

"Then I have no recourse but to sentence you to death by hanging. Your sentence will be carried out at noon tomorrow. However, I am in a generous mood, and in light of your relationship to Lady Miranda and the North Haven court, I am willing to grant you leniency in exchange for your cooperation. Assist my inquisitors and the Academy in their study of the Codex Arcana, and I will commute your sentence to imprisonment. Prove yourself useful, and even those accommodations need not be uncomfortable. What say you?"

Ellyssa glared balefully up at the duchess. "I say you can share the same stick with Fennrick."

The duchess narrowed her eyes and tilted her head slightly. "What does she mean by that, Fennrick?"

The inquisitor shuffled his feet nervously. "It is in regard to her response when I offered a similar proposition, Your Grace. It was rather untoward, and I would rather not repeat it."

"Explain, Inquisitor," Paullina demanded. "I am not some blushing little maiden."

Fennrick cleared his throat and answered, "She told me to go fornicate myself with a rough-hewn staff, Your Grace."

A few stifled chortles broke through the indignant muttering echoing around the chamber.

Paullina glared back at the girl just as fiercely. "We shall see if you hold such arrogant contempt when the rope is tightened around your neck tomorrow."

"I think we both know that's not going to happen," Ellyssa retorted with amusement.

"I beg your pardon?"

"We all know you cannot afford to kill me. I had time to think about this last night, and it all became quite clear. Fennrick overplayed his hand when he told me I could live if I played nice. Obviously, none of you can access the book, a book I hear the Academy and every practitioner of magic has been coveting for more than a millennium.

That pretty much makes me the most important person in the world right now, which really sucks for me because I was looking forward to my execution."

Duchess Paullina leaned forward and pierced Ellyssa with her glare. "Child, there are far worse things than death, I assure you. Continue this pointless obstinacy and I promise you will learn that very soon!"

Ellyssa could not control herself. Every eye in the chamber went wide as her near maniacal laughter rang off the walls.

The duchess leapt to her feet, shaking with rage. "Fennrick, take her below and get her cooperation! I don't care if you have to flay the skin from her body to do it!"

The same three guards marched Ellyssa from the chamber and down the hall, her continued laughter masking their heavy footfalls. Fennrick shoved her into her cell with enough force to make her fall onto her cot. Ellyssa rolled back to her feet and sneered.

"You insult the duchess and make a mockery of us all!" Fennrick shook in outrage. "Do you really think we are bluffing? You said it yourself; there is nothing more important than unlocking the secrets of the codex, certainly not the life or comfort of some willful, spoiled little girl who has found herself in the middle of something far bigger than herself."

Ellyssa's body tensed and contorted under the sudden magical assault. There was neither a flare of light nor arc of electricity, but she felt as though lightning danced across her skin and resonated in her bones. She could not completely stifle the animalistic grunt of pain escaping her clamped shut jaws.

Fennrick finally paused in administering his torture. "You bring this upon yourself. You can put an end to this pain any time you choose."

Ellyssa looked up at him through tearing eyes, and the room once again filled with her laughter. "You call that pain? Remove these shackles, take me out of this room, and I will show you pain. I have experienced pain beyond anything you have ever imagined! You are pathetic, Fennrick, you and the rest of your ilk."

Fennrick's blood boiled at the audacity of the girl, and he renewed his assault with vigor. But no matter what he tried, she just laughed at him even more whenever he stopped. Soon, not even his anger could keep him going. He was not a trained torturer, and his imagination was as limited as his stomach for causing continued pain, especially when doing so was garnering nothing in return.

Ellyssa looked up from where she lay sprawled on the floor and found herself alone. She climbed onto her cot and curled into a ball. Despite her bravado, pain was pain and nothing could ever completely inure her to its effects, but something inside her refused to relent.

She knew the pain would stop if she cooperated. It would be so easy. But doing so would mean she was in no better position than she had been in Bakhtaran. The duchess promised her a comfortable room if she simply supplied the Academy with answers, just as Vila Mushadan had provided her palatial surroundings for using her magic to help steal his country's throne. She was still a prisoner and still a slave, but she would fight them to the very end. Eventually, they would have to kill her, intentionally or by accident.

Either way, she would win. Even if she wanted to live and was willing to surrender, Ellyssa knew something in her mind would stop her from doing it. It was at that moment she knew she was broken and only death could fix her.

Fennrick needed to report his progress, or lack thereof. He relished reporting his failure as much as the thought of continuing his tortures. The inquisitor had never thought of himself as squeamish; he would kill the girl in an instant given the order to do so and not lose a wink of sleep, but to inflict pain on a girl barely out of childhood was not something he cared for.

His worst fears were borne out when he stepped into Elias's office. The senior inquisitor sat at his desk while Duchess Paullina reclined on a plush sedan drinking a glass of red wine. Fennrick took a deep breath and sat in a chair where he could capture the other two occupants in his field of view without undue head turning.

"I was hoping you would be wrapping up soon, Fennrick," the duchess said over her glass of wine. "Is the girl singing a different tune now?"

Fennrick looked to the ceiling then back at the duchess. "No. It is the same tune, same song, and louder than ever. I applied the most pain I thought advisable, and she laughed in my face."

"Then apply more!"

Fennrick shook his head. "I don't think it will help. It may even cause more harm than good, especially if it drives her over the edge and makes her completely unreachable."

Paullina swirled the wine in her glass before bolting down the remaining scarlet liquid. "Is she insane?"

"To a lesser degree, I believe so. She is not the sort of gibbering lunatic type of insane, but I believe her touched in the head. My reports indicated she suffered significant abuse in Bakhtaran, and she holds a great deal of remorse and guilt over the death of Lord Giles. It is this reason I fear pushing too hard. Her mind is in a fragile state, and pushing too hard could irrevocably shatter it. Doing so could lose the codex to us forever and that would not do."

"No, that certainly would not do at all," mused the duchess.

Although technically not under her control, having the inquisitors headquartered within her city gave a significant boost to her power base, more so even than the Academy did for Southport since the inquisitors actively patrolled and even defended against minor border issues while under the auspices of her command. Delving into the secrets of the Codex Arcana would increase her power. It could even one day give her the means to make the inquisitors a separate entity from the Academy and secure the throne.

"Perhaps the crudeness of brute force is not what we need here," the duchess supplied. "There are a plethora of torture techniques utilizing discomfort and mental strain instead of simple pain. Of course, we will still have to monitor her carefully, but I think that tree may yield more fruit."

"I think it would be best to err on the side of caution by not expecting instant results," Fennrick cautioned. "This will likely be a time-consuming process if done properly."

Paullina nodded. "I think you are right. I have a man who is skilled in such things. I shall put him at your disposal. Elias!" the duchess shouted. "Are you even awake over there or is there truly nothing intelligent you have to add to this discussion?"

The senior inquisitor practically jumped out of his chair. "No, Your Grace. I mean yes, Your Grace. All are very sound ideas and I fully agree."

"Idiot. Now, are you equally incompetent as a host, or is this glass going to magically fill itself?"

Elias leapt from his seat and grabbed the nearby bottle of wine. "Of course, Your Grace, forgive me."

CHAPTER 18

Azerick slowly opened his eyes and examined the room in which he lay. He was reclining on a pallet of furs laid over what he assumed was a mattress of stuffed straw atop a stone plinth. Several wool blankets were layered upon his unclothed body, which was protected from their coarse fibers by an undyed silk sheet.

The room was shaped like a half sphere. The circular walls and domed ceiling appeared smooth and polished with great effort given in their shaping. Natural crystals grew from much of its dark surface, a few of the larger ones glowing with a comfortable white light. Other than his pallet, there were no other furnishings.

Movement out of the corner of his eye caught his attention. Standing in the archway leading to a larger chamber was a woman unlike any he had ever seen. She was tall, very tall. It was hard for Azerick to gauge her exact height from his reclined position, but he guessed at least seven feet in height. However, her size was the least defining of her features.

Her skin was a pale blue and glimmered as if covered in millions of tiny diamonds. On closer inspection, Azerick saw they were extraordinarily fine, crystalline scales. Her eyes were large, almond-shaped, and the color of molten gold. The pupils looked like the blade of a black dagger splitting the iris down the middle. Her ears swept back slightly and came to a delicate point. A thick braid of hair like spun silver as fine as silk hung over her left shoulder where it nearly touched her waist.

She was incredibly thin, almost frail-looking, but Azerick sensed enormous power radiating from her. Even her voice held power as she spoke, sending a tremor through his body despite its soft tone.

"Good, you are awake. How do you feel?"

Azerick felt his panic rise as he discovered a great many things wrong. "I can barely move! What is wrong with me? Where am I? Who are you?"

"I will explain everything in its due course, but you must remain calm," the creature said softly. "I am Lissandra, and you are in my home. Do you know your name?"

Azerick searched his mind but found nothing except grey emptiness and a few vague recollections. "I don't know. I don't know anything! What is wrong with me? What happened?"

Lissandra pursed her lips in consternation. "It appears the process of bringing you here caused some damage to your mind. It is not unexpected, and as frightening as it seems now, it could have been much worse."

"I don't know who I am, where I am, or how I got here, and I cannot do more than twitch my body! How could it have been worse?" Azerick shouted, the fear making his voice tremble.

"Your mind could have been irrevocably destroyed, casting you into an incurable madness. Now, you must remain calm. I will do everything in my power to set things aright."

Azerick took several deep breaths to calm his frayed nerves. He realized panic would not help and only calm, rational discussion would improve his situation. It did not appear as though the creature meant to harm him, at least not at the moment, but there were a great many questions he needed answered.

Lissandra continued, "Your name is Azerick Giles and you are in my home. The process of bringing you here was monumentally difficult and the strain has caused some damage, particularly to your memory."

"Why did you bring me here?"

"That is a reasonable question with a very complex answer. There is much I do not know and even more I cannot tell you. Such discoveries of yourself you must find and process on your own. What I will tell you is that you are very important, and it is vital I return you to your former self, as much as is possible."

"Why am I so important, important to whom, and for what?"

"I cannot tell you that."

Azerick's anger washed away his fear like a strong rain. "I need to be able to trust you if you expect anything from me, and that starts with at least telling me who I am, why I am important, and why you brought me here. Your actions have done me enormous harm, and you owe me an explanation."

Lissandra paused to consider the young man's demands, piercing him with her strange reptilian eyes. "She warned me you could be difficult. Apparently, that was not lost with your memory."

"Who told you that?"

"Sharrellan, goddess of the abyss, from where I retrieved you."

"Why would a goddess know of me? Why was I in the abyss? Isn't that a place for evil people to go when they die? Was I dead? Was I an evil person?"

Lissandra let out a long breath. "This is going to be more tedious than I anticipated, but I suppose if I were in your position I would be asking much the same thing. You should know that if you were in mine, you would understand why I cannot tell you everything you want to know."

"Why not?"

"Your memories are what make you who you are," Lissandra explained. "They are more than a simple collection of facts. The emotions tied to every memory you possess, and how you dealt with the situations which caused them, define you. It is the difference between reading about a frightening event and living it. It is the difference between reading a poem about love and being in love. I must restore not just what you once knew, but who you once were. The fate of this world depends on it."

"The fate of the world? Who am I? How can I possibly be so important?"

"You are a powerful sorcerer, a wielder of magic. The gods saw you deeply entwined within the strands of fate and have watched over you since your birth."

"Surely I cannot be more powerful than the gods."

Lissandra did her best to explain. "Power is subjective and comes in many forms. The gods have the power to shift mountains and raise the seas, but they cannot alter the course of fate. Their power is limited, particularly where the races of our world are concerned. To affect the course of fate for the races, the gods must work through the mortals of our world. You are one such mortal."

"There are others like me?"

"Many people have been chosen, and though each of them is vitally important, none play a role as great as yours."

Azerick had a difficult time comprehending what the creature was telling him. How could he do what the gods could not? He certainly did not feel powerful. He could barely move more than his head.

"Can you fix me?"

"I believe so," Lissandra answered with a nod. "The process of bringing you from the abyss to here was enormously complex. It took years of this world's time to pull you out. Even then, you floated between worlds for months. It took all of my energy to maintain my hold upon you. Such an endeavor placed an enormous amount of stress on your body and mind. Had your soul not belonged here, such a task would not have been possible. It should be easy to restore function to your muscles, but reclaiming your memories will take time."

Azerick's hope soared. "You think you can get my memory back?"

"In time, yes, but be warned, it will take an emotional toll upon you," Lissandra said gravely. "You will relive every moment of each of those memories anew, and you have more terrible memories than most. What you experienced and came to terms with over the course of your life, you will do so again in only a matter of months. I pray you are as strong as Sharrellan said, or you may yet still go mad. It is something I have witnessed, and do not wish to repeat."

"You have done this before? Who was it?" Azerick asked.

Lissandra looked into the distance, beyond the stone walls of the room and deep into the past. "Once, for my grandson," she said quietly.

"Lissandra, why am I so important? What is it I am supposed to do?" Azerick asked again.

"I cannot tell you what to do, no one can. Not even the gods know what will happen before it occurs. They can only prepare for eventualities. I do know this: you must unite the races once again or all is lost."

Every explanation only created more questions, and it made Azerick increasingly frustrated. "I feel as though we are talking in

254 / Brock E. Deskins

circles! Unite them against what? Or is that something else I have to discover on my own?"

"I understand your frustration, Azerick," Lissandra said, straining to hold her own temper in check, "but you must be patient. You will understand more as we regain your memories. Most, if not all, are still within you, but they are like lost sheep wandering aimlessly through a strange, dark forest. I will be your shepherd and will bring them back to you, but you must be patient and trust me."

"Then tell me something, anything," Azerick pleaded. "I am lost in a darkness that has nothing to do with my eyes!"

"I suppose a simple lesson in history will do no harm," Lissandra yielded. "Nearly two millennia ago, the races rose up against the gods before our gods. These beings were known as the Scions. The Scions are ancient creatures, formed alongside the world upon which we reside. They were to shape the lesser creatures that came later, but instead of being the benevolent caretakers of the world and its inhabitants, the Scions became petty and capricious. They demanded more and more sacrifice and supplication.

"As the races became more independent, the Scions grew more jealous. They used dragons to control the races through fear and brutality because it was easier to control a few hundred dragons than hundreds of thousands of humans, elves, and other races. A few of the elves, always having been sensitive to the effects of the Source, discovered a way to harness its energy and shape it into magic. They were the first sorcerers. From them, other elves discovered a way to emulate these innate abilities, and they became the first wizards.

"When the Scions discovered the elves were tampering in the domain reserved for gods, they were furious. They unleashed the dragons and struck down several of the elven cities with their terrible power. Human cities soon followed. The Scions knew that with the curiosity of humans, it would only be a matter of time before the humans also stumbled upon wizardly ability.

"In a secret gathering of all the leaders of the races, it was decided they would rise up against their masters and cast off the heavy hand of oppression or die trying. The races knew even elvish magic was not enough to defeat the dragon watchdogs, much less the Scions, so they created tools of incredible power. The humans and dwarves constructed suits of armor that could withstand the awesome power of the dragons. They gave these suits to the most powerful warriors amongst the races to do battle against the creatures.

"It was left to elves to face the Scions themselves, which meant they needed a tool of great arcane power. By this time, the All Mother, the creator of everything, had been incubating new gods to replace the Scions for millennia, but she dared not make the same mistake with them. Therefore, she limited their ability to act directly upon this world. The new gods were born and created a book called the Codex Arcana. The codex contained a vast amount of magical knowledge and they gave it to the elves so they could find the answers they desperately needed. The codex showed the elves how to mix the life essence of a dragon with that of the elves. This created a being of extraordinary magical ability."

Azerick interrupted, "That is what you are. So you are two thousand years old? You fought these Scions?"

Lissandra inclined her head. "Indeed I did. The elves created twelve such creatures, of which I was one. We were called the Guardians, although we have gone by many names. Our duality of spirit prevented the Scions from simply dominating us as they did the dragons or any of the other lesser creatures. When the Great Revolution occurred, death beyond imagining cast its pall over the land. The Scions raised the mountains upon which we are now residing in just a day, effectively cutting the world in two. But even with the kingdoms divided, the races fought on, knowing that surrender would mean the death of their species, for the Scions would never allow them the opportunity to rise up again.

"By the end of the war, only a fraction of the races' original population survived along with one human hero, Magnus Ollander and his marvelous armor. He became the first true human king, and his descendants have ruled ever since. With the aid of the new gods, the Guardians managed to defeat the Scions, but they failed to destroy them. The Scions agreed to banishment, knowing that one day they would return. That day is fast approaching, and it is why you are so vital."

"How can I defeat the Scions if the gods could not? What about the other Guardians? Will they help me as they did once before?"

Lissandra's mask of pure calm slipped for a moment and her pain flashed briefly. "I am the last of the Guardians."

In that moment of shared loneliness, Azerick felt a kinship with Lissandra. "What happened to them?"

"The elves created twelve Guardians. By the time the Scions capitulated, only five still lived. The Guardians helped the gods banish the Scions within an alternate dimension and created a wall of magic to keep them confined. It was left to the Guardians to ensure the wall did not fail. We tried to live with the elves, whom we viewed as our surrogate parents, but over the centuries, the elves became distrustful of our power. Many feared we would attain the highest positions within the elven hierarchy. The elves did not like the idea of being second to something they created. It was foolish, but they asked us to leave and so we did. Not belonging anywhere, and fearing others may turn against us, we fled to the far corners of the lands to maintain our vigil over the Scions' prison."

"So where are the other four Guardians?"

"The prison walls were flawed, and the Scions have spent the last two millennia chipping away at them. On occasion, they managed to create enough of a breach to send through some of the minions they have spent the centuries creating. When that happened, the only thing strong enough to seal the breach was the entirety of our life force. The last breach occurred several years ago and the only other living Guardian gave his life to repair it. I am now the last, and my time is fading."

"Why?" Azerick exclaimed.

"I told you, prying you from the abyss was a phenomenally difficult task. It took everything I had and more to achieve even this flawed level of success. Like the barrier, it required me to expend a great deal of my life force to enact it. I knew this going in, but it was the only chance we all have."

Azerick did not know how to respond or even feel. This creature, who was seemingly immortal and fought to free him and the rest of the world from enslavement, had just told him she willingly sacrificed her life for his.

He swallowed in a desperate attempt to choke down the knot in his throat. "Why would you do that? Who am I to warrant such a sacrifice? I cannot even move!"

The Guardian smiled down at Azerick. "You will move again, and you will be the savior of the races."

"But I don't know how! I am not like you. I am not a Guardian. You said only the duality of your spirit allowed you to approach the Scions and bring the battle to them. How can I hope to do that?"

"Azerick, you also possess a dual spirit. You will regain your memory, and with it, your power."

Azerick shook his. "I just cannot see it. What dual spirit? I am not like you. I am only human."

"No, you are not like me, but you are not as different as you think. It is something I cannot tell you. You must come to understand it on your own. Simple might is not what will save the world. Your greatest duty will be uniting the races. Unfortunately, it will also be the most difficult. The elves are deeply secluded and distrustful of others, the dwarves have locked themselves away under the mountains, and humans cannot set aside their own petty desires to reach for a common good. The other races are equally divided or secluded, but fear not, you will not be alone. You have made many friends, even enemies, whom you may call upon for support. And there will be another, perhaps the greatest weapon since the elves created my kind, but that is for later."

Azerick wanted to raise a hand and run it through his hair, but it only twitched and flopped back down onto the bed. "Why does so much fall upon me? This All Mother created the gods, even the Scions. Why can she simply not destroy them?"

Lissandra smiled as if explaining to a child why the wind blew or the sun shone. "The All Mother is not a being or a creature as we are, or even as the Scions or gods are. She is the sun and stars. Her body is the universe in which we live. Her blood is the Source from which we draw all magic. Inside our bodies are tiny organisms. Some cause illness while others fight them to make us well and heal our wounds. To the All Mother, we are like those tiny creatures. She created the Scions, but they became malignant tumors, and like the disease, it is not so easy to be rid of them. It is up to us, the tiny creatures, to do battle and heal her. We cannot think of her in such a mortal way, for she cannot think of us in such a way."

Azerick's head hurt from trying to understand the Guardian, and he only marginally succeeded. He prayed he became smarter when he got his memory back, because right now he felt like a simpleton. He thought he understood what Lissandra was saying and knew his understanding was a partial one at best.

"This would be so much easier if I could remember," Azerick said dejectedly.

Lissandra smiled sympathetically. "Not necessarily. Much of what I have told you has been lost through the ages. The centuries following the Great Revolution were very hard times, especially for the humans. As a forward-looking people, much of your history was lost and forgotten. You must remind them."

"I just do not see how I can possibly do what you are asking."

"You have already accomplished amazing things in your short life. It is what makes humans so remarkable, and you are remarkable amongst humans. Now let us mend your body, for it is the foundation of your existence."

Azerick nodded and watched as Lissandra pulled a red crystal from the pocket of her sheer silken gown. Kneeling next to Azerick's prone form, the Guardian chanted softly as she ran the crystal from his head down his naked body. Azerick felt the crystal thrum against his skin in sync with Lissandra's chanting. His arms and legs tingled as the Guardian traced a path from his head and along each extremity.

He ached to ask what she was doing, but thought it best to leave her to her task uninterrupted. Eventually, his arms and legs began to feel less leaden and more responsive. When he had moved his arm earlier, it felt as if it were separate from his body, but now it felt more attached. After about an hour of treatment, Lissandra stopped her ministrations and stood.

"That should enable you to start your physical recovery."

Azerick pulled the silk sheet back over his body. "What did you do?"

"The journey created a disconnect in the neural pathways responsible for translating thought into motion."

"Uh, what?"

"Forgive me. I often forget most people, even those with their memories intact, are ignorant of our greater functions. Inside your brain are tiny pathways. Those pathways connect to your nerves, which allow your brain to make the muscles move," the Guardian explained. "It is much the same thing that is wrong with your memories. They are still there; we simply need to find them and reconnect them."

"I see," Azerick responded, staring across the room at nothing. "I guess it was a lot of bad luck to get both my memory and muscle connection broken, huh?"

Lissandra gave Azerick a serious look. "It was good luck that only the greater responses were broken. It could have just as easily been the unconscious commands controlling your breathing and the beating of your heart."

"Oh," Azerick said softly. "When do we start on getting back my memory?"

"We must work on your physical self first. You will need your strength when your memories return. Azerick, this will become very unpleasant for you. You will experience your entire life in a matter of weeks or months. All the joy and sorrow will smash into you like a wave from the sea. Such a thing is an exhausting experience, and if you are not strong, it will crush you. If you lose your mind, I will be forced to destroy you, even knowing I may doom the world by doing so."

"Thanks for the warning. I'll do my best not to do that."

"Rest today, but do not lie stagnant," Lissandra ordered. "Move your arms and legs as much as you can. Practice sitting up, but do not get out of bed. Enjoy this time. It will be the last pleasant day you have for a long time."

Lissandra vanished through the doorless entryway with that final warning. Azerick tried to sit up, made it about halfway, and fell back onto the bed. He realized his emaciated body was nowhere near typical for him and had indeed suffered a great deal of atrophy. His chest was sunken and the bones showed clearly through his pale flesh. He settled for raising first one leg and bending it at the knee until it hovered over his stomach. He then straightened it and did the same with the other.

Azerick grunted under the exertion and sweat soon beaded his brow and ran into his eyes. After only a few minutes, each repetition elicited a gasp and a struggled groan. He collapsed, panting and exhausted from what should have been a simple exercise. Catching his breath once more, Azerick settled for simply raising and lowering his arms until they also became so fatigued he could no longer lift them. He fought his body's desire to sleep and continued to alternate his exercises until he became too tired to continue.

He lay there in his bed, breathing hard and thinking about what Lissandra had told him. As Azerick wiped away his perspiration, a task taking significant effort, he wondered how she could think he had the ability to battle something with the power of a god when he could barely move, and unite multiple kingdoms when he did not even know who he was.

The entire situation was beyond overwhelming. Then there was Lissandra. She said he was important, but when she looked at him, he could not help but feel like a bug under a magnifying glass. She told him she was dying, dying because she rescued him from the abyss. Was she telling the truth? Was any of it true? He could think of no reason for her to lie, but then he could barely think at all. Lacking the strength for anything else, Azerick closed his eyes and slept.

That night, horrors filled Azerick's dreams. He found himself walking through the streets of a city, stepping over or walking carefully around bodies littering the ground. Faces he did not know cried out to him, covered in blood. Buildings burned and smoke hung heavy in the air, carrying the scent of death within its murky haze. He found himself at the foot of enormous stone steps and began climbing.

Here, in his dreams, his body worked fine. He felt power in his muscles and deep within himself. He looked up and saw a brilliant bolt of lightning sizzle across the sky as it cut through the smoke. He knew he could call it down and wield it with just a thought. His ascent took him above the smoke and only the cries of the few living and thousands slowly dying echoed their reminder of the carnage below.

As he cleared the smoke of the burning city, he discovered the steps climbed the side of a gargantuan pyramid of black stone. Upon reaching the top, Azerick stood before a shattered throne of the same black stone decorated with the skulls of humans and monsters. Without thinking why, he sat upon the macabre seat and looked down. As if commanded by his eyes, the smoke cleared. Horrible creatures, foul and grotesque, clung to the side of the citadel and flew overhead, but he was unafraid. With a wordless command, the creatures bowed before Azerick, and he smiled.

Azerick shot up and tumbled from his bed, sprawling in an undignified heap. He grabbed at the silk sheet and found it soaked in sweat. Before him was a pair of feet, their delicate bones standing out beneath their cover of sky-blue flesh. He looked up at Lissandra's expressionless face.

"I was going to wake you soon, but I see you are already up, however briefly. There are clothes next to your bed. If you can put them on, you may wear them. If you cannot, then we shall begin your training as you are."

Azerick turned his head and saw a black garment sitting at the foot of his pallet. He figured it was a gesture to appease his own sense of modesty and doubted Lissandra cared a whit about his nakedness. When he turned his head back, the Guardian was already stepping from the room.

He crawled to the folded stack of clothing and grabbed at the black fabric. Azerick found the entire bundle consisted of only a black robe and a pair of matching slippers with soft leather soles. He was relieved at the simplicity of the garment. He dreaded the effort and humiliation he would have suffered if it had been a tunic and trousers. Tossing the robe open on the floor, Azerick simply rolled onto it and slipped his arms into the sleeves. The slippers proved a little more difficult since he had to bring his feet up near his chest to slip them on.

Tying the robe closed, Azerick called for the Guardian. "Lissandra, I am ready."

The woman appeared almost instantly and looked down at him from the doorway. "You are dressed, but you are hardly ready. Food is available when you decide to get off the floor."

"Can you not help me up?" Azerick asked as he raised a hand toward her.

"I was told you were a man of exceptional spirit. Was I misinformed?" Lissandra's irritation was evident only in the slight narrowing of her eyes. "What you are going to experience during your recovery will take heroic effort, and I will not coddle you. Once you leave here, these tasks will seem like child's play. If you lack the discipline to even stand, then you are not what I was led to believe."

Lissandra turned then took a stutter step when Azerick's slipper struck her in the back of the head. Pausing, she looked back over her shoulder and said, "That's a start." She then walked away before Azerick could see the faint smile tug at the corner of her mouth.

Azerick crawled to the entranceway, retrieved his slipper, and used the arching doorframe to pull himself to his feet. He stood there for several moments gripping the stone as he got his breath back.

The room beyond looked much like the one he was in only larger. Lissandra sat at a stone table that looked like an enormous stone mushroom sprouting from the ground near the center. Smaller bulbs of rock framed it on two sides and acted as stools. The Guardian sat upon one of these sipping from a teacup. Two large plates of food and another cup sat on the table.

There was no wall against which to brace himself and at least twenty feet of open floor between him and the table. It was apparent she expected him to take a seat and to do it unassisted. Azerick took a deep breath, stiffened his legs, and began taking small, shuffling steps toward the table. The table felt a mile away and his legs would feel steadier on a ship in a storm than they did now.

Agonizing step after agonizing step, Azerick meticulously crept across the floor. He was grateful there were no obstacles to navigate or he would have been doomed. Azerick reached the table and grabbed it as if it were the only floating object in a storm-tossed sea. Ensuring his rump was positioned over the stone stool, he sat down heavily and smiled triumphantly at Lissandra.

"You look like you expect some sort of reward for walking to the breakfast table," Lissandra said dully over the top of her cup.

Azerick glared at the Guardian and replied, "And you sound like you want to get hit with another slipper."

The Guardian was thankful her cup hid the smile trying desperately to break her calm façade. "I have prepared you a meal that will help you regain your strength. Eat it, and then we can begin your training."

Azerick looked at the food set out for him and tried to identify what it was. A slab of meat seared on the outside but still oozing blood from within butted up against a pile of green vegetables that looked like leeks but were definitely not leeks. The meat was light in color, like pork, but had a strong gamey scent and taste.

He looked at the food on Lissandra's plate. The meat looked the same without the benefit of searing. If it were any rarer, it would probably try to flee. There were no vegetables, but she did have a palm-sized honeycomb on her plate.

The Guardian caught Azerick looking. "I like to indulge. It is what helps me keep my sweet disposition."

"And for that I am grateful," Azerick responded sardonically. "You may want to ease up on the salt, however. It appears to be nullifying whatever effect the honey has on you."

"Are you finished eating, or do you lack the manners to not speak with your mouth full?"

Azerick took the hint to shut up. He was certain the Guardian would not hesitate to take his food if he kept talking. The strange vegetables were bitter and spicy, like a pepper crossed with horseradish. Azerick coughed a mouthful back onto his plate.

"You need to eat those," Lissandra said. "They possess vital nutrients."

"I don't see you eating them!" Azerick snapped, then drank deeply from his cup; its contents he promptly spit out as the concoction burned the inside of his throat.

"I am not as weak as a newborn babe. And you need to drink that as well. Spit any more out and you will lick it off the table. It is not easy to brew."

"It can't be half as bad to brew as it is to drink," Azerick mumbled. "What is it, concentrated armpit sweat from an ogre?"

"I could say yes. It would make you feel better than if I told you the truth."

Azerick decided he did not want to know what any of it was, but if it helped return him to normal, he would consume it all. Feeling helpless was not something he liked. In fact, Azerick could not think of a single thing more distasteful. The more he thought about it the angrier he got. He tore into his food and ate without tasting. Only the foul liquid required him to consume it with care.

Lissandra dabbed at the corners of her mouth with a napkin. "We shall start with the simple exercise of walking. You will walk around this chamber, using the seat here to rest only when you cannot continue any longer. Once rested, you will resume walking."

"For how long?"

"Until I tell you to stop."

"So just walk? You don't want to make me carry you or throw rocks at me? Maybe pour some oil on the floor?" Azerick asked.

"Not yet."

Azerick bit back a retort and stood. Oddly enough, he already felt stronger. He stumbled once as he walked to the wall of the circular room but caught himself before he fell. Using his right hand to steady himself, Azerick circumnavigated the room with care.

The room was large and it took several minutes for him to complete each circuit with his dreadfully slow shuffling. Azerick made only two and a half circuits before fatigue forced him to shamble to the table to sit and rest.

"What do you think you are doing?" Lissandra asked.

"I am tired," Azerick responded shortly. "You told me I could use the seat when I got too tired to continue."

"You managed to walk to the table; therefore you are not too tired to walk the floor."

Azerick's face burned as he glowered at the Guardian. "What do you want me to do, walk until I collapse then drag myself to the table to rest? Or would you prefer if I just lay on the floor whimpering?"

Lissandra took a sip from a fresh cup of tea. "Either one is fine with me. I leave it for you to decide. If you are asking my opinion, I would tell you crawling is slightly more dignified than lying there like a dying animal in the street."

Azerick inwardly seethed with rage and humiliation, but he refused to rise to the bait. He felt certain Lissandra was intentionally stoking the fires of his anger and ego. He could not control his physical weakness, but he would control his temper. Azerick felt the craving for control over himself and his surroundings like a drunkard craved strong drink. Control was everything.

Azerick stood back up forcefully and fell. Using the stool and table, he hastily got on his feet and carefully made his way back to the wall to resume his walking. Barely-suppressed anger motivated and energized his steps. He stopped thinking about his weakness and exhaustion, letting his mind fantasize about the Guardian sprawled out on the floor, desperately trying to crawl to the table, and begging for Azerick's help.

So lost in his anger-induced daydreams was he, Azerick did not detect the approaching end of his physical limits. When he collapsed, it came as a complete surprise, almost as much as realizing he had made three more complete laps. This time he did crawl to the table. It took several minutes of monumental struggle to reach his seat.

When Azerick finally opened his eyes and looked at the tabletop, he was surprised to find another plate of food set out, identical to the previous meal. He had no idea when Lissandra had prepared and left it for him. The moment the scent of food wafted up and reached his nose, his stomach growled noisily and did not care if it was cold or how it tasted.

The next day was much like the previous, only Azerick was able to dress, get to the table, and walk much farther without resting than he had yesterday. By the end of the fourth day, he could walk almost like a normal man, an old man, but not someone infirm.

"So what will it be today?" Azerick asked as he sat down to eat. "Shall I walk on my hands for you?"

"Do you think you can?" Lissandra asked.

Azerick thought a moment. "No."

"Then we will save that for later. Today, you will continue to circle the room, but now I want you to bend down deeply with your foreleg while extending your trailing leg. You will dip low enough that your back knee almost touches the floor, but do not let it do so."

"What happens if it touches?"

"Then I shall throw rocks at you."

Azerick smiled and reminded himself not to give the Guardian any more ideas. He had slowly come to the opinion she was not as stern and dispassionate as she let on. He felt Lissandra's tough approach was partly for the benefit of his training and partly from not being accustomed to being around people. On a few occasions, out of the corner of his eye, Azerick caught the Guardian smiling when she thought he was not looking. Granted, the smile was subtle and mostly on the inside, but Azerick liked to think he saw it.

If walking had been difficult, the lunges were torture. Not only did it take extraordinary effort to get up after each dip, it took a lot of fine muscle control to keep from falling over, which he did several times. Azerick failed to make a single complete circuit of the room before collapsing, and this time he did choose to lie on the floor like a dead animal.

"Are you going to simply lie there all day?" Lissandra asked.

"No. It should be nightfall before too long," Azerick groaned.

"Shall I serve your supper on the floor as well?"

"It would probably be easier than moving the table."

The Guardian looked at her charge with annoyance. "I suppose I shall leave you with some small shred of dignity and put it in a bowl for you."

"You are all heart. You should not coddle me so much," Azerick quipped. "Could you do me a favor?"

"What?" Lissandra asked in exasperation.

"Pull off my slipper, and then hit yourself with it."

Azerick let out a yelp when a rock struck him in the shoulder with significant force and pinpoint accuracy. He rolled onto his hands and knees before struggling back to his feet. He rubbed at his bruised shoulder and took several deep breaths before returning to his exercises.

CHAPTER 19

Inquisitors Elias and Fennrick sat in plush chairs across from Duchess Paullina who reclined on a sedan sipping wine in her parlor.

"Fennrick, what progress on the girl and the codex have we made?" the duchess asked.

Both inquisitors shifted nervously in their chairs. "None, Your Grace."

Duchess Paullina set her glass on the low table separating her from her guests and sat up. "None? It has been almost four months since you brought her here. How is this possible?"

"The girl is extremely resilient," Fennrick explained defensively. "She has been subjected to torture before, and there appears to be little we administer that she has not already undergone. Couple that with her madness, and we face a significant challenge. I did inform you this would take time."

"Yes, and in this time I have been plagued with the company of nearly a hundred pilgrims from the Academy, a dozen requests, each more insistent than the last, to hand over the Codex Arcana, and another five hundred requests from every wizard and charlatan in the kingdom to view it to see if it will speak to them. Headmaster Florent has threatened to start sending journeymen wizards here by the wagonload if we do not gain access to it soon!"

"Perhaps Fennrick is being too gentle," Elias suggested. "If she has faced pain before, we simply need to apply more pain than those Sumaran barbarians did."

Fennrick shook his head. "It is not that easy. I have applied a great deal of pain. When it gets too much, she simply goes catatonic and becomes completely unreachable, for days sometimes. If we continue to push as we are, we risk sending her over the edge forever."

"Then what are we going to do?" the duchess demanded.

Elias stared at the ceiling and let out a slow breath. "I am at a loss, Your Grace."

"Of course you are! You always are because you are an idiot! Obviously I was asking Fennrick."

"I have concluded that we will not find the solution through physical means, even those of discomfort as we have been using. Sleep deprivation, near drowning, excessive heat and cold, none are working," the inquisitor said. "I think the resistance her emotional condition gives her against physical coercion could hold the solution."

Paullina leaned forward interestedly. "Explain."

"I have been studying the girl and doing research on mental abnormalities and think that if we are ever going to break her or convince her to help us, we must focus on her mind with no other physical stressors. We know there is a weakness already present. We simply need to find the most effective way to exploit it."

"I assume you have some ideas."

"I do. I think it is time she had some visitors."

Ellyssa sat on her cot, held her knees, and gently rocked back and forth. It had been days since they last tortured her, and she knew they would be coming again soon. She used to fear their coming with each beat of her heart, but not anymore. When the pain and turmoil got too bad, she simply went away. It was getting easier to go away these days. The first time it happened, she thought she had died, but then reality slammed home once again and she found herself back in this room.

She looked forward to going away even though it took so much pain and fear to get there, but it was worth it. When she went away, she was back home using her magic. Ellyssa realized it was not the huge, flashy, destructive magic that brought her the most joy. It was the simple things like the time she stalked Wolf through the forest while he was hunting. She created an illusion of a rabbit and watched as Wolf chased it for over an hour, cursing furiously every time he failed to hit it with one of his arrows. Ghost saw right through her magical camouflage and almost certainly knew the rabbit was a fake, but he never let on. That was one unusual wolf.

Thinking about her magic got her wondering about the spells used to keep her from reaching the Source within her cell. She had first thought the runes carved deeply into the walls made the entire interior a magic-free zone, but later realized the wizards here had no problem using magic to torture her.

It meant there had to be an associative spell in effect as well, one that either acted with the runes to prevent her from using magic or allowed the inquisitors to cast within her cell. She searched her body for any magical sigils but failed to locate any. There could be something on her back, but she had no mirror to check. More likely, those tasked with her torture wore an item, like a bracelet or pendant working in conjunction with the negation magic in her cell to give them access to the Source. If this was the case, all she needed to do was take it from one of them, and then she would bring this whole place down upon them all.

The problem would be getting it. Ellyssa needed to know precisely what it was and where they wore it. If she tried to relieve them of it and failed, she likely would never get another chance. So far, she had seen nothing that appeared to be what she was seeking, if it even existed. For this reason, she held on, waiting for the day one of them got careless and revealed it.

Ellyssa snapped out of her thoughts when she heard voices echoing through her door from the passageway beyond. She flinched and drew back on her cot at the sound of the heavy bolt being drawn back. A startled gasp escaped her mouth when she saw Allister and Miranda filling the doorway.

"Hello, dear," Allister said kindly. "How are you?"

Ellyssa looked down at her feet drawn up against the edge of the cot and remained as silent as Miranda.

Seeing he would get no response, Allister continued. "We wanted to come and tell you we did not abandon you. The Academy, particularly the Office of Inquisition, wanted to execute you for your crimes. I made a protest to the Academy and Miranda sent an official plea for leniency. Although we were able to achieve a stay of execution, we were unsuccessful in getting you a pardon or moving your incarceration to North Haven. We even beseeched the king, but the Academy has a significant amount of autonomy. We have exhausted our last resources to try and improve your situation despite the damage you have done to the school and those within it."

Ellyssa looked away and studied the runes on the far wall as tears cleaned away some of the accumulated grime on her face.

"Inquisitor Fennrick told me of his offer to move you to more comfortable accommodations if you helped them use the codex," Allister continued. "I know you feel responsible, and maybe some of your unwillingness to accept their offer is so you can continue being punished for killing Azerick. You do not have to do that, child. You have suffered enough. Help them, and help yourself, because none of us can help you anymore."

Ellyssa returned her gaze to her feet, refusing to meet the old wizard's eyes. "I can't."

"Why not? You are not just helping them or yourself, you are helping to advance magic as we know it for all wizards. Ellyssa. The things in the Codex Arcana could save countless lives."

Ellyssa shuddered and shook her head. "You wouldn't understand."

Miranda finally broke her silence as her anger reached its limits. "I understand perfectly! You have always been a stubborn, selfish child!"

"Miranda, please," Allister begged.

"No! I am sick and tired of pretending I forgive her, that I still give a damn about her! Her selfishness killed my husband, and I hope she clings to that same stubbornness so she can live in the same pain I do every day for the rest of her miserable life. I cannot stand to look at her anymore," Miranda declared, storming away, wiping the tears from her face as she retreated.

Allister watched Miranda for a moment before turning back to Ellyssa. "I'm very disappointed in you, as would be Azerick." He turned and followed Miranda.

Ellyssa flopped down onto her bed as sobs wracked her body. She desperately willed herself to go away again, but it was the wrong kind of pain to pay the fare, so she had no choice but to lie there and endure it.

Allister caught up with Miranda near the stairs leading out of the dungeon. Both stopped before Inquisitor Fennrick as he stepped into the hallway.

"How did it go?" Fennrick asked.

The couple's faces shimmered and contorted as they dropped their illusions. "Perfectly," Inquisitor Tamara answered.

"She is sobbing uncontrollably, her spirit seriously compromised if not broken," Inquisitor Parkes said. "A few more sessions like this and we will certainly have access to the Codex Arcana."

"And you will have your promotion to senior inquisitor," Tamara added.

Fennrick beamed under the successful report. "Then I had best go play my part."

Fennrick walked toward the sound of Ellyssa's sobbing and paused in the open door until she sat up and looked at him. He had watched the girl tortured, even inflicted a great deal of suffering himself, but her face showed more pain than he had seen from her before. He doubted she was broken yet, but they had certainly managed to create a flaw in her defenses. Now he just needed to exploit it.

"I could not help but overhear," the inquisitor said. "It sounds like you are truly on your own now. You don't have to be, you know. I have been thinking. You showed a great deal of strength and cleverness when we fought. You certainly humiliated those Academy weaklings. We could use those kinds of talents here. Our numbers are declining just as the Academy rolls are, and our mission is vital to the security of the kingdom. I know my associates would support me in requesting that you be given the chance to become one of us. It would be on a probationary basis and you would be guarded and limited in freedom for a time, but if you showed you were willing to act properly and worked with us, I am sure I could convince the Academy to give you a chance. Think about it."

Fennrick turned and walked away. Ellyssa was so lost in thought she did not even hear the door slam shut and the lock clank home. She wanted to ignore the inquisitor, wanted to spit in his face as she had at his previous offers, but this time she could not help but consider it. And for that, she hated herself.

CHAPTER 20

A zerick clung to the side of the soaring mountain like a spider on a wall and made the mistake of looking down. Through the tops of the wispy clouds below him, he could see the sheer mountain face descend an untold number of feet.

Farther out, where the mists did not cling to the mountainside, Azerick could see giant swaths of green, which he assumed were the tops of trees spreading out across the land and occasionally opening up to reveal lakes, rivers, and fields. He was so high up there were no distinctive features evident in the sprawling terrain, only a patchwork of colors, like a quilt blanketing the planet.

Looking up did not make him feel much better as thousands of feet of grey granite glared down at him, ready to send him plunging through miles of open air for his audacity in trespassing upon their heavenly heights. At this altitude, he should be freezing to death in his thin covering of silk, but his body maintained a comfortable temperature despite the massive plumes of fog erupting from his mouth as he breathed. He assumed it was due to Lissandra's magic.

"Is this really necessary?" Azerick called up to Lissandra.

The Guardian looked down from her perch on a ledge perhaps a hundred feet above Azerick's head, calmly sipping from the teacup that never seemed to leave her hand. "It is vital for your training, both physically and mentally."

Azerick had undergone a series of grueling tasks over the weeks, each one more strenuous than the last. The simple, yet fatiguing, tasks of walking and doing lunges became much more acrobatic ones like walking on his hands and performing stunts that required not just physical strength and endurance, but also significant balance and concentration. When Lissandra told him this morning that today was his last day of physical training, he had been overjoyed. When the Guardian then told him he would be climbing to the peak of the mountain in which they lived, he longed for his previous tortures.

He soon pulled himself up onto the ledge and sat next to Lissandra. "Is climbing to the top truly necessary?"

"It is important," answered Lissandra.

"Why? What can I get out of the climb from up there I cannot get from here? Nothing has really fatigued me for days now."

"I will tell you when we get there," Lissandra answered cryptically.

Before Azerick could protest further, the Guardian's teacup vanished and she lazily threw herself over the narrow ledge. The first time she did this had startled Azerick terribly. He had rushed to the ledge, expecting to witness Lissandra plummeting to her death only to see her sheer silken robes become a pair of great leathery wings of an azure hue.

Lissandra abruptly reappeared as she raced upward, soaring several hundred feet over Azerick's head until she found another ledge upon which to perch. She once again summoned her cup of tea and waited for Azerick to resume his climb. Azerick did not keep her waiting for long and continued his arduous trek up the mountain face. It took Azerick nearly two hours to reach the Guardian's newest roost.

"You are taking too long," Lissandra said as Azerick pulled himself onto the ledge. "I want to reach the summit early enough to return by nightfall."

Azerick gave her an annoyed look. "If you are in such a hurry, you could just fly me to the top."

"The air is too thin, and you are too heavy for me to carry. Besides, it would defeat half the purpose."

"The purpose being the amusement you take in watching me suffer?"

"Not entirely, but largely yes. Now hurry up. We are behind schedule."

Azerick sighed as Lissandra once again hurled herself into open air and flew upwards. "Give me your wings and then let us see who reaches the top first," he muttered.

With another grumble, Azerick picked out the best route for the ascent with his eyes before gripping the rock and climbing once more. The ascent was not that difficult. The face of the mountain was rough and provided ample hand and toeholds and his body felt very strong.

Azerick was not certain how strong he was before all this, but he had a feeling such unflagging strength was not normal for humans. What he did not know was whether the source of that strength was due to his rigorous training, the awful food and drink Lissandra forced him to eat, or something magical in nature.

Such a climb, especially by someone so ignorant about such an endeavor, should have been terrifying. However, Azerick knew Lissandra would never let him fall and, with such readily available support for his hands and feet, scaling the mountain was little more difficult than climbing a tree. That still did not mean Azerick was completely free from feeling nervous. There was simply no way to take his mind completely off the fact there was so much empty air between him and the ground.

Azerick finally attained the long, narrow ridge shrouded in snow and ice running up to the mountain peak like the monstrous spine of some colossal animal. Lissandra stood waiting only a few paces away, her silk gown fluttering in the breeze. She did not say anything, only turned and began walking along the steeply inclining ridge toward the rocky, snow-capped summit.

Azerick followed dutifully, plodding through the soft blanket of unmarred snow. It was then he noticed the Guardian left no footprints despite the fact that he sank to his knees in the white powder. Yet another advantage of mastering the arcane, he surmised.

He continued to trudge up the slope, which became steeper as he neared the final ascent to the summit. Fortunately, it never became so steep he had to start climbing again. Azerick finally reached Lissandra, who was sitting on a bare expanse of rock, and flopped down beside her.

"Now will you tell me why you forced me to climb to the top of the world?" Azerick asked exasperatedly.

Lissandra pointed out toward the expanse beyond them and the clouds cleared away to reveal the world beneath them. "Look out there, and look well."

Azerick did as he was told and studied the patchwork of colors thousands upon thousands of feet below him. Mile after mile of browns, greens, and golden swaths of land stretched out to the horizon. Blue ribbons of water looked like the veins and arteries of the land. Behind him, the peaks of grey stone and snow-capped summits, some nearly as tall as the one upon which he sat, stabbed at the sky in a jagged field as far as he could see.

"This is what you are fighting for," the Guardian said. "Those lands you see, and even more you cannot, are populated with hundreds of thousands of lives. Beyond the Great Barrier Mountains lies an even greater land where millions call home. The Scions will destroy it all should they be victorious."

"That is an enormous responsibility," Azerick stated, feeling overwhelmed under its weight.

"It is," Lissandra agreed, "but your entire life has been carefully directed to be capable of bearing it. You are strong, and you must remain strong and unwavering in your resolve. I want you to remember this view and what it represents, and use this memory whenever you feel your resolve slipping. Tomorrow, we will begin recovering your memory, and you will need every source of strength you possess to endure it. You will hurt, you will doubt, and you will not want to face what you will experience, but you must so you will become what you were and what you must be."

Azerick let Lissandra's words soak in and responded heavily, "I understand."

"I truly hope so. Come, it is time we returned."

The Guardian took Azerick by the hand, and the expansive vista from atop the mountain peak vanished and was replaced by the comforting walls of Lissandra's home. Food was set out and waiting, and of a variety far more palatable than he had previously enjoyed.

There was little conversation that night, and Lissandra encouraged Azerick to get as much sleep as he could. Despite his anxiety over what was to come, he had little trouble falling into a deep sleep, thankfully devoid of nightmares. When next he opened his eyes, Lissandra was seated next to his bed.

"We will begin now," the Guardian told him. "Your brain is at its least cluttered immediately after you awaken."

Azerick nodded. "Okay, so what do I do?"

"Just lie back and close your eyes." Lissandra held up a clear gem the size of a large hen's egg. "I will search your mind and store the memories I find in here, and then put them back in order, much like putting together a puzzle."

"Sounds easy enough."

"It is not. It will be challenging for me and positively overwhelming for you. Now close your eyes and let your mind go. You will sense little until I begin returning your memories to you. When you see them play out, you must focus on them and accept them back into you. Some you will joyfully welcome with open arms, others will make you want to flee and cause you great distress. You must fight the fear and pain of those unpleasant memories and take them in as deeply and completely as you do the others. It is part of who you are and you must not deny them. When you feel you cannot go on, remember what it is you are fighting for. The first day of battle starts now."

Azerick closed his eyes and did his best to relax. He felt the cool pressure of the gem as Lissandra touched it to his brow and began softly chanting. The jewel hummed and vibrated against his skin and grew warm as if heated by the sun.

For a long time, Azerick felt and saw nothing, but then he detected a change in the heat and vibration of the crystal. Images began flooding in and Azerick willed them to clarity. Visually, they were indistinct, but a wave of emotion hit him with great force. He felt the arms of his mother cradling him, heard her voice singing him a lullaby, and felt the love for him radiating out of her. Tears came unbidden and flowed down his face as he experienced such unfiltered emotions.

His life raced forward in a series of flashes. Azerick reached out, grabbed hold of a particularly clear image, and drew it to him. He was on his father's ship standing behind the huge wheel, controlling the rudder. He looked up and beamed into his father's strong face. Darius smiled down at his son, his calloused hands covering Azerick's as he gripped the big wooden wheel.

Azerick was in the courtyard of their home, the loud clack of wooden swords echoing off the walls as he and Master Ewen dueled in a mock battle. His old weapons instructor smacked him hard in the shoulder and berated him for leaving his guard open. The words of every book he ever read came flooding back to him, reminding him of how much he loved to read and learn.

The feelings he experienced were far more immersive and substantial than he had expected. Every sound, sight, and smell came to him with complete realism and solidity. Every emotion and sensation he had experienced over the years felt as fresh as if everything was happening at that very instant, but compressed and concentrated into a few short hours.

He opened his eyes and returned to the reality of the present when he felt Lissandra pull away the gem. Azerick's entire body trembled with pent-up emotion desperately seeking release and his breath came in ragged gasps.

"Why did you stop?" Azerick asked.

"It is enough for today."

"I thought you said it would be horrible, that what I saw would torment me. These memories are wonderful. I remember my father and mother and the love they hold for me."

"And that is why I chose this point to stop. I want you to imprint them into your mind fully. Tomorrow, the pain begins and you will need these joyous memories to bear it. When the pain becomes more than you think you can handle, you need to focus on these few pleasant memories and hold them tightly within your heart."

Once again, Lissandra warned him of impending emotional angst. Azerick wondered what could have happened in his life that would cause her so much concern and prompt such continued warnings. Was it the events of his life that were so terrible or just the process of retrieving them?

These first happy memories were certainly intense, and the unpleasant ones would most likely be equally strong, but could they be so bad they threatened to overwhelm him? Was it the things he saw and experienced that concerned Lissandra so greatly or the things he had done? She had pulled him from the abyss, a place for the souls of the damned. Was he evil? Did the Guardian fear he would return to his vile ways when he learned who he truly was?

Wonderful images of Azerick sailing with his father filled his dreams that night. He felt the salt spray upon his face and the taste of it upon his lips. He hastened across the gently rolling deck of the ship, carrying out his father's instructions with zeal. In another scene, his mother sat with him as he studied from a book, helping him with the harder words and answering his many questions. When he awoke, he saw the face of his mother for the briefest moment upon Lissandra's countenance.

"Today is when the true test of your resolve begins," Lissandra said. "Are you ready?"

Azerick nodded and the Guardian again touched the crystal to his forehead and began softly chanting. Azerick felt himself slip away into the familiar dreamlike state and watched as the images began pouring in. Seeing his life unfold at such an incredible speed should have made it impossible to comprehend, but his mind absorbed every image, sense, and emotion like a sponge.

Azerick gasped and jerked violently as he relived the loss of his father, mother, and home. He was able to recall his emotions the first time the tragedy struck. He experienced the agony again but compounded severalfold. The first time his parents died, he had time to process his emotions before facing the next horror in his life. Now those heart-rending moments came at him with crystal clarity and no time to mourn, process, and overcome his turmoil.

He tried to conjure the images and joyful feelings he felt yesterday, but the torment he felt now overwhelmed them and crushed him beneath its oppressive emotional weight. Azerick writhed in agony as he suffered a seemingly unending barrage of pain and misery-inducing events.

Lissandra finally relented when Allister took Azerick in to join the Academy. It was the happiest moment of his life after the death of his father, and he was grateful for the memory. He clung to it as he wept, trying to take comfort in the memory of his mother's loving arms and his father's strong, protective hands.

There was another source of strength as well. It was something deeper and more personal, a well of power growing from somewhere far beyond himself. It, more than anything, was what defined, shaped, and drove him. Azerick dipped his mind and soul into the silver essence of the Source and let it envelop him. His skin flushed from the shame he felt from feeling more comfort in his magic than in the caring arms of his loved ones. It was the first moment Azerick truly began to understand who and what he was.

If his experiences that day were terrible, the next proved to be unimaginable. Travis's death was only moderately difficult to accept and troubling mostly due to having to leave the Academy. Even his capture by the psylings, although terrifying, was not nearly as devastating as what he felt at the death of his family and friends.

It was difficult beyond imagining, but Azerick felt he could weather the session's emotional assaults—until Xornan murdered his beloved Delinda. The tormented sorcerer bolted upright, a scream of anguish and rage tearing from his throat. He slapped Lissandra's hand away, sending the jewel flying from her grip.

Azerick pushed the Guardian's steadying hands away and rolled out of the bed and onto the floor. With another primal scream, he scrambled to his feet and ran from the room. He sprinted across the large central chamber and ran for the archway opening directly to the open air of Lissandra's cliffside home.

Just as Azerick reached the opening and leapt to throw himself into the empty void more than ten thousand feet above the valley floor, magical strands wrapped around his body and jerked him back into the room and pinned him to the floor.

"No!" Azerick futilely tried to claw his way to the precipice. "Let me go! I cannot do this. Please, no more. For the love of the gods, no more!"

Lissandra laid a comforting hand on Azerick's shuddering body. "You must go on. I know this is difficult, more so than I can even imagine, but you must persevere."

"I can't," Azerick sobbed as his tears soaked the floor and great strands of drool trickled from his mouth. "It hurts too much. I cannot go on. I can't!"

"You can, and you will. You will see that once you are able to process this terrible memory. I looked into your mind after I brought you here, and I believe this to be the most traumatic memory you possess, as well as the most important. Return to your bed and rest. I will give you as much time as I can for you to recover."

"I have my magic back, isn't that enough?" he begged.

"No, I am afraid it is not. Your sorcery is only half of what you are. You must rediscover yourself in your entirety for there to be any hope."

Azerick felt himself float above the floor and be gently lowered back onto his bed. He curled into a ball and held his knees as he lay weeping until his body ached and exhaustion finally pulled him into a troubled sleep. That night, his dreams were a series of nightmares as he watched Delinda die repeatedly in a macabre montage painted with the brush of his anguished soul. Every death he had ever been a part of or witnessed, Delinda was there, taking the place of the victim.

It took days for Azerick to summon the strength to eat, and over a week before Lissandra pushed him to continue his treatment.

"We need to continue. I am running out of time."

Azerick hugged his arms around his chest and shook his head. "I'm sorry; I just don't think I can. I want to, but I just can't."

Lissandra extended her hand to him. "Come, it is time you saw the face of our enemy."

Azerick let the Guardian lead him from the room. She touched the wall of the main chamber and a section disappeared, revealing another chamber beyond. The room was empty except for a crystal sphere the size of his head cradled on a stone plinth.

Once inside, Lissandra gestured to the doorway and it vanished, plunging the room into total darkness. The crystal began to glow and Azerick could see again. The light continued to expand but the walls were now gone.

The light revealed a great shimmering barrier stretching beyond sight both horizontally and vertically. Suddenly, Azerick could see past the wall and his knees nearly buckled. Spread out across a desolate plain milled hordes of fearsome creatures of every size and description. Everywhere creatures fought and died, but their numbers were so great even their constant battles could do nothing to reduce them. Floating high above the plain was a massive crystal fortress twice as tall as its width.

"By the gods, there must be…" Azerick tried to count.

"Millions," Lissandra finished. "There are millions just waiting for the inevitable fall of this barrier, and they know the time is drawing near."

Before Azerick could form a response, an intense pressure began crushing his brain. Four ghostly, giant-sized figures appeared just beyond the shimmering wall. They were gaunt and covered in purple silk robes. Their heads were dull grey, hairless, and far too large for their emaciated bodies. No sign of a mouth broke the featureless plain of their face. The creatures' eyes were like looking into the nighttime sky. The twin black caverns twinkled with starlight, luminous eddies swirled, and an occasional comet streaked through them.

Guardian, I see you have brought us a tribute. Have you finally decided to save yourself and free us?

The chorus of voices crushed Azerick to the ground under their awesome assault. The mentally invasive power of the psylings was but the gentle whisper of a loved one in comparison. Azerick cried out as he fell to the ground, feeling as though the boot of a titan was grinding him under its heel.

Lissandra spoke a few words and gestured with her hand. Azerick gulped in air as the titanic pressure relented to a dull throb and an annoying buzz.

"No, Scions. I wished to show you the face of your ultimate destruction, and you to him. You know my time is nearing, and so I hand off my duty to one more capable."

Capable? He is certainly interesting, but hardly capable. We shall amuse ourselves with this strange creature before destroying him, his bloodline, and all those who trespass in the place of the true gods. Hear us, sorcerer, and live your final days in terror. We are coming, and we will destroy all who dared touch the power reserved for the gods and all who share their blood. Then we shall purge the world of all but a few of the most docile and tractable of your pathetic kind. The feeble creatures you worship as gods cannot help you. They cannot even help themselves. You are all insignificant to the true gods.

Azerick stood and faced the Scions' wavering image. "Only those who have fear in their hearts feel the need to threaten. Were we so feeble, we would be beneath your notice and such wasted words unnecessary. Stay behind your wall and save yourselves. Come to my world, and we shall be ready to meet you with steel, magic, and courage." Azerick turned to the Guardian. "Come, Lissandra, let us leave these posturing fools to their rightful desolation."

Lissandra smiled and gestured. The room went black once more before filling with natural light when the doorway reappeared. Azerick sank down and shuddered, gasping for air.

"What were those things?"

"Those were the Scions. That is what you shall have to face. Now you see why it is so incredibly vital for you to regain all you once were."

Azerick shook his head. "So much power, and that from behind a great barrier. How can I, any of us, hope to stand against it?"

"By standing together. You handled yourself well. Return to your bed and rest. We shall return to your ministrations tomorrow."

Azerick forced himself to stand and nodded his agreement. What he saw was so much bigger than himself. It was bigger than his pride, fear, and pain. It was the destruction of everything, and he would not let anything keep him from doing everything in his power to stop it.

The next several days were a mash of bad to horrible, but nothing approaching the intensity of Delinda's death. He even experienced a few pleasures like creating his school and watching Ellyssa develop into a very talented wizard. As angry and frustrating as many of her antics were at the time, he found himself laughing at his recollections.

Finally, after weeks of emotional turmoil, Lissandra called an end at the moment of his death in Sumara. "This is where I must stop."

Azerick looked at her quizzically. "But there is more. I was in the abyss. I must have memories of that place as well."

"That is so, and you shall experience those, but not today." The Guardian stared out at nothing. "Azerick, my time is drawing near, but you must go on. You must continue to fight and grow. You now know much of the source of your strength and perseverance. I have done everything I can to prepare you for what is to come."

Before Azerick could form any of the dozen questions racing through his mind, Lissandra swept from the room and vanished. Azerick wanted to chase after her, to demand answers to his many questions, but her departure left no doubt as to the finality of the gesture.

Azerick did not see the Guardian again. She did not show for the evening meal, but there was a plate set out for him. He figured he would see her in the morning, but when he awoke, he was alone in the room. A slender pillar of stone rose in the center of the chamber the moment his feet touched the floor. Upon it lay the memory crystal.

He crossed the room and lifted the crystal from its pedestal. Azerick jumped in surprise as Lissandra materialized near the column. A second look showed him that she was not truly there, but was a semi-translucent image much like the Scions had been, only normal-sized.

"Azerick, if you are seeing me then I am already gone," the image said. "The crystal holds the last of your memories. They are those I intentionally withheld until now and stored within the crystal for you to discover. Be warned, they are the most dangerous ones you possess. When you use the crystal, those memories will unlock a cage in which your other half has been contained since you left the abyss. That half is enormously powerful and will seek to dominate you. You must apply all your resolve to ensure that does not happen. This is your most dangerous task yet, but the most vital. You will need the strength your other self possesses."

The image stopped speaking but remained in the room, seemingly waiting. Azerick tried to understand what she meant by his other half, but none of his previous memories gave him a clue as to what it could be. He assumed it must be tied to his being in the abyss and was why Lissandra chose not to restore those memories yesterday.

Azerick considered not using the crystal. He had his magic back and could leave this place. Why risk what the Guardian said was so dangerous? Because he must. He had come to accept what was happening was far bigger and more important than he was. Azerick returned to his bed and pressed the crystal against his forehead.

It hummed against his cool skin a moment before it pulled his consciousness inside its faceted form. Azerick found himself chained to the summoning floor of the black tower. He recalled this from his previous recollections, but instead of his previous vague memory of escaping, he felt himself falling.

The scene raced forward as he relived Klaraxis's possession and his inner battles with the demon lord. He recounted every instance of the demon's existence and his struggles in maintaining control. Finally, he witnessed his death and return to the abyss. Azerick agonized over his encounter with Krade and the tortured images the devil had shown him. He found himself in his final battle with Drak'kar and the silver light tearing him from the abyssal realm.

Klaraxis felt his black void of a prison disintegrate with the return of Azerick's memory and ferociously charged forth, clawing at Azerick's consciousness with every ounce of strength he possessed. Azerick, taken by complete surprise despite Lissandra's warning, struggled desperately to fight off the demon's assault. He fought against his rising panic and forced himself to a state of calm.

Klaraxis raged as he brutally lashed at Azerick's mind. *You cannot imagine the awfulness of the prison I was in, barely cognizant of my own existence! There was nothing, just the black void of a semi-existence!*

Azerick mentally took hold of the demon and simply responded, "No," then pushed Klaraxis away from him.

Azerick shuddered as he shared Klaraxis's pervasive fear over his banishment. Whatever prison Azerick's loss of memory had thrust him into, it upset the demon more than anything he had ever felt from his host before. Azerick tuned out Klaraxis's furious howling and returned his focus to Lissandra's image as she spoke once more.

"You should now know who you are in your entirety. I pray you were successful in maintaining control. Your apprentice and the Codex Arcana are now being held in the Office of Inquisition in Argoth. You will need them both in the coming days. There is one more thing I must show you. Please follow me."

The illusion turned and strode from the room and Azerick dutifully followed. Lissandra came to a brief stop before the solid wall of an unfamiliar room. The stone before her vanished and revealed another large chamber beyond. Azerick assumed it was the Guardian's personal chambers. The room had a large bed and furnishings typical of any fine home, if a bit austere.

What caught his eye was a large crystalline egg the size of a keg of beer near the center of the room, and it moved. Azerick watched warily as it twitched and a crack formed along its side.

"I told you that there would be another who would be a great weapon against the Scions, and this is it," Lissandra explained. "As the elves did in my creation, I took from you your essence and combined it with my own. Here it has been growing for most of the year since I took you from the abyss. It is our son, a creature of human, dragon, elf, and demon spirit. The plurality of its soul and ability to wield the magic of all our races will make him truly formidable.

"It is up to you to ensure he learns not just power, but discipline, sacrifice, and decency. The demonic portion of his soul will encourage him to selfishness and destruction. You must defend him at all costs, even from his own nature. I have named him Raijaun and have spoken it to him frequently so that he will respond to it when he hatches. I have already given the last of myself to the barrier holding the Scions at bay in hopes of granting you the time you need to prepare for their invasion. I can only pray it is enough. Raijaun will grow swiftly, as his demonic nature, as well as that of mine, dictates. Take care of our son, teach him to be a good man, and civilization may have a chance. Goodbye."

Lissandra's image vanished, throwing the room into an eerie silence. The quiet was broken a moment later as another crack formed in the amber crystalline cocoon. A spiderweb of fractures began appearing as the creature inside struggled to break free of its incubatory prison. One final thrust sent shards of crystal skating across the floor as Raijaun exploded from the glassy shell.

Azerick's son spotted him, hissed loudly, and leapt away, placing the bed between him and his father. Azerick stood in disbelief as the creature emerged and fled from him. His skin was the color of granite, small black horns jutted slightly back from his head, and a pair of leathery blue-black wings sprouted from his back.

Azerick knelt and called out to his son. "Raijaun, it's all right. Come here."

Raijaun crept around the side of the bed, peeked around the corner, and narrowed his green-flecked, golden eyes at Azerick. He tilted his head upward and sniffed the air several times. He slinked forward as Azerick beckoned and gently called his name. Raijaun lightly touched the tips of Azerick's extended fingers with his clawed digits. Sensing something, a bond or perhaps just the knowledge this person was not going to harm him, Raijaun leapt into his father's arms and cooed as he nestled his head against Azerick's chest.

He certainly looks like his father, one of them anyway. Do you think you can prevent him from acting like me as well?

"You will have nothing to do with any of my children, demon," Azerick swore. "As I told you before, I will destroy us both before I let that happen."

And as I told you, we shall see.

Azerick set Raijaun on the edge of the bed, pulled off a small wool blanket, and created a sling he then draped around his neck. Securing his toddler-sized son within the fold, he stood at the edge of the entrance to Lissandra's lair and conjured his staff to his hand. Azerick gave an ecstatic sigh as he felt the familiar warmth of the artifact in his hand once again.

"Well, Raijaun, we have a great deal to do, so we had best get to it." Azerick shifted to his demonic form, and stepped out into the void, gliding down into the valley below.

EPILOGUE

The Rook flew through the endless streams of brilliant light, using all of his strength to keep the titanic dimensional forces from tearing apart his noncorporeal form. Time was lost in the ether of this place between worlds as the luminous currents whipped him about like a leaf in a hurricane.

After months, years, maybe even an eternity of being hurled about in the strange vortex, the assassin spotted an anomaly. It was a pinpoint of pure white light, unmarred by the silver flows shimmering with a rainbow sheen. The Rook willed himself toward the speck and watched it grow as he fought against the powerful currents of the intradimensional universe.

The point grew to become a portal, and the closer the Rook got, the harder the current tried to pull him away. The Rook fought against the awesome tidal forces working against him, a cry of effort born of rage and denial tearing soundlessly from his throat. He finally gained the portal, now shining so brightly it pained his eyes, grabbed the edges, and pulled himself through with a final, monumental effort of will.

Intense light flooded his entire existence, setting his very soul aflame. The Rook screeched in agony beyond anything imaginable as the light rapidly sought to destroy him. A short distance away, the orange flickering of a campfire and the dark silhouettes of two men pierced the overwhelming brilliance.

The Rook streaked toward the men, picked one at random, and thrust his ethereal blade into his unsuspecting body. The assassin poured his essence into the man, found his spirit, and engaged it in a battle for existence.

Birkar felt the foreign entity invade his mind and dropped to the snowy ground, writhing as the creature slashed mercilessly at his soul. His last thought was feeling something frigid pierce his consciousness before it devoured him.

"Birkar!" Magn cried out as he watched his friend go into some sort of seizure.

His friend thrashed about for just a few seconds before he went still, gasping for breath.

"Birkar, are you all right?" Magn asked as he helped the man to his feet.

Birkar nodded. "I'm fine."

"What happened? What is wrong with your eyes? They're glowing blue!"

Magn gasped as Birkar's skinning knife plunged into his guts. The Rook dispassionately watched the corpse fall to the ground, the hot blood painting an expanding crimson circle beneath him until freezing solid in just seconds. The Rook looked out at the frozen wasteland, nothing but snow and ice as far as he could see. Packing up as much food and supplies as he could drag on the sled, the Rook turned south and started the beginning of a very long walk in search of his prey.

The boys and girls surrounding the two duelists laughed and encouraged the much smaller boy as he landed another strike against his opponent. Daebian's foe significantly out-massed him, so he relied on his speed and skill to worry away at Daniel's defenses and landed several light blows while dancing away from the bigger boy's slower but powerful strokes.

Daniel flicked his eyes at the other martial students, their good-natured laughter and ribbing feeling like needles under his skin. It did not help that even though Daebian looked like a ten-year-old, he was still only five and already a better swordsman.

With a shout of frustrated anger, Daniel charged in, ignoring another light strike against his shoulder, and used his bulk to bash away at Daebian's defenses. Daebian found himself retreating as

Daniel's fury-driven slashes set his arm tingling from the vibrations ringing through his wooden sword and into his body.

Daebian caught his heel and tripped as he backpedaled. He landed heavily on his back, a grunt escaping his lips as the unyielding ground forced the air from his lungs. This should have declared an end to the mock battle, but Daniel, his anger clouding his judgment, pressed on and chopped at the defeated boy on the ground.

Daebian rolled to his side and covered his head as a pair of strokes abused his right shoulder, deeply bruising him even through the thickly padded training armor they wore. Several onlookers leapt to his defense and pulled Daniel away before he could elicit further punishment.

Snapped out of his fury, Daniel was able to enjoy his victory. "Good fight, but you're still too small to beat me. Maybe when you're bigger. That should only take a couple of weeks, you freak!"

"Come on, Dan, that's not right," one of the boys who pulled him off admonished. "That's Azerick's son after all."

"What do I care? He is a freak," Daniel replied cruelly.

"That's okay," Daebian said with a smile as he got up and dusted himself off. "I am getting bigger, and I look forward to a rematch. It's getting late and time for me to get going."

Daebian waved at everyone as he left the practice field. He absolutely loved sparring, but none of the kids his size proved much of a challenge, so he often chose bigger, stronger, and more experienced students to fight. Daniel was bigger than most he fought, but he knew the boy would not take it easy on him like so many others did, and he needed a true challenge to get better. The rudeness was uncalled for, however.

The evening's dinner was winding down as the original school faculty sat around the big dining table and discussed the issues of the day. It had been two years since the Academy took over, and the transition was not going well.

"Did you speak with the council today?" Rusty asked Magus Allister.

Allister's face darkened. "I did, and I got the same answer I have been getting the past two years. They need more time to gauge the ability of the students, and most of the students need far more general education before raising the level of applied magic."

"Many of the children do lack a fundamental education compared to those attending the Academy," Rusty replied.

"That is because every student at the Academy comes from a family who can afford private tutors! Every student in our applied magic class can read, write, and cipher well enough! They have an understanding of magical theory and history, and their knowledge grows daily. Harvey is intentionally strangling the advancement of magic in this school and I will not stand for it! Our most advanced students are learning little more than an Academy novice, and our novices are learning nothing at all!"

"Maybe everyone just needs a little more time," Joshua said. "I imagine there is still some fear at the Academy given the fact that the only previous source of structured magic education outside of the Academy was at the Black Tower."

"It's not about time, it's all about desire," Allister snapped.

The dining hall door swung open and Daebian took a seat at the table.

Miranda looked crossly at her son. "Daebian, where have you been all evening? Your supper is long cold."

"Sorry, Mother. I got distracted and lost track of time."

"Did you lose track of the sun as well? It set over an hour ago."

Daebian just smiled and shrugged his shoulders. Daebian had barely finished half his meal when one of the older martial students burst into the room

"Excuse me, but there has been an accident on the wall," the young man exclaimed excitedly.

"What happened?" Aggie asked.

"Someone fell, and he's hurt bad. Evan and Brother Thomas are with him at the infirmary and sent me to inform you."

Allister and Miranda stood abruptly and made haste to the infirmary. They arrived to find the field surgeon, Alex, and Brother Thomas next to the bed of a young man.

"What happened?" Allister asked.

Alex turned and answered, "He was on sentry duty. Apparently a stone gave way and he fell."

"Will he be all right?" Miranda asked fretfully.

"He will recover from the fall," Brother Thomas told them. "The biggest concern is that the stone landed on his arm and crushed it. It was everything Evan and I could do to save it. It is doubtful he will ever use it again, which is unfortunate since it was his sword arm."

"What is his name?" Allister inquired.

"That's Daniel," Daebian answered and stepped up to the bed. "We sparred today. I was looking forward to our next fight."

Miranda laid a comforting hand on her son's shoulder. "Pray for him, and he'll get better soon. Come; let us leave him to his rest."

"I think that is all we can do now," Thomas agreed.

"Can I stay a moment longer, Mother? I would like to make him a poem."

"All right, but just a minute." Miranda gave her son a tight-lipped smile and led the others out of the room.

Daebian watched the others step away and leaned close to Daniel's ear.

"A mighty warrior, so strong and tall,
So easily brought down by a little fall,
I'll tell you about winning,
In this rhyme I am spinning,
And teach you a lesson you'll never forget,
On the field, you may defeat me,
But if you make me your enemy,
Your prize will be a life of regret."

Daebian had lain in wait for nearly an hour as Daniel performed his sentry duty. He knew every stone in the wall and hid in the shadows near one he knew to be loose and which was made looser by his efforts. When Daniel strode near, Daebian burst from his hiding spot and shoved the boy off the wall. He then finished prying out the loose stone block and used it to crush Daniel's sword arm as he lay stunned on the ground.

Smiling contentedly, Daebian left the infirmary, crossed the grounds, and made for his room atop the new tower. As he reached the landing occupied by his mother's rooms, he paused and glanced into her chamber. His father's staff leaned in a corner within her solarium just as it had done for the past five years. As Daebian turned to walk away, a glimmer of movement caught his eye. When he turned back, the staff was gone.

Daebian tilted his head and pursed his lips in thought.

"The young prince, left all alone,
To care and tend to his mother.
The boy struggles to become a man.
The king gone, seemingly forever.
In his place, the prince does stand.
He does his best when put to the test,
But what happens when the king comes home?"

To be continued in:
THE SORCERER'S RETURN
Book Seven of The Sorcerer's Path

FROM THE AUTHOR

I hope you enjoyed this tale and will try my other works. Feel free to look me up on Facebook! You can also check me out on my website http://brockdeskins.com/ where I write serial fiction, free for your enjoyment, and answer questions!

Author page:
https://www.amazon.com/Brock-Deskins/e/B005M6VQ1O

Facebook:
https://www.facebook.com/brocksbooks/

Twitter:
@brockdeskins

PLEASE <u>**REVIEW**</u> **MY BOOKS** (Especially if you liked it). Customer reviews are the primary means of enticing others to purchase them. I am dependent upon the sales of my books to earn a living that will allow me to continue writing stories that I hope bring you some measure of entertainment. Thank you for your support.

OTHER BOOKS BY BROCK E. DESKINS

The Sorcerer's Path is an epic fantasy series.

The Sorcerer's Ascension: Torn from a life of comfort and luxury, his family destroyed by political intrigues and aspirations, a young boy must quickly grow into a man before the deadly streets of Southport devour him. Follow Azerick through a page-turning adventure that pits him against thieves, thugs, murderers, and men of power that will stop at nothing to achieve their goals.

Azerick must fight just to survive, but for him survival is not enough. A hunger to avenge the wrongs committed against him burns deep within. But that is not all that lies within the young man. There is a power waiting to be unleashed that may be the key to achieving the justice and security he seeks--if it does not destroy him first.

The Sorcerer's Torment: Azerick flees The Academy but quickly falls prey to powerful beings that use his skills and power for their own amusement. What these creatures do not understand is the power of the young sorcerer's will and the lengths he will go to for vengeance. Despite becoming a prisoner, Azerick finds his first true love, but can he keep it?

The Sorcerer's Legacy: Azerick has found himself a home and tries to settle down. He takes on an apprentice and tries to put all the death and desire for vengeance behind him. But when the Rook finds him, Azerick is once again pulled back into Ulric's schemes. Knowing that all he has worked toward and everyone close to him is in danger as long as these schemes are ongoing; Azerick decides to put an end to it, once and for all.

The Sorcerer's Vengeance: After narrowly avoiding being killed in his own bed by the land's most feared assassin, Azerick leaves his school behind to find out who sent him and to put an end to the threat once and for all. Azerick's search will take him to the very pits of the abyss and back to unleash hellish fury upon those that threaten him.

The Sorcerer's Scourge: With the siege broken and Ulric dead, Azerick can finally relax, study his magic, and run his school in peace. Unfortunately, Jarvin's reign is far from uncontested and the true usurper decides to make his move. Jarvin escapes with help from an unlikely source—a vampire named Landrin who still clings tenaciously to his own humanity. While Azerick and a large force from North Haven race to save the king in exile, evil forces are preparing to unleash a nightmare upon the kingdom that may well destroy them all.

The Sorcerer's Abyss: Now the master of the Fifth Circle of the abyss, Azerick is challenged by another demon lord for supremacy. Azerick must face this threat as well as his innermost demons, all the while searching for a way to escape his hellish prison.

Ellyssa fears she is going insane as she plagued by nightmares of her capture and enslavement. Deciding the key to saving herself lies in the total destruction of the object of her fears, she embarks on a crusade to find and kill the slaver, Captain Jake, and eradicate the slave trade.

Ellyssa's nightmares and battles spill out onto the streets of North Haven and gains the attention of The Academy. Fearing Azerick's school is turning out rogue wizards, The Academy decides to hunt down and destroy the rogue and place the school within their control.

The Sorcerer's Return: Azerick has come back from the abyss in order to try to unite all the races against the return of the old gods who seek to destroy them and subjugate the few they allow to survive a brutal purging. However, fighting ancient gods may be the least of his troubles as he battles to save a fractured kingdom, a brilliant son traveling a dark path, and the splintered soul of his own humanity.

The Sorcerer's Destiny: Brutally purged of his demonic influence, Azerick continues the struggle of uniting the kingdom to face the coming of the Scions, ancient gods banished by the mortal races during the Great Revolution two thousand years ago. The fallen gods' prison is crumbling, and Azerick is powerless to stop them from breaking free and enacting their cataclysmic vengeance upon the world.

The humans must ally with the other races in a final battle against impossible odds while their entire world crumbles to the ground and is trod beneath the feet of an unstoppable foe. How can they set aside their distrust of each other when they fear the very person trying to save them?

Rise of the Order: Banished to the abyss after helping defeat the Scions and saving the world from eternal darkness, Azerick languishes in perpetual misery as Lord of the Fifth Circle. The denizens of his hellish realm view him as a usurper and outsider. The chaotic creatures form an alliance with one goal in mind: destroy Azerick Giles, but Sharrellan stands in their way.

A powerful spell tears through the demonic planes, and when the dust settles, the dark goddess is nowhere to be found. It is up to Azerick to return her to her seat of power, but he has a price: return him to his mortal form and send him home.

Back home, a vast empire is on a crusade to conquer the world, and it has set its sights on Valeria. Their goal is to unite the world under a single banner, eradicate the spawn infestation unleashed by the Scions, and replace the gods who they feel have forsaken them with their mystical rulers.

Can Azerick save the dark goddess from the clutches of her demonic subjects and become mortal once again? Will he have the power to protect his people from The Order if he does?

Descent Into Chaos: The Order has arrived in force, and the fate of Valeria, and perhaps all the world, is poised to come under their iron-fisted control. Azerick and Daebian are forced to flee Southport and make a contentious alliance when King Miles capitulates to the invaders. Reduced to insurgent warfare, Azerick and his allies attempt to battle The Order's vastly superior forces in a series of hit and run strikes, but the enemy legions may not be his biggest threat.

Princess Sylvian Attar, daughter to The Order's godlike emperor and empress, has taken a personal interest in Azerick. Herself a powerful sorceress, Sylvian hunts Azerick in hopes of removing Valeria's legendary hero from the battlefield thus sapping her enemies' will to fight. Azerick decides there is but one course of action he can take against this unstoppable foe. It was time to inject a little chaos into The Order.

Brooklyn Shadows is a modern-day vampire tale. Full of action and snarky dialogue, Brooklyn Shadows is an enjoyable read for anyone who enjoys the supernatural underworld and butt-kicking vampires.

Shrouds of Darkness (Brooklyn Shadows Book 1) Leo Malone has been a vampire for the better part of the twentieth century. Once a prominent Sherriff (vampire cop), he now earns his living as a private eye and occasional bodyguard for anyone that requires some serious protection. Leo is hired by the daughter of a mob accountant who has gone missing.

The fact that her father is also a werewolf has Leo following a trail of grisly murders that will lead him through a web of intrigue and conspiracy involving his fellow vampires and the local werewolves that make New York their home, all the while trying to keep one particularly determined cop off his back and himself out of jail. Leo is not some pretty-boy vampire that all the girls ogle over, but a hard-eyed, remorseless killing machine who does not take crap from anyone.

Blood Conspiracy (Brooklyn Shadows Book 2): While dealing with the aftermath of the failed vampire council coup, Leo discovers that the modified Cure has fallen into the hands of a black ops government project designed to create vampiric super soldiers. When the inevitable happens, the off-book Homeland Security operation forcefully enlists Leo to help them resolve the situation. Worse yet, he has to work not only with an antagonistic werewolf named Meat, he is reunited with his hated creator, Lesile.

Primacy of Darkness (Brooklyn Shadows Book 3): Jack the Ripper, sadistic madman of old London, once thought long dead, has returned to New York in an effort to quench his thirst for blood and mayhem. When the city's vampire enclave finds itself insufficient to deal with a madman of Jack's caliber, Vincent, the enclave head, enlists Leo Malone to put the maniac down before he reveals the existence of vampires as he throws the city into the throes of chaos and terror. Leo soon finds that Jack is not the only monster with which he must contend. A ghost from his past has also seemingly crawled from its grave and seeks to put an end to him and the rest of his kind.

The Transcended Chronicles is the story of an outlandish young man as he goes from being a troublesome youth to one of the kingdom's greatest secret agents. Blessed (or cursed) with an amazing ability to both fight and abuse his body with every conceivable vice known to man, Garran Holt is either the kingdom's greatest hero or its biggest embarrassment.

<u>**The Miscreant**</u> **(The Transcended Chronicles Book 1):** Garran Holt is a troubled young man. Unable to tolerate his self-destructive ways, his mother sells him into indentured servitude as part of a work crew building King Remiel's new trade road. When mercenaries sent to disrupt the road's construction attack his work camp, Garran discovers an inner power capable of turning him into a warrior of unparalleled ability. When the leader of his work crew recognizes Garran as being one of the transcended (a fighter able to slip into the swifter currents of time), he is trained as an agent, one of the kingdom's elite spies. Crude, abrasive, and deeply committed to destroying himself with drugs, alcohol, and debauchery, Garran might be the kingdom's only hope against falling to The Guild, the powerful trade cartel bent on becoming the true and undisputed power in the land.

<u>**The Agent**</u> **(The Transcended Chronicles Book 2):** The Guild rules the kingdom through their puppet monarch, and Garran must race to save the last living heir to the throne before the powerful syndicate's assassins complete their extermination of anyone who could oppose them. Garran and Prince Adam Altena struggle to find allies in hopes of rescuing Adam's sister, who was forced to marry the usurper in order to prevent even the thought of rebellion, and raise an army

capable of defeating The Guild. With The Guild now in control of Anatolia's powerful army as well as their legion of mercenaries, their future is grim. How can a disreputable agent and a deposed prince convince their neighboring rulers to oppose The Guild, an organization that has had them cowed for decades?

Empire of Masks is an exciting and explosive new series that takes place in the world of Hedon and takes you across the land of Eidolan where ships sail through the skies and men and women wage war with magic, swords, muskets, and cannons.

<u>Highlords of Phaer</u> (**Book one of Empire of Masks**): Born a slave, descended of kings, Jareen Velarius just wants to provide the best life he can for his family, but Eidolan is a realm that challenges even the most stalwart of souls. Caught between his masters and those brave or foolish enough to strike against them, Jareen struggles to reconcile his role as a dutiful slave with that of a man who desires to be free. His goal: to return his people to a life stolen by the highlords more than a millennium ago.

Auberon Victore, sorcerer, alchemist, son of a powerful overlord, and Jareen's master, creates an alchemic compound he is certain will change the world; he just does not know how. Jareen sees it for the weapon that could break the sorcerers' iron grasp wrapped around the necks of every lowborn in the empire. It will change the world, but not in the way his master desires.

Across the Tempest Sea, a mighty storm has raged for a thousand years, keeping a terrible, long-forgotten enemy at bay, an enemy whose cruelty knows no bounds. Only the perpetual storm and their fear of the sorcerer highlords keep the Necrophages from returning to Eidolan and cloaking the empire in death and darkness. But the tempest is waning, and the dissidents' freedom may well come at the cost of their total destruction.

<u>Nightbird</u>: The Great Revolution ended the highlords' tyranny two hundred years ago, but the legacy of that epic war, and that of the principal architects' descendants, lives on. With the highlords' death and their taking magic, as it was once known, to their graves, Eidolan fell into a time of darkness and its cities lived in isolation. However, some people, dubbed arcanists, discovered a new form of magic and the airships returned to the skies, rejoining the cities in trade as well as conspiracy, but a new darkness, more dreadful and deadly than any they faced before, is coming.

Kiera is a fifteen-year-old nightbird, one of many who flit about after dark, stealing whatever they can find in order to survive. She lives on a derelict airship in the poorest part of the city with Wesley, a young man who plies his trade as an escort to wealthy older women, and his little brother Russel, an autistic savant who communicates only through sign but who could secretly be the most powerful techno-arcanist the empire has ever known. Deep in debt to the underlord Nimat, Kiera dives into evermore dangerous schemes that put her at the heart of a secret war that could spell the destruction of not just the city, but the very empire.

Kiera is caught in the center of several factions on the brink of war. When she can no longer tell friend from enemy, there is only one side she can trust—her own.

Mourningbird: A creature of darkness lurks in the shadows of Velaroth, wearing the skin of its victims, and grips the city in terror. Dorian, a Necrophage bent on sowing chaos and paving the way for his people's invasion, has declared war on the humans of Eidolan, and there appears to be no one capable of stopping him.

Kiera's world is shattered by those who hold power, and she is forced to seek an ally. The nightbird is coming into power of her own, but can she stay alive long enough to seize it? Russel's behavior has taken a turn for the worse, and his actions have drawn the attention of those who would use his amazing talents for their own gain...and everyone else's loss.

The battle for Velaroth, and perhaps the world, has begun. Who will win? Who will live to mourn the dead? Will there be anything left for the victor to claim as their prize?

Standalone books

<u>The Portal</u> is a fun and exciting story of some less than popular teenagers that accidentally open a portal to a mystical land during one of their role-playing games. Drew, a dour and anti-establishment teenager, is pulled through and captured by evil creatures lying in wait on the other side. Now it is up to his friends and older brother to rescue him, but who will rescue Drew's captors from him?

<u>Amelia (Battle for Ardentia)</u>: Amelia is a precocious, ten-year-old girl with a powerful imagination. In her alter-ego guise of a demi-goddess warrior princess, Amelia fights against a powerful demonic sorcerer named Romut and his horde of monsters in a never ending series of battles to protect the people of her imaginary world. However, the true battle strikes home when Amelia is diagnosed with a brain tumor. Now Amelia must fight not just the evil living in her imagination, but for her very life.

ABOUT THE AUTHOR

Brock Deskins was born in a small town located in rural Oregon. At age twenty, he joined the army and served as an M1A1 tank crewman, dental specialist, and computer analyst. While in the military, he became an accomplished traveler, husband, and father of three wonderful children. His military career completed, attended college to brush up on his skills as a computer analyst and gain new skills as a writer. Brock received his degree in computer networking and is now devoting his full time and limited attention span to writing.

BIBLIOGRAPHY

THE SORCERER'S PATH
The Sorcerer's Ascension
The Sorcerer's Torment
The Sorcerer's Legacy
The Sorcerer's Vengeance
The Sorcerer's Scourge
The Sorcerer's Abyss
The Sorcerer's Return

The Sorcerer's Destiny
Rise of the Order
Descent Into Chaos

BROOKLYN SHADOWS
Shrouds of Darkness
Blood Conspiracy

THE TRANSCENDED CHRONICLES
The Miscreant
The Agent

EMPIRE OF MASKS
Highlords of Phaer
Nightbird
Mourningbird

OTHER BOOKS BY BROCK E. DESKINS
The Portal
Amelia: Battle for Ardentia

Curious about other Crossroad Press books? Stop by our website:
http://crossroadpress.com
We offer quality writing
in digital, audio, and print formats.

Subscribe to our newsletter on the website homepage and receive a
free eBook.